MURDER AMONG THE PYRAMIDS

MURDER AMONG THE PYRAMIDS

RETAILER EDITION

LADY TRAVELER IN EGYPT

SARA ROSETT

McGuffin Ink

MURDER AMONG THE PYRAMIDS

Book One in the 1920s Lady Traveler in Egypt series

Published by McGuffin Ink

Hardcover Special Edition: 978-1-950054-87-9

Paperback Special Edition: 978-1-950054-90-9

Trade paperback: 978-1-950054-69-5

Large Print Hardcover: 978-1-950054-71-8

Audiobook: 978-1-950054-72-5

Copyright © 2022 by Sara Rosett

Cover Design: Qamber Designs

Editing: Historical Editorial

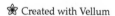 Created with Vellum

ABOUT MURDER AMONG THE PYRAMIDS

Book One in the 1920s *Lady Traveler in Egypt* series

Escape on an Egyptian Excursion to the Land of the Pyramids!
Tour highlights include: Hieroglyphics and high tea in the desert, followed by murder after sunset . . .

It's 1924 and Blix Windway has made a career out of her wanderlust, giving lectures to ladies' groups about everything from the flora of the American desert to the beauty of the Swiss Alps, but she needs new material for her talks.

She strikes what seems to be an ideal agreement with an eccentric older lady. Blix will be her travel companion during her journey to Egypt, helping to smooth the way through customs and coordinate sightseeing tours. The arrangement will provide Blix with the perfect opportunity to photograph the pyramids and gather material for her next lecture series.

But they've barely left England before the trouble begins — rough seas, attempted robbery, and the disturbing certainty that someone has very carefully searched their belongings.

Then a murder occurs during a tour of the pyramids. Despite the attempts of the British officials to sweep the death under the rug, Blix becomes increasingly convinced that one of their tour party is a murderer.

Blix's search for the truth takes her from the posh sporting clubs and lavish gardens of Cairo to the narrow, twisting lanes of the city's centuries-old bazaar and the vast desert around the Giza Plateau.

Can Blix unearth the truth before the killer makes this journey her last?

Join Blix on this classic murder mystery set in glamorous 1920s Cairo.

CHAPTER ONE

"*I*t's of direst importance. Please, Blix. The package *must* get to Cairo. You're on your way there. You could pop it in your bag . . ."

Percy Smitherington's brown eyes reminded me of Lucky, the housekeeper's spaniel and my constant companion during my solitary childhood. I steeled myself against Percy's pitiful expression. Even if I was traveling to Egypt, I wasn't a package service. "Why not send it in the diplomatic pouch? It will get there faster than if I take it."

The waitress arrived at our table, and Percy waited until she'd delivered the teapot and left. I had to strain to hear him over the noisy chatter of the tearoom as he said, "The thing is, I can't send it that way. I intended to, but I mucked things up. Old Featherhead would be furious if he knew what happened."

"Featherhead? You mean Sir Gerald Feathering?" Sir Gerald held an important position at Whitehall, which was where Percy also worked.

"Yes. Featherhead is a nickname." He chuckled. "Bit of a joke. Of course, we don't call him that to his face."

Since Sir Gerald was bald, I said, "I imagine not." I stirred my tea as I looked out the window, where rain was sheeting down. "You should explain to Sir Gerald, especially if it's urgent."

Percy shifted, his gaze on his teacup. "I can't. He's already given me a warning. He nearly sacked me last month. If I do anything else wrong"—he shrugged—"that'll be my job, and I'll be back as one of the great unemployed."

I sipped my tea, watching him over the rim. I'd known Percy for years. He was about half a dozen years younger than me. He'd been one of the few people who hadn't dropped me when Father cut me off. Percy's sister had been especially cruel, spreading some rather vile rumors about me, but their father had died at Ypres, and Percy was the breadwinner for his sister and mother.

"Please, Blix. It's hush-hush, but seeing as your father is a diplomat, I know I can trust you. Sometimes we have to do things a bit out of the ordinary. It's critical that the package get there before the twenty-second."

I put my tea down. I'd never been good at putting off Lucky when he wanted a walk, and I found I couldn't turn down Percy either. "What do you need me to do?"

"Hardly anything." He took a package wrapped in brown paper from his pocket. Handling it as if it contained fine china, he gently set it on the table. "Just hand this off to Mr. George Rhodes. He's staying at Shepheard's in Cairo. That's it. Nothing to it."

CHAPTER TWO

"*I*'m dying!" Miss Spalding clamped her hand over her mouth for a moment, then removed it again to add, "I feel so terribly wretched!"

I took a clean handkerchief from my handbag and held it out to her. "I understand you feel ghastly at the moment, but I believe such a grim outcome is quite rare when it comes to seasickness."

Miss Spalding pressed the fabric to her mouth and moaned. When we'd chugged away from the brilliant white cliffs of Dover, one of the ferry's crew had noticed Miss Spalding's sickly demeanor and returned with a bucket. Miss Spalding had been hunched over it ever since.

"Only a little longer." I nodded, indicating the view beyond the ferry's railing. "Look, you can see the train waiting for us at the quay."

Miss Spalding daubed her mouth. "I pray you are correct. I can't—"

The ferry surged heavenward. Miss Spalding groaned. We hung for a moment, poised between the sky and the sea, then plummeted. I hadn't been plagued with *mal de mer*. And it was a good thing too. As Miss Spalding's hired traveling compan-

3

ion, it was my job to ensure she made it across the English Channel, then on through France and finally to Egypt.

I found riding the swells of the rolling sea thrilling—the spray of water as the waves broke against our little craft, the dramatic rush as we rose, then the drop that was so speedy it seemed as if the very deck would fall away from under our feet. But I kept my exhilaration to myself. Miss Spalding was suffering so. I doubted she'd appreciate any commentary on nature's intense display. The ferry's crew went about their business, and their faces weren't the least bit worried, so I assumed the crossing was nothing out of the ordinary. If they weren't frightened, there was no reason for me to be anxious. My only twinge of concern was for my lecture lantern and glass slides. I'd nestled them in layers of my clothing deep in my suitcase, which had been loaded with the rest of the large luggage. Hopefully, my careful packing would protect them during the rough crossing.

I waited for the next wind-driven assent, but it didn't come. The ferry settled into a less dramatic motion as we bobbed along like a cork in a washtub.

We rode the more gentle swells for a few moments, then Miss Spalding leaned back and pressed the handkerchief to her eyes with one hand and shoved the bucket in my direction with the other. "Have that removed."

"Of course, Miss Spalding." I caught a steward's eye, and he took the bucket away.

A plump woman in a cobalt-blue traveling suit who was passing along the deck stopped in front of us. The wind tossed the rather excessive amount of feathers on her collar and hat as she addressed Miss Spalding. "Forgive me for intruding, but you're in such distress. I find watching the horizon to be quite helpful."

"There is no horizon," Miss Spalding said from under the handkerchief, which she still held to her face, shielding her eyes. "Only a never-ending bank of gloomy fog out there."

That wasn't quite true. The day was misty and overcast, but land was visible.

"Or a stroll along the deck," the lady in blue added. "A change of situation might help."

Miss Spalding whipped the handkerchief down. Her face was ashen. Somehow she managed to both pinch her lips and turn them down into a frown. "I thank you for your concern, but I do not require your assistance or misguided advice."

I would have cringed if Miss Spalding had spoken to me in that manner, but the woman in blue didn't seem concerned. Miss Spalding replaced the handkerchief, and the woman addressed me. "I believe we are quite near France. Not long now. Good day." The feathers rippled as she turned away.

The waves seemed to drop away from under the ferry, and we catapulted down again. The woman in blue gripped the railing as the ferry roiled.

Miss Spalding dropped the handkerchief. "Bucket! Where is it? Oh, why did you take it away, you wretched girl?"

One of the ferry's attendants must have been keeping an eye on Miss Spalding because she'd barely finished speaking when he hurried up with another metal pail.

Head bent, Miss Spalding spoke into the bucket. "Why did I ever leave on this horrible journey?"

I was beginning to ask myself that same question. My previous stints as a paid travel companion hadn't been like this at all. I'd toured the American West with Miss Henry, an English widow with a placid temperament who enjoyed reading and needlework. She hadn't felt confident about crossing an ocean and a continent alone, and I'd been happy to escort her from Liverpool to New York, then travel by train to San Francisco with her for a visit with her brother. Unfortunately, my correspondence with Miss Spalding hadn't revealed that she was a different type of woman altogether from Miss Henry.

I'd met Miss Spalding for the first time this morning at

Victoria Station, and I was beginning to suspect that agreeing to align myself with her for several weeks sight unseen had been a rather colossal mistake.

But I couldn't back out now. My only source of income depended on visits to new destinations. Everyone in England was agog over King Tut and the Nile. A travel lecture on the Wonders of Egypt would ensure I could keep myself fed and clothed for the next few years. If I was lucky, the new lecture series might also allow me to save funds for a future trip. But I had to get to Egypt first. And then there was Percy. I'd given him my word. I *must* get to Egypt. No matter how difficult Miss Spalding was, I could endure her for a few weeks.

The woman in the feathered blue hat and suit adjusted her stance at the rail and glanced at Miss Spalding, then sent me a commiserating smile—which I thought probably had more to do with my traveling companion than the choppy sea—before she moved carefully away, still gripping the handrail. I dearly hoped the lady in blue was correct and we landed soon. I only had one more clean handkerchief.

A short time later we arrived in Calais. "There." I stood and settled my handbag on my wrist, then reached for Miss Spalding's valise as well as my ladies' traveling case. "The worst is over. You'll feel much better after a cup of tea on the train." Amid the bustle of departing passengers, Miss Spalding sat unmoving, her hands still clenched on the rim of the pail. "Miss Spalding? We've arrived. You can put the bucket down."

She stirred and tucked the bucket closer to her chest. "No. I must keep it. I'll need it for the return journey."

"What do you mean? We're taking the train to Paris."

"No. We're returning to Dover." She shuddered. "And then I'll never set foot on a boat again."

CHAPTER THREE

I was by nature an optimistic person, but unease fluttered through me. I traced my hand over my vest pocket Kodak as I thought of the notebook with pristine pages, waiting to be filled with details that I could recount to the audiences who would come to hear about Egypt.

I'd only been acquainted with Miss Spalding for a short time, but I already could see that she wasn't the wishy-washy type. I was going to have a time convincing her to continue the journey. She still looked shaken from the rough crossing. Her face was pallid, and when she smoothed the creases in the skirt of her wool traveling suit and straightened her hat, her fingers trembled.

"But, Miss Spalding—"

"No," she said. "Travel isn't for me—especially boat travel."

I had to jolly her along. I only needed to get her off the boat, across the quay, and onto the train. I used my brightest tone. "Come now, Miss Spalding, you want to see Egypt. Pyramids and tombs. Hieroglyphics and high tea in the desert. The Sphinx and—"

She released her grip on the bucket and chopped her hand through the air, cutting me off. "I'm not crossing the Mediter-

7

ranean, and I'm certainly not traveling down the Nile in a boat."

"But the Nile is calm. It's nothing like the English Channel." Well, the upper Nile wasn't, but I wouldn't mention that now. "And we'll be on a ship when we cross the Mediterranean. It will be much larger. You'll hardly feel the waves at all."

"I most certainly won't. I'll be in England and—if I survive the return crossing—I'll never leave again."

Worry settled like a heavy rock on my chest. "But the reservations . . . the hotels, the tours—"

"Nothing that can't be canceled. You'll send a few telegrams, and the whole thing will be handled."

Oh my. This was dreadful. All my plans—my very livelihood for the next few months hinged on traveling to Egypt with Miss Spalding. If she turned back . . . well, that didn't bear thinking about.

I sat down beside her. If she'd been another sort of woman, I'd have taken her hand in mine. Instead, I leaned forward to convey my earnestness. "Not many people have the opportunity to travel to Egypt. Won't you regret it if you go back to England?"

"The only thing I would regret is continuing this journey, which will necessitate getting on another boat, and that's something I'll never do again."

I gestured at the choppy gray waves in the channel. "But you have to make the return journey. Why not press on today and take the train? By the time we return in a few weeks—"

"No. I've made up my mind. You there!" She motioned at an attendant who'd rushed by. He paused. "I'm returning to Dover on this ferry. Arrange it."

The young man looked bewildered. She flapped her hand, waving him into motion. "Go on. Let the person in charge know. I'll pay any fees that are needed. And keep my luggage on the ferry. Do not have it unloaded for customs."

"Yes, ma'am. I'll see to it."

I glanced across the quay. The customs line that snaked across the cobbles was rapidly diminishing. I could still make the train, but I didn't have long.

The wind had disarranged Miss Spalding's hair, and she tucked a few wayward strands under the brim of her hat as she said, "Now, Miss Windway, I expect you—"

I transferred my valise from one hand to the other as I stood. "I'm sorry, Miss Spalding, but I can't go back to England."

"Nonsense. I'm returning to England. You will come with me."

"That's impossible."

"What? You made a commitment to me. You can't abandon me. You're my traveling companion."

"But my promise was to accompany you to Egypt. One could argue that you're the one doing the abandoning."

There must have been something in the tone of my voice that indicated I wouldn't waver. I wasn't sure how I would get to Egypt without Miss Spalding, but I would sort out something. I separated my traveling case from Miss Spalding's luggage.

Miss Spalding's chin tucked in as her head reared back. "Well. I've not been around many young people, but I can see that everything I've read in the newspapers about the selfishness of your generation is true."

"My generation?"

She swished her hand through the air. "Flappers. Bright Young People and such."

I couldn't help but chuckle as I buttoned my coat of turquoise gabardine. "I'm rather closer to a spinster than a Bright Young Person."

She squinted up at me. "Yes, now that the sun is coming out from behind the clouds, I can see the fine lines around your eyes. Closer to thirty than twenty, I imagine." She looked beyond me to the train. "Now I understand. You're hoping to catch a husband in Egypt. Well, *that* at least is a sensible decision. Cairo is a place where a young woman can shine if her debut did not go well in London."

Irritation fizzed up in me, but I pushed it down. It was true that my season—and those that followed—hadn't gone according to my family's plan, but I wasn't about to delve into that subject with Miss Spalding. "That's not why I agreed to accompany you to Egypt."

"Then what was the reason?"

I checked the train. Steam billowed around the engine as figures scurried across the quay toward it. "I want to see the Sphinx and the pyramids and experience the intoxicatingly clear desert air. I want to float along the Nile and see crocodiles. Then I want to share that experience with others through my lectures."

"So, for adventure." Her tone indicated that adventure was a frivolous pursuit. She ran her gaze over me, then said, "Well, that's an excellent story. Although I think my version is closer to the truth. Since it's too late to cancel the ticket to Paris, you may continue on with the train ticket I purchased for you. I'll have the rest of the arrangements canceled when I return to England. I'm sure your journey will be better than my return trip on this despicable ferry."

A blast of steam from the train engine set my heartbeat racing. There was no time to lose. As Miss Spalding's companion, I held all the tickets for the journey. I opened my handbag and removed my train ticket, then handed the remaining tickets —a thick bundle—to her. "Thank you for the train ticket." I settled Miss Spalding's case on the chair beside her and said goodbye. She was already looking back across the channel.

The deck around me had grown quiet, and the throng of people who'd been filtering through customs had thinned. Only a smattering of people remained. I flew down the gangway, one hand clamped on my hat, then dodged around a few people lingering on the stretch of the quay between the ferry and the train, my thoughts spinning. I'd lost my sponsor. How would I get from Paris to Egypt?

I'd work it out somehow. I'd have to. But the first order of business was to get on the train. I collected my large suitcase and navigated through customs quickly. The bored official only gave my luggage and passport a cursory glance before I dashed for the train.

I'd almost reached the first-class carriage when a cry carried through the air.

CHAPTER FOUR

$\mathcal{I}$t was more of a yelp of surprise than a scream. I sidestepped around a mound of luggage and saw the woman in the blue suit from the ferry trying to wrestle her handbag from a small man who had his hands clamped on it. He was tugging at it, but she was holding fast to the strap, feet planted. The metal clasp popped open, but the man didn't loosen his grip.

"Hey!" I called. "Stop that!"

The man glanced at me, released the handbag, and shoved the woman to the ground before sprinting away in the opposite direction.

I hurried over to the woman and knelt down. "Are you all right?"

She levered herself into a sitting position. "I believe so. Thank you." Her hat had been knocked off, and the beautiful cobalt-blue fabric of her suit was streaked with mud, but she wasn't grimacing in pain. "That man offered to help me carry my case, but he was actually a thief. Imagine! Me, the target of a thief." She seemed to find the idea quite amusing, but I could see why the man had singled her out. Her clothing was of the best quality, and the number of feathers on her hat and collar indicated she was wealthy.

A shrill whistle cut through the air. A few of her belongings had fallen out of her handbag, and she snagged a thin lace handkerchief before the breeze whipped it away. I picked up a heavy gold tube of lipstick as a blast of steam hissed from the engine.

I handed her the lipstick and picked up her hat, which looked much worse than her suit. "We must hurry. The train's about to leave." I held her arm and helped her to stand. "Do you feel dizzy?"

"No, I'm not wobbly at all." She picked up her handbag.

The wheels of the train were beginning to turn as it slowly rolled away. I grabbed my case, and we dashed for the carriage where an attendant leaned out, hand extended. He gripped the woman's arm and heaved her up. I jumped up after her as the cadence of the wheels increased and the train picked up speed. The brim of my cloche shifted as a gust of wind lifted it. I tilted my head down into the wind so the breeze wouldn't snatch it off my head, then I ducked into the carriage behind the woman. The attendant escorted us to our seats, padded armchairs across the aisle from each other. He promised to return with water.

I held out her hat. "I'm afraid it's rather squashed."

"Oh well. I'm sure it can be repaired." She smoothed the disarranged feathers. "Thank you. So kind of you." She popped the flattened crown back into place and settled it on her hair, which was a light brown going gray, done up in a bun. Several of the blue feathers that had arched along the brim were broken and dangled over her eye, but she didn't seem to give her appearance another thought. She extended her hand, and the feathers swayed back and forth in front of her eyes. "I'm Hildy Honeyworth."

"How do you do? I'm Blix Windway."

"Oh, the lady traveler! I attended one of your lectures in Manchester. Your slides were fascinating."

"Thank you. I'm so glad you enjoyed it."

"I must thank you as well for frightening away that man and helping me catch the train. I had no idea travel could be so thrilling. You must experience this sort of thing all the time. Tell me, are charlatans who pretend to be helpful fellow travelers quite common?"

"Personally, I've not experienced that sort of thing. But there are always those seeking to take advantage of travelers."

She took out her handkerchief and brushed at her muddy skirt. "Yes, especially those of us who are rather naïve. This is my first time traveling."

"To France?"

"To anywhere, actually. I've never been farther than Manchester."

The thought boggled my mind. I'd been traveling for years. Of course, that had only happened after the Incident. Up until that point, my life had been confined to a small geographic circle around Burywood. "And you're going to Paris. Brilliant choice."

"I'll spend a few days there before going on to Egypt."

"Egypt is my destination as well, at least—that's my plan." Now that I was on the train, I knew I'd make it to Paris, but I'd given the Paris-to-Marseille ticket back to Miss Spalding.

A deep guff of laughter drew my attention to another set of armchairs, where a pair of young men sat facing each other. One of them must have sensed my gaze and looked toward me. He sprang up and strolled across the carriage. "Well, if it isn't Blix. Were you on the ferry? I didn't see you."

"Yes, I was." I searched my mind for his name. Nash? Nicolas? I had an excellent memory for names and faces, but I'd met him only once, and it had been nearly a decade ago. His chubby face had thinned as he matured. He'd been seven when I went to stay with Edith during the school holidays. Noah? Nathan? At that time, he'd been rather whiny and bothersome, and I'd

14

been glad to see the last of him when I departed. "How are you . . . um . . . Ned?" That was it—Ned.

"Very well. Just popping down to Cairo."

"How nice. That's my destination as well." How wonderful to be able to travel across Europe and the Mediterranean with scarcely a thought.

The carriage swayed, and Ned braced his hand on the back of my seat. "I have a hankering to bag a few crocodiles."

"What of the pyramids and the tombs?"

"Oh, that too. That's more Timothy's line." He tilted his head to indicate his traveling companion, who had joined us. He was a slight man who looked to be in his early twenties with spectacles and curly black hair. "Timothy Noviss, this is Blix Windway. She gads about taking pictures, then tells ladies' groups about them. I suppose you'll give Egypt the 'Blix Windway' treatment? I know how you enjoy dabbling with your camera."

His mocking tone rankled, but I only said, "I plan to give travel lectures about it, yes."

"Well, if you need to know anything about Egypt, ask Timothy. He reads hieroglyphics."

"How fascinating to be able to understand them," I said. "Are you an archeologist, Mr. Noviss?"

He looked down at his shoes as he gave a little shake of his head. "Oh no. My interest is purely as an amateur enthusiast, Miss Windway. My area is art. I've done some paintings for a few excavations. One can't help but pick up on the meaning of some of the symbols."

"Is your work on display, Mr. Noviss?"

"Oh no. I'm commissioned to create copies of the walls of the tombs to capture them before they decay or are destroyed. It's more a scientific record than a creative expression."

Ned said, "Edith wants him to paint a family portrait, but I don't know how he'd ever accomplish that. Her little brats are never still."

"And how is Edith?" I asked.

"Fine, I suppose. She and Henry are a truly stodgy married couple. She's got several squalling hellions. Let's see, is it three or four now? I lose count."

"Three, I believe. Little Charlie was born in the spring." I hadn't been fond of Edith's younger brother when I stayed with her during a school holiday, and I was finding it hard to warm up to Ned now.

"Yes, she was over the moon about that," Ned said. "Succession secured and all that. Although, strangely, she dotes on each one. Even seems to actually enjoy having them around. Insists they take tea and dine at the table with us."

It wasn't the accepted way to raise children, but it sounded lovely, especially compared to the upbringing I'd had, but I didn't voice my opinions. "I'm happy to hear she's well."

"And your family? Is your father still off on a foreign posting? Bogota, wasn't it?"

"Berlin."

Across the aisle, Miss Honeyworth had put away her handkerchief, and I turned to include her in the conversation. "Let me introduce you. This is Edward Breen—called Ned—and his friend Mr. Timothy Noviss. Ned's older sister was a school chum of mine. Ned, this is Miss Honeyworth, who is also traveling on to Egypt."

Something flickered across Ned's features, but his face settled into a bland mask before I could identify it. He bent over Miss Honeyworth's hand. "Charmed, I'm sure." The words were entirely correct, but a subtle undercurrent in his voice indicated he didn't like Miss Honeyworth.

The conductor arrived, and Ned returned to his seat. Later, over tea, I invited Miss Honeyworth to join me. She moved to the empty seat across from mine, and we chatted about the sites we intended to visit in Egypt. Eventually, she asked, "And your traveling companion, the woman who you were with on the ferry, will she meet you in Paris and continue on to Egypt?"

"No, she decided sea voyages were not to her liking. She decided to return to England."

Miss Honeyworth stirred her tea. "I'm sure it will disrupt your travel plans somewhat, but overall, probably the best outcome."

"I agree. We didn't suit."

Ned and Mr. Noviss got up from their seats. Ned gave me a quick nod. When they came even with me and Ned saw Miss Honeyworth had changed seats and was now across from me, he frowned, but only for a moment, then the two men passed on down the aisle.

Miss Honeyworth placed a tiny sandwich on her plate. "Perhaps Mr. Breen will escort you to some of the dances in Cairo."

"I doubt it. I'm nearly ten years older than he is. If he thinks of me at all, it will be in an aunt-like way."

"Well, he seems a nice young man."

"Perhaps."

She tilted her head, and the broken feather flopped into her line of sight. She swished it away. "You don't agree."

"He was rather a terror when he was a child." I explained how I knew Edith and Ned, then added, "During my visit, he spent his time playing pranks on us. All the usual sort of thing —a frog in my tooth mug and spiders in my bed. But by far his favorite activity had been to wait in a window above the entry door with a pitcher of water. When Edith and I left the house, he'd soak us."

"Youthful high jinks, I'm sure." She peered at me a moment, her gaze suddenly as intent as a searchlight. "But I do believe you're correct. He wouldn't do for you at all. You need someone who is interested in more than sport and dancing with pretty girls. But it's none of my business, of course. Thank you for tea. Now I believe I'll attend to a few letters."

Miss Honeyworth returned to her seat and took out a writing desk along with a sheaf of envelopes. Something of my surprise at the amount of post she'd taken out must have shown on my face. She tapped the letters into alignment. "I always have a copious amount of correspondence to deal with."

"Then I'll leave you to it. I believe I'll stretch my legs." I strolled through the carriage to the window in the vestibule. I leaned against the glass, swaying with the motion of the train. As we'd moved away from the coast, the clouds had cleared. The muted russet and beige of the winter countryside raced by. In a few hours, we'd arrive at Gare du Nord. How could I get to Egypt? I twisted the buttons on my gloves as I ran through possibilities.

I had enough cash to cover a night's stay—possibly two—in Paris. I was speaking to the Paris Ladies' Society tomorrow, which would bring in a little money. British ex-pats, mostly wives of diplomats and businessmen, had formed the club, and they paid speakers a small stipend.

My original travel itinerary with Miss Spalding had included two days of Paris sightseeing, but I had afternoons and evenings free. I'd booked with the society to present one of my travel lectures during one of the afternoons. But even adding the stipend to my meager stash of money wouldn't get me to Marseille. And then I still had to come up with the passage to Alexandria.

I ran through my list of acquaintances and where they were in the world at the moment. Had anyone mentioned going to Paris lately? Perhaps I could convince someone they must see Marseille and take me along with them? That strategy would get me as far as the coast. Then if I could book a few more lectures, I might possibly be able to raise the cash for third-class passage on a ship to Alexandria. I sighed. The plan had merit, but many groups only gave a pittance for lecturers, and I hadn't prepared the ground. It could take weeks for me to raise the funds.

A footfall behind me drew me out of my reverie. Ned joined me, leaning a shoulder against the window. "I'm glad you're alone, Blix. I wanted to have a word."

"You sound quite grave."

"It is serious." He ducked his head closer to mine and lowered his voice. "Are you traveling with Miss Honeyworth?"

"No." I was somewhat surprised that he'd sought me out, but the fact that he wanted to converse about Miss Honeyworth was odd.

He let out a breath, a sigh of relief. "Oh, that's jolly good, then. She's the worst sort of female."

Ned had positioned himself with his back to the sun, and I had to squint against the light to see his face. "I beg your pardon?"

He cast his gaze up to the carriage's decorative inlay, then shot a look over my shoulder to the area where Miss Honeyworth was seated. "She's a tigress."

"Whatever do you mean?" I knew what he was insinuating, but I found it so distasteful that I pretended not to understand.

"You know—a tigress."

"In regards to the jungle, I'm aware of what a tigress is, but you clearly mean something else . . ." Character assignation was one of my least favorite aspects of high society and one I refused to participate in.

He let out an impatient snort. "She's a social climber, Blix. She's on the hunt for prey—susceptible women who will bring her into our circle. From there, she'll be able to worm herself even more deeply into society."

"Our circle?" I crossed my arms.

He hadn't picked up the icy edge to my words because he nodded. "Exactly! *Good* society."

"And where did you get this idea?"

"You only have to look at her clothing to see she's new money. Not our sort. Obviously, she comes from a low background and has come into funds somehow."

"That's not a reason—"

He went on as if I hadn't spoken. "Her coat and hat are quality, of course, but that ridiculous amount of feathers—it borders on vulgar. She's obviously anxious to ingratiate herself with you. If you let her fasten on to you, she'll see herself settled very comfortably in Cairo society."

I forced myself to take a slow, deep breath. Anger on behalf of Miss Honeyworth simmered inside of me, but I kept my voice low. I didn't want to alert her to the poisonous things being said about her. "You're assuming quite a lot from her appearance."

"Edith said this Miss Honeyworth tried to scrape up a friendship with Leticia Murray. Claimed they were girlhood friends."

"Well, they would seem to be about the same age. And isn't Leticia's family from the area around Manchester? Miss Honeyworth mentioned that she lived there. It wouldn't be beyond the bounds of believability that they could be acquainted. And wasn't Leticia's family rather stony when she married?"

Ned drew himself away from the window. "I can see you're close-minded on the subject. How long have you known her?"

"Only a few hours. I met her on the ferry, and then she had that unfortunate incident with the man who tried to steal her handbag."

"All staged, I'm sure. Very shrewd. The little show went a long way toward gaining your sympathy. Probably exactly what it was set up to do."

"Ned, that's a ghastly thing to say! If someone is attacked, one must do something."

He tilted his head toward a passing attendant. "Plenty of porters and attendants about. One of them could have helped her—if it were a legitimate attempt at robbery."

"I'm disappointed in you, Ned." I sounded like one of my governesses, the tedious ones who were forever moralizing, so I added, "Miss Honeyworth has shown herself to be a kind person."

"All an act, I'm sure."

My anger spilled over into words. "You've got some cheek.

If you feel that way, why did you speak to her politely and say you were charmed to meet her?"

"I couldn't do anything else. You put me in a very awkward situation. I don't appreciate that."

I'd thought Ned was an insufferable little twit years ago. It was obvious that he hadn't changed. However, I wouldn't make a scene on the train. My words were clipped and my tone as frosty as my mother at her most haughty. "I'll keep that in mind should our paths ever cross in Egypt."

He caught at my sleeve. "I'm only trying to help you."

I shook him off. "Then please keep your *help* to yourself. It's rather vile." I made my way back to my seat. Miss Honeyworth was still bent over her writing desk, scribbling away, her broken feather trembling with each movement.

I took out my lecture notes and read over them to prepare for the event at the ladies' society, but I found it hard to concentrate. Ned had also returned to his seat, and his voice carried as he spoke to Mr. Noviss. ". . . hired a Delage. I've always done the train, but it'll make a nice change to drive to Marseille, if the weather holds. It should be cold but sunny."

Snippets of Mr. Noviss' reply weren't as distinct. ". . . second place . . . road rally . . ."

I felt the corners of my mouth turn up as I thought of one of my governesses who'd been a gem, Megs. Her full name had been Mary Megsgrop, and she'd taught me to drive a motor. Her brother had raced in road rallies and had won several. He'd taught Megs to drive, and Megs had insisted I should learn as well.

As usual, Father had been away—St. Petersburg, I think it was—and Dowers, the butler, had frowned on the idea, but Megs had insisted that Father instructed her to give me a well-rounded education. "In today's world, a young lady needs to master the skill of motoring," she'd said and arranged with the chauffeur to have the motor at our disposal three mornings each week. Looking back now, I thought it was probably also a good excuse for Megs to get out of the schoolroom during a particularly fine stretch of spring weather, but she'd certainly known how to drive a motor. By the end of the month, I did as well.

I lost all interest in my lecture notes as an idea sparked. I did some rapid maths and decided it just might work.

It was dark by the time we steamed into Gare du Nord. I made sure I was striding along the platform so that my path would cross with Ned's. He and Mr. Noviss raised their hats as I approached. Ned glanced around, apparently checking to see if Miss Honeyworth was with me. She wasn't. She'd struck up a conversation with another lady about Lincolnshire and lingered to talk with her.

"Ned," I said, "I couldn't help but overhear that you hired a Delage to drive to Marseille."

His wariness had dropped away when he saw that I was alone. "Finest machine out there."

"I'm sure you'll make excellent time."

"Of course."

"Then what would you say to a little wager?"

He tilted his head. "What did you have in mind?"

CHAPTER FIVE

"*A* race," I said. "I'll wager thirty pounds that I can beat you in a race through Paris." That amount combined with the cash I had would be enough to cover my fare to Alexandria, then on to Cairo, and also pay for lodging once I arrived.

He stepped back. "That is intriguing, but it doesn't seem cricket to wager against a lady, especially when it comes to motoring."

"You don't need to worry about that. I assure you, I'm a skilled driver."

Ned looked at Mr. Noviss, who said, "Sounds like good sport to me."

I could tell Ned was teetering on the edge of accepting, so I added, "You'd be able to put the Delage through its paces. Really see what it can do."

"Well, I suppose I might do it. Of course, it would only be sporting to give you a head start."

"I don't want a handicap. We'll start from the same spot. Shall we meet tomorrow morning and plot out a course?

"All right, then. Tomorrow morning."

I put out my hand.

He shook it, then a thought struck him. "I say, do you have a motor?"

"I'll hire one."

"No need." The voice came from over my shoulder. I turned to find Miss Honeyworth standing beside a porter with a luggage trolley piled so high I could barely see the porter's hat. A frown traced across Ned's face.

Miss Honeyworth stepped closer to me. "A race is a splendid idea! And *I* have a motor. I intended to amble through the French countryside with a driver, but you're welcome to use my motor, Miss Windway. I'm delighted to put it at your service."

"Thank you, Miss Honeyworth. That's very kind of you. I'm pleased to accept." Her offer would save me the cost of hiring a motor and also goad Ned, who was sending me a dark look. I ignored it.

Miss Honeyworth noticed Ned's reaction. "You don't approve, Mr. Breen?"

His face transformed into a tight smile. "How Blix arranges her transportation is no concern of mine."

"Excellent. Until tomorrow, then."

I turned and walked away with Miss Honeyworth, the porter following us. "Thank you, Miss Honeyworth."

"It's the least I could do to repay you for your kindness in frightening that thief away. And I'll be glad to have the company of another lady. My cousin had planned to travel with me, but at the last moment family commitments prevented her."

"And you set out alone? On your first journey to Europe?"

"Well, I wasn't about to cancel everything and sit at home."

"I admire your spirit, Miss Honeyworth," I said. And I did. Her fashion sense might be a bit over the top, and sticklers like Ned might turn up their noses at her, but I thought she showed enormous pluck. "By the way, what sort of motor is it?" I asked. "Do you know?"

"Oh yes. I wanted something French and beautiful and expensive. The hotel arranged it. It's a Bugatti."

I laughed. "Wonderful."

∼

NED LOOKED up from the map I'd spread across the small round table. "So we agree on the route?"

"Yes, first one to cross through one of the archways at the south side of the Louvre wins. And remember it's a complete loop around the Arc de Triomphe at the beginning of the race." I wanted to make sure we were both clear on the details. My ability to get to Egypt was riding on it. The smallest miscommunication could cost me dearly.

He nodded as he stubbed out his cigarette. "Right. Once around." He went to push back his chair, but then stopped. "And I propose we bring back something to prove our presence at the last checkpoint."

I jerked up my map from the table. "If you're insinuating that I'll have to cheat to win, I assure you I'll follow our planned route exactly. However, I have no objection to your suggestion."

He flushed. "I say, I didn't mean to offend you. I just thought—you know, with a chap, one's sure of their sense of fair play, and with you being a lady—um—well, I only meant—"

"I suggest you stop now." I held up my hand as I blew out a breath. He was young—just a puppy. Barely out of school and flush with his own importance. "I'll have you know that ladies have a sense of fair play that is every bit as well-developed as any chap's. But since you've brought it up, we must have something . . ."

I drummed my fingers on the table. It had to be something that could only be obtained along the route, but I needed it to be something inexpensive. I wouldn't waste my money to prove to Ned I wasn't a cheat. My gaze fell on the remains of breakfast on the table next to ours. "Ah!" I picked up the crumpled paper wrapper with the name of one of the city's hotels printed on it. "A sugar cube from a hotel. Where shall we get it? Let's see . . ." I scanned my map. "The Hotel les Rives is practically across the road from Notre-Dame." The cathedral was the farthest point on our route.

"Fine." He pushed back his chair, his color still high.

I checked my wristwatch. "Shall we meet in a quarter of an hour at Place de la Concorde?"

He nodded, and we strode off in opposite directions. As I left the shelter of the bistro, the cold morning air enveloped me, and my breath bloomed out in little foggy bursts as I hurried back to the Hotel du Louvre. It had stormed during the night, and the fragrance of rain lingered in the air.

I set a quick pace, covering the flagstoned pavement rapidly. Miss Honeyworth had stayed at the hotel to oversee the delivery of the motor while I'd gone to meet Ned at the little café a few streets over to sort out our route.

The sun was just beginning to rise. Above the tall mansard roofs of the buildings that lined the street, the sky was a washed-out blue. Ned had sent a note around to my hotel last night saying that we should hold our contest that evening, but I'd put him off until this morning. Partly because Miss Honeyworth's motor wasn't scheduled to arrive until today, but also because the roads were crowded in the evening. Paris was still sleepy at the moment, and the streets were quieter now than they would be at the end of the day.

I turned the corner and let out a sigh of relief. A Bugatti sat in front of the hotel, its maroon curves reflecting the lights from the hotel. Even at a distance, Miss Honeyworth was easy to spot in her dark green tweed coat that was trimmed with pale fur. Her tight-fitting cap of a hat was completely covered with cream-colored ostrich feathers, and they floated around her head as she waved. She reminded me of a fuzzy dandelion. She asked, "What do you think? Will it do?"

I circled the motor. The top was folded back, revealing a dark coffee-colored leather seat. "I'll say." I ran my gloved hand along the swoop of the wheel well. The engine was running, radiating waves of toasty air. "We're to meet at the Place de la Concorde shortly." I took out the map and spread it across the bonnet. "Let me show you our route."

Miss Honeyworth tilted her head. "*Our* route?"

"Yes, you're coming along, aren't you?"

"I hadn't intended to."

"Nonsense. You don't want to miss out on the fun, and I must have a navigator. Otherwise, I might take a wrong turn."

"Oh dear." Miss Honeyworth looked at the map as if it were a viper. "I'm afraid my sense of direction is—well—to be completely honest—terrible."

"You'll do fine. There are landmarks all the way. You won't be able to miss them."

I traced the route with my finger. "You see, we start here at the Place de la Concorde, and it's a straight shot to the Arc de Triomphe. Next, down this way, across the Seine, then along to Notre-Dame. We'll backtrack a bit, cross the Pont du Carrousel, and end at the Louvre. Simple."

Under the poof of ostrich feathers, Miss Honeyworth's powdered brow furrowed. "I suppose so."

"Here. I'll mark it down for you." The desk clerk had let me borrow a pencil, and I drew a heavy line along the course as Miss Honeyworth watched. "See? Very straightforward."

She murmured, "Yes, it does look that way when one looks at the map."

The hand on my watch was nearing a quarter after. I opened the door to the motor. "In you go."

She climbed in, and I squished in next to her.

"Goodness," Miss Honeyworth said, "one begins to understand how the sardines feel in the tin. I suppose you'd better take a turn around the block. You're not nervous, are you? You don't look nervous."

I looked over the metal dash, locating the various dials. "Of course I am. That's part of the excitement."

The engine gave a throaty roar as I pressed down on the accelerator.

The map fluttered, and Miss Honeyworth made a grab for it, catching it before the wind whipped it away. "Oh my. I'm not sure this is a good idea. Not a good idea at all."

The motor glided along as we pulled away from the hotel. "Just focus on finding our starting point."

"Oh. Right." The map crinkled as Miss Honeyworth fought with it against the breeze.

I took a few turns through the streets to get the feel of the motor while Miss Honeyworth tamed the map. Eventually, she wrangled it into a smaller shape.

She looked back and forth from the map to the street several times, then said, "I believe you turn right here."

"See, you'll make an excellent navigator." The Egyptian obelisk at the center of the Place de la Concorde came into sight as I spun the wheel. Ned was parked near one of the fountains. I coasted to a stop beside his motor, a black Delage. Mr. Noviss was in the passenger seat. He raised his hat and made a move to climb out, but Ned waved him back as he said, "I thought you might have forfeited, but I know how you ladies like to make an entrance."

"I'm never fashionably late." I looked at my watch. "In fact, I'm right on time."

Something over my shoulder caught Ned's attention, and he said, "We'd best be off."

I twisted around. A policeman was strolling down the middle of the plaza, pacing from the obelisk at the center to the fountain near us.

"What's wrong?" Miss Honeyworth asked.

"Motorsports in the middle of cities are rather frowned upon."

Miss Honeyworth pivoted toward me—not an easy thing to

do in the close quarters of the motor. "What do you mean? Is this illegal?"

"Of course not. Not technically. It's not an official race. Just a little friendly jaunt to see the landmarks." I leaned forward so that I could see around her. I caught Ned's eye and gave a nod. He nodded back, and we both accelerated away. The Bugatti surged forward, and we took the lead as I turned away from the obelisk and shot up the Champs-Élysées. A smattering of motors and lorries were on the road, and I easily navigated through them as the tall white buildings with their tiers of iron balconies whipped by. I raised my voice over the purr of the engine. "Which street do I take after the loop around the Arc de Triomphe?"

Miss Honeyworth had both hands braced on the dash, and the map had slipped to the floor. "What? Oh yes. Let me see." She picked up the map and hunched over it as the wind flicked at the edges of it in a noisy rattle. "It's the"—she counted under her breath—"the eighth, no, the ninth road after the Champs-Élysées."

"Perfect." The morning sunlight turned the Arc de Triomphe a buttery gold, but there was no time to admire it. A splotch of black came into my peripheral vision, and Ned inched the Delage forward until he was even with us. He shouted something, but I kept my gaze focused on the road, counting intersections as we circled the monument. A man left the pavement to cross the street in front of us, and I stepped on the brake. The Delage shifted to the far lane, looped around the man, and shot ahead, disappearing down the tree-lined avenue.

As soon as the man was out of our path, the engine roared as I worked up through the gears again, racing along, looking for the midnight black of the Delage as the stately facades of the Parisian neighborhood blurred.

Miss Honeyworth said, "Next we're looking for the Pont d'Iéna." Above the bare branches of the trees, the peak of the

Eiffel Tower came into sight, and Miss Honeyworth gave a cry of delight.

I slowed and picked out the sign for the bridge. I made the turn, and we zipped over the Seine. The Eiffel Tower rose directly in front of us, its fretted outline dark against the pale morning sky.

Miss Honeyworth tilted her head back, hand on her hat. "How marvelous!"

"Where is the next turn?" I scanned the motors in front of me for the Delage, but it wasn't in sight. There were any number of routes to take to Notre-Dame. There was no way to know if we were in the lead or lagging behind.

She twisted the map this way and that and then finally said, "You've marked the one called Bourdonnais."

I hit the brake, and we just made the turn. My hands tightened on the wheel as Miss Honeyworth read off the street names, guiding us past the open space of the Esplanade des Invalides and through the confusion of streets to the Hotel les Rives.

"Oh, look," Miss Honeyworth said, "I can see the gothic towers and the rose window of Notre-Dame from here." I jerked the motor to a stop in front of the hotel. Before the doorman reached us, I hopped out and called to Miss Honeyworth, "Don't let them move the motor. Back in a jiffy."

"What? Is the race over? I thought the finish line was at the Louvre."

"It is. This is just a short stop."

I sprinted across the pavement, then slowed my steps to a more sedate pace once I was inside the marble-tiled and columned lobby. There was no sign of Ned. I scooted over to the restaurant, which was open for breakfast. I approached the maître d' and said in my best French, "Excusez-moi," then switched to English. "Could I trouble you for a sugar cube? It's for a contest."

He lowered his brows. "How many more people will bother me this morning?"

My heart sank. There went my passage to Egypt. Ned had already been here and left. "No one else. I'm the last." I couldn't squash the sigh that welled up. Well, at least I'd given Miss Honeyworth a lightning tour of Paris.

The maître d' picked up a bowl from a nearby empty table. "Because you asked politely and didn't storm in and frighten the guests like the young man did, I will indulge you." He held out the bowl.

I picked a wrapped cube from the stack. "Thank you."

As I left the hotel, a shriek drew my attention to a man dodging along the pavement, scattering people and pigeons as he went. It was Ned. He'd had to park farther away. I shifted from a brisk walk to an all-out run, my blood thrumming. I still had a chance!

I threw myself into the motor and had it moving the second I closed the door. Miss Honeyworth said, "I do believe I saw Mr. Breen running down the street." She pointed to an intersection. "Turn left."

"Yes, it was Ned." I handed her the sugar cube. "Please keep this safe."

She pinched it between her fingers and peered at the blue text printed on the white wrapper. "Part of the competition?"

"Yes. Sorry. I forgot to tell you."

"No matter." She dropped the cube into her coat pocket and swept her hand toward the Seine as we sped by Pont Neuf. "This has been the most exciting tour of Paris I could have imagined."

I grinned. "It's the adrenaline. Rather a rush, isn't it?"

She laughed, then her face changed. "There! Isn't that our turn coming up? The Pont du Carrousel?"

I downshifted and swung the steering wheel. A black Delage whizzed by.

"Oh no!" Miss Honeyworth cried. Ned swung wide, going around us at speed, and drove into oncoming traffic.

Horns blared. Pedestrians sprinted to the safety of the pavement. I completed my tight turn, then shifted gears. The engine growled, and we skimmed over the narrow bridge. The intersection on the far side of the bridge was empty. I pointed the nose of the Bugatti at the three stone arches at the edge of the Louvre and pressed down on the accelerator.

The Delage shuddered as Ned jerked the wheel to bring it back into the lane. He'd passed us, but his wide turn meant that we had a shorter distance to travel to the arches than he did. A little burst of happiness bloomed in my chest. I was going to win. I was going to Egypt!

Ned must have realized it too, because instead of making for the arches, he cut across the lane, the nose of his motor aimed at us, a threatening move meant to make me veer off course.

Miss Honeyworth squished the map to her chest and let out a squeak.

My calf tensed to lift my foot from the accelerator. The amount of money that Miss Honeyworth would owe if there was a crash flashed through my mind.

I checked the distance to the arches. Megs' voice sounded in my head. "If you're sure, Blix, don't doubt yourself."

CHAPTER SIX

$\mathcal{I}$ changed gears and stomped on the gas pedal. The motor lunged forward, pressing me back into the seat. We squeezed by the Delage and careened through the central arch into the Louvre's courtyard.

I pulled to the side of the road, my breath coming in little huffs as if I'd run the race instead of driving it. I'd bested Ned! Even with him resorting to underhanded tactics and trying to run me off the course. And he'd had the gall to insinuate that *I* might cheat! Ned passed us without turning his head to make eye contact. Then he coasted to a stop ahead of us.

Miss Honeyworth sat immobile, the map pressed to her chest as she stared straight ahead.

"Miss Honeyworth? Are you all right?"

She stirred, and the map crinkled as she released her claw-like hold on it.

"I'm sorry about how the race ended," I said. "That was rather frightful."

"Sorry?" The wind flicked the long cream feathers on her hat back and forth as she turned toward me. "That was the most exciting thing that's ever happened to me—well, aside from a thief attempting to steal my handbag. Well done, Miss Windway. Jolly good. This calls for a celebratory lunch. Will you join me?"

"I'd be delighted. Oh, wait. I'm sorry, but I have a lecture in an hour."

"One of your travel lectures?"

"Yes, about the American West," I said.

"Sounds fascinating. I'll attend, and then we'll go to dinner this evening. I'll even treat the losers—"

Ned slammed the door of the Delage and strode back to us.

"Or perhaps not," Miss Honeyworth murmured.

"He doesn't look as if he's in the mood for a pleasant dinner. Do you still have the sugar cube?"

Miss Honeyworth patted her pocket. "Yes, here it is." She handed it to me, and I tossed it to Ned as he approached. The action surprised him. He stepped back and bobbled the little cube, then dropped it. He snatched it up. The scowl on his face deepened as he examined the print on the paper, then clinched it in his fist.

"Where's yours?" I asked.

"What?"

"Your sugar cube. That was part of the race. Don't tell me you don't have it."

"Of course I have it." He dug into his jacket pocket and slammed a second cube onto the bonnet. "It was an idiotic idea."

"Have a care with Miss Honeyworth's motor, Ned." I stood up, feet planted in the foot well, reached around the windshield, and picked up the cube. I brushed the shiny finish of the motor, relieved that he hadn't marred the paint. "It was your idiotic idea to require a token to prove we'd kept to the route. Do you want to pay up now or later today?"

He tossed a sheaf of banknotes at me. "I'll have you know that the road was slick. I would've won if it hadn't been for that."

I shuffled the notes into a stack as I sat down in the driver's seat. I didn't want the wind to carry away even one of the precious bills. "My governess Megs taught me how to drive, and she always said, 'You must take the road surface into account—otherwise, you may end up *on* the road surface.'"

He gripped the edge of the Bugatti's door, his fingers biting into the leather of the interior. "Don't mention this to anyone. If you do, I'll write to your father and inform him of your unlady-like behavior. Betting. Racing wantonly through a foreign city." His gaze flickered to Miss Honeyworth. "Associating with people not of our class. Very unfeminine behavior."

"Go right ahead. My father is well acquainted with my ways." I let out the clutch and rolled forward, forcing him to let go of the door as I called, "I doubt very much this morning's events would shock him."

I SWIVELED AWAY from the rows of upturned faces in the audience and looked at the screen, the signal for my volunteer. One of the society's members had been happy to help with my slides. She was seated at the back of the room beside my lecture lantern. Thankfully, my lantern and all my glass slides had survived the ferry crossing perfectly intact.

The current slide, which was projected on the wall of the meeting hall, a view of the Grand Canyon, disappeared and an image of me appeared. I raised my voice over the murmurs of surprise. "I'm standing here beside a saguaro cactus. As you can see, it's taller than I am. The saguaro in this photo is about eight feet tall, but they can grow to be forty, even sixty feet tall. They're covered with prickly, needle-like spikes and can live for one hundred to two hundred years."

A woman at the side of the room leaned over and said to her neighbor in a carrying voice, "What an evil-looking plant."

Instead of ignoring the comment and plowing on through my speech, I moved around to the side of the podium. "I can assure you I gave these plants a wide berth." A few chuckles rippled through the audience. "They may look odd to us. I agree that they're not at all like our sturdy English oaks or our maple and chestnut trees, but it's quite a sight to see hundreds of them on a hillside. This slide doesn't do their color justice. They're a rich, vivid green. And when the desert blooms, their prickly appearance changes. Pretty white flowers as large as teacup saucers appear." I returned to the podium. "I have another amazing tree that I saw in America." I turned to the screen, which now displayed an image of a giant sequoia. "As you can see, this tree is so large a tunnel was cut through it in 1881. It's only one amazing sight in California."

I'd given the lecture many times, and it delighted me to see the audience's reaction to the images, their amazement and surprise. Even the occasional snide comment didn't bother me as it gave me an opportunity to engage with the audience, maybe even challenge their perspective. I finished the lecture, and Miss Honeyworth, her fuzz of a hat bobbing in the front row, applauded.

I lingered, chatting with attendees, then went to pack away my lecture lantern once the audience had thinned. Miss Honeyworth appeared beside me. "Well done, Miss Windway. Entertaining and informative."

"Thank you. I'm glad you enjoyed it. Are you off to see more sites of Paris before we reconvene for dinner?"

"I am. I believe Notre-Dame is quite near here."

"No, it's actually on the other side of the city." I stowed my slides in my bag and picked up the lantern. "I have a suggestion. Perhaps we could take a tour around Paris—a much slower tour—this afternoon. Would you like me to drive the motor?"

"That would be ideal."

LATER THAT EVENING the waiter removed my plate and then Miss Honeyworth's before asking if we'd like dessert.

"No, nothing for me," I said.

Miss Honeyworth tilted her head. "Are you sure? I hear the chocolate torte is rather spectacular."

"Well, if you plan to order a slice . . ."

"I most certainly do. It's not every day that I'm able to dine at a restaurant such as this. I intend to enjoy every course."

"I don't know how I'll eat any more," I said, "but I'm sure I'll find a way."

"That's the spirit." Miss Honeyworth nodded to the waiter. "Bring on the chocolate torte, my good man."

"Superb choice," he said and departed.

"Thank you so much for a lovely dinner, Miss Honeyworth."

"Surely we can dispense with the formalities. Please call me Hildy. After all, participants who've completed a race across Paris together should be on a first-name basis."

"It's hard to argue with that statement. All right, but if I'm to call you Hildy, then you must call me Blix."

The waiter returned with coffee and the torte. As I plunged my fork into the layers of chocolate, the buzz of conversation subsided. Heads turned, and my attention was drawn to the entrance to the restaurant, where a beautiful woman followed the maître d' through the tables.

CHAPTER SEVEN

*H*ildy nodded toward the woman who'd caused a stir in the restaurant as she followed the maître d'. "I do believe that's Mrs. Jenkins. Do you remember her from the lecture?"

"It would be hard *not* to remember her. She's quite striking. I didn't speak to her, though."

Mrs. Jenkins was the antithesis of the current standards of beauty, which ran to a slender, flat-chested silhouette. The modern style of dropped-waist evening gown couldn't hide her curvy figure, and her dark chestnut hair wasn't bobbed. Instead, it was in an elaborate coiffure more reminiscent of the turn of the century. A few long, curling tendrils brushed her shoulders. She was easily the most beautiful woman in the room with her mass of dark hair, perfectly pale skin, and pink lips.

Hildy said, "She looks like a fragile china doll, doesn't she? I've known her donkey's years, and she's always had that delicate aura about her. But her poor daughter. One can't help but feel sorry for her."

It was only then that I noticed the tall young woman loping along behind Mrs. Jenkins. She looked to be around twenty.

Pale brown hair in an Eton crop frizzed around her freckled face. She was dressed in a stylish evening gown, but her shoulders rounded forward as she slumped, which caused the long lines of the dress to wrinkle and sag. The designs of the dresses were similar, but with Mrs. Jenkins, one noticed a beautiful woman. With Miss Jenkins, one noticed the beauty of the dress.

As they moved through the room, Mrs. Jenkins sailed along like a boat skimming across the water, while her daughter tromped along in her wake. Mrs. Jenkins inclined her head at some of the diners and smiled at others as she passed, but when her gaze fell on Hildy, she glided to a stop. "Miss Honeyworth. It's so nice to see you again."

Miss Jenkins halted abruptly, almost knocking into the maître d', who'd paused.

Hildy said, "I feel the same, Mrs. Jenkins. I understand you didn't meet Miss Windway today. Let me introduce you. This is Miss Blix Windway. Blix, this is Mrs. Louise Jenkins and her daughter, Rose. They're traveling on to Egypt as well."

"Then perhaps we'll see you there," I said. "How soon do you leave Paris?"

"Not for several days. We're waiting for our frocks. You can't come to Paris without ordering new gowns."

"Indeed," I said.

Mrs. Jenkins touched her daughter's arm. "We're waiting on one for Rose in particular. It's the most lovely gown. She'll cause a sensation when we get to Cairo, won't you, my dear?"

"That's unlikely," Rose said in an undertone.

Mrs. Jenkins shot a quick, embarrassed look at Hildy and me, then she said in a low voice to Rose, "Nonsense. You will look every bit as lovely as any of the other young women there."

To rescue us from the awkward situation, I said to Rose, "What are you most looking forward to seeing in Egypt?"

"It's difficult to narrow it down to a single thing. But if I had to pick only one thing, it would be the Egyptian Museum. I understand that the pyramids are empty inside and that the most interesting tombs are some distance from Cairo. But the museum is full to the brim with interesting artifacts, many of them with hieroglyphics."

Hildy said, "We met a nice young man on the train who paints copies of hieroglyphics for research."

Rose's face became animated. "Oh, I adore hieroglyphics. Did you know that they could be written in any direction? Up, down, right, or left?"

Mrs. Jenkins' smile tightened. "I'm sure these ladies don't want to hear such details at this moment. The guides will tell them all about it once they're in Egypt. The maître d' has been kindly waiting for us," she said as she sent him an apologetic smile. "We should move on. It was lovely to meet you in person, Miss Windway. I look forward to furthering our acquaintance in Egypt."

Mrs. Jenkins turned away in an elegant pirouette. Rose lifted her hand in a half-hearted wave, then tromped after her.

After they left, a beat of silence sat between us, then Hildy said, "Oh dear. It would be difficult for anyone to have a mother that beautiful, but it seems poor Rose is particularly ill-equipped to deal with the situation. Perhaps we can introduce her to the young man who paints the tombs. Mr. Noviss, wasn't it?"

"Yes, of course. But I'm sure Rose will have plenty of opportunities to meet young men who are interested in archaeology. Cairo should be the perfect place for her."

"You're right. I'm too much of a matchmaker. Modern young people don't want any interference in that area."

"Well, with the war, finding an eligible chap is rather difficult—especially when one gets to my age."

Hildy picked up her tiny coffee cup. "Surely not."

"It's true. Most of my school chums have been married for nearly a decade. I'm considered an odd duck, but the fellows I meet . . . well, Ned is a prime example."

"Much better to be single than tied to a man one doesn't admire."

"I agree completely. However, my family doesn't. Goodness, how rude of me to turn the conversation to me." I folded my napkin and put it beside my plate. "I must thank you again for a lovely dinner. And for being my navigator today," I said to change the subject.

"Your victory was all down to your driving. I had an enormous amount of fun. In fact, the whole day has been memorable. Thank you for escorting me around Paris."

"It was the least I could do after that helter-skelter tour this morning."

We'd spent a few hours in the Louvre and then revisited the Eiffel Tower and Notre-Dame at a more leisurely pace.

She studied me over the rim of her cup. "I have a proposal. Would you like to travel with me to Egypt? I hadn't originally planned to travel unaccompanied, and when the situation changed, I thought I could handle it, but I've come to realize that I'm not an experienced traveler. You are. My naïveté may be a liability in some situations, such as with the man in Calais who duped me into believing he wanted to help me, then tried to steal my bag. It would be practical to have someone to help with all the intricacies of travel routes. And, most importantly, I find I enjoy your company. I have a two-bedroom suite booked in both Alexandria and Cairo. You can have the second room at my expense. You don't have to answer right now. Think on it, and let me know. If you decide you'd rather not travel with an old woman, there'll be no hard feelings."

"What happened to your original travel plans?" I asked.

"My cousin was to accompany me. At the last moment, her husband convinced her she shouldn't leave her children for such an extended amount of time—although one is in boarding school and the other one has a governess and two tutors." Hildy made a harrumphing sound. "I didn't see how it would be a hardship on the children, but her husband insisted that it was

41

unmotherly for her to abandon her children for an extended period of time. Since she was adamant she wasn't coming with me, I canceled her train ticket and her cabin on the ship, but I've left her travel arrangements in Egypt in place. I'd hoped she would change her mind and join me there, but I've had a cable from her this morning. She's definitely not traveling, so you're welcome to her room in Cairo. I wouldn't expect you to be at my beck and call, like that terrifying woman on the ferry. I simply want someone to help me through the rough spots of travel and perhaps tour the monuments, if you feel so inclined."

Excitement mixed with relief bubbled up in me. "I don't have to think about it. It's an extremely generous offer, besides being a wonderful idea. I'm delighted to accept."

"Marvelous! Then how soon do you think we can leave for Egypt?"

"Well, it's up to you," I said. "What else would you like to see in Paris?"

"I really should see Versailles and the Opera House and perhaps revisit the Louvre. It's rather enormous. One can't take in the Louvre in one day."

"I agree. Well, if that's your ideal agenda, then I think another three or four days in Paris should do it."

"Sounds reasonable. Then we'll depart on Thursday."

CHAPTER EIGHT

I stood beside Hildy at the railing of the ship, the sun washing over me, heating my bare neck. Below us, the Cairo dock teamed with movement. The crew was unloading mounds of luggage and cargo. Egyptians in long white robes—some wearing a tarboosh, others a turban—called out about their wares or offered their services as guides to the line of passengers inching down the gangway. Soldiers, men in business suits, sailors, and even nuns in black habits brushed shoulders with each other as they threaded through the crowd.

Hildy's grip on the rail tightened. She wore a wide-brimmed hat that resembled an oversized pith helmet. It was swathed in a lightweight purple scarf that fluttered and flapped around her shoulders in the strong breeze. "Oh my. That looks rather overwhelming. Perhaps we should wait a bit before we disembark— let it thin out down there."

"I doubt it will become less crowded. More ships are arriving today. Best to just plunge right in and experience it all at once." I hooked my arm through hers and steered across the deck. "We'll stay together."

"But our luggage . . ."

"The steward said we'll be reunited with our bags . . . somewhere . . . down there." Hildy sent me a doubtful look, so I added, "Even though it looks chaotic, he assured me it would be fine. And you have your most valuable things in your handbag, don't you?"

"Yes, of course. I made sure to transfer my few bits and bobs of jewelry, my correspondence, and my money."

"I did the same." The strap of my handbag rested on my wrist. I tucked my arm closer to my body as we joined the jostle of passengers converging on the gangway. Besides my money, my handbag also contained my pocket camera and the package that Percy had asked me to bring to Egypt.

As we merged into the throng going down the incline at a snaillike pace, we met a man with a slight stoop, who transferred his cane to his left hand and raised his bowler hat, revealing a fringe of curly gray hair. "Miss Honeyworth and Miss Windway."

We'd met Mr. Chambers, a retired clergyman, the day the ship departed. He'd told us he'd been forced to retire years ago because of ill health and had come to Egypt as many invalids did, seeking a warm, dry climate. He'd recovered and had "discovered his life's work," as he'd called it, founding an orphanage in Cairo.

Hildy said, "Mr. Chambers. How are you? We haven't seen you since we departed from Marseille."

"That's because I'm a terrible sailor. I spent the entirety of the journey in my stateroom."

He looked rather like someone recovering from a bout with a serious illness. His already narrow face was thinner, and his complexion, which had been ruddy when we met him, now had a pale and washed-out tone. "I'm sorry to hear that."

"Thank you, Miss Windway. I'm quite looking forward to being back on terra firma. How was your journey across the Mediterranean?"

Hildy shuffled forward a step. "I must admit I found the rough sea rather awful."

"I commiserate with you," he said. "An amazing display of creation's power, but nonetheless one I'm not anxious to experience again. How long are you staying in Alexandria?"

"Only today," Hildy said. "We leave for Cairo tomorrow. The pyramids await."

"Indeed." Mr. Chambers leaned heavily on his cane as we worked our way down the gangway with tiny steps. "My plan is the same."

"And how long will you be in Cairo?" I asked.

"Indefinitely, it seems." Dejection infused his words.

When we'd spoken to him about the orphanage, his passion for helping the children in Cairo had been clear. My face must have shown my surprise at his tone because he grimaced. "That sounded as if I'm being sent to a penal colony, didn't it? Don't mind me. I'm in a bit of a blue mood. I'm sorry to have shared it with you."

"Why should you be sorry?" Hildy asked. "I don't see any reason you should keep something like that to yourself. In fact, you'll probably feel better for speaking about it."

Mr. Chambers chuckled. "Ah, but even if I'm retired, I'm still a clergyman, Miss Honeyworth. People expect a clergyman to listen to their troubles, not share his own."

"That's rubbish. You're a person, not an automaton. People have feelings—even the clergy."

He tilted his head. "Curiously, that is a fact that many people forget."

His tone was lighter, but I wondered who in his life expected him to behave as if he didn't have feelings.

A gust of wind, dry and hot, ruffled my hair, and Mr. Chambers positioned his hat more firmly on his head. "Egypt—Cairo in particular—has been my life for the last twenty years, and I'll be delighted to see the children again, but I confess my heart longs to return to England."

"Then why did you come back to Egypt?" Hildy asked.

"Needs must."

We reached the end of the gangway and merged with the noisy throng on the dock.

"Miss! Very nice fly whisk."

"Sir, good dragoman at your service."

"Lady, fine shawls and beads."

"Oh dear." Hildy went up on her tiptoes. "We've been separated from Mr. Chambers." In the press of the crowd, his stooped figure had been borne away like a reed swept along a river current.

"We're fine on our own. We're almost through . . ." I pressed on, sidestepping the most insistent vendors. Hildy, following along in my wake, raised her voice over the hubbub. "A parasol would come in quite handy."

"Pity that the good stout ones have gone out of style and they're mostly flimsy paper things now," I said over my shoulder.

"Well, flimsy or not, I intend to buy one at the first opportunity. I'll use it to prod people out of my way, just as my grandmother did. Look, I do believe that's one of my trunks. Good heavens, that tiny man is carrying it on his back! How can he even stand, much less move so quickly?"

The young man was bent over almost double, the trunk balanced on his shoulder blades as he trotted up to us. One hand extended over his head, holding the handle in a loose grip. He tapped the trunk with his free hand. "The Savoy Palace?" At my nod, he pirouetted away and motioned to a few other porters who were laden down with various pieces of our luggage. The group converged and set off to our hotel down the street.

As Hildy and I hurried to catch up with the porters, I noticed a man standing very still at the edge of the crowd. His lack of motion drew my eye. He was a short, middle-aged European in a dark suit with a pencil mustache. The sun glinted on the gold watch chain stretched across his vest. What caught my attention was his intense stare as he watched Hildy.

His gaze was fastened on her. He took a step in her direction, then checked himself. The crowd shifted, and a large cart with a hillock of luggage blocked my view of him. When the cart rolled by, he was gone.

≈

LATER THAT AFTERNOON Hildy and I again stood side by side, but this time, instead of peering down from the ship, our heads were tilted back as we squinted against the brilliant sunlight. Pompey's Pillar, a Corinthian column of red granite, rose nearly ninety feet in the air. "Well," Hildy said, "at least *this* is from antiquity."

"You're not impressed with Alexandria, then?"

"I might as well be in any European city. It's nice, of course, but one goes to Egypt to see ancient things. So far, everything we've seen except this"—Hildy waved her hand at the pillar—"is only a few decades old." Hildy shaded her eyes. "It's hard to believe people picnicked at the top."

I pulled the pocket camera away from my face. "What? On top of the column?"

"Apparently, it was quite the thing to do a few decades ago. It could comfortably accommodate fifteen people. Imagine!"

"How did they get up there?"

"They ran a rope over the top and hoisted people up in a basket-like contraption."

I centered the pillar in the viewfinder of my folding camera. "Too bad that's fallen out of fashion. Imagine the view."

"Goodness, I do believe you're serious. Does nothing frighten you?"

"Plenty of things. Long footbridges. Mirrors in dark rooms—those always make my heart jump. And people with small minds and too much time on their hands." I waved Hildy into the shot and snapped a picture. "Since we can't go up, perhaps we should go underground to the catacombs."

"Yes, that's true. They date from . . ." Hildy took out her *Baedeker's* and flipped through the pages. "I have it marked right here. Catacombs of Kom El Shoqafa, the Mound of Shards, from the second century."

"Old enough for a look?"

"Certainly."

"Just one more photograph, then I'll be ready to move on." I stepped back to get a shot of the people mingling around the base of the column.

I was about to turn away, but then I saw the man who'd been staring at Hildy when we disembarked. He was several yards away, but I was sure it was the same person. He'd been looking in our direction, but as soon as I noticed him, he melded with a group of tourists.

"Ready?" Hildy asked.

"What? Oh . . . yes."

As we picked our way through the debris of ancient pieces of columns and shards of pottery, I looked back over my shoulder several times.

"Is something the matter?" Hildy asked as we descended to the catacombs along the stone steps of a circular staircase that wrapped around a central light shaft. "If staircases bother you, we can skip this."

"No. It's fine. I noticed a man at Pompey's Pillar. I also saw him as we disembarked."

"Someone from the ship?"

"No, I didn't recognize him."

Hildy's voice reverberated in the enclosed space. "He's probably following you."

"It was you he was watching."

Hildy almost missed a step. She braced her hand on the rough stone wall. "Me? Nonsense." She marched down the steps, her purple scarf fluttering behind her.

I hurried down after her and plunged into the cool darkness. The voices of the tourists chatting at the top of the stairs faded.

We crossed a rotunda and moved through an intricate layout of rooms with stone sarcophagi and square wall niches. The shelf-like tombs must have held other sarcophagi or mummies. A winged disk was carved over the entrance to one chamber, and columns bracketed the doorway. Reliefs on stone walls portrayed a mixture of ancient gods. I spotted Medusa, Horus, Anubis, Isis, and Osiris as well as decorative carvings of grapes and wreaths. I'd spent time reading up on the ancient Egyptian deities when we crossed the Mediterranean.

Footfalls echoed through the air along with snatches of French and Italian. As Hildy and I moved out of the inner chamber to give the next group access, I caught her sleeve. "Do you know that man across there in the black suit with the pencil mustache and the gold watch chain? The one looking at the relief of the snake with a crown. Reminds me of Douglas Fairbanks in the *Robin Hood* film."

She paused, her forehead wrinkled into a frown, then she lifted her voice. "George?"

The man turned, and a smile spread across his face. He came around a sarcophagus, hand extended. "Hildy! Is it really you?"

"Yes, it is," she said, delight in her voice. He and Hildy shook hands as she said, "I haven't seen you for an age."

"Well, I have been here in Egypt for nearly a decade."

"And Vita? Is she here as well?" Hildy asked.

He continued to hold Hildy's hand between both of his. "Yes, in Cairo. I have a new post, and we're in the midst of a move. I worked out of Alexandria for years, but now I'm transferring to Luxor. I'll take up my post there next month. In the meantime, Vita and I are staying in Cairo. I'm only in Alexandria for the day. I saw a colleague off at the dock." He stepped back, shaking his head. "I thought that was you, but then I decided it couldn't be."

"So you followed us to Pompey's Pillar?" I asked as I glanced at their still-linked hands.

He looked down, surprised, as if he hadn't realized he was

still holding her hand. He released her and stepped back. "I confess, I did. The thought of Hildy in Egypt . . . well, I couldn't believe it." He answered my question, but he gazed at Hildy, all his attention fixed on her. "But it looked so like you."

Hildy didn't seem to notice his scrutiny and said in her normal tone of voice. "Poor Cecil passed away, and I found I have a great desire to travel."

Hand on his chest, he said, "My deepest sympathies on the loss of your brother. I heard about it at the club."

"Thank you," Hildy said.

A group of German tourists entered, and we moved to one of the side chambers with rows of grave niches. He asked, "Are you in Alexandria long?"

Hildy shook her head. "We're traveling on to Cairo tomorrow."

"Then you must join Vita and me for dinner once you're settled in." He took out a gold pen and a business card. He propped the card against one of the rough walls and curled his left hand over the top to write. "I'll jot down our location for you. We're at Shepheard's for a few weeks."

"So are we," Hildy said.

"Oh—well, then. I'll just put down the number of our suite." He handed the card to Hildy. His attention throughout the conversation had been fixed on her, but now he glanced at me as he put his pen away. "Both of you."

Hildy said, "Oh goodness. I've completely forgotten propriety. Let me introduce you. Blix, this is George Rhodes. George, this is Miss Blix Windway."

I'd been poised to say "how do you do," but hearing the name that Percy mentioned surprised me. Before I could say anything, his eyes widened in surprise. "Not the Jilter herself?"

I forced a smile. "The lady traveler now."

"Of course. Of course," he said, but he stared at me as if I were a mummy about to be unwrapped.

Eager to keep the topic from returning to my past, I quickly said, "It's quite fortuitous that we've met. I have a package for you. I brought it from England. If you'd like to return to the hotel, I can have it retrieved from the hotel safe."

He looked startled. "For me?"

"Yes, from Percy Smitherington."

His face cleared. "No, you've got it wrong. It'll be for Vita, then. One of her—er—little hobbies. She's been going on and on about a book that would arrive soon via a helpful courier. Had a letter informing her it was on the way. I don't know why Smitherington didn't use the post. I'm glad you had a safe journey, Miss Windway. Vita was quite worried that your ship would go down and the book would be lost."

Rhodes seemed awfully flippant about the subject. And why would Percy send something to this man's wife? Was she in the diplomatic corps? I didn't know of any lady diplomats in Father's embassy circle, but I thought it was a jolly good thing if there was a female on the staff here in Egypt. "Yes, I imagine so. My friend Percy—do you know him? He impressed on me the urgency of getting it to Egypt."

Rhodes rolled his gaze to the shadowy ceiling of the catacomb. "Yes, I know Percy. Another follower of Mr. Duncan."

The way he spoke of Mr. Duncan indicated the man was a well-known person, but I didn't recognize the name. Rhodes must have misinterpreted my expression because his tone became contrite. "Excuse me. Are you also an adherent of pyramidology?"

It seemed an odd turn for the conversation to take, but I replied, "No, I've only read about it in the guidebooks."

"Oh, there's more to it than what you'll read in *Baedeker's* or *Murray's*." He blew out a sigh. "Much more."

Hildy said, "You mean those daft theories about measurements and magic and whatnot about the pyramids?"

"Ah. You're neophytes. And it sounds as if you have a healthy dose of skepticism, so a word of warning for you. Don't ask Vita about it. She'll pin you to the wall and natter on. You won't free yourself for eons. She's obsessed with it."

"Vita? And pyramidology?" Hildy gave a little shake of her head. "I can't see it."

"Surely you remember how she loves anything new and different. She must be the first one to delve into anything strange, unusual, or undiscovered. I don't understand the attraction myself. All jiggery-pokery in my opinion, but there it is. Vita's lost herself in the study of this so-called science. Pseudo-science, I say. Miss Windway, this package you've brought—it's the jottings of one of the leading lights of the pyramidology movement. One of the early chaps who was interested in the subject, apparently. All claptrap, of course, but Vita will be pleased it's arrived."

I drew in a breath of the dusty air and let it out slowly through my nose, cross with myself for being taken in. Percy's face had been so earnest, and the way he'd carefully handled the parcel had convinced me it was something valuable. And the words he'd used—*urgent, direst importance,* and *hush-hush.* I'd thought it was something that bordered on a diplomatic emergency, some sort of delicate political matter. I should have asked for details, but he'd been so cagey. Father had situations with the same veiled secrecy that he couldn't speak about outright.

I pressed my lips together, anger sparking through me. "So you're *not* with the embassy, Mr. Rhodes?"

"What? No, certainly not. I'm in banking."

I let out a huff, thoroughly annoyed with myself. "Then I was completely taken in. Percy hinted that the package—the book, apparently—didn't make it into the diplomatic pouch because of some mistake and that it was imperative it get to Egypt." To explain to Hildy, I said in an aside to her, "Percy works at Whitehall."

Rhodes said, "And since your father is with the diplomatic service—yes, met him a few times, fine chap—Percy led you to believe you'd be taking it to someone in the diplomatic circle. Had you by the nose, didn't he?"

I felt my cheeks heat with a blush. I should have insisted Percy tell me all the details. "I'm such a goose."

Hildy patted my arm. "Don't feel too bad. You simply did a favor for a friend. And you were traveling to Egypt anyway. It's not as if you made the trip only at his request."

Rhodes said, "You ladies have seen Pompey's Pillar and the catacombs. What else would you like to tour?"

Hildy said, "According to the guidebooks, we should return to the hotel, as we've seen all Alexandria has to offer."

"Rubbish. Alexandria always gets short shrift." He extended his arm to Hildy. "Allow me to be your escort for the rest of the day. I can show you the city's highlights."

LATER AT DINNER at the Savoy Palace Hotel I said to Hildy, "Mr. Rhodes was delighted to see you." He'd taken us through Alexandria's European-like boulevards to view churches and mosques and then escorted us through the museum, which he'd termed "minimally impressive." It contained artifacts mostly from the Greek and Roman eras, which seemed to lower its value in Mr. Rhodes' opinion, but I'd found my first sight of a mummy—along with the statues, coffins, plaster masks, coins, and jewelry—fascinating. Some of the exhibits were dusty and unlabeled, and I could tell that the disarray and lack of order bothered Hildy.

Hildy waved her knife as if she were brushing the comment away. "That means nothing."

"He was certainly attentive."

"That's just his way." She looked across the dining room. "Something Louise didn't understand."

I followed her gaze to Mrs. Jenkins and Rose. They were also staying at the Savoy Palace. We'd checked in at the same time. Tonight Mrs. Jenkins looked stunning with her dark hair piled high on her head, which highlighted her slender neck. An amethyst-and-diamond pendant dipped toward the neckline of her purple evening gown. Rose wore white and seemed to blend in with the tablecloth as she hunched over her plate.

"What do you mean?"

"I acted as a chaperone for my niece years ago. She's the same age as Louise, so I saw quite a lot of Louise that season. Louise and George . . ." She paused as she buttered a roll and sighed. "She set her cap for George, and of course he flirted with her, but he flirted with everyone. Still does, as you saw this afternoon. At the time—during that season, you know—it was difficult to watch. I tried to warn Louise, but she was so confident of his devotion."

I looked from Mrs. Jenkins to Hildy. I thought Mrs. Jenkins was in her late thirties. Mr. Rhodes had to be nearly two decades older than her, which made him more a contemporary of Hildy. But there were plenty of society weddings with bridegrooms twenty years older than the bride. "What happened?"

"She thought George was on the verge of making an offer, but I knew it wouldn't happen."

"Why not?"

"George's family needed money, so of course he married Vita, whose family had pots and pots of it—she was a Filmore before she married. New money, but George's family couldn't be too particular. An infusion of American money was what the Silverthorne estate needed."

I was cutting a piece of lamb, but I paused. "Vita is Victoria Filmore, the sweets heiress?"

"Yes. Victoria is her given name, but everyone calls her by her nickname, Vita. Her father makes what they call *candies* in America. The press nicknamed her the Lollipop Princess, which I thought was rather uncalled for."

I speared a morsel of the tender meat. "Still, it's hard to

imagine someone as beautiful as Mrs. Jenkins not bringing the man she wanted up to snuff."

"Oh, it wasn't the man she wanted—though he would've been a nice addition—it was Silverthorne."

"Silverthorne? What do you mean?"

"Her family expected her to marry the son of the family who owned Silverthorne. It was assumed from the time they were children that the two would marry and that she'd be the mistress of Silverthorne. Unfortunately, the son was killed in the Boer War, and his cousin, George, inherited. George was determined to rescue Silverthorne, so he married the sweets heiress."

I gave a warning shake of my head, and Hildy broke off as Mrs. Jenkins sailed by our table with a nod of acknowledgment. Rose trooped along behind her, head down, her gaze on the carpet. Once they were past, Hildy reached for her glass. "That will teach me to gossip."

"You weren't saying anything malicious."

"Nevertheless, let's speak of something else. What time do we depart for Cairo tomorrow?" Her question turned the conversation, and we discussed our plan for the city where we intended to spend at least a week. We were still chatting about the subject as we made our way upstairs after dinner.

"The guidebook suggests at least two separate visits to the Egyptian Museum, so perhaps we should—" Hildy broke off as I swung the door open. Our sitting room was in disarray.

I stepped inside and picked up a cushion from the floor. "Goodness. What happened?" The drawers of a little console table had been pulled out. Hildy's lap desk had been upended, and crinkled envelopes and papers covered the rug.

Hildy let out a strangled sound and crossed the room. She flipped her writing desk right side up. I crisscrossed the suite and checked our bedrooms, which were on either side of the sitting room.

They were in similar states. I returned to the sitting room and replaced a few more cushions. "Our trunks and cases have been emptied on the floor, but it appears nothing of mine is missing,"

Hildy looked up from the stack of papers she was gathering up. "Nothing of value can be missing from my room either. I put my jewelry and checkbook in the hotel safe earlier today."

"Thank goodness." I picked up another cushion. "We'd best ring the front desk and let them know someone has vandalized our room."

"Yes. It's just like what happened on the ship—only worse."

CHAPTER NINE

J pressed the button to summon an attendant. "What do you mean, this is just like on the ship?"

Hildy reached under the sofa and retrieved another envelope. "It was the day that the sea became rough so suddenly. I went below first, you remember?"

"Oh yes." That day I'd been glad that Miss Spalding hadn't continued on to Egypt. I'd enjoyed riding the rolling waves as we crossed the English Channel, but the heaving Mediterranean Sea was something else entirely. I hadn't lasted much longer on the deck than Hildy before I'd retreated to my stateroom. On the ship, we'd had rooms on the same passageway, but other than peeking in to check on Hildy the next day, I hadn't spent any time in her room.

"When I went to my stateroom, I noticed a familiar scent, hair oil. I supposed it was a new attendant who'd been in my room. I wouldn't have thought anything more about it, except that when I went to put away my gloves, I noticed my clothes had been shifted around. Not tidied like the attendant arranged them. They were squashed together as if someone had shoved them aside. So then I began to really look. Everything had been moved—my clothes, my writing desk, even my toiletries."

"Gracious. Did you tell anyone?"

"Yes, I rang for the steward, who informed the purser, but nothing had been taken, and with the storm . . . well, nothing came of it. In fact, by the time the purser left, I felt extremely silly for summoning the crew when so many other passengers were in such distress. The storm was ghastly, and the crew had their hands full caring for those who were ill. I decided to let it go."

A tap on the door sounded. "Well, to have it happen a second time—we can't ignore it."

"No, I agree. Let me check my room," Hildy said as I opened the door. The attendant who'd brought our luggage up from the lobby stood on the threshold. I motioned him inside. "As you can see, someone has been here, riffling through our belongings."

He wore a long-sleeved red jacket and vest with loose white trousers. His trousers were gathered at his ankles, and the fabric billowed as he followed me across the suite to glance into my room. "What is missing, madam?"

"Nothing of mine as far as I can tell at the moment." I turned to Hildy, who had re-entered the sitting room.

"It's the same for me. I don't think anything is missing, but my room is a muddle."

"Do not worry, madams." The tassel on his tarboosh moved as he glanced around. "We will straighten your rooms."

"We're less concerned about the mess than the fact that this has happened before," I said.

His eyebrows shot up. "Here? At the Savoy?"

"No," Hildy said. "In my stateroom on the ship."

His tone changed. "Oh. Well, that is out of our control."

I detected a hint of skepticism as his gaze became more assessing, running over our scattered belongings. Irritation prickled like a rash on my skin. "Surely you don't think we manufactured this situation?"

Hildy frowned at me and said to the man, "I'm sure he doesn't think that."

His gaze traveled from Hildy's obviously expensive discarded hat and gloves to the sparkling diamonds in her hair combs. "No, not at all. I will speak to the manager."

"Frankly, I don't see how that will help," I said.

His voice turned soothing, "Yes, very disturbing. I assure you it won't happen again. This floor will be monitored throughout the evening. I'll speak to the manager and make sure of it." He offered to send someone to help us clean up, but we declined.

I closed the door after him. "Sorry. When someone doesn't believe me, it rather sets me off."

"Your reaction did seem a tad over the top."

"Yes, I suppose so. In any case, he wasn't helpful at all."

"No, but what can the hotel do? Thank goodness I put the jewelry I wasn't wearing in the hotel safe. Not that it's incredibly valuable, but I'd hate to lose my great-aunt's pearl earrings."

"My things are there as well."

When Mr. Rhodes had returned us to the hotel earlier in the afternoon, I'd offered to have the book retrieved from the hotel safe, but he'd waved off the idea. "Don't trouble yourself. I'd rather you give it to Vita. She'll be delighted to meet the courier."

I'd considered asking for it tonight because it would help expedite our departure in the morning, but now I was glad I'd left it where it was.

I said good night to Hildy and went to tidy my guest chamber, all the while wondering if perhaps Mr. Rhodes had not been quite honest with me about the book. Or perhaps there was more to it than he understood.

~

THE NEXT DAY as the train chugged out of Alexandria, we passed by villages of mud houses fringed with palms, sycamores, and banyans.

I settled back in my seat with the package Percy had given me. He'd misled me about the contents of it and the importance of it. After the disturbance of our hotel room last night, I wanted to see what I'd been toting around. I'd found nothing amiss in my room after tidying it, but I couldn't quite put to rest the idea that the package might be the reason that someone had rummaged through our hotel suite. It had been Hildy's stateroom that had been searched on the ship, but during the sea voyage she'd almost missed the invasion of her privacy. The fact that her diamond combs and other valuable items weren't taken from her stateroom on the ship indicated that the intruder hadn't been a typical thief on the hunt for jewelry or cash.

Perhaps I'd been less observant than Hildy. Had someone been in my stateroom as well? We were traveling together. If someone were looking for something one of us possessed, then that person might have searched both our staterooms—and our hotel suite. The fact that I'd kept the package in my handbag while on the ship would have meant anyone looking through my belongings would come up empty and might turn to my traveling companion's room as their next place to search. And a search at the hotel would be fruitless as well since the parcel was in the manager's safe.

The parcel was small, about the same size as my *Baedeker's*, only thinner. It was wrapped in brown paper and tied with string. I worked the knots loose and folded the paper back, revealing a slender leather-bound notebook. The crinkling of the wrapping paper didn't disturb Hildy, who sat across from me, her head bowed over her writing desk as she scribbled away on another letter.

The notebook was dark blue with the word *Diary* embossed in gold letters above the image of a dragonfly. The pages were a faded lemon color and the cursive handwriting a faint brown, but I was able to read it. The name on the flyleaf indicated it belonged to Cornelius Duncan. According to the entries, he'd journeyed from England to Egypt in the 1800s and traveled quite extensively through the country, recording his impressions of the sites and the people he met.

I skimmed a dozen or so pages. It all seemed rather mediocre stuff, more travelogue than anything else as he described in great detail the meals he ate, the people he met, and each day's weather. It was only when he reached Cairo and toured the pyramids that I began to understand why it might interest someone decades later.

Duncan had been fascinated by the pyramids and spent days there, visiting them repeatedly, even camping there overnight. I turned the pages quickly, skimming detailed notations of pyramid measurements and his rhapsody over the Giza Plateau at sunset. I slowed and read his summaries of multiple conversations he'd had with fellow pyramid enthusiasts more carefully. Several people were convinced that the pyramids had inherent power that could be captured, but only at certain times of the year and at certain times of the day or night. As far as I could tell, he spent much of his time searching for these manifestations, but not experiencing them himself. Although another person in his party claimed that the time spent at the pyramids cured his tuberculosis.

Eventually, Duncan traveled to Luxor and his interest in pyramidology waned after he met a young woman named Gwendolyn. From that point on, he was more interested in pursuing her dahabeeyah as it traveled up the Nile. He planned to propose during a moonlight tour of Abu Simbel. She must have said yes because the diary entries halted after that, except for several drafts of a love poem about her eyebrows.

I flicked through the rest of the pages, which were blank. At the end of the notebook, a series of long lists on the final few pages detailed what he needed to purchase before his return to England. Since the list included new stationery for Mr. and Mrs.

Duncan, I assumed they either married or planned to marry soon after their return journey.

I closed the book and watched a string of pelicans flap alongside the train. We rattled over a bridge, crossing one of the tributaries of the Nile. The pelicans peeled off, angling toward the dark water. I caught a glimpse of more brown-toned villages, some with slender minarets rising against the pale blue sky. The pyramids, their outlines hazy and indistinct, came into view in the distance. Soon Cairo, with its multitude of minarets, was visible, a sprawling metropolis of stone buildings and clusters of palms, a sharp contrast to the open vistas of the desert.

The train slowed to a lazy pace and rolled into the station. As we gathered our belongings, Hildy said, "Oh, I forgot to tell you. I received a note this morning at the hotel in Alexandria."

"More correspondence?" I asked as I took down my small case from the rack. "You must be the most faithful letter writer in all of the empire."

"I doubt that. It was from Vita. George must have sent her a message last night about us. She's invited us to tea on the terrace this afternoon."

"How nice."

Hildy picked up her handbag. "Yes, it's very thoughtful, but she didn't give me the location."

"There's no need," I said. "There's only one terrace in Cairo that matters—the terrace at Shepheard's."

CHAPTER TEN

*O*nce we'd freshened up after the train journey, we went down the staircase and through Shepheard's impressive lobby. Soaring pillars with capitals crafted to resemble palm branches lined the immense area. A pattern of tiny stars covered the high ceiling, and the walls and doorframes were decorated with Egyptian motifs.

A short, effete man in a white linen suit stepped into our path and removed his pith helmet. "Good afternoon, ladies. Please allow me to introduce myself. Casper Denby, at your service." He looked to be in his middle thirties and was whippet-thin with a face that reminded me of the joker in a deck of cards. He had dark brown eyes, and his wavy brown hair was receding at the temples. He'd slicked his hair back, but a few wiry curls had sprung free and dangled on one side of his forehead. He made an elaborate bow, then swept the curls back with a careless, fluid movement. "Miss Windway, I believe we have a mutual friend in Prudence Brinkle. The last time I was in jolly olde England, I made her my cocktail creation called Desert Sunset, and we've been fast friends ever since."

"She does have a fondness for cocktails," I said.

"*Fondness* is far too anemic a description. She adores them."

I couldn't help but smile. "Too true. Allow me to present Miss Hildy Honeyworth."

"*Enchanté.*" He raised Hildy's hand to his lips, and she lowered her chin in a coquettish manner. "I won't keep you lovely ladies, but here is my card. I'd particularly like to chat with you, Miss Windway, about Cairo. I write a little column for *The Nile*, the local English-language rag, you know. It has all the details on social events, including the upcoming fancy dress ball. You'll want to arrange costumes for that right away."

"Yes, I've heard of *The Nile*." The desk clerk had asked if we'd like a copy of the weekly newspaper delivered to our room.

"I know *The Nile's* readers would be fascinated to hear the lady traveler's impressions of Cairo."

"Well, I've hardly seen any of it, so I can't give an opinion. Perhaps after I've at least seen the pyramids . . ."

He waved a languid hand. "Oh, don't worry about that. Half the visitors to Cairo never venture farther than the ballrooms of the various hotels." He pressed the card into my hand. "Do get in touch after you've settled in. I'll treat you to tea—a cocktail—and Cairo's very best gossip. Toodle pip."

Hildy and I exchanged glances, then continued on through the lobby. A multitude of Oriental rugs blanketed the stone floor like a patchwork quilt and muffled our footsteps as we crossed to the shady raised terrace that overlooked one of Cairo's busiest streets. On the boulevard, motors, pedestrians, and men pushing carts along with horse-drawn carriages jostled against each other. On the right and left sides of the terrace, stairs went down to the gardens that ran along the front of the hotel. A babble of voices rose up from beyond the wrought-iron balustrade as vendors on the pavement touted their wares to the tourists.

Hildy scanned the tables. "Vita's not here yet. Let's get a table. I'm sure she'll be along shortly." Hildy ordered tea, then said, "I really should have expected it. Vita is one of those people who has a tendency to be tardy." She shifted her rattan chair so she could look out toward the street. "At least we have plenty to watch. It's quite a spectacle."

"Rather like a play, isn't it?" Turbaned men waved everything from beads and fly whisks to postcards and fruit. One young man walked back and forth with a stuffed crocodile. A lady in a cloche and dropped-waist dress leaned over the banister to examine an ivory statue. I took out my camera and snapped a few pictures. "I hope I brought enough film. Everything is so interesting and unusual. I want to record it all."

"I'm sure you can find more film. In fact, I bet someone down there either sells film or knows where you can buy some." Hildy sat up straighter. "I believe that's Vita. She's in tangerine and is pressing through the crowd like a frigate cutting through a harbor filled with sailboats."

Vita was a statuesque woman and moved with purpose. The throng of vendors fell back from her headlong rush, creating a path. She climbed the shallow steps and disappeared into the main entrance. A few moments later she was striding toward our table, the maître d' trotting along behind her in an effort to catch up.

She threw her arms out. "Hildy! I was so thrilled to learn you would be in Cairo."

"It's wonderful to see you again," Hildy said, looking a bit caught off guard as Vita hugged her. The maître d' called for another chair, and Hildy introduced me.

As we took our seats, I said, "Delighted to meet you, Mrs. Rhodes."

"Likewise, but you must call me Vita. We'll have none of this Mr. and Mrs. Rhodes. George and Vita, please." A few heads turned at the combination of her nasal voice and her American accent, but she seemed to be unaware of the scrutiny as she continued, "And I'll call you Blix, if that's all right? It's no use being formal. It's such a small community. We're very friendly here. I don't understand these people who arrive and try to replicate England. They never venture out into the real Cairo. They're only interested in dances and teas and lawn tennis. They might as well be in London."

"But not you, Vita. Tell me, is this native dress?" Hildy waved a hand at Vita's bright clothing.

"It's my own creation, a combination of the two. I find Western clothing hot and unimaginative, whereas this"—she waved an arm, and her long bell sleeve, the edge of which was decorated with embroidered lotus flowers and tiny tassels, fluttered through the air—"is beautiful and comfortable."

She also wore a turban in the same shade of orange as her dress. While turbans were fashionable in London, Vita's was different than what a society woman would wear with an evening gown. Those turbans tended to be close-fitting and had a pin or two as decoration. Vita's turban was more intricate. Gold thread was woven into the cloth and sparkled when she turned her head. The fabric was twisted in an intricate crisscross pattern, and a swath of the tangerine fabric hung down on one side of her face and draped over her shoulder. Dark black curls peeked out from the edge of the turban around her forehead. Gold hoops swung from her earlobes as she leaned forward to accept the cup of tea Hildy poured for her.

Vita sipped it and let out a satisfied sigh. "I do enjoy a good cup of tea. Oh, you must think me a hypocrite, Blix, after my little rant about English travelers, but it's my only indulgence to colonial life, I assure you. Now tell me, Hildy, what have you seen?"

"Of Cairo?" Hildy asked. "The train station and Shepheard's."

"Then you must let me show you around. In fact—yes, this will be perfect. I'm going to the pyramids tomorrow, and you must come."

Hildy glanced at me and said, "We'd intended to visit a few sites around Cairo first."

"Nonsense. You must come with me tomorrow. It'll be perfect. You'll avoid the crowds. So tedious with the masses of tourists swarming all over the pyramids. No, this way you'll see the pyramids at their best—in the moonlight."

Hildy looked at me. "Blix, what do you think?"

"The pyramids by night? I don't see how we can pass up the offer."

"Then, yes, thank you for inviting us," Hildy said.

"Excellent. I've been planning a small dinner party at the pyramids for weeks, then we'll camp on the plateau overnight. I've invited several friends. I'm so happy you'll be there as well."

"Is that allowed?" I asked. "Having a dinner at the pyramids and camping at Giza?"

"Of course. One simply has to know who to ask. It's quite easy to obtain the correct permissions. Now you'll need to pack a small case. I've arranged for tents to be set up so we can spend the night—there will be a full moon. Then the next morning, we'll watch the sunrise. It will be spectacular."

"If all the arrangements have been made, then perhaps Blix and I should wait and visit the pyramids on our own."

"It's no trouble at all. I'll send word that we need another tent. And don't worry. You'll have all the comforts of civilization. It will be like a Shepheard's guest room transported to Giza."

I imagined that it would be quite a lot of work for someone else, something that Vita clearly didn't trouble herself about.

She went on, "Adding you to the guest list will round out things nicely. My nephew has recently arrived in Cairo. He and his friend will be in attendance. His friend is quite taken with all things Egyptian. He should enjoy the setting, even if Ned doesn't appreciate it."

"Would that be Ned Breen?" I asked.

"Oh, do you know him?"

"Yes, I do." I managed not to add the word *unfortunately*.

Vita's cup was almost empty, and Hildy reached for the teapot, but Vita set her cup down and pushed her chair back. "No, I'll leave you to settle."

It seemed Vita did everything at top speed. She'd only been at our table a few minutes. Since she was leaving, I took out the package from my handbag. I'd carefully rewrapped it and retied the string. "Before you go, let me give you this. It's from Percy Smitherington. I gathered from your husband—um—George, that you were quite anxious to get it."

She'd been poised to rise from her chair, but she subsided into it, her attention focused on the package. "I'm so, so glad it's arrived. Such an important book! I couldn't believe Percy was so foolish as to not make a copy of it before he sent it. The hours of sleep I've lost worrying about it." She untied the string. "But that doesn't matter. It's here now." The cadence of her words had been quick, a staccato beat. But as soon as she tugged the paper and it fell away, she went silent, staring at the book. I looked at Hildy, and she lifted one shoulder slightly, indicating she didn't know what to make of Vita's actions.

Vita ran her hand across the cover, her fingers tracing over the word *Diary* and the outline of the dragonfly, then she delicately opened it. The swath of fabric that hung from her turban slid off her shoulder as she bent over the notebook. She flipped through the pages. "Thank you, Blix."

"It was no trouble."

She looked up sharply. "You do realize what you've been carrying around, don't you?"

I knew what I'd read. The diary was nothing but a travelogue—a rather boring one at that, but the intensity of her gaze was disconcerting. I shifted in my chair, guilt pricking at me as I thought of my snooping. Whether or not I thought the diary was important, Vita clearly felt it was special.

She closed the book and placed her hand on the cover. Her tone reverent, she said, "These are the words of Cornelius Duncan."

"I'm not familiar with him."

"Never heard of him?" Vita tossed the swath of fabric from her turban back over her shoulder, in a *there's much work to do here* manner.

"Well, you will be. Soon everyone will know him."

CHAPTER ELEVEN

*V*ita scooted her chair closer and leaned her forearms on the table, her gaze fixed on me. "Surely you've heard of his book, *Visions in Egypt*?"

I hated to contradict her, but I didn't want to lie. "No, I'm afraid not."

"I'll lend you a copy," Vita said with the air of someone who was righting a great wrong.

"Thank you, but there's no—"

"I have several copies. You *must* read it. He's extraordinary! The first time he visited Egypt, he saw a vision of the woman who would become his wife while touring the pyramids."

He did? I managed to stop myself before I blurted out the words. There hadn't been anything about that in his diary, and it had been clear from the bits I'd read that the diary recorded his first visit to Egypt.

"He wrote about the experience extensively in *Visions in Egypt*. Such amazing intelligence. You see, he had an extraordinary gift of deciphering things that most of us can't see. It's amazing! I can tell both of you are doubtful, but you'll see tomorrow."

Hildy said, "What do you mean?"

"Now that I have his diary, we can do exactly what he did when he saw his visions."

"Visions?" Hildy asked. "Plural?"

"Oh yes. He returned to the pyramids many times and had several revelations." She caressed the cover of the diary. "Now that I have Cornelius' diary, we can do exactly what he did and replicate the results."

"You mean you think you'll also see a vision at the pyramids?"

"Of course. I'll go to the precise location where he stood and repeat his actions. He describes in *Visions in Egypt* how he recited certain Egyptian charms, and because he was standing at the perfect location—he worked that out later—he was able to see visions. Unfortunately, in his book, he forgot to be exact in describing his location on the plateau when he saw the visions, which was such a loss. He passed away before the war, so we thought the knowledge was lost. But now that I have his diary, I can work it out."

A noise came from Hildy that sounded suspiciously like a snort. "Vita, you can't be serious."

Vita's expression shifted from enraptured to mulish. "I most certainly am."

"I'm sorry, Vita. I can see that you take this incredibly seriously, but you can't really believe that he was able to discern the future? No one can do that. An educated guess is the most anyone can manage."

"But he did it. Besides seeing the face of the woman who would become his wife, he also saw the horrible carnage that came with the war. He tried to warn people, but no one believed him. And he's not the only person to experience it. Other people who visited the pyramids were healed of truly awful diseases. I tell you, there's incredible knowledge and power tied up with the pyramids. We just have to learn to access it. And once we do, I have such plans! Classes and lectures and so much more."

Hildy shifted in her chair.

Vita carefully re-wrapped the paper around the diary and tied the string again. "I know not everyone thinks as I do. A little skepticism is healthy, but you'll see. I'll study his diary tonight so that I can do exactly what he did. He camped at the pyramids and saw his first vision as the sun rose the next morning. He returned several times and had the same experience. I realize you don't believe now, but you'll see the results. When the sun rises, I'll be in the exact location he was. I intend to go about it in a methodical manner. That's why it was so urgent that I have his diary—so I can repeat exactly what he did. Isn't that the essence of science? To replicate an experiment and assess the outcome?"

"Yes, I suppose so," Hildy allowed.

Vita nodded and pushed back her chair. "So don't be hasty in your judgment. You'll see the results. You won't be able to argue about it then."

As HILDY AND I climbed the stairs to our suite to change for dinner, Hildy said, "I'd forgotten how impressionable Vita is. The conversation on the terrace brought to mind several times when she took up some idea or cause and pursued it wholeheartedly, almost blindly."

We came to our room, and I opened the door. No one locked their doors at Shepheard's. "What are your thoughts on this Cornelius Duncan?"

"A charlatan, I'm sure. But no one will convince Vita of that. It's something she'll have to discover herself, which will occur tomorrow when absolutely nothing happens at the pyramids."

"I wonder what vision she hopes to see?"

Hildy put her handbag down and turned to the mirror to remove her hat. "I don't think it's the vision so much as experiencing something new, something that few have experienced, that is the attraction."

"Seeing the pyramids by moonlight sounds lovely, but the outing could turn awkward when Vita's disappointed."

"Only for a short time. She'll be disillusioned, but it won't be long before she latches on to her next new thing."

~

WHEN WE ARRIVED at the Giza Plateau the next afternoon, the sun was already low, a great orange ball tracking toward the horizon and the pyramids.

Hildy pressed a hand to her chest. "Oh my. I knew they were immense, but to actually see them—and we're still so far away. What do you think, Blix?"

I stopped taking pictures long enough to say, "I think they're one of the most amazing things I've ever seen." The three largest pyramids dominated the view, but I was also intrigued by the smaller ones dotted around the larger ones, which *Baedeker's* said were for the wives of the pharaohs.

Hildy tilted her parasol to block the sun and moved to another position to see the site from another angle. We'd both purchased parasols from the vendors outside the train station in Alexandria along with a few other trinkets, including a letter opener for me with oval turquoise stones on the handle. I'd been assured the stones were rare ancient scarabs, but I doubted it because the handle of Hildy's paper knife was identical. We'd had a good laugh when we'd compared purchases.

Fortunately, our parasols were different. Hildy's was painted with a bright burst of flowers, while a geometric pattern in blues and grays decorated mine. Knowing that I'd want to take plenty of pictures, and that would require having my hands free, I'd left my parasol at the hotel and opted for a large-brimmed hat secured against the wind with a scarf tied under my chin.

The sun and stiff winds didn't seem to bother Vita. She stood facing into the gusts as she surveyed the plateau. "It will be even more spectacular tonight when the tourists aren't swarming over them." Tiny forms, dark specks, were moving up and down the massive stone blocks of the pyramids.

We stood on the edge of the desert. Behind us stretched a band of green vegetation and palms. The fertile area was threaded through with strings of canals flowing with the Nile's blue-green water.

Hildy and I had taken the tram to the Mena House Hotel, then made our way through a cluster of buildings—a few shops, a post office, a police station, and a drug store—then we'd climbed the steep curves of a road until we'd reached the plateau. The Sphinx, swathed in golden brown sand up to its neck, had greeted us, and I hadn't stopped taking photos since.

The area where we'd paused was full of motion. Tourists, some of them with their feet almost dragging the ground, trotted by on donkeys. A row of camels waited, their handlers calling out to us, "Good camel, ladies. No biting. No spitting." A photographer, camera set up on a tripod, posed group after group so that the pyramids would be in the background of the picture.

I shifted my attention from the pyramids to Vita. Her necklace, which looked like the ancient jewelry I'd seen in the museum in Alexandria, shifted as she drew in a deep breath of the dry air. Wind whipped at the skirt and bell sleeves of her simple white linen shift dress as she stared across the plateau. Her turban today was white with fringe on the scarf-like portion of it that hung down over her shoulder. "Really, I can't believe people are allowed to clamber over the pyramids. The pyramids' power, their energy, their spiritual—"

She broke off as a group of children closed around us, calling out for money while a young boy tugged a donkey to my side. "Nice donkey. Ride, miss?"

I shook my head while Hildy pressed coins into a few grimy

hands. Vita swished her hand through the air and said some-thing in Arabic. I don't know if it was her words or her commanding tone, but the children dropped back, and the donkey boy turned to speak to another group of tourists. "Never give them piastres, Hildy."

"Poor little mites," Hildy said. "It's only a few coins."

"If I wasn't with you, they'd plague you all day."

A man in a turban and striped caftan over his dark gallibaya, leading a donkey mounded with our luggage, caught Vita's attention. Her tone became sharp as she strode over to him. "Tadros! Not this way. Take those to the campsite." Maybe it was because he was looking into the sun as he replied, but he seemed to be scowling.

Hildy said, "Oh, look. Here's Mr. Chambers." He'd traveled with us on the tram from Cairo, but he'd stepped into one of the shops and told us to go ahead to the plateau. A day or two on land appeared to suit him. The ruddiness was back in his cheeks, and his face didn't look quite so thin. "Mr. Chambers," Hildy said, "I'd be quite interested in your thoughts on the pyramids."

He stopped beside Hildy and braced his hands on his cane. "They're impressive and fascinating, scientifically and archaeo-logically."

"No spiritual aspect to them?" Hildy pressed.

"Not in my book." His gaze went to Vita, who was now motioning for us to join her as she led the way to a line of camels. "Of course, others disagree with me. I don't share the opinion of our hostess."

I collapsed the camera and put it in my pocket. "Then I'm surprised you joined us, Mr. Chambers."

"Needs must."

It was a curious response. Hadn't he said something similar when we departed the ship? I would have asked what he meant, but Mrs. Jenkins paused beside me. "Where is Vita? Oh, I see her there. Come along, Rose."

She and Rose were also part of Vita's overnight camping party. Unlike Vita, who'd raced up to the plateau, Mrs. Jenkins had refused to hurry, and she insisted Rose stay by her side as she maintained a stately pace.

Mrs. Jenkins wore an apricot linen traveling suit and tilted a matching parasol to shade her face. Rose, in a white shirt and breeches, with a red scarf knotted around her throat, trailed along a few steps behind her mother. While Mrs. Jenkins looked immaculate, Rose's boots were already dusty, and the strap of her heavy satchel slung on one shoulder wrinkled her long-sleeved shirt. "Since we can't go to the museum today, I don't see why we can't see the inside of the pyramids."

"Because they're dusty, dirty places." Mrs. Jenkins increased her pace, and I made no effort to keep up with them. I recognized the tension in the air around the mother and daughter and had no desire to be part of their argument. "I don't understand why you want to crawl about in one," Mrs. Jenkins continued. "Now I expect you to participate in the conversation this evening . . ."

Vita turned and waved. "Come on, then. Our transportation to the campsite is waiting."

The camels were kneeling, their legs folded under them. I went to one camel and stroked its neck. In one long, sinuous movement, it turned its head and looked back at me. I'd heard that camels had rather bad manners and tended to spit, but this one only blinked its long-lashed eyes and sniffed at my arm.

"Oh, how darling." Hildy stroked her camel's shoulder. "Look at those lashes. I'm jealous, you pretty thing." But after she climbed into the saddle, she shrieked when the camel came to its feet. "Goodness. It's quite high, isn't it? And I'm not a very good horsewoman."

I snapped her picture. "I think they're quite tame. I'm sure they'll follow each other—they must do it all day." I motioned to the other tourists in the distance who were mounted on camels trekking around the pyramids.

"Yes, I suppose so," she said, her words barely audible.

"I'll stay with you," I said, but I had to admit that it was a little intimidating when I approached my camel again and climbed into the saddle. When the guide made a clicking sound, the camel raised its back legs first, tipping me forward. I felt as if I was about to tumble head-first into the sand, but then the camel straightened its front legs, and the world righted itself. I gave Hildy a wave, and she sent me a weak smile in return.

Once everyone was mounted, Vita looked around. "Where are the rest of the men? George promised me they wouldn't linger in the bar in the Mena House."

After leaving the tram, George, Ned, and Mr. Noviss—Timothy, I mentally corrected myself since Vita insisted we use Christian names—had stopped off for a drink in the bar at the hotel. They weren't interested in a camel tour of the pyramids. Vita motioned to the guide to move out. "We won't wait for them. George knows where the campsite is."

We set off on a route around the Great Pyramid with Vita shouting back facts about length and orientation to the four cardinal points and diagonal lines between it and the other smaller pyramids on the plain. I didn't take in much of what she was saying. The wind was strong. It peppered me with sand and whisked Vita's words away, which was fine with me. I only wanted to take my photos and then absorb the scene, which was difficult to do since every few moments I had to brace my hand over my hat to keep it on my head as the wind tore at it.

We skirted around an archaeological excavation, made a circuit around the Great Pyramid, and admired the head of the Sphinx. The camel's rolling, soft-footed gait reminded me of the movement of walking on the deck while at sea.

Mr. Chambers shaded his eyes and called, "I believe I see George." Everyone continued to address Mr. Chambers formally, probably because he was the oldest of the group. The men were mounted—if one could use that word—on donkeys. They looked comical with their long legs nearly brushing the ground. We waited for them, the windblown sand prickling against my face. The trio trotted up, and my camel shied to the side. Hildy gripped the reins of hers, but it turned its long neck and looked in the other direction as if bored with the whole venture.

George paused only long enough to shout, "We'll meet you at the camp," then he put his heels to the donkey's sides and bounced away with Ned and Timothy following, kicking up a trail of dust that engulfed us.

CHAPTER TWELVE

*W*e set off at a more moderate pace, the pyramids at our backs. With no prompting from me, my camel fell into line behind the guide. He moved along a track that meandered across the uneven texture of the plateau. Sandy hills scattered with rocks occasionally dropped down in sharp little escarpments to a lower layer of shard-strewn sand. The path cut like a riverbed through the sand and rock, undulating through the small elevation changes of the high plain. We kept to the packed, dusty trail and arrived at the campsite about a quarter of an hour later. A grouping of tents, their bright white sides pulsing in the strong breeze, were positioned so that we'd have a view of the pyramids. As we drew closer, I realized there was more to the campsite.

Beyond the string of small tents, a larger tent had been set up. Three sides were enclosed, but the fourth had been left open. A canopy stretched out from the open side, shading the interior. In the dimness of the enclosed area, I could make out wooden-framed sling-back chairs with canvas seats, tables, and even a sofa arranged on an Oriental carpet.

A few feet away sat another large tent with one side open to the view of the pyramids. A long table draped in white linen and set with crystal and china looked like it had been lifted from a country house dining room and magically transported to the desert. Silver candelabras sat on either side of a flower arrangement of roses and lotus flowers.

The smell of roasting meat and a column of smoke came from a smattering of smaller tents positioned beyond the two larger tents. Servants in white gallibayas hurried back and forth across the area, carrying luggage from the enclosure where the donkeys had been corralled to the row of small tents. The guide made a clicking noise, and my camel folded its legs and lowered itself to the ground, but I was prepared for the tilting descent and managed to dismount gracefully.

Hildy gave her camel's neck a last pat, then surveyed the campsite. "This is quite impressive, Vita."

"Thank you. As I said to George, there's no reason we can't be comfortable. I'll show you to your tents. Take a few moments to refresh yourselves, then meet in the lounge—that's the large tent with the chairs and sofa—for drinks before dinner."

Mrs. Jenkins brushed down her shirt, but she looked as flawless as she had when we'd departed. Not a single hair was out of place. "We're dining so soon?"

"Yes, it is early, but it will become quite cool once the sun goes down. We'll eat now, then we can bundle up in blankets and admire the pyramids in the moonlight from the lounge tent." Vita took us to the line of small tents set off to the side. "Ladies are on this end. George and I are in the middle, and the rest of the men are down at the other end."

I'd expected to share a tent with Hildy, but we each had our own. Vita motioned me toward the third tent from the end. "You'll find water in the pitcher, Blix. Ring the bell if you need anything else."

I stepped over the ropes that anchored the tent, lifted the flap, and ducked inside. Because of the well-appointed lounge tent, I expected the individual tents to be comfortable, but I was shocked at the luxuriousness I found inside. I spun in a slow circle, taking it all in.

A stiff woven mat covered the ground, and an Oriental carpet had been placed over it. White netting was tied back from a single bed where a fluffy eiderdown covered a thick mattress. My luggage had been delivered and placed at the end of the bed. A chest of drawers filled one corner, while a wash-stand and a small bedside table sat on either side of the bed.

Besides the sturdy furnishings, several other small touches showed no expense had been spared in preparing the tents. A pitcher and tumbler sat on a small bedside table. The floral scent from a vase of peach-colored roses on another table filled the tent. A lantern, a torch, and a stack of postcards and notepaper rested beside the vase. Another lantern hung from a hook on the pole at the center of the tent. And on the opposite side of the tent, a sling-back chair and table formed a comfort-able reading nook.

"Knock-knock." Hildy's voice carried through the flap that formed the tent door.

"Come in."

She poked her head in and surveyed the interior. "Every-thing to your liking?"

"It's amazing."

"Vita never does things by halves. I'm pleased your tent is as nice as mine."

"It would be perfectly fine if it wasn't."

Hildy drew in a breath, and her chest expanded out. "Non-sense. It would have been a slight—and I wouldn't have put up with that." She folded back the tent flap. "Are you coming along to the lounge tent? For all her prosing on about the absur-dity of colonial life, Vita's not gone as native as she likes one to think."

"Yes, but I must change and tidy up." I'd removed my hat, and my hair had expanded with static electricity in the dry air, haloing my dusty face.

"Just tamp it down with a bit of water. You look fine."

"I can't go to dinner like this." I waved a hand at my wrinkled clothes. "I look a fright."

"Nonsense. We're in the desert. You don't have to look as if you emerged from a bandbox."

"One must change for dinner." My governesses had been very keen on looking presentable at all times, but especially at dinner. And they had nothing on my mother. She'd once sent me to bed without dinner because my hair ribbon was creased.

"Well, I'll see you there." The flap fell back into place after Hildy left.

I unfolded a lavender-scented towel and poured cool water into the basin. Hildy was easygoing in many ways. Why was she so prickly about a slight to me? I was her traveling companion. A more Spartan setup for me would have been perfectly acceptable. I put the thought aside to ponder later as I shook out a fresh dress. Vita had sent a note to us at the hotel, informing us that the dinner that evening would be informal, so I changed into a fresh frock, not an evening gown.

The path that ran from the sleeping tents to the lounge tent had been cleared of rocks and shards, but sand filtered into my T-straps after only a few steps. I shook it out as best I could and followed the scent of cigars that drifted from the large tent.

It resembled a lounge in an exclusive hotel in every way except for the canvas walls. Ned, Timothy, and George were sprawled in the canvas sling-back chairs at the back of the tent, a fug of smoke hanging around them. Mr. Chambers' stooped figure hovered on the outside of their circle, a drink in one hand, his cane hooked over his arm as he listened to the conversation.

Ned stabbed his cigar at Timothy. "He saw it. It was ten feet long, I tell you. Just lying there on the bank, sunning itself."

"It was a beauty," Timothy confirmed. "Unusually large for a crocodile, I believe."

Ned threw out his arms to show the length of the animal.

Unfortunately, he was holding a whiskey, and his arm collided with Mr. Chambers. The amber liquid sloshed out of the glass and splashed over Mr. Chambers' shirtfront. Ned pulled himself to his feet and produced a wrinkled handkerchief. "Sorry, old chap. Forgot you were there."

"It's fine." Mr. Chambers put down his own glass and daubed at the stain. "I brought a change of clothes."

Ned settled back into his chair. "I tell you, if I'd had a clear shot, I would've bagged that crocodile."

"Of course you would, my boy," George said as he stroked his thin mustache. None of the men were in formal dinner attire, but while the younger men had taken off their jackets and rolled up their sleeves, George still wore a three-piece suit and his gold watch chain.

Vita was in another white dress, this one with the shimmer of silk. She'd also changed her jewelry and wore an elaborate necklace of lapis and gold. She'd removed her turban, and now a gold headdress rested on her short dark curls. Tassels attached to the headdress dangled at her temples. She greeted me, then introduced the man at her side. "Allow me to introduce Sir Abner Sapp." From the lines around his eyes and his thick middle, I presumed he was in his fifties. His sandy hair had been oiled into a Marcel wave that swept back from his pale face. Heavy brows formed a straight line over close-set faded blue eyes. "Sir Abner, this is Miss Blix Windway." He shifted his whiskey from one chubby hand to another and reached out as Vita added, "Sir Abner is the commandant of the Cairo police."

"How interesting," I said. "You must know Cairo well."

He tilted his head in agreement. "Yes, I've spent over a decade here."

Vita said to Sir Abner, "Blix is traveling with Hildy—Miss Honeyworth. They've recently arrived."

"How do you find Cairo?"

"We haven't seen much of it. We toured two mosques this morning and walked in the Ezbekiyeh Garden."

Sir Abner's gaze drifted to the men across the room as he asked, "Are you staying here long, or do you travel up the Nile?"

"We plan to stay for several days, possibly a week. The bazaar is on our agenda for tomorrow afternoon."

"Good choice. Mondays and Thursdays are the main market days, so you'll see it at its busiest." From the singsong cadence of his reply, I imagined he'd repeated the words to many new arrivals.

George shifted and threw his arm across the back of his chair as he called out, "Sir Abner, you were out south of Cairo not too long ago. How's the hunting there?"

"Ladies," he said with a small bow of his head. "Pleasure to meet you, Miss Winn."

"It's Windway," I said with a smile, and he apologized, but he was already moving away. I doubted he'd actually taken in what I said.

Vita shook her head as he walked away. "Men and their hunting. Their quest for a crocodile is quite absurd."

"Is it?"

"Oh yes. They see a stuffed crocodile as a testament to their manhood. All foolishness in my opinion. George has wanted one since we came out. He's been thwarted at every season. Hard to believe, but it's true. Ah, here's Hildy."

"My, Vita, that's a beautiful necklace," Hildy said as she joined us.

Vita stroked the lapis and gold. "It's a pectoral collar. Isn't the workmanship splendid?"

"It's exquisite. Do you collect Egyptian jewelry?"

"Yes, I find it irresistible. So much better to wear one's collection rather than hang it on a wall. And I find that wearing authentic jewelry helps me to be closer to the power that I feel here on the plateau. Now, Hildy, what would you like to drink?" The man who'd been in charge of the donkey with our luggage had changed into a lighter-colored gallibaya and stood behind a drinks cart, a sullen look on his face. A scar ran from his temple to his brow, causing one eyebrow to hitch up slightly.

"A gin and tonic for me," Hildy said, and the man reached for a glass.

Vita said, "Smile, Tadros! It's a party."

The corners of his mouth turned up, but it was far from a genuine smile. "Of course, madam."

Vita sighed. "Despite Tadros' tetchiness, he's clever with the cocktail shaker. Blix?"

"I'll have the same."

A few moments later he brought us our drinks on a tray. "Thank you, Tadros," I said. Startled, his gaze flashed from the tray up to my face, then back down to the empty tray before he went back to his position by the drinks.

Vita leaned in and lowered her voice. "You don't have to remember their names. Just snap your fingers or clap."

Hildy frowned, and I said, "It's only polite to learn some-one's name, though, isn't it?"

"But there's really no need," Vita said. "The servant problem isn't as severe here as it is in England."

Hildy closed her eyes briefly. Vita moved toward Mrs. Jenkins and Rose, who'd entered the tent. George surged to his feet and went over to greet Mrs. Jenkins as well. Both Vita and Mrs. Jenkins were taller than George, and the two women completely blocked him from view.

Mrs. Jenkins' dress wasn't quite an evening gown, but it was more formal than the linen frock she'd worn earlier. The midnight-blue fabric was shot through with tiny beads and silver thread that glittered as she moved. Rose, in a fussy peach lace gown, went to the edge of the room and stood in the shadows.

I made a mental note to speak to Rose later and see if I could draw her out. It was distressing to be the odd one out. I took a few sips of my drink, then put it down on a table. "I must get some pictures of the pyramids in the sunset," I said to Hildy and slipped away.

I photographed the pyramids as well as the campsite. One shot in particular intrigued me. I stood in the dining tent with the elaborate table setting in the foreground and the pyramids in the viewfinder. Tadros must have finished his duties as bartender because he was directing several men as they brought food to a small tent off to the side of the dining tent, a staging area for the meal. I nodded to them as I left the dining tent. No one returned my greeting. I went to the far side of the campsite and took some photos of the tents with the empty plain in the background.

A dark-haired man strode across the campsite and stepped into the frame of one of my photos just as I hit the shutter. I didn't remember seeing him before and wondered if he was another dinner guest. He moved with an easy stride that was different from the way the servants scurried from one tent to another, but he wasn't dressed for dinner. He wore dark trousers, tall boots, and a khaki jacket.

The dark-haired man stopped to speak to Tadros, then a ripple of laughter floated through the air. The scowl was gone from Tadros' face as he grinned at something the other man had said. I returned to the lounge just as Vita rousted the men from their corner for dinner.

CHAPTER THIRTEEN

It was probably the al fresco setting with the sunset burnishing the pyramids a bright gold on one side and casting their sharp-edged shadows across the plain that gave the dinner party an informal feeling. Instead of speaking only to the guests seated on either side, the conversation ranged back and forth across the table. At one point, Mr. Chambers suggested various sites that Hildy and I would enjoy. "And, of course, don't miss the bazaar. It's fascinating."

"Yes, that's our plan for tomorrow."

Mrs. Jenkins and George had been carrying on a quiet conversation, leaning toward each other, but at the word *bazaar*, Mrs. Jenkins turned away from George. "But is it safe?"

Rose rolled her eyes. "Everyone goes to the bazaar, Mother. There's nothing to worry about."

Mrs. Jenkins sent her daughter a warning expression reminiscent of many stern looks I'd received from my many governesses. Mrs. Jenkins maintained eye contact with Rose until Rose looked away, then Mrs. Jenkins said, "Sir Abner, what is your recommendation? I'm concerned because of the recent riots and unrest. Is it sensible to go into the native quarters of the city?"

He reluctantly put down his fork and knife, looking a bit perturbed that Mrs. Jenkins had directed the question at him. Most of his comments throughout the meal had been to praise Vita on the food and wine. "Your motherly concern is to be commended, Mrs. Jenkins, but I assure you it is quite safe. The natives don't want things stirred up any more than we do."

A choking sound came from Mr. Chambers, and he reached for his wine. His complexion had turned a deeper shade of red. "I disagree."

"You mean it's not safe?" A shrillness edged Mrs. Jenkins' voice.

Wind whistled through the tent, ruffling Sir Abner's hair. As he smoothed the wave back into place, the candlelight winked on the rings on his fat fingers. "No, I'm sure you won't encounter any problems touring the market."

Mr. Chambers, his voice tight, as if he was restraining a flood of words, said, "I disagree about the feelings of the Egyptians, Sir Abner. They are upset, and rightly so, that we've reneged on our promise of autonomous rule."

A servant approached the head of the table and handed a note to George.

Sir Abner twitched his shoulders. "Nonsense. The recent issues were nothing but rabble-rousing from a few troublemakers. We removed the instigators." He turned back to Mrs. Jenkins. "You have nothing to worry about. I assure you that Cairo is quite as safe as London or any other European city."

Mr. Chambers drew a breath, but George folded the note and raised his voice so that it carried. "I'm sorry, but it seems I'll miss pudding. My apologies, but I must return to Cairo," he announced to the table, but his gaze lingered on Mrs. Jenkins. I wasn't sure, but it looked as if he mouthed the word *sorry* to her as he stood. He waved a servant over. "Have a donkey saddled."

Vita, her knife and fork in her hands, rested her wrists on the

edge of the table. "But surely you don't have to depart immediately."

"I'm sorry, my dear. It's an urgent matter, but—" He turned
to Mrs. Jenkins and reached for her hand. "It's purely related to
banking. Nothing for a beautiful lady to concern herself with." I
thought he would kiss Mrs. Jenkins' hand, but he only bowed
over it.

Mrs. Jenkins tilted her chin down in a manner more typi-
cally employed by debutants than society matrons. "Thank you
for your assurances. You're too kind."

"Not at all."

They maintained eye contact until Vita's strident voice cut
through the air. "But you'll return, won't you, George? We have
the sunrise ceremony at the pyramids."

"No, by the time I handle it, it will be too late to return." He
checked his pocket watch as he pushed back his chair. "I'll stay
at Shepheard's tonight. One doesn't want to travel across the
desert by night. I'm sure your sunrise—um—event will go
splendidly. Again, my apologies. I bid you all good evening,"
he said and left the tent.

Vita's stare bored into his back, and an awkward silence
came over the dinner party until Hildy said, "What's this about
a sunrise ceremony, Vita?"

She dragged her gaze back and raised her eyebrows. "What
was that?"

"Sunrise ceremony?" Hildy prompted.

Vita's face became animated. "Remember, I told you. Now
that I have Cornelius Duncan's diary, we can replicate what he
did. I found the passages that described his first visit to the
pyramids. Our campsite is in the same location where he was.
We'll rise at dawn and trek to the Great Pyramid."

Hildy's eyebrows lifted. "Walk?"

Vita nodded, her gaze across the plain. "And then we'll
climb to the top and recite the lines of an ancient Egyptian
poem."

"Not from *The Book of the Dead*, I hope," Ned said. He and Timothy had been quiet throughout dinner, except when the conversation turned to the topic of hunting.

Vita frowned at him. "They're love poems. I've had copies made for each of you."

Ned opened his mouth, but Vita cut him off. "And no, you can't beg off, Ned. You departed before dawn for your hunting expedition this morning. I expect you and Timothy to go with us tomorrow. I'll send a servant to wake you."

"Yes, Aunt Vita."

She ran her gaze around the table. "Of course, everyone else may attend or not, according to their wishes, but please do come. The more people we have reciting the lines, the stronger the energy will be."

I wished I'd paid more careful attention to the diary when I skimmed it. I remembered a brief mention of sunrise at the pyramids in the diary, but nothing so elaborate as what Vita had described. "Duncan was that specific in his diary?" I asked.

"There are a few points that are a bit . . . nebulous, shall we say. But the diary combined with his other writings allowed me to piece everything together. It's fortunate I have such an in-depth knowledge of his writings. Ah, good, here's the pudding."

As we sat in the lounge after dinner, Vita read aloud sections of Duncan's diary, what she called "a little foretaste of what we could expect in the morning." The passages described a beautiful sunrise, but I didn't hear anything about visions or powerful energy emanating from the pyramids.

I said that I'd like to have a look at the diary, but Vita had said it was too fragile to pass around. Once she closed the diary, she kept it in her lap, occasionally running her hand over the leather binding.

Hildy chatted with Mrs. Jenkins a bit, then came over and took a seat beside me. I'd positioned my chair so that I could see the pyramids, which were silver-tinged from the wash of moonlight. "Lovely view, isn't it? Were you able to photograph it?"

"I tried. I haven't taken many pictures at night, so I'm not sure how they'll turn out."

"Well, the attempt is the important thing. And you'll be able to take some from the top of the Great Pyramid in the morning."

We both looked over at Vita, who was now snuggled into a fur coat as she spoke to Mr. Chambers, the gold tassels on her headdress swinging whenever she turned her head. Hildy leaned forward and said in an undertone, "I'm just thankful this Cornelius Duncan climbed the pyramids at dawn and not midnight."

"Oh, I hadn't thought of that. Good point."

"I'm turning in. Good night, Blix."

"Good night. I'll see you in the early hours of the morning."

I USUALLY FELL ASLEEP QUICKLY, but I found myself rolling from one side to the other. Perhaps it was the occasional distant howls of the jackals that kept me awake or the noise other members of the party made as they turned in for the night. I imagined Vita would say it was power vibrating out from the pyramids that prevented me from sleeping.

I chuckled at the thought and plumped my pillow into a new shape. I made sure the mosquito netting still enclosed the bed, then settled down again. The camp and the jackals quietened, and I drifted off, but it was a fitful doze. I never plunged into a deep dreaming state, but floated on the surface of sleep.

I woke, then rolled over to look at the flap that formed the door of my tent to see if any light was seeping in, but it was still dark. A low murmur of voices in the distance and the scent of smoke indicated the servants were at work. I snaked my arm out through the netting into the chilly air and patted along the bedside table until I found my torch and watch. A quarter after five.

I snuggled back into the warm layers of blankets. Even though I had a predawn appointment at the top of a pyramid, it was too early to emerge from my warm cocoon into the nippy atmosphere. Vita had said the servants would bring fresh water to wash in and a cup of tea at half past five. If we departed from the camp at six, we'd have plenty of time to travel back to the pyramids and make the ascent before sunrise, which occurred around seven.

Watching the day break from the top of the pyramid sounded romantic. It was a once-in-a-lifetime experience, but thinking about it from the toasty comfort of the bed, I suddenly found it singularly unattractive. But once I was on the top of the pyramid with the sun creeping over the horizon, I'd probably feel differently.

A shriek followed by the jingle of shattering crockery brought me upright. Hurried footfalls sounded on the path as someone ran toward the large tents. The sound had come from the direction of Hildy's tent. I pushed back the blankets and the netting, intending to dart over to her tent and check on her, but the frosty air slithered around my bare ankles. I shoved my feet into my climbing boots, which I'd put out the night before along with my climbing clothes—a sturdy divided tweed skirt and matching jacket. I left the tweed clothes where they were and slipped on my dressing gown, then shrugged into my coat.

I picked up the torch and poked my head out of my tent. The sky overhead was still dark with a sprinkling of stars, but the horizon to the east beyond Cairo was a dusty blue instead of midnight black.

Hildy's tent was next to mine. I switched the torch on and aimed it down at the ground as I made my way to it. I leaned close to the tent flap and drew a breath to softly call her name, but then I heard a petite snore. The snap of canvas drew my attention to the next tent, Vita's tent. The flap was unfastened and flicked in the breeze. A light glowed from the tent's interior, reflecting off a silver tray that lay on the path. Shards of a broken teapot sat in a puddle of liquid that had soaked into the sand.

I looked around for a servant hurrying back to clean up the mess, but the track was deserted. I went to her tent. "Vita? Are you all right? Should I call—"

The breeze teased the flap open for an instant, and I stumbled back, my hand at my mouth. She was lying on the ground in a pool of congealed blood, a gash in her throat.

CHAPTER FOURTEEN

a quick glimpse was enough to tell me that Vita was gone. The amount of blood around her was indication enough, but besides that awful sight, her skin was tinged a strange blueish hue. And her open, staring eyes . . . I dropped the tent flap and turned away, sucking in great gulps of the frigid desert air.

I dashed down the little path, the beam of the torch bobbing as I jogged. Last night Sir Abner had mentioned the "long trek" to his tent, which was at the far end of the row. I paused outside the last tent, unsure of the etiquette. One didn't burst into a tent, and there was no way to knock. I tucked the torch under my arm, took hold of one of the taut support ropes, and shook it, which sent ripples through the canvas covering, as I called his name repeatedly.

After a few moments, fabric rustled, then a slit appeared at the tent flap. The light from my torch cut across the opening, and Sir Abner rubbed his eyes. "Miss—er—"

"Thank goodness." I let go of the anchor rope and aimed the light at the ground. "It's Miss Windway, and you need to come immediately. Vita has been murdered."

His hand dropped from his face. "Vita murdered? Nonsense!

No one would be so foolish as to commit a murder with the police commandant a few yards away. You had a vivid dream. Are you of a nervous disposition?"

"No, of course not. It wasn't a dr—"

"Then you must be partaking of the narcotics that have been making their way into Cairo. I suggest you return to your tent and sleep off the hallucinations."

"No, it's not a hallucination or a dream or my imagination. She's been murdered."

He waved me off as he yawned and began to refasten the tent opening. "Go away, Miss Wind—"

I gripped the canvas and pulled it back open. "I won't return to my tent. You must come and see."

He murmured something under his breath. I caught the words *infernal women* before he said, "Give me a moment."

I stepped back, arms crossed, and blew out a long breath.

He emerged a second later wrapped in a silk dressing gown. He wore soft leather loafers and—I blinked and tilted my torch so that its glow lit his face—a hairnet, which held his Marcel wave in place.

"Well?" he snapped. "After you." He made an impatient flick of his hand toward the line of tents.

"Right." I turned and headed down the path without informing him he'd forgotten to remove his hairnet. Let someone else tell him.

When we reached Vita's tent, I pointed to the tumbled tea tray and spoke in a low voice. "I was awake and heard the servants on the path, then the crash of this when they dropped it. I thought something had happened at Hildy's tent, so I went to check on her, but she's asleep. I realized the noise had come from here. When I saw the tray on the ground, I came over to ask Vita if she was all right. The wind blew back the opening of the tent, and I saw—well—" I swallowed hard. "I saw her."

Sir Abner made a tsking sound and leaned close to the tent. "Vita? I hate to disturb you, but Miss—um—Windmere—"

"Windway."

"Miss Windway insisted. I do apologize. Vita . . . ?"

The only sound was the whistle of the wind between the tents, which caused the flap to fold back, and Sir Abner caught a glimpse of Vita.

"Good Lord." He snatched the torch from my hand and stepped quickly around the fallen tea things. He went inside, pausing beside Vita, his loafers a few inches from the pool of blood that had soaked the carpet.

I followed him but waited just inside the perimeter of the tent. He swept the beam of light around. The bed had been turned down, but it hadn't been slept in. No indention or wrinkle marred the smooth surface of the sheets. The white silk gown Vita had worn at dinner had been tossed across a sling-back chair, and her discarded shoes lay on the floor beside it. Everything else in the tent was in place and looked normal. The drawers of the chest were closed, water shimmered in the bowl on the washstand, and the vase of flowers and the glowing kerosene lantern on the table were undisturbed. The sight of Vita's body among such neat surroundings made it all the more shocking.

Sir Abner played the light over the table. She must have been sitting in the straight-back chair at the table when she was attacked. A sheet of paper lay on the surface, turned at a slight angle. I inched forward and was able to make out yesterday's date in the upper corner. A smattering of dark red dashes traced across the lower portion of the paper.

He shifted the beam to Vita's body as he bent over and studied her neck. She had fallen sideways out of the chair and lay on her side between the desk and the chair.

My breath caught in my throat, and I suddenly felt woozy. I looked away. I drew in deep breaths and looked to the other side of the tent at Vita's open suitcase. I focused on the jumbled mound of her clothes.

"Most unfortunate," Sir Abner said. "At least she didn't suffer."

"How can you tell?" I asked, my gaze pulled back to Vita. "It certainly looks like a ghastly way to die."

"It would have been quick. A single swift cut from under her left ear across her throat in a downward motion with the depth of the cut becoming more shallow from left to right. Typical of the assassinations we've seen in the native quarters among the less reputable of Cairo's inhabitants." The torchlight juddered across the tent until it found me. Light dazzled, blinding me. "What have you touched in here?"

I held my hand up to shade my eyes. "Nothing. Please move the light. I didn't even step inside the tent. I could tell she was . . ."

The light disappeared, and I couldn't see anything for a few moments.

"Quite. Well, that's a small mercy. Most women are nosy and would have poked about."

As my vision cleared, his attitude burned away some of the unsteadiness. "I can assure you the only thing on my mind was finding you so that you could begin your investigation."

He'd moved to the chest of drawers. "Which won't take long." He spoke with his back to me as he nudged at a silver-backed brush and several open jewelry cases on the table.

"What do you mean?"

The flap of the tent rustled, and I turned to find Mr. Chambers behind me, "Are we meeting in here . . ." He trailed off and whispered, "Good gracious!" He took a step backward, and his heel caught on the edge of the rug. He almost fell but used his cane to catch himself. "Excuse me. What a shock." He took out his handkerchief and wiped his forehead, then cleared his throat. "How tragic. What happened?"

A dark spot on Mr. Chambers' white cuff drew my attention. Was it blood? Surely not. The sight of so much of it on the ground must have muddled my thinking. His jacket sleeve slipped down, and I gave myself a mental shake. It had probably been an ink blot or a smear of dirt.

Sir Abner lifted one of the velvet-lined jewelry trays. "An attack, obviously. Mr. Chambers, if you would be so good as to round up the natives? I suppose they'll be about the cooking area. If you could keep them there, I'll be along shortly."

"Yes, of course." Mr. Chambers' handkerchief fluttered to the ground. He hooked his cane over one arm and braced his hand on the bedside table as he leaned over. I reached down and retrieved it for him.

I frowned as I stepped back. Had Mr. Chambers just surreptitiously palmed a piece of paper from the little table into his pocket as he straightened up? Surely my eyes were playing tricks on me.

Sir Abner said, "Please go now, Phillip. Time is of the essence."

Mr. Chambers blotted his forehead. "Yes. Right. Of course." He must not have really looked at Sir Abner until that moment because Mr. Chambers had been on the point of wheeling about to leave, but he stopped and stared at Sir Abner.

"Yes?" Sir Abner asked.

Mr. Chambers hesitated, then motioned to his own head, his fingers tracing against his thin gray hair. "You have a—um . . ."

Sir Abner's eyes widened. He turned away, jerked the hairnet off, and stuffed it in the pocket of his dressing gown. Mr. Chambers sent me a small smile and whispered, "Vanity of vanities," before he slipped out of the tent.

"Why is time of the essence?" I asked Sir Abner as I glanced at Vita's body, then looked quickly away. There was no rush. Nothing would help her now.

Sir Abner checked his reflection in the mirror on the washstand, soothing the waves in his hair back into place. "Obviously, one of them is the culprit. If I can nab the man now, it will save legwork."

"Them?"

"The natives, of course."

"But couldn't it be anyone in the camp?"

"As I said, slashing of the throat is a very common method of assassination in the native quarters of Cairo. We come across it frequently." He motioned to the open jewelry cases. "You see? Robbery. The pectoral collar she wore last evening along with the golden headdress are gone."

I wrapped my coat tighter around my body. "But even if someone stole her jewelry, it still could have been any one of us. It doesn't mean one of the servants is to blame."

"Come now, Miss Windy. Everyone else here is British." He looked from the empty jewelry boxes to Vita's body. "This is the work of a native. Run along and tell Miss Honeyworth to go to the lounge tent. I'll summon the others. Rest assured I'll keep the inconvenience to a minimum. Everyone will be able to go about their sightseeing shortly."

I didn't bother to correct him about my surname. "Everyone except for Vita."

CHAPTER FIFTEEN

J went directly to Hildy's tent and found her in a flustered state. She wore a rough-weave linen skirt, a white shirt, and thick boots. She stood at the washing table, peering into its mirror as she coiled her hair into a chignon. "Hello, Blix," she said around the hairpins she gripped in her teeth. She smoothed her hair into place, then secured it with the pins. "There. The servant didn't wake me, so I'm running behind. I won't be a minute more. You're still in your dressing gown! You must change, and be quick about it. It's true that Vita is always late, but I have a feeling this is the one time in her life that she'll be ready to depart on time."

Her hands were still at the nape of her neck, smoothing a stray hair into place, when she turned away from the mirror and saw my face. She slowly lowered her arms to her sides. "What's wrong?"

"Why don't you sit down?" I motioned to the sling-back chair.

"Goodness, Blix, you're scaring me."

I waited until she was seated, then said, "It's not good news. It's Vita. She's . . ." I debated how I should phrase my news. *She's passed to the other side? She's no longer with us?*

"Is she hurt? I have nursing experience." Hildy pressed the arms of the chair, preparing to stand. "Perhaps I can help."

"No. I'm afraid you can't do anything."

She subsided back into the canvas of the chair. "You don't mean . . . ?"

"I'm afraid so. Vita's dead." I explained how I'd found her and then called Sir Abner.

Hildy slumped, her gaze unfocused as her back curved into the shape of the chair. "How utterly horrible."

"Yes, it is."

"And shocking," Hildy added. "It's difficult to believe something like that could happen . . ."

I'd expected tears, but she was calm and self-possessed. I'd grabbed a handkerchief from my tent on the way, but it didn't look as if Hildy would need it. I put it in my pocket. "Sir Abner would like all of us to gather in the lounge tent. Do you feel able to go there? If you don't, I'm sure it will be fine to stay here."

Hildy stood up and pulled on a hip-length jacket. "It's terrible, and I feel a bit stunned—it's the shock, you know—but I'm perfectly able to function. I have enough experience in nursing that someone dying—even a friend—isn't something that will make me go wobbly." She did up the buttons, and I said, "I'll get dressed and meet you there."

By the time I'd changed, the sky was seashell pink and the sun had crept halfway over the horizon, bathing the plateau and pyramids in a soft golden light. I met Ned and Timothy on the path. They both must have rolled out of bed only moments before. Ned looked like a schoolboy with his hair sticking up at the back of his head, and Timothy was still doing up his tie.

Ned said, "If we're not going up the blasted pyramid—good morning, Blix—then why the mandatory formation? It's inexcusable! A chap should be allowed to sleep if the climb up the pyramid is canceled."

It was the first sentence he'd addressed to me. He'd avoided me yesterday, clearly still annoyed that I'd bested him in the motor race. He didn't really seem to expect a reply. I was simply a convenient target for his grousing.

"Yes, most annoying," Timothy agreed as he worked his tie into place. "There's nothing wrong, is there, Blix?"

"Why do you say that?"

"It was Sir Abner himself who roused us. Bit unusual, that."

Our arrival at the lounge tent saved me from having to answer. Mrs. Jenkins and Rose were already there. They had obviously been up for a while. Both were fully dressed, and Mrs. Jenkins' hair was arranged in an elaborate coiffure under a dainty sunhat that matched her flowing sleeveless dress. Her T-strap shoes made no sound on the thick carpet, but her stalking gait telegraphed her annoyance. "What's this about our excursion being canceled?"

Rose sat at the back of the tent, reading a book about hieroglyphics. She had on another outdoorsy outfit like the one she'd worn yesterday. Today's version was an olive green. She turned a page. "Mother, we'll find out soon enough."

Sir Abner stepped into the tent. The hairnet was not in evidence. The waves of his sandy hair would have been the envy of any woman who'd just left the beauty salon. He'd changed into a dark suit and had on all his rings, including a pinkie signet ring. "Good morning to you all. I assume Miss—er —Windly has informed you of the tragic news?"

"It's Windway, and no, I haven't. Only Hildy knows."

"Oh, in that case." He cleared his throat and swiveled to speak to everyone. "An unfortunate thing has happened. Vita's life has been taken in a violent manner."

Mrs. Jenkins let out a sharp cry. "Oh, surely not!"

"I'm sorry to be the bearer of such disturbing news, Mrs. Jenkins, but I assure you it is true."

Ned shook his head like a dog waking from a nap. "Aunt Vita? Dead? But that's not possible."

Timothy didn't say anything. He shoved his hands into his pockets and moved a step back, as if signaling he wasn't part of the family group and would remove himself. Mr. Chambers hurried in and made his apologies.

Rose closed her book. "But what happened? I don't understand. What does that mean, *a violent manner*? Does that mean—"

"Hush, Rose." Mrs. Jenkins' sharp tone cut through Rose's questions.

"She was killed, yes," Sir Abner said reluctantly.

No one said anything for a moment, then Ned went to the drinks cart, poured himself a whiskey, and tossed it back in one gulp. He grimaced. "Poor old girl."

"Then she was murdered during the night," Rose whispered, but her voice carried through the silence as her gaze cut to her mother.

Sir Abner dipped his head. "It's tragic. Very tragic, but I'm pleased to inform you that there will be no need to interrupt any plans you have for today."

Mr. Chambers asked, "Then you know who did it?"

"Indeed, I do."

The book Rose had been holding hit the carpet with a soft thud. She picked it up and ran her hand over the spine in an absent-minded way.

Mrs. Jenkins pulled a handkerchief from a pocket and daubed at her eyes. "I need to sit down." Mr. Chambers offered his arm. He guided her to a chair, where she sank down in a graceful flutter of silk. His movements caused his sleeve to ride up and exposed a bright red blotch on his cuff. With the sunlight streaming in through the large opening, there was no doubt about the color of the mark.

"Mr. Chambers, is that blood on your cuff?" I was so shocked to see the dark splotch that I spoke before I thought. The words popped out.

"What?" He twisted his arm up and tugged at this sleeve. "Oh. Yes, it is. I cut myself shaving this morning." He touched a tiny red slit on his jawline.

Sir Abner scowled. "Miss Windton, please—"

"It's Windway."

"Apologies. Miss Windway, please do not interrupt." He turned so that his portly figure faced the group, but he aimed his next words at me. "One of the natives, Tadros, has disappeared. As has Vita's ancient Egyptian jewelry, which I'm sure you all understand is incredibly valuable. Tadros robbed her during the night and fled. The lure of the jewelry had to be especially tempting for someone of Tadros' station. I've sent word to my officers in Cairo to be on alert at the train station and to set up roadblocks. Unfortunately, Tadros has a head start. It may take us a few days to find him. But once again, let me assure you that you're safe, and we have the matter well in hand. You are all free to go about your normal activities."

Ned swallowed, his Adam's apple working. He sniffed, and I was surprised to see his eyes were glassy as he worked to keep his emotions hidden. "Then I should go back to Cairo and tell Uncle George."

"Yes, you should. Where is he staying?"

"At Shepheard's."

"Of course. I'll go with you." Sir Abner swept back the covering at the tent's entrance.

Ned followed him out, and an uncomfortable silence enveloped the rest of us.

Rose leaned forward and picked up the book from the carpet. "Did anyone hear anything during the night?"

CHAPTER SIXTEEN

"*R*ose!" Mrs. Jenkins said. "Of course, no one heard anything. You know the natives move in a way that you never hear their approach."

"That's not necessarily true. I believe they're trying to be silent," Mr. Chambers said.

"I suppose that's correct," Mrs. Jenkins allowed. "The best servants are invisible."

"But some people are light sleepers, Mother. Someone might have heard something. Just because you sleep so deeply that you snore—"

"Rose!"

Rose subsided back in her chair as she murmured, "Well, it's true."

Mrs. Jenkins fanned herself with her handkerchief. "This is so distressing. I don't feel well. Rose, run along and get my tonic for me."

"Yes, Mother." Rose didn't bother to muffle her sigh as she left the tent.

Hildy said, "So no one heard anything of significance last night?"

Mrs. Jenkins stopped fanning herself for a moment. "Really,

105

Miss Honeyworth! What an absurd question. The police know who did it. We all saw how surly that man Tadros looked last night. I'm not at all surprised he's the culprit."

"But that's not Tadros' normal disposition," Mr. Chambers said. "He's been in the Rhodes' employ for years. I've often visited their home, and Tadros has never looked as he did last night. I asked him if anything was wrong, and he said he had a toothache. That's why he was frowning. But to your question, Miss Honeyworth, no, I'm afraid I didn't hear anything—other than the jackals, of course."

Mrs. Jenkins waved her scrap of lace faster. "I heard nothing. I find the desert air so refreshing that I sleep soundly."

I said, "I didn't sleep well, but I didn't hear anything during the night that I could attribute to someone moving along the path."

"Neither did I. What about you, Timothy?" Hildy asked, continuing to address him informally. Since we'd delved into casual address yesterday, it would be odd to transition back to *Mr.*, *Mrs.*, and *Miss.*

He'd picked up the book that Rose had left in her chair. He looked up from the pages. "I didn't hear anything, but I'll admit that I had quite a bit to drink. I must have slept the whole night through without even turning over."

Rose returned with a small bottle and a glass tumbler like the one that had been placed on my bedside table. She poured a measure of the tonic into the tumbler. "Here you are, Mother." Her voice was breathless, as if she'd been running, and her color was high. I looked more closely at Mrs. Jenkins. I'd thought her malady was probably an act to get Rose out of the tent and to stop her from asking questions about Vita's death, but now I wondered if Mrs. Jenkins had a legitimate illness. Rose had certainly hurried with her mother's medicine.

Mrs. Jenkins swallowed the topaz liquid, then laid her head back against the chair and closed her eyes. "Thank you, my dear."

I felt a little pang at the last two words. What was it like to hear your mother say the words "my dear" in that offhand yet affectionate way?

Mr. Chambers asked Rose, "Is your mother well? Should we summon a doctor?"

"No. She just needs to rest for a moment." Rose took the tumbler from her mother's hand.

Mrs. Jenkins kept her eyes closed as she spoke. "Thank you for your concern, Mr. Chambers, but I will be fine."

"Well, if you're sure . . ."

Rose said, "Mother will feel much better very soon. She always does."

"In that case," Mr. Chambers said, "I plan to return to Cairo and put myself at George's disposal. There will be much he needs to see to."

Hildy said, "Oh, that's right. The service for Vita. I still haven't quite taken everything in. I suppose she'll be buried here?"

"Yes, it will be as soon as possible. With the heat . . ."

"Of course. Poor George. He'll have to see to all that on top of this horrible tragedy."

Mr. Chambers nodded. "It will be difficult. I'll help in any way possible. Perhaps you'd like to offer to assist as well, Miss Honeyworth? I'm sure a woman's perspective would be welcome."

"Yes, anything I can do."

Mrs. Jenkins stirred and opened her eyes. "Rose, it's not a day for pyramid-climbing."

Rose nodded. "I wouldn't enjoy it now anyway." Mrs. Jenkins gripped the arms of the chair. Rose put a hand under her mother's elbow as she stood. Mrs. Jenkins said, "Mr. Chambers, Rose and I will accompany you back to Cairo, if you don't mind."

"Of course not. You're most welcome."

Hildy and I agreed that we'd return another day to climb the pyramid. It was the appropriate thing to do. One couldn't continue with a sightseeing agenda when one's host had been murdered.

Hildy looked to Timothy. "And you, Timothy, are you staying on?"

"No, I'll return with you. Ned might need me."

Mr. Chambers offered Mrs. Jenkins his arm, and I paused to let them file out of the tent before me. Hildy followed them. Timothy handed the book back to Rose as they fell into step together behind me. He said, "I wouldn't spend too much time on this if I were you."

Rose tucked the book into the crook of her arm. "Why not?"

"This sort of thing is too taxing for the feminine brain. Just enjoy the pretty silhouettes of the hieroglyphics. Don't try to understand them."

Rose's voice was tight. "I find the glyphs incredibly interesting. I will continue to study them. Not that it's any of your concern." She brushed by me as she surged around me on the path.

I glanced back at Timothy, who lifted a shoulder. "I was just trying to tell her it's difficult. It's not something one can pick up in an afternoon."

"I don't think Rose is only spending a few hours on it. She seems keen to understand hieroglyphics."

"I doubt it. Girls are notoriously fickle."

I'd been irritated on Rose's behalf, and now I was annoyed in my own right. "Sweeping generalizations are rarely true. Pondering that fact is probably a better use of your own brain than worrying about Rose overworking hers."

I increased my pace, leaving him behind as I went to my tent. I had to pack my things, and then someone would need to coordinate with the camel handler. I hoped my smattering of Arabic was up to the task.

CHAPTER SEVENTEEN

he next Monday I was in the bazaar, perched on a bench called a *mastaba* outside a small shop, waiting for the proprietor to bring out silk scarves for me to examine. The bazaar was made up of crowded, dusty lanes. Buildings on either side of the higgledy-piggledy streets gave it a cavern-like atmosphere. Scarves and rugs had been tacked up between the roofs of the buildings to block the blistering sun, which created shady patches that contrasted with the light that filtered in around the edges of the makeshift canopies. Some areas were quite dim, while in others bright sunlight beat down, illuminating the muck and dirt.

I'd been tightening the string around one of my purchases, but my hands froze at the words of a passing tourist. "It's no surprise, really. Hildy Honeyworth always had a *fondness*, shall we say, for George Rhodes."

My head jerked up. Two women, their heads close together, walked by, their boots stirring up the dust as they strolled.

The other woman tittered. "Mrs. Philpott! What a scandalous thing to say!"

"Is it? It's completely true."

"But she was a chaperone. You're not saying . . . ?"

SARA ROSETT

"Oh, I don't think anything happened then. But now . . . well, the way is clear, isn't it?"

A hot rush of indignation flooded through me on behalf of Hildy. How could they insinuate such a thing? I recognized the two ladies. Mrs. Philpott and Mrs. Canning were also staying at Shepheard's. Hildy and I had taken tea with them. The two women had been nice, if somewhat reserved. I'd put their reticence down to Hildy and I being new acquaintances, but a definite malicious tone had laced through Mrs. Philpott's voice a moment ago. They paused to look at the shopkeeper's wares beside me, and I couldn't help but overhear more of their conversation.

It wasn't surprising they didn't notice me. The press of the bodies as well as the sun and shadow made it difficult to see. I shifted uncomfortably on the bench and wished they'd move on, but Mrs. Canning lingered, fingering a rug. "Well, Miss Honeyworth has certainly set her cap for him now, all in the guise of helping him."

Mrs. Philpott tugged at the fringe on the rug, testing its strength. "It's outrageous what she's gotten away with, but there you go. Sir Abner is convinced it was a native, and you know he'll never change his mind." She waved away the proprietor of a little shop who had emerged with another carpet. They turned away, but Mrs. Canning's voice carried back to me. "Hildy had nursing experience—and not just her brother. She worked in a hospital during the war, so I'm sure the sight of all that blood didn't trouble her at all."

"And Hildy has that young woman accompanying her—the lady traveler person. I'm sure Hildy's paying her rather well. It wouldn't be difficult for Hildy to convince her to provide an alibi."

"Or perhaps even convince her to do the deed?"

The women's voices faded as they moved away down the lane. A nauseous surge of revulsion swept through me. *No, no, no.* It couldn't be happening again. Not that I'd ever been accused of murder. The gossips hadn't had that possibility to play with, but they'd been vicious enough with the details they'd scraped up. My body went hot then cold as the familiar feeling of humiliation mixed with frustration came over me. Not here. Not now. Not when I felt as if I'd finally put the last of those rumors behind me. I closed my eyes and fought to calm my breathing.

At my elbow, a voice said, "Mademoiselle?"

My guide for the day, a young man named Asim who spoke Arabic, English, and French, directed my attention to the shopkeeper, who now stood beside me with scarves in a rainbow of colors—daisy yellow, crimson, amethyst, seafoam blue, and turquoise green. I rubbed the smooth silk between my fingers and nodded, my actions rote while my mind ran through what I'd overheard. The shopkeeper said, "Good quality," and named a price that seemed ridiculously low. Asim spoke to him in Arabic, haggling over the cost, I assumed.

"I'll take the turquoise at the price he named," I said to Asim and handed the man the coins. A few moments later the scarf was wrapped in brown paper and tied with string.

Asim and I threaded through the crowd. "You could have gotten it for much less. You should let me negotiate."

"It doesn't matter. I'm ready to return to the hotel."

"But there are some fine copper pots just around this corner. Let me show you." He increased his pace toward an area where the sound of metal on metal rang out. Since he knew the way out of the twisty and confusing little streets, I trailed along behind him, examining pots and jewelry and fake antiquities, but I couldn't bring myself to consider any other purchases.

I followed Asim's nimble movements through the press of the market, but I was preoccupied, the last few days running like a newsreel in my mind. Several times when Hildy and I had entered the dining room, conversation had dropped off suddenly, but I'd put it down to the fact that we'd been present when the "murder among the pyramids" had happened, which was what the newspapers had dubbed the event. But the conversation between Mrs. Philpott and Mrs. Canning made the situation worse—so much worse.

They actually believed either Hildy or I had murdered Vita! It was an impossible thought. Hildy had been nothing but kind to me, and I couldn't imagine her doing anything so vicious and cold-blooded as to murder a friend in order to clear the way for her to be with George. He had been delighted to see her, but Mrs. Philpott's insinuations were repugnant. And they thought I'd helped Hildy cover it up—or even committed the murder myself. My heart rate kicked up, and bile rose in my throat. It was sickening—all of it.

It was true that Hildy had been quite involved in helping George prepare for the funeral and make the burial arrangements for Vita, but the women were being unfair. It was at Mr. Chambers' invitation that she'd become involved in helping with funeral arrangements. They'd worked together to help George, who had needed their assistance.

He'd been listless and couldn't seem to make any decisions at all. Ned hadn't been much help either. He kept saying he had no idea what his aunt would want. Hildy had taken things in hand, arranging the service while Mr. Chambers had spent hours sending cables, notifying relatives and friends, but Mr. Chambers' help had been less public than Hildy's.

The service had been on Saturday at the Anglican church in Cairo, St. Mary's. Then we'd had a quiet day on Sunday, attending church and returning to the hotel so Hildy could rest. She'd been exhausted.

Even if Mrs. Philpott and Mrs. Canning didn't recognize the sorrow that Hildy felt since her friend's death, I could. It was clear to me that Hildy was upset and fatigued. I'd convinced her to stay at the hotel and rest this morning while I visited the bazaar, promising that we'd return again together when she was feeling more the thing.

But the thought that rumors were circulating about her and

George—it was revolting. Mrs. Philpott was a leader in the British community, and her view of the situation would already be percolating through the rest of Cairo's colonial society. My stomach clenched at the thought.

"Mademoiselle, your photos." We were now back in the brilliant sunlight on the road that would take us back to the hotel, and Asim had paused at a shop where I'd dropped off my film a few days ago to be developed.

"Of course. Thank you for remembering." I stepped into the cave-like atmosphere of the shop and asked for my photos. When they were handed across, I paid for them but didn't bother to look at them. I put them in my bag and continued the walk to the hotel with Asim in the lead.

Was there any way to scotch the rumors Mrs. Philpott was spreading? I knew that the hint of scandal might only be a tiny spark, but rumors flamed up quickly, no matter what one said or how much one contradicted them. Like embers, it only took a few words to breathe new life into an old scandal, making it flame up like a phoenix.

My heartbeat kicked up as the thoughts raced through my mind, and I took a deep, steadying breath. I couldn't let that happen. I'd worked too hard to tamp down the gossip about me.

At the hotel, I tipped Asim and went inside. A discarded copy of *The Nile* lay on one of the rattan chairs in the lobby. I skimmed the articles as I climbed the stairs. Still no mention of the investigation or the capture of Tadros, which was most disconcerting. It seemed Tadros had disappeared from Cairo, and I doubted he would return anytime soon.

I'd expected to be formally interviewed by the police and to have to sign a statement, but the single time I'd seen Sir Abner since Vita died, it had been at dinner one evening at Shepheard's. When I'd asked him about making a statement, he'd waved his hand. "No need. As I told you at the pyramids, that's all sorted. No need to trouble yourself or Miss Honeyworth any further."

I entered our suite, and seeing that Hildy's door and all the windows in the three adjoining rooms were open, I called out that I was back. Hildy bustled from her bedchamber into the sitting room. "Hello, Blix. What did you find at the bazaar?"

I'd been so preoccupied with Mrs. Philpott's nasty insinuations that I'd forgotten about my purchase. "A scarf."

I unwrapped it, and Hildy said, "Oh, it's lovely. It matches your eyes. You'll have to take me back there. Have you seen my letter opener? The one with the turquoise on the handle that I purchased in Alexandria from those vendors outside the hotel?"

"No, I haven't. I thought you were resting."

Hildy tucked a few stray hairs back into the coil of her chignon. "I can't. I tried. Thoughts keep going around like a whirligig about George and poor Vita. It's just unbelievable. I can't quite seem to take it in that she's really gone, even though we've had her funeral. Since I couldn't rest, I thought I'd catch up on my correspondence. At least that's something productive I can do, but my search for the letter opener sidetracked me. I haven't seen it since we returned from the campsite."

"You didn't take your letters to the campsite, did you?"

"Of course. I had a few moments to spare in the evening, and I answered some of them then."

I shook my head. "I've never seen anyone be so diligent. It's not as if it's your job."

She turned and ran her hands around the sofa cushions. "It may be surprising to you, but until recently my life was very isolated. My friendships were conducted through letters." She paused and looked toward the open window. The cries of the street vendors floated faintly through the air, and the fronds of the tall palm clacked in a gentle breeze. "How dreadfully Victorian that sounds." She moved to a chair and checked under its seat cushion. "But I can't abandon my letter-writing friends. They've been so faithful. I must continue."

"I'm not criticizing. I'm impressed. Hildy, I must tell you something."

She dropped the cushion back into place. "Oh dear. You look somber."

I motioned for her to sit down, and once she had, I perched on the sofa. "I overheard some ladies in the market today. They were saying quite dreadful things about you—and about me as well. Apparently, there's a rumor circulating about why you've helped George with the arrangements."

"Whatever do you mean? George couldn't think straight. He needed help."

"Yes, I know he did, but the rumor is that you didn't help him out of Christian charity and kindness. You had an ulterior motive."

Hildy's forehead wrinkled. "I don't understand what you're saying."

"They think you have 'set your cap' for him, as one of them said."

Hildy let out a peal of laughter.

"Hildy, this isn't funny!"

She drew in a deep breath as she patted her chest. "Oh, it does feel strange to laugh after the last few days. I'm sorry. It's just that it's so far from the truth. I'll never align myself with a man. I'm enjoying my freedom far too much. I have no need to marry, and I'm not interested in flirtation. I'm past the age when one wants romance. No, I was under a man's thumb for far too long, and I'm not about to put myself back there now."

"But George did seem to be delighted to see you in Alexandria, and he was very attentive. I'm sure that's partly why the rumors have started."

"Oh pish! George has always behaved like that. He's a terrible flirt. Not at the moment, of course. He's devastated now, and there's not an ounce of the lothario in him, but I'm sure he'll return to his ways once he recovers."

"But, Hildy, these women think you—"

She shook her head. "It'll blow over in a day or two. Something else will happen. Someone new will arrive, and those silly rumors will be forgotten." She stood. "Perhaps I put the letter opener in my travel case?" As she sailed out of the room, she called over her shoulder, "Don't worry, Blix. It will all be fine. Tempest in a teapot and all that."

CHAPTER EIGHTEEN

J'd hoped Hildy was right, but when we entered the dining room for lunch, the noise level dropped and picked up again like the sea receding away from the shore, then sweeping back in again. A few people darted glances at us as we were escorted to our table, but most of the ladies didn't make eye contact.

A little line appeared between Hildy's brows as we were seated. I did my best to carry on as if the whole thing wasn't incredibly awkward, but then to make matters worse, the maître d' arrived at our table with George.

George's physical appearance hadn't changed. He didn't look thinner or suddenly have more lines etched into his face, but his buoyant, attentive manner and his quick, teasing smile were gone.

He placed a hand on the back of an empty chair. "May I join you ladies? I find I dislike dining alone."

I gave a little warning shake of my head to Hildy, but she said, "We'd be delighted, George. I'd like your advice about the steamers to Luxor."

Was it my imagination, or did the buzz of conversation in the room increase another notch as George pulled out the chair?

He took a seat and shifted his chair closer to Hildy. "You're not planning to leave Cairo soon, are you?"

"Not for a while, but I must make steamer reservations soon. Is there one in particular you'd recommend?"

The conversation about the benefits and drawbacks of various steamers as well as George's sightseeing recommendations carried us through lunch. The conversation between Hildy and George wasn't romantic in the least. But a few tables away, Mrs. Philpott exchanged a glance with Mrs. Canning. An ache began to pulse behind my eyes.

As soon as lunch was over and George had departed, I pulled Hildy to a quiet table under one of the lattice balconies in the Arab Hall. The octagonal dome-topped Arab Hall sat at the center of Shepheard's, inside the square of surrounding guest rooms.

"Hildy, I know you felt the atmosphere at lunch. People are whispering about you and George. By allowing him to join us, you've made matters worse."

"You worry too much, Blix. Let them say whatever they want. I simply don't care."

"How can you say that? Women like Mrs. Philpott can ruin your reputation."

Hildy tilted her head to adjust her rather large pearl earring. "The Mrs. Philpotts of this world always have something horrible to say about someone. Today she's whispering about me. Tomorrow it will be someone else. And the truth will out. I'll never marry George. I'll never have an affair with him. All their murmurings will come to nothing. Now I'm off to change into something suitable for the bazaar. George said he'd return in an hour to escort me there. Would you like to come?"

"No! And that's the worst thing you could do. If you continue to be seen in his company, you'll only give Mrs. Philpott and her cronies more ammunition for their gossip."

The corners of Hildy's mouth turned down, and I realized she was disappointed in me. "Blix, I'm touched that you're concerned for me, but you shouldn't be so worried about what people think. It's frightfully fatiguing and doesn't change a thing." She patted my hand and sent me a small smile before rising. "I'll be back before dinner."

I fell back against the rattan chair and let out a huff of air as she walked away. I massaged my temples. Despite her age, Hildy was naïve about the ways of high society. She didn't realize *everything* hinged on her reputation. If things continued in this manner, I knew exactly what would happen. It wouldn't be long before invitations dried up and people would snub her. I let out another sigh and pushed back my chair. Perhaps some fresh air would help my headache.

The hotel garden was extensive, but I wanted space to roam without encountering other guests, so I walked down the street and paid my admission fee to the Ezbekiyeh Garden. Hildy and I had visited it when we first arrived, but we had only seen a tiny portion of its twenty acres. I hoped to be able to find some solitude there.

Before I arrived, I'd pictured Cairo as a windswept city on the edge of the desert sands, but I'd been surprised to find Cairo had several extensive gardens. The Ezbekiyeh Garden was an expansive park with man-made features dotted among the mature trees.

I strolled along the wide paths, skirting around the grotto, where clusters of people lingered, admiring the waterfalls. I kept moving until I reached a quieter area where the only sound was the burble of a fountain that fed a small channel. The citrusy scent of verbena was heavy in the air. I wandered along beside the water, moving in and out of the shade of figs and acacias as the palm fronds rustled overhead. In the distance, the silver thread of water widened into a small lake.

I walked for about a quarter of an hour, seeing only a few pelicans. The tension in my shoulders uncoiled, and the throbbing in my temples faded. I knew how malicious gossip could be. I wanted to save Hildy from the awful experience I'd had.

However, I couldn't convince her to behave in a certain way. But to be thought a murderer, well, I couldn't let that stand. I hadn't reconstructed my reputation only to have it shredded again.

It seemed the police were confident that Tadros was to blame for Vita's death, but it still seemed strange that a long-time retainer would kill his employer for jewelry, even valuable jewelry. And if he did decide to murder Vita, why would he choose to do it during the expedition to the pyramids? Surely he could have taken the jewelry at the hotel. Vita had said she liked to wear it often. It sounded as if it wouldn't have been continually locked away in the safe at Shepheard's.

If Tadros had taken it at the hotel, there would be many more suspects, and he could slip away down the broad streets to the train station instead of navigating through the desert in the darkness. Despite Sir Abner's confidence in Tadros' guilt, I wasn't so sure he'd killed Vita. But if he didn't take the jewelry or murder Vita, then why did he leave the camp during the middle of the night?

The path had curved, taking me back in the direction of the grotto and waterfalls. Perhaps Tadros had left because he saw something—or someone. Yes, that made sense. If Tadros saw the murder committed or somehow worked out who had done it . . . then the safest thing for him to do would be to disappear. Sir Abner's first thought was that the culprit was one of the servants. If Tadros had information that pointed to someone else, I doubted Sir Abner would have even heard Tadros out, much less believed him. If Tadros was a frightened witness, then the murderer had to be someone Vita had invited to Giza.

A bird that I didn't recognize with bright plumage flapped from one of the hedges and settled on the limb of an acacia. I paced along, the sun hot on my back, throwing my shadow ahead of me on the path. The splash of water indicated I was nearing the grotto.

A female voice called, "Puck! Come back! Come back here now!"

Metal jingled, and then a small brown dog with a wiry coat burst through a low-growing shrub. The dog's short legs churned across the path, heading for the green expanse of grass and hedges. In the distance, the woman's voice warbled again.

I whistled. The dog paused and turned its head, ears pricked. He had something in his mouth. I hunched down and whistled again, and the dog trotted in my direction. A woman came barreling around the bush. "Puck, there you are, you little wretch!" Her words were scolding, but her voice was relieved.

The dog hesitated, then changed course and went to her. As she swept up the dog, he released what he held in his mouth.

She rubbed his ears. "You must come when I call, Puck, or I'll lose you."

The dog didn't look at all repentant. He gazed up at the woman, his little pink tongue lolling to the side of his mouth as he panted. He tilted his head back and licked her neck. She gave the dog a final pat, then put him down and clipped a lead onto his collar. "No more privileges for you." She turned to me. "Thank you so much."

"You're welcome. What breed is he?"

"He's a mutt—and a lot of trouble."

"He's charming."

"It's how he gets away with so much."

I laughed and was about to turn away to continue walking, but I halted, my attention caught by what had fallen from Puck's mouth. A string of smooth narrow blue stones connected with thin gold wire lay in the grass. "Why, it's jewelry."

The woman bent down. "How odd. That's lapis lazuli—and, goodness, there are several stones."

I pushed the grass away from the stones. "How did Puck get this?"

"He was digging. He'd been behaving beautifully, so I let him off the lead, but that's how they lull you into complacency, isn't it? He shot off, away from the path, and when I found him, he was churning up dirt, the naughty boy. When I went toward him, he snatched that"—she pointed to the stones—"and streaked away." Her hat had slipped back on her head as she ran. She pushed it back into place and bent down for a closer look. "Oh my. It might be valuable."

"Quite. It's an ancient Egyptian collar. Can you show me where Puck found it?"

"Yes, it was over by the large fig tree with the twisty trunk. Why?"

"Because I bet there's more stones than just these."

"Well, then. Follow me."

We left the path and circled around the large bush. With Puck trotting obediently at her side, I walked with her across the lawn-like expanse to a small grove of trees. "There it is." A pile of freshly dug earth sprayed out from a small hole. A bit of white nestled in the small pit. I picked up a stick and poked at the bundle. It was a handkerchief. The fabric fell back, and the sun glinted on gold intertwined with lapis lazuli. "We must contact the police."

"Why?"

I tossed the stick away and dusted my hands. "Because this jewelry was stolen from a woman who was murdered."

CHAPTER NINETEEN

*L*ater that evening Hildy's beaded evening gown swished as she took a seat on the sofa in our suite. "It would seem that the Ezbekiyeh Garden would be an unusual place for Tadros to hide Vita's stolen jewelry."

"Exactly!" I dropped into a chair, exasperation still simmering through me at the attitude of the police in general and Sir Abner in particular. "I pointed that out to Sir Abner, but he didn't agree."

It had taken hours to hand off the jewelry to the correct person at the police. I'd had to explain the significance of it again and again as I worked my way up from an underling until I spoke to someone actually associated with the investigation into Vita's murder.

Eventually, I'd managed to convince them to contact Sir Abner. He'd reluctantly dispatched an officer to go to the garden to take down the exact location where the jewelry had been buried. I'd returned to Shepheard's and asked for a roast beef sandwich and coffee to be sent to the room. I was too agitated to join the crowd in the dining room and make polite chitchat during the meal. I'd paced back and forth, fuming about Sir Abner's attitude while I waited for Hildy to return from dinner so I could tell her about the jewelry.

I dropped my head to the back of the chair and rubbed my temples. "If only Sir Abner had your mental acuity." My conversation with him had made my head ache again. Sir Abner and I agreed on the fact that Tadros wanted to disappear, but I thought it was because he was a witness to the murder and was frightened.

Sir Abner had laughed at the idea. He was still sure Tadros was in hiding because he'd committed the murder. The discovery of the jewelry didn't sway him from his theory.

Hildy bent over and removed her shoes. "But it's mostly European visitors who go to the Ezbekiyeh Garden."

"Yes, and if Tadros was trying to disappear, burying stolen items there would be a foolish thing to do. His gallibaya and tarboosh would stand out. He'd also have to pay the entrance fee, and the attendant might remember him."

Hildy tilted her head one way and the other as she removed her earrings. "And why wouldn't he just sell the jewelry to an antiquities dealer, either here or in Alexandria? Why bury it at all?"

"I pointed that out to Sir Abner as well. I'm sure there are disreputable dealers who'd have bought it." I gripped the arms of the chair and pulled myself upright. "The buried jewelry is another reason there should be a real investigation into what happened to Vita. I can't believe Tadros would kill her to steal the jewelry and then bury it in the Ezbekiyeh Garden, but Sir Abner refuses to see it that way. He's posted a man in the garden to watch for Tadros and arrest him when he returns to dig up the jewelry."

"I suppose Tadros could have buried it until he found a dealer who would buy it," Hildy said.

"But that brings us back to the location. Why would he bury it in the Ezbekiyeh Garden?"

"You're right. That doesn't make sense."

"Sir Abner was hasty and prejudiced at the campsite, and now he doesn't want to admit that he could have been wrong. If he can't blame Vita's death on a native, it means Sir Abner will have to investigate everyone else who was there. The thought that it could be someone British seems to make his brain short-circuit. He can't comprehend it."

Hildy put her earrings on the side table. "It's admirable that you're pressing for the truth, but might it be better to leave things as they are?"

"Leave things as they are? With the gossips saying that you were involved in Vita's death and that I helped you? Don't you see? If Sir Abner is forced to truly investigate and he finds the real culprit, that will put an end to the whispers. There are several things he should check."

"What do you mean?" Hildy asked.

"Mr. Chambers had blood on his cuff, for one thing."

"He explained that. He cut himself shaving. He did have a nick on his jawline. I saw it."

"I did as well, but who's to say he didn't make that cut himself? Ned spilled his drink on Mr. Chambers' shirt before dinner, remember? Mr. Chambers probably only brought one change of clothing. If he got blood on his second shirt, he'd need some sort of story to explain it. He couldn't very well put on the whiskey-stained shirt again in the morning. And then there was the whole thing about the paper." The more I thought about it, the more confident I was that he'd palmed something from the bedside table.

"Blix, stop."

I stared at her, surprised at her sharp tone. "Why?"

Hildy looked out the open window at the night sky for a moment before she spoke. "I do see what you mean about the . . . atmosphere in the dining room. It was worse at dinner." She turned back to me, her back straight and head high. "While the gossip makes it incredibly awkward, the fact remains that I had nothing to do with what happened to Vita. Anyone who thinks I did isn't a true friend. It's shown me who I can count on." She smiled at me, then her expression sobered. "You have to consider that uncovering the truth may also reveal some rather unsavory things—things that people might prefer to keep hidden. And other people may have some sort of harmless secret that they don't want exposed."

"But—"

Hildy spoke over me. "Discovering the truth is all well and good, as long as the truth isn't a wrecking ball that's used to destroy the reputations of people who are perfectly innocent."

"That's exactly what's happening to you, but it's gossip, not the truth that's the wrecking ball. You're innocent, and your reputation is being shredded by gossips like Mrs. Philpott." I ran my thumb over a seam in my skirt. "I know what it's like to have people think the worst of you."

"Ah, but as I've told you, I don't care about what people think of me. It's irrelevant."

My head snapped up. "I don't think you understand. People will avoid you, and the whispers won't stop. Believe me. I know. It's been years and years, and they *still* whisper about me."

Hildy leaned forward and gently touched my hand. "I'm sorry. I can see that you've been badly hurt."

"I'm the Jilter—that's what the newspapers called me."

"Ah yes. George said something about that, didn't he? I had no idea what he was referring to."

"You must be the only person in all of England who hasn't heard."

"You broke off an engagement, then? That's frowned on, but not very scandalous these days."

I smoothed the fabric of my skirt over my knees and schooled my breathing. It was something I'd learned to do.

Whenever the subject came up, my heart raced, just as it had the first time I'd seen the headline over my picture.

"I learned . . . something . . . about my fiancé, and I couldn't go through with the wedding. I was living in London at the time, and I had to get away, somewhere far away. I got on a train and went to Switzerland. I'd gone to school there and knew of a small hotel in the Alps." I drew in a breath and let it out slowly. "I didn't truly understand the character of my former fiancé. I'd embarrassed him. I had actually left him at the altar. Horrible thing to do, I know, but it was on the wedding day that I found out . . . well, no need to go into all that at the moment."

I shifted in my chair. "I see now that I should have said I was ill and couldn't go through with the ceremony. That would have allowed him to preserve his dignity. Then I could have broken it off later, but I wasn't thinking clearly. I simply wanted to get away. Two days after our wedding date, he gave an interview to a reporter and claimed I was in a sanatorium—that I'd had a mental breakdown. My parents didn't ask me what had happened. They just cut me off."

"Oh, Blix, how awful."

"It was. But I'm not telling you for your sympathy. I want you to understand the power of rumors. Everyone sees me through that lens now."

A smile flickered across Hildy's face. "Not everyone. You're a lovely young woman. That's my opinion."

"Thank you," I said, touched by her words. Had she grasped my point? I wasn't sure. A tap sounded on the door. I stood, grateful for the interruption. I hardly ever spoke about my aborted wedding day, and I was glad to drop the subject. "That'll be my sandwich."

One of the hotel's attendants, a young man in a tarboosh wearing a white tunic and wide-leg pants gathered at the ankle, brought in a tray and set it on the coffee table. I took some coins from my handbag for a tip and met him at the door. As the attendant left, two European men, deep in conversation, passed down the hall. I half closed the door, then pulled it open again to look at the men who'd walked by, but they'd already turned the corner at the end of the corridor.

I closed the door and picked up the sandwich as I returned to my chair. "The man with the dark hair and broad shoulders who passed by when the door was open, did you see him?"

"No. Why?"

"He looked familiar. I've seen him somewhere, but I can't place it."

"There's quite a few dark-haired men in Egypt."

"Yes, but there was something distinctive about his stride. It was very . . . confident."

"So a confident, broad-shouldered, dark-haired man. That narrows it down."

I grinned as I said, "I don't know why, but I think it's impor-tant—where I saw him."

I heard Hildy say something about going to bed, but my mind was clicking through the possibilities of where I could have seen the man. It wasn't on the ship. It wasn't in Alexan-dria. It wasn't at the bazaar. "Oh! The pyramids." Still holding my sandwich, I dashed into my bedchamber and returned with the photos I'd had developed.

I put my sandwich back on the tray as I flipped through the images. "I think I have a photo of him. He was talking with Tadros when I photographed the sunset before dinner. Yes, here he is." I handed it to Hildy. "Do you remember seeing him?"

"No, but I was in the lounge tent at that time." She handed it back to me, then gathered up her shoes and earrings.

"I don't think you understand." I wiggled the photo at her. "The dark-haired man is another suspect. If he was there, he could have murdered Vita. I'll take this to Sir Abner first thing in the morning."

Hildy, shoes in one hand and earrings in the other, had taken a few steps toward her room. She turned back, her hands dropping to her sides. "You're not going to leave it alone, are you?"

"No, I'm not. I thought sharing what happened to me would help you see that we have to learn the truth. Finding out what really happened to Vita will shut down the rumors. You don't understand the urgency of this. The necessity of it!"

I realized with a start that a paid companion didn't speak in that tone. Hildy's welcoming manner had lulled me into a state where I felt as if we were friends rather than employer and employee. I braced myself, waiting for her to dismiss me, my mind already whirring through possible options. I had enough money to stay at Shepheard's for a few days, but it would make sense to move somewhere more economical.

With a concerned expression on her face, Hildy said, "Be careful."

I'd already taken half a step toward my door. "I'm sorry. I'll be out of your way in a few moments—" I stopped as her words registered. "Wait. You're not dismissing me?"

"Dismissing you? Whatever for?"

"For being . . . um, rather pigheaded, I suppose." I wrinkled my nose. "That's how my governess Megs always described it. Father called it obdurate."

Hildy chuckled. "Perhaps just plain stubborn is a better descriptor? And why would I dismiss you for having an opinion?"

"It's the opposite of yours."

"Blix, I think we know each other well enough that we can disagree and remain friends."

"Oh. So you won't try to prevent me from finding out the truth about Vita's death?"

Hildy drew herself up, back straight and chin up. "Of course not. You're a modern and imminently capable young woman. Besides, there's nothing more infuriating than having your actions dictated by someone in *authority* over you." I took the sarcastic twist of her inflection of the word to mean that she was speaking from personal experience.

She relaxed her shoulders, and her tone softened. "I consider you much more than a paid companion, Blix. I consider you my friend. Your actions in defending me and your concern for me show that you're truly that to me. Do what you feel you should without worrying what an old woman thinks of you. Just remember, knowledge can be a dangerous thing."

CHAPTER TWENTY

I had to wait an hour to see Sir Abner the next morning. Phones rang, typewriters clacked, and the low hum of conversation carried on around me as I sat on a wooden bench outside his office at Cairo's police headquarters. As I waited, I pondered the exchange Hildy and I had had last night. She considered me her friend. Had I ever had a friend? A true friend?

I'd had school chums, but most of my so-called friends, like Percy's sister, had evaporated from my life when Father cut me off. I'd carved out a place for myself as a travel lecturer, cultivating acquaintances and connections with society matrons who ran clubs and groups, but my relationships were gossamer thin.

I'd built up a web of connections, but it was as shallow as the first frost that melted away when the sun came out. When Miss Spalding decided to return to England, I hadn't been able to think of a single person I could rely on to help me out of my travel muddle.

The ding of the typewriter brought me back to the present. Directly across from me, a young man in a British police uniform with a sunburned nose hunched over a desk, his fingers pounding away on a typewriter at such a rapid rate that it shook the swath of ginger hair that fell over his forehead.

Another officer stopped beside the desk and reached into a cardboard box that was positioned by the typist's elbow. He took an object from the box, and I had to force myself not to sprint up from the bench for a closer look.

He waggled it beside the typist's head. "Is this the weapon that did the old woman in?"

The typist paused, glanced up, then returned his attention to the keyboard. "Don't be daft. That's just a letter opener. Too dull."

I inched down the bench to get closer.

The man rotated the letter opener, giving me a clear view of the turquoise stones on the handle. It looked exactly like the letter openers that Hildy and I had bought from the street vendor in Alexandria.

The man swished it through the air experimentally, then lunged forward with it as if he were striking a fencing opponent. "It would work for puncturing someone, I suppose."

"But she wasn't stabbed. Her throat was slit."

The man caught the small dangling tag that had been tied to the letter opener and examined the writing on it. "Found in her tent, was it?"

The typist apparently didn't think this question deserved a reply.

The man returned the letter opener to the box. "McMillan and I are going to the café down the street. Like to come along?"

"Can't. I have to finish this. Sir Abner wants the inventory typed this morning."

The other man shrugged and walked away.

The noise and movement around the office faded as I focused in on the man who was typing. He removed an object from the box, read the tag, then stabbed at the typewriter keys, adding it to the list. When he completed the description, he laid the item on his desk. By the time he finished, he had several neat rows.

Apparently, the police hadn't collected Vita's clothes, only the small objects from around her tent, which included pots of face cream, several pens, a silver brush and mirror set, the letter opener, two hardbound books, and the empty jewelry cases.

The typist rolled his chair back and pulled the paper from the typewriter in a fluid motion, then read over it, swiveling the chair a quarter inch this way and that. He must have been satisfied with it because he returned everything to the box, settled a lid on it, and handed it off to another officer.

How incredibly bizarre. Hildy's letter opener had been cataloged as evidence. Had it been on the table where Vita had been sitting when she was killed? I hadn't seen it, but Vita's dead body had drawn all my attention. Why had it been in Vita's tent? Had Hildy been in Vita's tent? She hadn't said anything about that. Surely Hildy would have mentioned if she'd visited Vita's tent? But if she had, why would she take a letter opener along?

"Miss Windway?"

I hadn't noticed a different officer approach, and I started when he spoke my name. "Sir Abner will see you now."

Sir Abner's office was an oasis of silence. His head was bent over a folder on his desk. He didn't bother to look at me when I entered. He lifted a finger to point me to a chair as he continued his reading.

I sat down and removed two photographs from my handbag. I'd found a few pictures of the dark-headed man with a broad-shouldered build. Most of the photos were focused on the pyramids with the foreground softly out of focus, but I did have two images that showed the man clearly.

For about five minutes, the only sound in the office was the crinkle of paper as Sir Abner turned a page. He kept his head down, showing that every wave of his sandy hair was perfectly aligned, like ripples on a beach after the tide withdrew. I began to suspect that he wasn't reading anything at all because his eyes weren't tracking over the words. He stared at the page for a moment, then turned to the next.

If he hoped I'd become bored and leave, he'd have no joy on that score. One of the things travel teaches is patience. No matter how one wishes the miles would fly by or that the line would move faster, the fact remains that you have to wait it out. I let my gaze range around his office. Certificates and photos covered the walls along with big-game trophies, including some gazelle and a lion with rather mangy fur.

Eventually, he closed the folder and clasped his hands on top of it. "Well, Miss Wingway, to what do I owe the pleasure of this visit?"

I kept a smile on my face as I corrected him. "It's Miss Windway."

"Right, right. How can I help you, Miss Windway?"

I'd thought all morning about the best approach to take. No one liked to admit they were wrong, and I knew that Sir Abner was clinging to his original theory despite the fact that the discovery of the buried jewelry made it seem more unlikely. I'd try a different angle—an angle that the longer I considered it, the more sense it made.

"I think it would be quite odd for Tadros to steal the jewelry and then bury it in the Ezbekiyeh Garden. It would be more likely for him to sell the jewelry to an antiquities dealer straight-away, don't you agree?" I didn't pause long enough for him to answer. "Then it occurred to me that perhaps Tadros didn't act alone."

Sir Abner had been fiddling with the position of the tele-phone on his desk. His hand stilled. "An accomplice?"

"Yes. What if Tadros took the jewelry, left the campsite, and handed it off to an accomplice? After all, isn't it doubtful that Tadros would bury the jewels in the first place? And in the unlikely event that he did bury them, why would he choose a location frequented mostly by Europeans?" I scooted forward in the chair. "However, if he had an accomplice whose role was to sell the jewelry to a dealer, what would stop the accomplice from betraying Tadros and burying the jewelry . . ."

Sir Abner pulled his hand back slowly from the telephone, lost in his thought. ". . . in the Ezbekiyeh Garden to hide them from Tadros?"

"It's a possibility, isn't it? The accomplice could return to the garden, retrieve the jewelry, and sell it when it wasn't at the forefront of everyone's mind. What could Tadros do in that situation? He couldn't come forward and accuse his partner without implicating himself."

Sir Abner linked his hands together again on top of the folder. "No, I don't see how that could have happened. We questioned all the natives. Except for Tadros, they were within view of each other at all times. Only Tadros was unaccompanied. He attended to the guests because he speaks English. All of the guests are familiar and well-known to us. You can't possibly think that one of *us* would liaison with Tadros to steal valuables and commit a murder?"

"But there was someone else there that day—someone who wasn't a servant and wasn't part of our party."

"What?"

"This man. He might very well have been Tadros' partner. He might be a murderer." I handed the photos to Sir Abner. "I took these photographs of the pyramids before dinner. As you can see, the dark-haired man spoke to Tadros that day."

He made an odd choking sound. "Sir Abner, are you all right?"

"Yes. Yes." He coughed, cleared his throat, and reached for his telephone. He murmured something in a low voice that I couldn't catch. Then he aligned the photos on top of the folder. "One moment, Miss Wind—ah—Wind . . ."

The door opened, and a man came in, speaking as he closed it behind him. "Thank you for seeing me so quickly. I have a few—"

The man broke off as his gaze fell on me. It was the man from the photographs. Today he wore a suit and hat, but his dark hair and physique combined with his quick, confident movements were unmistakable.

"So sorry," he said. "I didn't realize you were already with someone, Sir Abner."

Sir Abner held up his hand. "It's fine. Do come in. In fact, this lady is here about you."

The man's brows came down into a frown. "Me?"

"Indeed," Sir Abner said with the air of someone who was holding a secret close. "She thinks you might be a murderer."

"Sir Abner! I merely informed you that he could be a suspect."

The man turned a cold glance on me. "We haven't even met. Most ladies wait until they've been introduced to me before they make dire accusations about my character."

He switched his attention to Sir Abner, and they exchanged a silent communication that I couldn't decipher. The dark-headed man continued to look cross, but the corner of Sir Abner's lips twitched.

I stood. I felt at a disadvantage with the dark-haired man towering over me like one of the carvings on the catacombs in Alexandria. I moved around behind my chair. "This isn't some sort of joke, Sir Abner. I assure you this is the man that I saw at the Giza campsite speaking with Tadros."

"Oh, I'm sure it is." Sir Abner made that strange sound again as he stood, and I realized it was smothered laughter. "He was there at my request."

"What?"

Sir Abner drew a breath and tamped down his mirth. "Yes indeed. Let me introduce you to Mr. Briarcliff. Mr. Briarcliff, this is Miss Windham—"

"Miss Windway," I corrected him automatically without looking away from the man's face. In contrast to Sir Abner, he certainly didn't find the situation amusing.

Sir Abner continued, "Mr. Briarcliff, this is Miss Windway, who is newly arrived in Cairo."

"How do you do?" I was gobsmacked, but my long rotation of governesses had drilled me so often that the words came to me automatically despite my stunned state.

"Pleasure to meet you, Miss Windway." The words were correct, but his curt tone conveyed his feelings were actually the opposite.

"Mr. Briarcliff is in the personal employ of Harold Martin," Sir Abner went on, his tone jovial, as if we were meeting at a social occasion like a fancy dress ball. "Perhaps you've met Mr. Martin? No? He owns Shepheard's along with the other major hotels in Cairo as well as several in Alexandria and Luxor. Mr. Briarcliff keeps an eye on things for Mr. Martin."

My fingers dug into the back of the chair. "Keeps an eye on things? What does that mean?"

Mr. Briarcliff's topaz eyes narrowed as he studied me, antipathy flickering across his face. "It means that British travelers such as yourself"—he made a little motion with his fingers, indicating everything from my stylish hat and dress to my gloves and my handbag—"don't enjoy it when their Egyptian tours are interrupted. They want to attend dances every night of the week and perhaps visit a pyramid or float down the Nile. Pesky things like pickpockets and petty criminals put a damper on their travels. I make sure things run smoothly for the tourists. They never have to sully their white gloves or mar their shiny shoes with Cairo's unsavory elements."

I blinked at the bite in his tone but only asked, "And that's why you were at the campsite?"

He gave a curt nod.

Sir Abner added, "They'd had word from the hotel in Alexandria about the disturbance to your rooms there. Mr. Martin asked that Mr. Briarcliff check on the campsite at Giza as a precaution."

"And yet there was a murder that evening." I shouldn't have made the dig, but the words were out before I could censor myself. Mr. Briarcliff's sneering assessment of tourists had annoyed me, even though I knew it was true of some visitors to Egypt. The fact that he'd lumped me in with the selfish and shortsighted travelers annoyed me.

His expression didn't change. "I advise you to go back to your fancy dress balls and antiquities tours. You know nothing of Cairo. We'll run the culprit to ground soon."

Anger fizzed through me at his dismissive attitude. "Then I'll find the murderer before you do."

His nostrils flared in a snort. "Oh, you think so, do you?"

"I do. It's more likely that Vita's murderer is among the British, and they'll be found at fancy dress balls and on antiquities tours." A cold, set look came over his features, which intensified as I continued, "Sir Abner—and you, apparently—have had days and days to find Vita's murderer. You've both been spectacularly unsuccessful."

He closed his eyes briefly. "Unfortunately, yes." Were his next words tinged with regret? It was difficult to tell because his expression was about as lively as the marble busts of Roman emperors Hildy and I had seen in the Louvre. "I didn't see anything untoward at the campsite and returned to Cairo that evening. I wish I'd stayed. However, I'm making every effort to bring the culprit to Sir Abner."

"But isn't that Sir Abner's job?"

Sir Abner patted the waves of his hair. "Normally, yes, but this is a delicate situation. Guests who arrive at Shepheard's are of a certain caliber. One cannot go poking about their business."

"You mean one can't insinuate that one of them is a murderer—or helping a murderer," I said. "You leave that to Mr. Briarcliff?"

Sir Abner came around the desk. "There's every indication that we'll have Tadros in custody shortly. Very shortly indeed. Isn't that right, Mr. Briarcliff?"

He gave Sir Abner a perfunctory nod. "As I said, I'm doing everything I can to bring the culprit to justice."

"Very good. Very good." Sir Abner opened the door for me. "As you can see, things are well in hand. Have you been to the Egyptian Museum? I recommend you see it. Perhaps today. I wish you a good morning, Miss Wingham." He steered me to the other side of the threshold and closed the door.

I stood there for a moment, bristling with indignation, but I wouldn't make a scene. That wouldn't help things.

I turned and was making my way through the desks when I heard the name *Tadros*. I slowed my pace. A young officer holding a slip of paper hurried to Sir Abner's door and knocked. I opened my handbag and shifted its contents around as if I were searching for something.

I lingered long enough to hear the young officer say, "Sir Abner, pardon me for interrupting, but I thought you'd want to know immediately. We have a report that Tadros has been found near the Wagh el-Birket, at a house called Beit el Lutis."

I snapped my handbag closed and left.

CHAPTER TWENTY-ONE

*T*n the street outside, I waved down a horse-drawn cab. The driver, a man with a wrinkled face and gnarled hands, half turned his head toward me as I climbed in. "Beit el Lutis," I said.

He twisted around, a frown deepening his wrinkles. "Not good place, not for"—he searched for the English word—"ladies."

I glanced back at the police headquarters. No one had emerged yet, but it wouldn't be long. "I must go there quickly." I reached into my handbag and pulled out several bills. "I'll pay all this."

The driver looked at the money, sent me a doubtful look, but made a motion with his gnarled hands, which held the reins, indicating indifference. He made a clicking noise, and the cab rolled forward.

I fell back against the scratchy fabric of the seat. I'd been moving on instinct, my desire to show up Mr. Briarcliff spurring me on, but also there was still the question of who had actually killed Vita.

I still didn't think Tadros would murder his employer—but his accomplice might have. And while Sir Abner seemed to think Mr. Briarcliff was above reproach, I wasn't ready to remove him from my suspect list. What's to say he didn't leave the camp and return later? And even if I was wrong and Mr. Briarcliff wasn't the guilty party or an accomplice, someone else from the camp could be Tadros' accomplice.

At the very least, Tadros could pinpoint his partner. Sir Abner was fixed on Tadros as the guilty party. Would the police even ask Tadros what had happened, or would they simply push for a confession? I was pretty sure of the answer to that question. If I could find Tadros first, I might be able to find out what really happened.

The driver flicked the reins, and the clip-clop of the horse's hooves sped up, bringing me out of my thoughts. Voices chanting a phrase in Arabic carried through the air. I craned my neck and caught a glimpse of a throng, mostly young men, moving along one of the side streets toward the larger thoroughfare we were traveling on. We passed the side street seconds before they spilled into the main road. Behind the cab, shouts filled the air, and a motor horn blared.

The driver flicked the reins again, bringing the horse to a canter, then a gallop. I gripped the edge of the seat as the cab rocked. I'd read about the unrest in the papers, but I'd never seen it firsthand. "What will they do?" I called over the clatter of the horse's hooves.

The driver shrugged. "Stop traffic and shout, if they're lucky. If they're unlucky, they'll shout and later be beaten."

"By the police?"

"And the army, yes." His tone was matter-of-fact.

After we'd carried on for a few more blocks without seeing any more groups of people, he slowed the horse. We left the wide boulevard with its European-style buildings, streetlights, and clear pavements. The roads became narrow dirt lanes lined with dingy three- and four-story buildings that blocked out the light. He made several more turns, each one taking us farther

SARA ROSETT

into the warren of streets, which became more decrepit with
each yard.

He stopped the cab in front of a building that listed to one
side, its wood lattice balconies tilting toward a gloomy alleyway. The driver angled his head toward an alley. "This is as far
as I can go. Beit el Lutis is through there."

I almost told him to drive on, but then I spotted a familiar
whippet-thin figure in a white suit a few yards down the alley.

I thanked him, handed over the money, and delved into the
alley. A few feet into the narrow passage, a rancid odor
engulfed me. I pressed my handkerchief to my nose. I hurried
along, kicking up dirt and skirting around animal droppings
and rubbish.

Three men stood around one of the doors that lined the
alley. Their gazes felt heavy as they tracked my movement. I
wished I'd worn a cloche that completely covered my head
instead of the small floppy-brimmed hat. My light hair had
always drawn attention, which was annoying at times, but I'd
never felt the prickle of unease that I did now as the men stared.
People had gawked in the bazaar, but this was different.

At the market, an air of commerce predominated. Interactions had been formal, an elaborate dance of debate over price.
Here, the men's gazes were direct and assessing. I skimmed
over the uneven ground and focused on keeping the linen suit
in view, which was easy to do even in the dim alley.

I scurried, glancing down a narrow lane that ran perpendic-
ular to the one I was on before crossing it. My steps stumbled as
what I was seeing registered, buildings with women behind
iron bars. Men strolled along the passage, surveying them. My
stomach roiled at the sight. In the distance directly ahead of me,
the figure in the white suit was moving away from me, deeper
into the maze of streets, his pace close to a jog. He turned a
corner. I darted forward and broke into a run. I certainly didn't
want to lose sight of him. I rounded the corner and called, "Mr.
Denby! Please wait!"

He spun around. "Miss Windway?"

I removed the handkerchief from my nose. "Yes, it's me."

"Good heavens, what are you doing here?"

I pocketed the handkerchief. Either the smell wasn't as strong in this area or I was becoming used to it. "I heard Tadros had been seen in the area. I want to speak to him."

"Angling for my job? If you fancy adding *reporter* to your resume, I assure you there are better—and safer—ways to go about it."

"It's not that at all. I simply need to speak to Tadros. Do you know where he is?"

"No, I don't. Let me find you a cab, Miss Windway. You'll be back at Shepheard's in no time." He motioned for me to come with him.

I didn't move. "I *must* speak to Tadros. Let me come with you. You do know where he is, don't you? Why else would you be in this area?"

"Perhaps I'm visiting one of the nearby—er—I mean to say—"

"Brothels?

I'd shocked him into silence, but only for a moment. "You surprise me, Miss Windway."

"Establishments of that sort can be found in every city. I'm not saying I approve"—a wave of revulsion swept through me at thinking of the caged women—"merely stating a fact, but I don't believe you're here for that."

"No, I'm not." He looked uncomfortable. "But escorting ladies around the slums of Cairo isn't the done thing. Frowned on, don't you know?"

"I'll give you that interview if you let me come with you."

He contemplated me for a moment, then let out a sigh. "All right. I can't leave you to wander this area alone."

"Excellent. I look forward to sharing my thoughts about Cairo with you. I probably won't mention this bit. Now how do we find Tadros?"

"I don't know where he is, but this young chap does." He motioned to a thin boy of about eight or nine who stood a few yards in front of us. He was barefoot and wore a dusty tunic. His stance was tense, and his alert gaze bounced between Mr. Denby and me.

"An informant?" I asked.

"Something like that. Well, come along." He nodded to the boy, who spun around and took off at a fast clip.

Mr. Denby took my arm, and as we paced along, I said, "Thank you. I'd never find my way out of here."

"Neither would I. Amet is my passport back to the European area. Now how did you learn Tadros was here?"

"It was something I heard in passing." I wasn't about to tell him I'd been to visit Sir Abner in regard to Vita's murder.

"Come now, Miss Windway. Surely you don't think you can palm me off with such piffle. There hasn't been a whisper about Tadros among the Brits. You must have an informant of your own." We passed another cluster of men, then turned a corner and followed Amet down an alley that was so narrow we couldn't walk side by side.

Mr. Denby motioned for me to go first. "Hardly. It was something I overheard," I insisted. "I can't reveal my source. Surely you understand that," I tossed over my shoulder as I kept my gaze fixed on the dusty hem of Amet's tunic and his cracked heels as they skimmed along the hard-packed dirt. He veered to the right, and for a moment I thought he'd disappeared, then I realized he must have slipped inside the nearest building.

In a deep recessed doorway, a few boards had been broken away from the tall double doors, creating a small gap. Amet peered out of the opening and waved me forward.

I stepped toward the doors. "Is this it, then?"

"I believe so. I'll go first, shall I?" Mr. Denby took off his pith helmet and stepped sideways through the crevice.

The rough edge of the wood caught at my dress as I wiggled

through. I emerged into a dim corridor. I was glad for Mr. Denby's white suit, which was easy to follow despite the cave-like atmosphere. Amet led us down the short hallway that turned back on itself, then ran up a shallow flight of stairs into a wide room. A few cracked marble floor tiles remained along the edges, but most had been removed.

"Scavenged," Mr. Denby said. "It's a shame. This was probably a fine mosaic floor."

The room was two stories high. Light filtered through the broken wooden *mashrabiya* screens over the windows, illuminating elaborately carved ceiling beams. "What beautiful woodwork," I said as I picked my way across the pitted floor to a doorway, a square of white sunlight, where Amet stood waiting for us. "I wonder why no one lives here now."

Mr. Denby said something to Amet, who replied. Then Mr. Denby said, "Amet says the house is abandoned. It's thought to be haunted."

We paused in the doorway, which opened into a colonnaded courtyard with a toppled fountain in what must have once been a central square of greenery. Only a few plants remained, a scattering of spindly low-growing palms and a ground cover that had sent tendrils out across the stone pavement enclosing the central garden area. A second-story balcony with wrought-iron balustrades running between stone columns enclosed the courtyard. *Ablaq*, alternating dark and light stones, outlined each peaked arch between the columns. A few shell-like alcoves carved in the shape of lotus flowers with marble basins below them were set into the masonry, and I wondered if they'd been fountains that had filled the space with the burble and splash of water.

The sounds of a donkey braying and a child crying floated faintly through the air, but the tall, thick walls of the house insulated the abandoned courtyard, giving it a forlorn atmosphere.

"Interesting mixture of Islamic and French styles," Mr.

Denby said, gesturing to the balcony as he looked around. "Amet?"

The boy had paused beside us. He took a step forward into the sun but halted when a small groan whispered through the hush of the courtyard.

Amet dropped behind us with a whimper. A tinkling, like pebbles falling, came from the far right corner of the courtyard.

I turned and let out a sharp shriek before I clamped my hand over my lips. A man hung from a noose, his limp body rotating slowly as it dangled, suspended between the iron balustrade on the balcony and the courtyard.

CHAPTER TWENTY-TWO

*B*its of masonry sprinkled down from either end of the balustrade where it was attached to the columns as the weight of the body pulled the already sagging iron railing away from its fastenings.

Mr. Denby looked around. "There's a staircase at the other end. I'll go up and—"

The iron fixtures in the stone gave way, and the body plummeted to the ground as stone and dust rained down.

I turned away, my shoulders hunched as the metal clanged against the stone. I froze in that position for a moment, listening for more crumbling sounds. After a few seconds of silence, I turned around slowly. Dust filled the air, and hot sunlight beat down on the body. It lay on the pavement on its side with its back toward me. The section of balustrade had landed on top of the body.

"Are you all right, Miss Windway?"

I swallowed and mentally wrapped myself in the mantle of detachment that I'd employed to get me through the war. "Yes. You?"

He nodded, and we both looked at the body. Mr. Denby went to move the balustrade but jerked his hand away from the hot metal. He shook out his handkerchief and used it to shield his hand before lifting it. The thick, rough rope was still knotted to the metal.

I took off a glove as I picked my way through the rubble.

"There's nothing we can do for him," Mr. Denby said.

"No, but one must check." The rope ran under the man's chin and behind his ear. I touched the skin below the rope. It was cool, and there wasn't a flutter under my fingertips. I shook my head and pulled my hand back.

"Is it Tadros?" Denby asked. "I've never met the man."

"Yes. I'm afraid it is." I could only see his ear and the side of his face as far as his cheekbone, but I recognized the scar that ran from his temple to his eyebrow. Even in death, the seam of the scar pulled the eyebrow upward.

"Poor bugger," Mr. Denby said. "Remorse for killing Vita must have driven him to this."

I'd been about to stand, but I paused and leaned closer. "Perhaps not . . . look at this red line across his throat." It ran all the way around his frail neck.

Mr. Denby's attention was on the balcony. "That will be from the rope."

"No, it's lower and much thinner than the rope. Have a look." I stood and stepped back.

Mr. Denby leaned over and let out a low whistle. "It looks as if he's been garroted."

"So he must have been dead before he was hanged from the balustrade. Someone tried to make his death look like suicide instead of murder."

"Yes, and went about it in a very clumsy way."

I pulled on my glove. "We should notify the authorities."

"Of course, but I'm not anxious to spend any time with the authorities. I propose we have a quick look around, then send an anonymous note to the police. I'm sure Amet will be happy to do it. I'll reward him handsomely—" He looked around. "Where is he? Amet!"

A high, thin voice floated out from the shadowy doorway to the house. "Here, mister."

"Ah, good. He hasn't abandoned us."

They had a short exchange in Arabic, then Mr. Denby said, "He doesn't like dead bodies, but he's agreed to wait for us."

"Can't blame him. And I certainly don't want to explain my presence here to Sir Abner or any of his officials, so I agree to your plan."

"Excellent."

"You'd better put the balustrade back over his body."

"Right. Good point." He used his handkerchief to move the railing back, then lifted the pith helmet and blotted his forehead. "Let's get out of the sun, shall we?"

"Will you write about it this?" I gestured to Tadros' body.

He put away his handkerchief and settled his hat on his head. "Unfortunately, macabre stories sell papers. Until I finish my novel—and find a publisher—I have to think of that." His gaze skimmed the courtyard. "What was Tadros doing here? Did he meet someone here?"

"It is isolated and private." The dust had settled, and the only movement was the flicker of a tiny lizard as it scurried up a wall. "Is that . . . ?" I took a few steps to the shady side of the courtyard. Under the balcony, a door was propped open with a piece of broken masonry. I looked up at the balcony, but it didn't appear that it was in danger of collapsing within the next few minutes, so I had a quick look. "It appears he was living here."

Mr. Denby joined me at the doorway. A thin blanket and a mat rested in one corner. Unopened tins of food and a candle stood on a rickety table.

"Spartan," I said.

"He'd been here for days, apparently." I turned. Mr. Denby had left my shoulder and was nudging a pile of open, empty tins that had been discarded under a stubby bush that had grown up through the pavement. "Two or three days, by the looks of it. There's coffee grounds here as well. He was settled in."

I looked back at the crumpled body. "So someone came to visit him."

"It appears so."

The crack of wood breaking cut through the air like a gunshot.

The noise, which had come from the front of the house, spurred Amet out of the shadows. He flew across the courtyard, his tunic flapping like a butterfly flitting over the ground cover, which muffled his steps. He waved for us to follow him to the far end of the courtyard. We didn't hesitate.

Mr. Denby, hand to his pith helmet as he jogged, called, "That sounds as if someone else informed the police about Tadros. Best not to be found here."

"I agree." If the police arrived and I was practically standing over Tadros' dead body—well, I couldn't imagine what they would make of that. I didn't want to wait around and find out.

Amet led us through two more cavernous rooms, both with high windows covered with rotting wood shutters. I didn't hear any noises behind us, but the solid walls muted sound. My heartbeat pulsed in my ears, drowning out our steps as we crunched across the broken mosaic floor of a long dim corridor.

Finally, Amet slid to a stop and opened a door an inch. A swath of sunlight cut through the darkness. After a quick glance, he opened the door wide, and we followed him into a small back courtyard. A tiny wooden door with reinforcing iron slats was set into a high stone wall.

Amet unlatched the door, and we spilled out into a tiny deserted alleyway. The solid stone wall continued many yards on either side of us, enclosing the house we'd just left. Barely an arm's length away on the other side of the alley's dirt track, another high solid wall stretched out with a smaller door set into it.

Mr. Denby pulled the door closed, and Amet beckoned us to

the right. I hurried along, stepping over rubbish and waving off the flies we stirred up. When we reached the end of the alley where it met a street, Amet paused. At the corner, British military officers blocked the road. Fortunately, a group of people had gathered in the street, and their presence shielded us from the view of the officials. Amet pointed us in the opposite direction, down another alley, a dark slit in a line of battered buildings, and said something to Mr. Denby in Arabic.

Mr. Denby nodded, gave Amet a few coins, and pulled a napkin from his pocket. It was wrapped around something bulky. As Amet took the bundle, the napkin fell back, revealing a golden loaf of bread. Amet's face broke into a smile before he sprinted away.

We went in the direction Amet had indicated. Mr. Denby said, "Bit narrow. Shall I lead?"

"Please do." I followed him into the dark crevice, and a rancid smell assaulted us. I tried to breathe shallowly as I hurried along in his wake. It felt as if we'd entered a tunnel. The only indications that we weren't heading underground were the tiny slashes of blue sky that appeared between the rows of drying clothing strung up on lines between the buildings.

Mr. Denby half turned as he walked. "Amet said the European quarter is only a short distance away."

"Excellent." I waved away flies buzzing around my face. Over Mr. Denby's shoulder, I could see through the fissure where the buildings ended. A horse cab trotted by, which meant it was a boulevard, and I'd be able to flag one down once we reached the street.

We passed an old man, toothless and wrinkled, sitting by a rickety door, then we came to a gap, another alley that crossed perpendicularly. We paused as a group of three men, their voices echoing up the steep cavern-like walls, approached. They fell silent when they saw us and watched us as they crossed. Mr. Denby dipped his head, acknowledging them, then we hurried on our way down the next section of the alley, which was wide enough that Mr. Denby and I could almost walk side by side.

"I can see why you rely on Amet," I said.

"Yes, he's invaluable—"

I let out a little gasp as a hand gripped my elbow and turned me around.

CHAPTER TWENTY-THREE

"*I* thought it was you. The gold of your hair is unmistakable."

I jerked my arm away as it registered that the tall figure was Mr. Briarcliff. "What are you doing?" My voice was shrill and had a breathless edge of panic.

He stepped back and raised his hand, palm up. "I apologize. I didn't mean to scare you. What are you doing here? This is no place for an English lady."

"I agree." He'd drawn a breath—to launch into a lecture, I was sure—but my answer had thrown him, startling him into silence. "That's why I have an escort." I motioned to the spot where Mr. Denby should have been standing. There was nothing there except air.

I twisted around and caught a glimpse of a white-clad shoulder disappearing into the crowd of the boulevard in the distance.

Briarcliff said, "It seems Mr. Denby's journalistic drive is stronger than his chivalrous impulses. Allow me to walk with you to the Ezbekiyeh Garden?" He extended his arm. I debated turning on my heel and striding away. It was only a few more yards, but Mr. Briarcliff was connected with the police. He could be a useful source of information. Was he truly serious about searching for Vita's murderer, or was he simply going through the motions? Was his attempt to "bring the culprit to justice" a sham investigation to make Sir Abner believe someone was on the case? And who was to say he hadn't been Tadros' visitor who'd made a bad job of covering up a murder? All those factors played into my decision, but the one that tipped the scale was that I didn't relish traversing the alleyways of Cairo on my own. He wasn't the companion I would have picked, but when one is abandoned in the alleyways of an Egyptian city, one has to make do with what one can find.

I took his arm. "All right, but shouldn't you stay here? You have an investigation to complete at Beit el Lutis, don't you?" I watched his face to gauge his reaction. But his features had the same mobility as Stonehenge—none.

He stopped. "You know about that?"

Drat, that was a misstep on my part. I should have realized questioning him would reveal my own knowledge of the situation. My thoughts spun as I tried to come up with a likely reason I'd be in this part of Cairo. Before I could concoct a plausible story—was there even a remote chance I'd be in this neighborhood?—Mr. Briarcliff said, "Interesting. How do you know there's been an—um—incident—at Beit el Lutis?"

"Why is everyone so interested in how I learned about it?"

Mr. Briarcliff didn't reply for a moment. His gaze was unfocused as he stared up at the clothes flapping on the lines strung up between the buildings. He returned his attention to me, his gaze piercing into mine. "You overheard when you left Sir Abner's office."

"All right, yes. That's exactly how it happened. Bully for you for figuring it out. However, the more important fact is that Tadros is dead. And Sir Abner's closed-minded view of the motives around Vita's death means that your time would be better spent at Beit el Lutis than walking with me."

"I agree with you, but it will be a long time before I'm allowed in, if at all."

A group of British officers passed us, giving us curious looks as they edged around us. They must have been called out to Beit el Lutis because I heard that name along with the word *suicide*.

After they'd gone by, Mr. Briarcliff stared at me for a moment. "The suicide isn't news to you, is it?"

I tried to assimilate a shocked expression on my face. "I'm sure I don't know what you mean."

"Most women would have let out a gasp or reacted in some way." He looked speculatively back down the alley. "You came from Beit el Lutis, didn't you? Well, well, well. It appears you're not the typical tourist after all." He scanned my face again. "And you've been inside—you and Denby! Good gracious. Sir Abner would be furious if he knew." The prospect seemed to delight him. A smile flashed across his face, but the expression came and went so quickly it was like a lightning strike. If I'd blinked, I might have missed it.

There didn't seem to be any point in denying what had happened now that he'd guessed, so I stayed silent as we paced through the alley.

Briarcliff added, "You have a terribly transparent face, by the way."

"Yes, I'm a ghastly bridge partner. I wanted to speak to Tadros. I didn't realize he was dead."

"The two of you found him?" Briarcliff asked, turning serious.

"Yes. His body was hanging from the courtyard railing, which collapsed while we were there."

All the mirth disappeared from his manner. "I see. That must have been awful, but it seems that you take death in stride. War work? Nursing?"

"Hardly. I did work in a hospital, but nothing so as exalted as a nurse. My duties were more along the lines of mopping up."

"But still."

"Yes, but still." We emerged from the alley and stepped onto the pavement. Petrol fumes and horse dung replaced the odors of the alleyway. Briarcliff raised his hand at an approaching cab, but it whizzed by without the driver looking our way.

"I have plenty of time to take you back to the European quarter. Shepheard's, wasn't it?"

"Why won't Sir Abner let you in Beit el Lutis?"

"He's quick to take credit. It will only be later—if things don't go well—that he'll call in help."

"What do you mean, quick to take credit?" I asked as we passed a café and two respectable-looking shops. It was hard to believe that a slum existed literally behind the storefronts.

"Sir Abner will take the suicide as confirmation that Tadros murdered Vita. He'll be quick to close the case now."

A cab approached from the other direction, and I waved energetically. The driver turned in my direction. "Then you'd do well to make sure you see the body."

I climbed up and said to the driver, "Shepheard's Hotel, please." As the cab rolled away, I turned and called out to Briarcliff, "Thank you for escorting me out of the alley. If you really want to know what happened, take a good look at the man's neck. It wasn't suicide." The frown on his face deepening, he turned and strode toward the alleyway.

I WAS HALFWAY through Shepheard's lobby when Rose rushed up to me, her face flushed. "Miss Windway, may I speak to you? It's rather urgent."

"Of course. Perhaps we can find a quiet table in the Arab Hall?"

We passed under a pointed arch with its *ablaq* edging and

entered one of the antechambers that connected the hotel with the octagonal Arab Hall.

"It looks rather crowded in the center." Rose set off at a diagonal toward a table under one of the balconies decorated with *mashrabiya* screens of intricate wooden lattice. The balcony was empty, but soon the hotel's orchestra would emerge from behind the carved wooden doors to play while guests chatted and had tea in the lounge below.

Once we were settled and had ordered glasses of lemonade, and Rose had caught her breath, she said, "I apologize for accosting you, but I've been looking for you for quite a while. I spoke to George, but he was no help at all."

"What seems to be the problem?"

Her abrupt, breathy pace slowed. "It's a—um—delicate matter. I'm afraid I can't go into all the details, but I assure you that it's quite urgent that I find out what happened to Vita's book."

"Her book? You mean Cornelius Duncan's diary?"

"Yes. I asked George if I could see it, and he said he doesn't know where it is."

"Well, it would've been in her tent . . ."

"That's just the thing." She paused while the waiter set two glasses of lemonade in front of us. "George says it wasn't there, but she had it. We all saw her reading from it after dinner. And I know she took it with her when she went to bed. Mother and I left the lounge tent at the same time she did, and I saw her carrying it." Rose demonstrated, bending her arm at the elbow and curling her hand up over her breastbone.

"Well perhaps the police . . ." I let the sentence trail off, barely speaking the last few words as I remembered the items spread across the typist's desk after he emptied the box. The diary with the gold letters and the dragonfly hadn't been among Vita's possessions.

Rose swallowed a gulp of her lemonade, then twisted her hands together on the inlay pattern of the tabletop. "I wanted to speak to you because you—well—you found Vita. Did you see the diary in her tent?"

"Let me think . . ." So many important items connected with Vita's tent. First Hildy's letter opener appeared there. And now it seemed the diary had disappeared from the tent. I wished I'd been more observant. I looked across the room, reliving that moment when the tent flap flicked open. I'd been too shocked to notice anything but Vita at that moment, but later, when I returned with Sir Abner, I'd looked everywhere but at Vita. "I don't remember seeing it."

"Then who stole it?"

"I might have just missed noticing it—"

She gripped her hands, interlacing her fingers. She shook her head, tiny little jerks of movement because her body was tense.

"It's too valuable. The killer must've taken it. Mother needs it—" The flow of Rose's words cut off as abruptly as when one shut off the wireless in the middle of a weather report. She dropped her gaze to her glass.

"What do you mean about the diary being valuable? It's only a travelogue."

She stood, her chair screeching across the floor. "I'm sorry. I must get back to Mother."

CHAPTER TWENTY-FOUR

I finished my lemonade, my thoughts on Rose. Of course, it was absurd that the diary contained anything of value. I'd read it. Well, I'd skimmed it, and it was nothing but a travelogue—and a rather boring one at that.

But Rose thinks it's valuable. The thought whispered through my mind as I climbed the stairs to our suite. I drew a bath and had a long soak in the cool water.

As I sponged away the sand and grime, my thoughts kept going round and round from Vita to Tadros with an occasional detour to ponder what Rose had said. Mrs. Jenkins had seemed unwell after the discovery of Vita's body, and Rose had rushed off to get her mother's medicine so quickly. Was Mrs. Jenkins seriously ill? Vita had mentioned something about pyramids and people claiming they'd been cured of diseases. Surely Rose didn't think that some mumbo jumbo from a traveler's diary could cure her mother? Was Rose's nerviness linked to Vita's death?

I belted my silk kimono and settled at the small writing desk in the sitting room. I took a sheaf of hotel notepaper and aligned it beside the photos I'd taken. Using the images to jog my memory about the campsite, I wrote down everything that had happened from the moment I discovered Vita sprawled on the rug in her tent.

I was an enthusiastic list-maker, and my prose was dotted with columns of words. I noted the items I could remember seeing in Vita's room (a pitifully small list), Vita's possessions that had been spread across the typist's desk at the police station (a longer list), as well as the items in the room where Tadros had apparently been living (a pitifully short list that indicated a threadbare existence—especially for someone believed to be a jewel thief).

I'd taken out a fresh sheet and jotted down a new list when the door to the corridor opened and Hildy entered the sitting room. "Hello, Blix."

I returned her greeting and swiveled toward her, ready to launch into a description of everything that had happened that morning, but her face had a pinched look about it. "Are you all right?"

She dropped her paper parasol and handbag on one of the chairs, then pressed her palm down on the back of the sofa as she moved with slow steps across the room. "I'm feeling a little under the weather. Too much sun. My head feels as if one of those jazz bands is playing inside it." She ran her fingers back and forth across her forehead.

Now was not the time to tell her about Tadros. I put my pen down. "I have some aspirin. Would you like some?"

She paused by the desk and squinted at me from under her hand. "Yes, please."

I retrieved the medicine tin from my room and gave her two tablets along with a glass of water. "I'm sorry you're not feeling well."

"It's my own fault. Sometimes I have these episodes." She circled her hand at her temple. "The best thing I can do is retreat to a dark room and lie down for a few hours, but I ignored the first twinges because I wanted to see the mosque."

"What was it like?"

"Magnificent. *Such* intricate geometric mosaics. And the dome! Amazing." She swallowed the tablets, then pointed with the glass at my list. "You should add it to your sightseeing list."

"Oh, those aren't places to visit. It's everyone who went on the camping expedition to the pyramids. I've had an eventful morning."

"Why?" she asked before she took a sip of water.

"It's a rather long story. Perhaps I should tell you about it after you get some rest."

"Yes, good idea. I can't concentrate while this horrible drumbeat is pounding behind my eyes." She set the glass down on the blotter, then leaned closer to the paper, her forehead wrinkled. "You're missing one person—George."

"But he left in the middle of dinner."

She turned and made her way slowly toward her room. "But you said it was a list of people who went to Giza. Even though he left, he was there for a while." She paused, her hand braced on the doorframe. "I may not feel up to accompanying you to dinner. If I'm able to get to sleep, I may be out until tomorrow morning. Hopefully, I'll be recovered for tomorrow's trip to visit Mr. Chambers at the orphanage."

"I won't disturb you."

She nodded, winced, and then closed the door.

I stood over the desk, tapping the back of the chair as I looked over the list again. Then I took a seat, picked up my pen, and added George's name to the top. Hildy was right. Even though George had left Giza, he could have returned to the campsite during the night. He had probably inherited Vita's wealth, and that was a strong motive.

And that was really what it came down to—motive. Everyone at the campsite had the opportunity to slip into Vita's tent during the night. I rolled my pen between my palms. And considering the means didn't narrow the list either. Anyone could have brought a knife in their luggage—or probably even retrieved one from the trunks of supplies that contained utensils to prepare and serve a formal dinner. The key question came down to motive. Who wanted Vita dead?

I headed a second column *Motive* and wrote *inheritance* beside George's name. I tapped the pen against my lips as I considered the rest of the list. Did Mrs. Jenkins or Rose have a reason to want Vita dead? Rose had been concerned about the diary going missing, but if she and Mrs. Jenkins wanted to see it, they'd only have to ask Vita. There was no need to kill her to get it.

I skimmed down the list. Ned was Vita's nephew. Had he inherited anything from her? I put a question mark beside his name, then frowned at the last two people on my list: Timothy and Mr. Chambers. I couldn't picture either one of them as a murderer, and I couldn't think of a motive for either of them. But there had been that oddity of Mr. Chambers palming a piece of paper from Vita's tent. What had that been about?

I added Mr. Briarcliff's name to the bottom of the list because he was in the same category as George. He'd left, but he had been at the campsite.

I sat back and read over it again, then nodded to myself. I'd have to make some inquiries to fill in the blanks on my list. And I might as well start at the top with George.

I cleared the desk and put the papers and photographs away in my room. Then I rang for the attendant, a young man with a tarboosh and a large mustache that dwarfed his delicate features. Fidel always had a smile on his face, and this time was no exception to that rule. "Good afternoon, mademoiselle. How may I help you?"

"Good afternoon, Fidel. I hope that you can help me with something. It's a rather unusual request."

"Yes, mademoiselle. I will try."

"You see to everyone on this floor of the hotel, is that correct?"

"I care for the guests in the rooms on this side of the hotel. Where the corridor turns, that is another's area."

"And you work in shifts?"

"Yes, I am the day attendant. Another person takes care of guests in the evening."

"I see. Now I understand Mr. George Rhodes is staying in this hotel. Do you know where his room is?"

"Of course. He is on the third floor." He gestured to the ceiling. "On the west side."

I wasn't surprised that he knew where George's room was. The news about Vita's death would have traveled through the hotel, and I'm sure everyone who worked at Shepheard's had heard about it and knew which rooms the Rhodes party had. I was counting on that notoriety, hoping that the attendants would remember that night in particular. When something shocking and out of the ordinary happened, it was human nature for the events around that time to stick in one's mind.

"I'd like to speak to the night attendant on Mr. Rhodes' floor. Could that be arranged this evening when he comes on duty?"

He looked away to the corner of the room. The longer my questions had gone on, his smile had faded by degrees, and his manner had become more and more guarded. I needed his help with my strange request, but it was clear he was wary.

Mentally, I flicked through several tactics I might use to ensure his assistance, settling on a combination of a small fib and a large tip.

I leaned forward and lowered my voice a touch as if I were confiding a secret. "You see, the thing is, I have a little wager with a friend. I need to find out if Mr. Rhodes returned to the hotel in the evening and stayed here on the night Mrs. Rhodes died. If you'd introduce me to the attendant who was on duty that night, I could settle our bet. And since this sort of thing is above and beyond any of your normal duties . . ." I picked up my handbag from where I'd left it on the desk and took out several banknotes. I folded them in half and held them out. "Would that be possible?"

He took the notes. "More than possible." His typical smile

was back in place. "Rahim is on duty now. He was promoted to day attendant this week."

"Excellent. Thank you."

"If you'll come with me?" Fidel moved to the door, held it open for me, and then closed it gently. "If you'd please meet me on the third floor at the end of the corridor." He set off down the hallway in the opposite direction from the stairs.

"But the stairs are this way." I gestured the other way.

"Yes, but I must take the back staircase. Attendants must not be seen unless absolutely necessary." He motioned to a door that was set into the wall that I hadn't noticed before.

Of course, the hotel functioned along the same lines as an English county house, where the servants were to be invisible. "Right, then. I'll meet you on the third floor." He went through the door to the back staircase, and I climbed the wide staircase.

Fidel's route must have been more direct because by the time I arrived at the appointed spot, he was already there. "Rahim is here." He knocked on a door in an alcove set back from the hallway. A voice called out, and we entered a room barely bigger than a closet. Shelves stacked with sheets, towels, and soap lined three of the walls, and the scent of freshly laundered linens filled the air. A battered wooden desk sat against the fourth wall under an open window. A desk-top fan whirred, ruffling the papers on the desk and circulating the hot breeze that came in through the tiny open window.

Two men were in the room. One, in a tunic and tarboosh, was apparently Rahim, because he'd been flicking through the pages of the ledger. The other man wore European clothes, but I knew who it was before he turned. That white linen suit, while more wrinkled and a bit dustier than it had been earlier today, was unmistakable.

Fidel and Rahim spoke in Arabic as I said, "Mr. Denby, what a surprise. I didn't expect to see you here."

"The feeling is mutual."

"As you can see, I made it back to the hotel despite your disappearing act."

His pith helmet had been tucked under his arm as he bent to study the ledger, but now he used it to fan his face. "Never had a doubt about that. Briarcliff, despite his rather curmudgeonly manner, is too chivalrous to leave you."

"Unlike someone else I could mention."

"You're the plucky sort. You would have been fine with or without Briarcliff."

Fidel and Rahim finished their conversation, then Fidel introduced me to Rahim, who said, "It is a pleasure to meet you, Miss Windway. I understand you're here with a question for me?"

"Yes, I have a little wager riding on your answer."

Rahim said, "But Mr. Denby has a wager to settle as well. Is it between the two of you?"

Mr. Denby transferred his pith helmet from hand to hand. "Well—er—that is—"

"Yes," I said firmly, "we do. It's about Mr. Rhodes." I raised my eyebrows and tilted my head toward him, indicating he should take over.

"Yes," he said somewhat reluctantly. "I'm sure Mr. Rhodes returned to the hotel last Wednesday and stayed here . . . the night of the—er—unfortunate event with his wife."

I said, "And I disagree. I think he went out again. Can you help us settle this?"

"But of course," Rahim said. "Mr. Rhodes rang at midnight, and I spoke to him then."

"You're sure about that?" Mr. Denby and I both said at the same time.

"Oh yes. I noted it in the ledger." The tassel on Rahim's tarboosh swung as he leaned over and traced one of the hand-written lines on the book. "He requested fresh towels, which I delivered myself."

"You actually spoke to him?" Mr. Denby asked.

"I said good evening. He said it was indeed a good evening because he didn't have to sleep in a tent that night." Rahim smiled. "That is why I remember. Most people do not share a joke with me."

"And would you have noticed if he left the hotel that evening?" I asked.

"I can't see the stairs from here, so I wouldn't know. But he'd have had to ask the front desk to call the night manager to unlock the doors. Since the riots, the doors are locked at midnight."

Mr. Denby said, "Thank you, Rahim, you've helped me win my bet. Miss Windway, I'm looking forward to that drink you owe me. I think the Long Bar has a new cocktail that I'll enjoy immensely."

But we didn't go to the Long Bar. Fifteen minutes later, having left a message requesting to speak to the night manager when he came on duty, we rounded the corner to the garden at the back of the hotel. I increased my pace to keep up with Mr. Denby's darting figure. "I should have asked exactly which room Mr. Rhodes is staying in."

"Third from the corner of the building," Mr. Denby said.

"Oh, how did you find that out?"

"Despite my unwilling membership in the brotherhood of Fleet Street, I do know some rudimentary tricks. Rahim pointed the room out to me on the way to his closet-cum-office, and I counted the doors to the end of the corridor."

We paused in the shade of an acacia tree, and Mr. Denby ticked off the windows, counting under his breath. "There. Smack in the middle of the wall."

"And no matter which room was his, I can't imagine he'd be able to leave through the window." While many parts of Shepheard's were ornate, the windows of the third floor were simple, with no lintels or embellishments. If George had been barmy enough to try to climb out his window to the roof or any other direction, he wouldn't have had a handhold. It would require an acrobat to reach the cornice that topped the building, and George was certainly not that. He was a middle-aged man. I couldn't see him doing anything more athletic than the quick-step. And he couldn't have gone down either. The drop to the ground from the third floor was enough to make my stomach tighten at the thought of trying to leave the building that way.

"It does make one wonder about preparation in case of fire, doesn't it?" Mr. Denby said.

The facade didn't have any handy vegetation or drainpipes to shimmy down. A few spindly palms reached the middle floor, but not the top story. None of them were close enough to the building that even the most desperate person could climb down.

"Denby! What's this I hear about you agitating the staff?" Mr. Briarcliff's tall form powered across the grass. "Can't have you upsetting people and starting rumors—"

The trunk of the tree had blocked me from his view, but as soon as I came into his line of vision, he broke off. "And Miss Windway. I shouldn't be surprised to see you here. You keep turning up."

"Like a bad penny. You really shouldn't harass Mr. Denby. He's simply doing his job."

"But his questions have repercussions, which Mr. Martin will not be happy about. If you'd come to me, Denby, I could've saved you quite a bit of time."

Mr. Denby pulled his notebook out of his pocket. Pencil poised over it, he said, "Do tell."

"Mr. Rhodes finished whatever business he had at the bank and arrived at the hotel around ten. He and I had a drink in the Long Bar, played a few hands of cards, and then he retired to his room around midnight."

Mr. Denby murmured as he scribbled. "Drink at ten—Long Bar—retired, midnight—according to . . ." He raised his eyebrows and waited.

"An unnamed but reliable source," Mr. Briarcliff said.

167

Mr. Denby sighed but nodded. "And I suppose you've talked to the night manager?"

"Of course. And the doorman as well. Mr. Rhodes did not leave the hotel after midnight."

"Well." Mr. Denby slapped the notebook closed and pocketed it. "That will please my editor to no end. He's licking his chops at the thought of the newspaper sales that come with a notorious murder case, but he's a friend of Mr. Rhodes, which puts him in an awkward spot. Between the three of us, I believe he wants to run this piece so that everyone in the community understands that Mr. Rhodes is in the clear."

"And what about Tadros? Will you write about that?" Mr. Briarcliff asked.

"Sadly, the death of an Egyptian *will* make the papers when it relates to the death of a British woman."

CHAPTER TWENTY-FIVE

I went down to dinner alone. I hadn't heard a peep from Hildy's room, so I didn't disturb her. Before I went to the dining room, I stopped off to chat with the doorman. I wasn't about to accept a secondhand recounting of what happened at the hotel last Wednesday. Mr. Denby might be happy to take Mr. Briarcliff at his word, but I wanted to follow up on that detail myself.

It took a few minutes to run the appropriate person to the ground, but eventually I was introduced to Zaham, a dignified man who wore a white turban with his gallibaya. He'd been on duty that night and confirmed that Mr. George Rhodes hadn't left the hotel after he returned late Wednesday night.

"And Mr. Briarcliff?" I asked. "Did he leave?"

Zaham looked puzzled. "No, why would he leave his room after midnight?"

"Oh, he stays here?"

Zaham nodded. "Yes. He handles the difficult guests and any problems that arise. He must be on hand for that."

"I see. You're sure he definitely didn't leave the hotel that night?"

"No, miss. No one left. It was a quiet night. I didn't unlock the door for anyone."

I thanked him and went to dinner, making some mental adjustments to my list of possible suspects. I was seated at a table with Mrs. Jenkins and Rose. I didn't mention any of the events concerning Tadros. It would be unseemly to discuss it at dinner. But we didn't struggle to carry on a conversation. Rose's anxious demeanor was gone. She and Mrs. Jenkins had visited the museum that afternoon, and Rose was animated, almost bouncing in her seat as she said, "The hieroglyphics! It was truly fascinating. I was able to read a few of them off to Mother, which gave me a thrill, let me tell you. We'll have to return, of course. There was so much we didn't see."

Mrs. Jenkins said, "So many tiny statues and scarabs and funeral things. The ancient Egyptians were certainly fixated on death. Rather sad."

"It wasn't sad at all," Rose countered. "It was an effort to make sure they could continue doing the things they enjoyed in the next life."

Mrs. Jenkins looked as if she would argue, but her attention shifted to George, who had approached our table.

"Good evening, ladies."

Mrs. Jenkins wafted a hand toward the empty chair at her side. "Do join us, George."

"Thank you. I've spent the day on the Nile with Ned and his friend, hunting for crocodile. No luck, unfortunately." That explained the pink tinge of his face. Above his dark pencil mustache, his nose was a bright salmon color. "It will be a pleasure to dine with three beautiful women," he said as he held his gaze on Mrs. Jenkins, who wore a wine-colored evening gown that showed off her figure. It was the first time since Vita had died that I'd seen any flicker of his previous flirtatious manner.

Mrs. Jenkins tilted her chin down and smiled at him in a coquettish way. "You're too kind."

Rose rolled her eyes before turning her attention to buttering her roll. She wore a ruffled white dress, which washed out her pale complexion.

After the waiter took George's order, Rose said, "We were just telling Blix about our visit to the museum. Mother and I were having a bit of a debate—"

She seemed to suddenly realize it wouldn't be the done thing to bring up the topic of death and funeral practices with a man whose wife had just died.

I jumped in to rescue her from her conversational misstep. "I imagine you were there the whole afternoon? I understand it's quite an extensive collection."

"No, only a few hours." Mrs. Jenkins worked her eyelashes—full-force flickering—as she added to George, "It's all so confusing. I can't keep the names of the pharaohs straight."

"Of course, we didn't have time to see everything," Rose said. "And then we had to go from one antique dealer to another." Resentment underlined her tone.

"Did you find any treasures?" I asked Rose.

"No. We were searching for Mr. Duncan's diary. I told Mother it was a useless task."

"It still hasn't turned up?" My thoughts had been so full of Tadros that I'd completely forgotten about the diary.

Mrs. Jenkins' trill of laughter sounded forced. "But, of course, we were looking at other things too. We happened to ask after it in a few shops."

A wrinkle appeared between Rose's brows. "No, it was the reason—"

Mrs. Jenkins, her cheeks flushing, spoke over Rose. "Nonsense. We looked at those carpets as well as those rather disturbing-looking scarabs that you like with the tiny writing on the back."

"Are you a follower of pyramidology, Mrs. Jenkins?" I asked, curious about why Mrs. Jenkins was so interested in the diary.

"Me? Heavens, no." From her tone, you'd have thought I'd asked her something outrageous, like, *Are you a cannibal*?

"I wasn't familiar with pyramidology until recently," I said, "but I understand it's quite popular."

"Especially here in Cairo," George added.

"Well, I find it absurd," Mrs. Jenkins said emphatically as she plucked at her neckline. She sipped some water. "Since the diary has gone missing and we stopped in a few shops, I asked after it. If we ran across it, I could return it to you, George."

"How very thoughtful of you," he said. "I've been haggling with the antique chaps myself. I purchased a few rugs and sent them back to Silverthorne Hall."

The stiffness went out of Mrs. Jenkins. Her shoulders relaxed as her face became more animated. "You have?"

"The old hall needs a bit of a refresher. I've instructed my estate steward to begin repairing the roof as well."

"How wonderful. Silverthorne was always so elegant and beautiful. Have you changed anything else since I've been there?" Mrs. Jenkins asked.

"Let me think . . . we added a yew walk."

"On the east side?"

"Yes," George said, his chin tucking in as his head pulled back in surprise. "How did you know?"

"I always thought it was the perfect spot for something like that. It's so flat and open. And when you come out of it, you'd have the wonderful view of the lake."

"Just so," George said with a nod and a bemused look on his face. "Any other improvements you'd recommend?"

"Oh! Well!" Mrs. Jenkins looked like a child presented with a birthday cake. "There's so much, isn't there? The hillock that gives the view to the lake would be an excellent place for a folly. And did you update that awful brocade in the yellow drawing room?"

"Still there, I regret to report."

"You simply *must* have it down. A pale blue would be more soothing than that ghastly shade of burnt mustard."

"Do you know, I believe you're right."

George and Mrs. Jenkins had been turning more and more toward each other as they spoke, and now they were in a little conversational bubble that completely excluded Rose and me.

Rose said in a low voice to me, "Mother's always been quite fond of Silverthorne."

Mrs. Jenkins heard her remark and swiveled toward Rose. "Of course I take an interest in Silverthorne. I practically grew up there."

George chuckled. "That she did. Always dodging my footsteps, your mother was. She'd tag along and pull at my arm, demanding to be included."

Mrs. Jenkins frowned. "George, that makes me sound like a beastly pest."

"Oh, you were. But you always had your way. All you had to do was turn those big blue eyes on me. I couldn't say no. And you knew it too. You were a little minx."

I was seated across the table from Mrs. Jenkins, but I could see a tiny line, a fine sheet of perspiration, had appeared along her hairline. She swept her fingers across the top of her forehead, wiping away the glistening trace on her skin. Then she patted her hair as if she'd been checking to make sure her coiffure was still in place. "Really, George. That's not how I remember it at all. I only wanted to be part of the fun."

The pudding arrived, and after the waiter departed, George asked, "Have you ladies been out to Gezira?"

"Not yet," Mrs. Jenkins said, and I shook my head.

"Well, then. You must come out with me. Be my guests."

"What is Gezira?" Rose asked.

Mrs. Jenkins waved off the waiter, who'd indicated he'd refill her wineglass. She sipped her water instead. "It's a sporting club, dear. You'd know that if you read anything besides your hieroglyphic books."

"Polo, horse racing, golf, squash, tennis, croquet," George elaborated.

"Oh, I adore tennis," Rose said.

"As do I," I said.

"I prefer croquet," Mrs. Jenkins said.

"Well, then, you and I can have a nice game of croquet while Rose and Blix play tennis. Or I'm sure you could find partners for doubles," George said. "And if you're not interested in athletic pursuits, it's set among the gardens, which the ladies seem to find pleasant. Shall we plan on tomorrow?"

"I'm afraid I won't be able to join you. Hildy and I are visiting Mr. Chambers' orphanage."

"Perhaps later in the week, then?" George said.

I considered declining on behalf of Hildy and myself, but if George continued with his attentions to Mrs. Jenkins, surely that would help scotch the rumors that linked his name with Hildy. "Sounds delightful," I said, and Mrs. Jenkins agreed.

"Excellent. I look forward to it," George said. I looked around to see if Miss Philpott had noticed George's attentiveness to Mrs. Jenkins, but unfortunately Miss Philpott and Mrs. Canning were seated with their backs to our table.

CHAPTER TWENTY-SIX

I wasn't able to tell Hildy anything about Tadros because she emerged from her room moments before we were due to leave the next morning.

"Sorry," she said as we went downstairs. "I didn't sleep well until the early hours of the morning, which made it difficult to wake up."

"I'm sure Mr. Chambers would understand if you want to postpone our visit."

"No, I'm fine today and looking forward to the outing."

"I have quite a lot to tell you on the drive—"

A short elderly woman intercepted us as we crossed the hotel lobby and planted herself in our path. "I understand you're going to the orphanage. Might I ride along with you? I'm Mrs. Treeford, by the way."

Of course we invited her to join us. In the horse cab, I took the seat with my back to the driver to allow the two older ladies to face forward. Mrs. Treeford opened a silk-and-lace parasol with a canopy that curved like the domes of the Arabic mosques. It made the paper parasols that Hildy and I had brought along look like flimsy children's toys.

Mrs. Treeford propped the thick wooden shaft of her parasol

on her shoulder and tilted it to protect her crinkled skin from the sun. "Thank you for allowing me to accompany you. I'm afraid I'm not the adventurous kind. I find traveling alone around Cairo rather intimidating." She braced a hand on the seat as the cab swerved to avoid a donkey pulling a cart of produce. "And it's so nice to have someone to converse with."

She was a little dumpling of a woman with fluffy white hair peeking out from under her hat. I was much taller than Hildy, but even Hildy towered over the petite Mrs. Treeford. Behind gold-rimmed spectacles, Mrs. Treeford's bright brown eyes surveyed the street scene as the driver threaded through the bustle of Cairo, avoiding pedestrians—men in business suits, workers in tunics, women in dark headdresses and long robes that swished along the pavement, and children who darted in and out of the throng.

I put the news about Tadros aside and focused on being sociable. "Did you arrive in Cairo recently, Mrs. Treeford?"

"A few days ago. But this is my second stop here. I've been up the Nile to see the temples—amazing structures. Quite unbelievable! And indescribable too. My attempts to recount what I saw in letters home failed miserably to do them justice. But now that I'm back in Cairo, I must visit dear Phillip again. I'm delighted to finally be able to see the orphanage's new location. I didn't have time to do that before my steamer departed."

Hildy shifted the angle of her paper parasol as we turned a corner. "You've been acquainted with him for a long time, then?"

"Oh my, yes. Phillip and I have known each other since we were children. We've kept up a correspondence, and I've followed his work with the orphanage closely over the years. My late husband and I often wintered in Egypt. Each time we arrived we'd stop and see Phillip."

Hildy said, "Blix and I met him on the ship on the way over. It was clear to both of us that he's deeply passionate about the orphanage."

MURDER AMONG THE PYRAMIDS

"It's been his life's work. It's so sad that he can't hand it off to Mr. McKinney. I never understood Vita's opposition to it."

"What do you mean?" I asked. This was the first hint I'd heard about any discord between Mr. Chambers and Vita, and since I'd determined to find out who might have wanted Vita dead, I was interested in any disagreements in her life.

"Well . . ." Mrs. Treeford flattened her lips. "One doesn't like to cast aspersions, and Vita was a lovely person—so helpful with the orphanage in many ways—but she could be rather set in her opinions. She felt that only Phillip was qualified to run the orphanage. And him in his eighties! It should have been handed off long ago to Mr. McKinney. Chasing around after energetic children is quite beyond Phillip. Mr. McKinney has been Phillip's second-in-command for over a decade. Very capable man, good to the children, and an excellent administrator, but could Vita see that? No."

"So Vita was a patron of the orphanage?"

"She was a patron of *Phillip*," Mrs. Treeford said tartly. Then she sighed, and her tone shifted to a more conciliatory note. "Vita provided a great deal of support to the orphanage, which was admirable, I'll grant that, but her patronage was conditional. She refused to see that Mr. McKinney was imminently capable. She told me herself a few weeks ago that if Phillip wasn't in charge, she'd withdraw her support. I attempted to convince her that Phillip deserves a little rest, the opportunity to return to England and see his grandchildren. He's trained up Mr. McKinney to take over, but Vita wouldn't hear a word of it. 'I couldn't trust anyone else,' she said."

Hildy frowned. "That seems rather rigid and shortsighted."

Mrs. Treeford said, "I don't know how well you knew Vita, but she was never one to take suggestions."

Hildy tilted her head in agreement. "Yes, she was so sure of herself."

Mrs. Treeford looked beyond the driver of the cab. "It's never a good combination. Scads of money and an intractable disposition. Makes one a bit of a tyrant." I was beginning to think that Mrs. Treeford would get along swimmingly with the gossipy Mrs. Philpott and Mrs. Canning, but she did know the people who had been in Vita's life, so instead of changing the topic, I let her twittery voice ramble on. "And such distressing news about the man the police thought was guilty."

"What news?" Hildy asked.

"You haven't heard? There was talk of nothing else at breakfast." Mrs. Treeford took a folded newspaper from her handbag and gave it to Hildy.

Under *The Nile's* masthead, the headline read, *Second Murder Linked to Death at the Pyramids.*

Hildy smoothed the creases from the newspaper. "Oh dear. What's happened?"

"They found the man who the police thought was guilty of murdering Vita. *He'd* been murdered. But it was clear his murder was intended to look like a suicide."

"Goodness. Tadros murdered. And Sir Abner seemed so sure about him," Hildy said as she looked up at me.

"It just goes to show that Sir Abner isn't always correct in his assumptions, doesn't it?" I leaned in to skim the article under Mr. Denby's byline.

"I suppose so," Hildy murmured, her expression troubled as she read.

"The police are making progress, though," Mrs. Treeford said. "They've ruled out that nice Mr. Rhodes. He is a bit of rouge, but he's kind enough to dance with all the ladies at the fancy dress balls, which so many men won't do."

I'd read the article this morning. Mr. Denby had managed to work in a few mentions of George's whereabouts during the night in question, which put him in the clear for his wife's murder. "Someone's doing investigative work, but it's not the police."

Hildy looked at me, a question in her gaze, and I said

quietly, "I'll tell you later," while Mrs. Treeford was occupied with straightening the lace on her collar.

The cab pulled up in front of a high wall that had once been white but was now a dusty beige. The brilliant sunlight high-lighted the cracks that ran through the flaky stucco like a pattern of marbling. "Oh, how nice. It looks as if this building is much larger than the last one," Mrs. Treeford said as she climbed down from the carriage and pulled on a string by a narrow arched wooden door set into the wall.

Hildy remained seated as she surveyed the wall and the dilapidated building across the street with broken lattice. A dog with matted fur rested in the shade of the building eyed us but didn't move. "Are we sure this is the right address? It looks rather forbidding."

"I agree, but Mrs. Treeford seems to be confident that this is it." I climbed down.

The door opened, and Mr. Chambers appeared. "Welcome! Do come in." He clasped Mrs. Treeford's hand in both of his own. "What a delight to see you, Imogene."

"And it's always a pleasure to see you, Phillip. I'm so looking forward to touring your new location."

"Miss Honeyworth and Miss Windway," he said as he turned to us, "thank you for taking the time to visit. This way."

Hildy and I followed them through the door single file. We crossed a narrow strip of bare dirt, then went through a set of double wooden doors.

"Let me give you a bit of a tour." Leaning on his cane, Mr. Chambers led us along a wide, cool hallway with dark-paneled walls. Sunlight streamed in from high windows, illuminating a beautiful geometric mosaic of white and blue that ran the length of the corridor. "We won't disturb their studies," Mr. Chambers said as we passed rooms of students, their dark heads bent. "Arabic here, English across the hall, maths down here at the end. And here is the creative section around the corner, art and

SARA ROSETT

music." The tones of children's voices penetrated a closed door, singing a song in Arabic to the accompaniment of a piano.

At the end of the corridor, shouts and laughter sounded as we descended three shallow stone steps and entered the central courtyard. Palms and flowering shrubs grew on the margins. The wide area in the middle was an open swath of grass, where a group of children ran back and forth, kicking a ball. "And games, the favorite of most of the children."

A young woman with dark hair in a pale blue dress blew a whistle. "That's Miss Daglish, our matron and games mistress." The children lined up and she led them to a door on the opposite side of the courtyard.

"I thought you might like to join us for lunch," Mr. Chambers said as we entered a long room lined with trestle tables. The smell of fresh bread wafted through the air.

"Excellent idea," Hildy said, and Mrs. Treeford and I agreed.

Instead of the staff sitting together at a single table, Mr. Chambers paired each one of us with a teacher and dispersed us around the room to sit with the children. I joined Miss Daglish, who spoke both English and Arabic and translated for me so I could talk to the children as we ate lamb, bread, and fruit. They confirmed that Mr. Chambers had a good grasp of their likes and dislikes. Games was indeed their favorite activity. Maths and penmanship ranked on the low end of their preferences.

After lunch, Hildy, who had been matched with the science teacher, asked for a tour of the laboratory, and they set off together, with Mrs. Treeford accompanying them. When we left the dining hall, I matched my pace to Mr. Chambers' slower stride as he leaned on his cane. "You've done an amazing thing here."

"Thank you. It's only through the generous donations of our patrons that we've been able to carry on as long as we have."

"Patrons like Vita?

His face flooded with emotion, but I couldn't tell if it was regret or simply sadness. "She was one of the driving forces in keeping the orphanage open."

We reached the central courtyard and stopped to watch Miss Daglish with a new group of children.

"Have you seen *The Nile* newspaper this morning?" I asked.

"Yes, terrible news about Tadros."

"It is." I didn't elaborate on my firsthand involvement with the discovery of his body. I studied Mr. Chambers' face a moment more, then decided to ask a bold question. I'd spent my childhood living with a rotating parade of nannies and then governesses—some of them kind and conscientious and some of them cruel tyrants—and I'd developed the ability to take the measure of a person. I sensed that Mr. Chambers was essentially honest, not nefarious. The best thing to do would be to ask him my question straightaway. As we both looked out across the courtyard, I said, "May I bring up a delicate question?"

The children were now running races, kicking up dust as they scampered over the patchy grass. "Yes, of course. Something about the orphanage?"

"No. It's to do with that morning in Vita's tent."

CHAPTER TWENTY-SEVEN

*A*t my words, Mr. Chambers' head dipped, and he looked down at his hands, which he'd braced one on top of the other on the head of his cane. "Ah, I believe I know what your question is. You saw me take a piece of paper from Vita's tent. Was that it?"

"Yes, exactly that. I realize it's none of my business, but—"

He waved off my explanation of why I wanted to know. "Not one of my finer moments." His chest rose and fell as he took a deep breath. "I'd written a letter to Vita that was an attempt to convince her that the best course for the future of the orphanage was for me to hand off the reins to Mr. McKinney. Physically and mentally, I'm finding it more difficult to keep up with things. Vita is—was—our foremost donor, so her support of the plan was essential. I'd floated the idea before—several times, in fact. But each time she rejected that plan. She was adamant that her continued support was tied to whether or not I stayed on. I made a rash statement in the letter, that she would regret it if she didn't come to see things my way."

Chirps of laughter came from two girls as they walked across the courtyard back to the beginning of the race lines. Mr. Chambers straightened and looked at me. "We'd discussed the

182

topic a few days earlier. I'd given Vita an ultimatum then. I told her I would finish out the term, then I was returning to England. If she didn't support Mr. McKinney after my departure, then the orphanage would close. I'd hoped to force her hand—that's what I meant when I said she'd regret it. She'd be the one turning the orphans onto the streets."

A sharp cry came from the courtyard. A small girl had tripped during a race and grazed her knee. Miss Daglish swept her up, cuddled her a moment, then examined her knee. She let the girl curl against her shoulder as she called for the other children to start the next race.

"On the morning you found Vita—" Mr. Chambers paused and ran his hand over his mouth. "As soon as I walked into the tent and saw what had happened, I realized that although Vita understood the implication of my note, the police would not."

"I can see how that could be misconstrued. Did Vita come around to seeing things your way?"

He gave a dry chuckle. "She ripped my note in half."

"I see. So you gave it to her that day at the campsite?"

"That evening," he said. "Vita announced she was turning in, and I said I would as well. That was after you and Miss Honeyworth retired. I walked with Vita to her tent and gave her the letter. I asked her to read it after I'd left, then we could speak about it in the morning, but that wasn't her way. She skimmed it immediately and then tore it in half. She told me she wouldn't change her mind about my retirement. I'll admit that I was quite frustrated and stalked away—as much as one can stalk through the desert sand," he added with a brief smile. "So when I saw my note the next morning, I snatched it up." He took an envelope from his pocket and handed it to me. "See for yourself."

"You kept it?" The envelope contained what had been a single sheet of paper, but it had been torn in two. Each piece had a jagged tear along one side where it had been ripped in half. A quick look showed Mr. Chambers' shaky penmanship, a

183

duplicate of the handwriting on the invitation he'd sent to Hildy and me to tour the orphanage.

I tucked the note into the envelope and handed it back as he said, "Rather absurd of me to do so, isn't it? But my conscience wouldn't let me destroy it. Foul play and all that. And I didn't believe Tadros was the culprit, as the sad news of the day has borne out."

"What will you do with it?"

"Hand it over to the officials." He looked at his pocket watch. "In fact, someone should be along shortly to collect it."

"I won't take up any more of your time, then. I'll find Hildy." I walked a few steps away and turned back. "Mr. Chambers, what will happen to the orphanage now?"

"Its future is secure. Vita's solicitor has been in touch. She left a very generous endowment. The funds are to be in a trust that's managed by a solicitor and distributed to the orphanage on a quarterly basis."

"Are there any stipulations as to you remaining in charge?" I asked, thinking the question was nosy and he might not answer.

"No. No stipulations," he said, sadness tinging his features.

So he'd gotten exactly what he wanted, but looking at his face, I couldn't believe he'd been the one to kill Vita. But then I remembered the blood on his cuff, and my confidence in my assessment of him wavered.

Footsteps rang out as a man strode along the tiled passageway toward us. The light was behind him, silhouetting the man's broad shoulders and trim waist. I knew it was Mr. Briarcliff before he stepped into the sunlight.

"Miss Windway," he said. "Of course you're here." Before I could reply, he turned to Mr. Chambers and greeted him.

"Sir Abner drafted you, did he?" Mr. Chambers said as he handed over the envelope with the torn letter.

Mr. Briarcliff took it but didn't open the envelope. "I'm little more than an errand boy."

"I very much doubt that." Mr. Chambers tapped the envelope. "Now I'm sure you'll have a few questions about that. Why don't you come along to my office? Miss Windway, would you care to join us?"

Mr. Briarcliff sent him a warning look, but Mr. Chambers added, "No need to be concerned. Miss Windway knows all about that." He motioned to the envelope.

"I should have known."

"She was there at the campsite, you know," Mr. Chambers said. "Very observant. You should talk with her."

"Oh, I intend to."

I smiled at him sweetly, thinking that he was probably thinking *grill* instead of *talk*. "I'm afraid we'll have to chat another time, Mr. Briarcliff. I promised to meet Hildy. Good day, gentlemen."

HILDY CLOSED her *Baedeker's* with a snap that made the blue feathers on the cuff of her suit jacket tremble. "I can't concentrate on anything in the museum today, not with everything you told me about Tadros filling up all the space in my head."

"I understand. I feel the same." I ran my gaze around the rows and rows of mummies lying in their glass cases. "Perhaps we should return another day."

"Let's do."

After leaving the orphanage, we'd invited Mrs. Treeford to join us for an afternoon at the Egyptian Museum, but she had declined, saying one outing a day was her limit. We'd dropped her at Shepheard's. During the drive to the museum, I'd told Hildy about the discovery of Tadros' body as well as the details about why it was clear the death was not a suicide.

I'd expected her to be upset, but I should have remembered how calm she was after Vita's death. Hildy wasn't a woman who suffered from the vapors. She'd said, "Oh dear. How tragic for Tadros," then she'd gone quiet. After a moment, she'd said, "Blix, my dear, you must be very careful. I was worried about you discovering unsavory details in people's lives, but this is worse. So much worse. Vita's murderer is desperate to make sure he—or she—isn't discovered."

Her warning was like an ominous low note that carried on under a light melody, a hint that a shift to a darker tone was coming in the composition. I couldn't disagree with her. I'd been so focused on scotching any rumors that might damage my reputation—and Hildy's as well—that I'd barely given any thought to the fact that there was an evil person behind the deaths of Vita and Tadros. I'd been caught up in figuring out who was guilty, but I hadn't stopped to consider how desperate that person must be to keep their deeds hidden.

Hildy was right. Someone was doing whatever was necessary to keep the truth of Vita's death from coming to light, even to the point of attempting to make a murder appear to be suicide. If the marks on Tadros' neck hadn't been noticed, I was sure Sir Abner would have been quick to accept that Tadros killed Vita, then committed suicide out of remorse. The investigation—such as it was—would have been closed.

Hildy's worries filled my thoughts, and from that point on it was as if a veil descended, blurring and muting everything around me. I'd viewed the museum's statuary, artifacts, grave goods, and mummies with a sense of detachment, wrapped in my thoughts about Vita and Tadros.

While we were moving through the galleries to leave the museum, my steps checked at a display case filled with objects carved of ivory, lapis lazuli, and malachite, which reminded me of the letter opener that I'd seen when Vita's belongings were spread out across the desktop at the police station.

Hildy hadn't realized I'd slowed down. She'd continued walking at a quick pace, the blue feathers on her cloche rippling with her swift movement. I hurried to catch up with her as she led the way down the stairs to the main floor and through the two-story central atrium. Colonnaded balconies ran along each side of the second story, and beyond the balconies a multitude of galleries held the treasures unearthed throughout Egypt.

As we navigated around a large wooden boat in the atrium and headed for the main doors, I asked, "Hildy, did you go into Vita's tent when we were at the campsite?"

It took her a moment to answer. It seemed that she had to pull her thoughts from one track to another. "No. Why?"

I described what I'd seen at the police station. "A letter opener like the one you're missing was there among the things taken from Vita's tent."

"How very peculiar. I didn't take it to Vita's tent. I may be a tad forgetful about some things, but I certainly know I didn't do that." We resumed walking, threading through the busy rotunda in front of the entrance.

"Do you think—oh, hello, Mrs. Jenkins," I said.

"So sorry." She stepped back after nearly running me down. "Quite a crush today." Under her chic hat, her color was high. She fanned her flushed face with a folded map while daubing her forehead with her handkerchief.

"Is Rose here?" I asked, scanning the throng. The murmur of conversation mixed with the click of hundreds of heels across the starburst-tile floor echoed through the rotunda and up to the lofty ceiling.

Mrs. Jenkins waved her handkerchief toward the tall double entry doors. "She's out in the gardens. She saw an acquaintance and stopped to speak to her, but I didn't want to stay a moment longer in that scorching sun. Oh, look, there's George." She bounced up on her tiptoes and flapped the map. "Yoo-hoo, George!"

He'd been heading for the door, but at the sound of his name, he turned. He spotted Mrs. Jenkins and smoothed down his thin mustache as he worked through the crowd. "Hello, ladies," he said as he removed his straw boater. "Aren't you all looking lovely today. Enjoying the museum?"

Hildy and I had been too preoccupied with Tadros' death to take in much about the exhibits, but she was too much of a lady to mention it. Hildy answered in keeping with the vein of social chitchat. "It's fascinating."

"Rather a lot to take in during one visit," I added. "We plan to return later."

"It's our third visit," Mrs. Jenkins said. "Rose wants to see the papyrus room today." She sounded resigned, not delighted. "Of course, I'd rather have her here than touring the desert. The silly girl went and had the concierge arrange an outing. She hired a guide at sunrise this morning and toured Sakkara."

"How enterprising." I should ask her if she'd recommend her guide because I wanted to travel farther afield. Hildy was all for visiting the sites in Cairo, but the incident at the pyramids had put her off traveling into the desert.

"But she went all on her own! Thank goodness she returned before luncheon, otherwise I would have insisted on a search party."

"I'm sure that with Shepheard's arranging the guide, she was as safe as could be," George said, then added, "If I'd known you were coming here, I could have driven you in my new motor. I just came a few moments ago to hand off a document to one of the museum's directors."

Mrs. Jenkins looked at him out of the corner of her eye. "Is that cream-colored Rolls Royce Phantom parked by the gate yours? Goodness! What a gorgeous motor."

I caught Hildy's attention and tilted my head toward the door. She gave an infinitesimal nod, agreeing that she was ready to depart. It was clear that Mrs. Jenkins and George could converse for hours. Hildy drew a breath to break into the conversation to say our goodbyes, but George, his attention on Mrs. Jenkins, was saying, ". . . topping machine, if I do say so myself. I'd be delighted to give you—and Rose too, of course—a lift back to Shepheard's whenever you're ready to return."

"You're a dear to offer." Mrs. Jenkins gripped his arm to

emphasize her words, or she just wanted to latch on to him in every sense of the phrase. "But I couldn't ask you to wait. It will be a while. Once Rose gets into the museum, it's rather difficult to extract her. She's quite mad on Egyptomania."

"It's no problem. Ned is at the café across the square. I'll join him for a late lunch and wait for you there."

Hildy finally managed to get in a few words. "Blix and I must—"

A high-pitched scream startled everyone. The noisy rotunda went silent for a second. Mrs. Jenkins clamped down on George's forearm, nearly pulling him off-balance. "Rose is out there."

Our group was swept up in a general surge toward the doors. As we spilled out into the garden, the sunlight dazzled. I shaded my eyes and spotted two young women, one petite and the other tall and gangly. "There's Rose."

She and the other young woman stood beside a fragment of an obelisk, the upper triangular portion. It was one of the antiquities that were on display in the gardens around the museum. Hildy had pointed it out on our way into the museum, reading from her guidebook. It was the pyramidion to Queen Hatshepsut's obelisk, and we'd had a look at its hieroglyphics.

Rose had one hand braced on the stone while the other covered her mouth as she stared down at something hidden from our view on the ground behind the obelisk. Her companion was backing away, still shrieking at a volume that rivaled the performances of some opera sopranos.

Mrs. Jenkins flew down the flight of steps to the garden and shoved her way through the tourists, many of whom were striding toward the two young women. I followed, slipping through the gaps in the crowd, and shouldered my way to the edge of the throng. Mrs. Jenkins was pulling Rose back. "Come away, dear. Don't look again."

A young man lay motionless on his side with his back to me, a red stain spreading out from his head. His hat—a bowler—

had tumbled away, and a satchel with the flap thrown back lay near a notebook that was splayed open, the wind riffling the pages, which were filled with sketches of hieroglyphics.

A flare of shock and anger coursed through me. Another body? "This is horrible!" I whispered, too shocked to move.

Out of the corner of my eye, Hildy's floaty blue-feathered ensemble emerged from the crowd. She paused beside Rose, then went and knelt by the man. "Why, it's Mr. Noviss." She crouched closer. "And, thank goodness, he's breathing." She gently shook his shoulder. "Mr. Noviss?"

There was no response.

She leaned down and said in a loud voice, "Timothy, you really must wake up."

He gave a little groan and moved his shoulder, which caused him to roll onto his back. All color had been leached from his face, and his dark eyelashes contrasted with his washed-out complexion. Hildy took off her jacket, folded it into a square, and pressed it to the wound at his temple. "Go for help, Blix. Best hurry."

As I backed up, my foot kicked the satchel and some more of the contents tumbled out—a sketchpad, pencils, and some books. I shoved everything back inside, pausing only for a second when I recognized the cover of one of the books with gold lettering and a dragonfly. It was Cornelius Duncan's diary.

CHAPTER TWENTY-EIGHT

*T*houghts coursed through my mind as I shoved the books back into the leather satchel and closed the flap. Why did Timothy have it? Had he taken it from Vita's tent?

I tucked the satchel to my side and sprinted toward the museum's horseshoe arch entrance at the center of the soft pink stucco building to find someone who could telephone for help. George caught up with me on the steps. "The fastest way to get help for the boy will be for me to take him to the hospital. My motor is across the square at the café where Ned is waiting. I'll have him bring it around."

Before I could reply, he ran in the direction of the museum's gate, his gold watch chain jangling as his short figure retreated. I hurried back across the garden and pushed through the crowd to tell Hildy the plan.

Her brows lowered so that they were visible under the low rim of her cloche. "I don't like it. Moving Timothy to the motor might jar him, to say nothing of the drive."

George jogged up a few moments later, his face flushed under his boater hat. "Clear a path," he commanded, motioning for the people to move aside. "Ned's on his way with the motor."

SARA ROSETT

Hildy was still kneeling beside Timothy, pressing her jacket to his head wound. "I don't think it's a good idea to move him."

George leaned down and put a hand on her shoulder. "Time is of the essence, correct?"

Hildy surveyed Timothy's gray skin and limp limbs. "Yes, it is."

"Then trust me, Hildy. The motor is the most expedient course."

She gave a quick nod, then picked two sturdy young men from the crowd and had them lift Timothy by the shoulders and feet. She held his head steady and kept the pressure on the makeshift bandage. The three of them carried him out of the garden and to the motor, where Ned was opening the back door. He climbed in the back with Timothy, and Hildy said, "Keep that fabric pressed to his head." Ned nodded, his face nearly as pale as Timothy's. George got into the driver's seat, checked over his shoulder to see that Timothy was settled, then put the motor in gear.

"Oh, wait!" I called, but the motor was already too far away for them to hear me. "I still have his satchel," I said to Hildy. "I kicked it when I went for help. I picked it up so it wouldn't be trampled."

Hildy splayed her hands, which were covered with spatters of blood. "I think you should hold on to it for now."

I shifted the satchel to my other hand and removed a handkerchief from my handbag, which hung from my wrist, and gave it to Hildy.

She wiped the traces of blood from her hands. "We'll pay him a visit at the hospital tomorrow. You can return it then."

"You think he'll recover?"

Hildy scrubbed at her palm. "I don't know, but I find it's always best to take an optimistic view." She gave a little smile. "That comes from years of nursing my brother when he was ill. You never let on if the prognosis is doubtful or gloomy."

"Then we'll hope for the best," I said as Mrs. Jenkins bundled Rose and her friend into a horse cab and departed.

"I left my handbag by the obelisk fragment," Hildy said, and we crossed the garden to it. The crowd had dispersed, and the area around the pyramidion was deserted. The sun beat down, casting tiny shadows within the carvings of the hieroglyphics.

Hildy picked up her handbag and brushed off several blades of grass. "What is the protocol in a situation such as this? One does wonder."

"What do you mean?" I asked.

"The poor boy was attacked. Do we contact the police? Does the hospital?"

"Normally, yes, I think that would be the correct action to take, but it looks like it will be an exercise in futility."

"I know you're not fond of Sir Abner, but surely he won't ignore an attack on a British citizen."

"Oh, I'm sure he'll give that his full attention, but unless someone who saw the attack comes forward . . ."

"Yes, I suppose you're right. There's no sign of what was used to hit him."

We returned to the museum and asked to use their telephone to contact the police, but museum officials had already done so. The director himself took down our names and said he'd pass the information on to the police. "There's no need for you to stay on." He put down his pen and whisked us out of the building as if he were sweeping a couple of annoying beetles outside.

As we made our way back to the hotel, Hildy said, "I begin to see why you have little faith that things will be handled correctly." When we arrived at the hotel, we went directly up to our suite. Hildy paused at the doorway to her room. "I intend to have a long soak in the bath and then have something sent up on a tray. I'm not up to the dining room this evening."

"Me either."

"I'll ring and order dinner for both of us," she said before she closed her door.

I took the satchel into my room and settled into a chair by the open window. A thin breeze stirred, hot and dry, and I lifted the hair off the back of my neck for a moment. I opened the leather flap and took out each item, placing them on the small table beside me.

It took a few minutes to smooth the wrinkled pages of one of Timothy's notebooks, which were covered with his minute handwriting mixed with exact drawings of hieroglyphics. Besides the gold embossed diary, the satchel contained two sketchpads, several pencils, an Arabic phrasebook, and a well-thumbed *Journal of the British Archaeological Association*.

I picked up the diary and began reading. Fortunately, Cornelius Duncan's handwriting was clear, if a little faded. By the time the call for prayer rang out over the city, I'd read each entry.

Hildy tapped on my door, and I called out for her to come in.

She held a plate. "Would you like a sandwich?"

"Yes, please." I showed her the diary. "This was in Timothy's satchel. I couldn't resist reading it," I said as I took a sandwich.

Hildy sank down onto my bed as she took the diary from me. "The diary of that man Vita was so fascinated by? Cornelius . . ."

"Duncan," I supplied. "It went missing from Vita's tent." I ate while Hildy turned pages.

I swallowed a bite of the sandwich and said, "I spent the last few hours reading it, and I can't see any reason someone would steal it from Vita's tent. It's a boringly detailed travelogue."

"I see what you mean. If I ever had insomnia, this would cure it."

"Not exactly scintillating reading."

Hildy closed the diary and looked at the satchel on the floor by my chair. "Timothy took it from Vita's tent? I'm so surprised. I wouldn't have thought it of him."

"Me either. He doesn't seem like a thief—or what I imagine a thief would look like," I said with a quick smile. "But, more than that, there's nothing in it about hieroglyphics, not a single word about them. If there had been some notes about hieroglyphics or something fascinating about one of the sites and it related to hieroglyphics, then I could almost imagine Timothy taking the diary, but there's nothing like that."

Hildy twisted it around and looked at the cover. "Perhaps it's not the contents of the diary that makes it valuable. Perhaps it's simply because it belonged to Mr. Duncan. What did Vita say? Something about it being the only thing in existence to fill in some gaps in pyramidology . . . um . . . ideology, I suppose you'd call it. I didn't pay too much attention to what she was saying about that, I'm afraid."

"I don't remember much of it either, but I believe you're right that she said this was the only copy of the diary." I tapped the cover. "Perhaps you're right, and *that's* why it's valuable."

"I suspect from the state of Timothy's clothes that he's not well-off. George mentioned that Ned was covering Timothy's travel expenses."

I shifted in the chair. Timothy wasn't the only one whose travel expenses were being picked up by someone else. Hildy didn't notice my discomfort. She was staring at the brocade drapes. "Perhaps Timothy thought he could sell it? Would the pyramidology people pay a high price for it?"

"I have no idea. It would be a small market, though. It wouldn't seem to be a good plan for raising cash. Perhaps it's something else . . ." I took the diary from her and felt along the end pages and held it up so that I could peer into the crevice that formed the spine.

Hildy tilted her head. "You think there might be something hidden within the book?"

"Apparently not. It was the only other thing I could think of that would induce Timothy to take it from Vita's tent. However, as far as I can tell, it's just a diary. There's nothing in the spine, and there's no lumps or bumps on the end pages." I ran my fingers over the gold embossing.

"We'll just have to wait and see what the police can find out."

"Yes, I expect they'll be along soon to interview us."

BUT THE POLICE didn't arrive that evening or the next morning. I telephoned police headquarters and was transferred from one person to another until I finally spoke to a very junior officer, who said they would send someone around eventually. I relayed the news to Hildy and said, "There's no need for us to delay our trip to the hospital. Apparently, investigating what happened to Timothy isn't a priority for the police."

"That's rather disturbing."

"I agree, but I have an idea of how to make sure the police look into the attack."

Hildy sent me a wary look. "You're not thinking of putting off our visit to the hospital? You don't want to go to the police in person again, do you? Because I have no desire to visit a police station, even in the role of a guest."

"No, nothing like that." Her expression didn't change, so I added, "No police stations, I promise. I'll see that someone comes here to the hotel, which means—as much as it pains me to do it—I must write a note before we leave."

"Oh, I like that plan much better. I'll put on my hat, then," Hildy said as I sat down at the desk. I paused, hand poised over the fresh sheet of paper, to order my thoughts. It rankled to write the note, but it had to be done. I squished down my distaste at the task and began writing.

Dear Mr. Briarcliff,

I apologize in advance for intruding upon your time, but I believe you are the best person to contact about a matter that has come up.

You may have heard of the attack on Mr. Timothy Noviss yesterday at the Egyptian Museum. I took charge of his satchel, which was left behind. The contents of the satchel were mostly personal items related to his sketching and interest in hieroglyphics. However, there was one item that I think would interest the police: Cornelius Duncan's diary. It went missing from Vita's tent after her death. I contacted the police, but they do not seem to be interested in interviewing us. I believe you could convince them of the importance of the diary.

I've examined it and don't see any intrinsic value in it, but there must be something useful or worthy about it because it was stolen. I'll leave it in the hotel safe, and I'm happy to meet you to retrieve it at any time that is convenient for you. I will be at the hospital this morning, visiting Mr. Noviss, but I'll return this afternoon and await a message from you.

Sincerely,
Blix Windway

I SEALED the letter and took it down to the front desk along with the diary. The manager stored the diary for me, then took the letter. "I'll see that Mr. Briarcliff receives this as soon as he returns."

Hildy strained to see the name on the envelope before the manager turned away. As we moved away from the front desk, she said, "Mr. Briarcliff? Here in Egypt? What an amazing coincidence."

She seemed delighted with the idea. "You know him?"

"Yes. A fine young man."

I was gobsmacked. "A fine young man?"

Hildy didn't hear the tone of astonishment in my voice. She was lost in thought, and her expression sobered as we moved slowly across the Oriental carpets to the main entrance. "Although it was through sad circumstances that I met him. He and my nephew Christopher were in the same hospital ward during the war." She swallowed and pursed her lips before saying, "My nephew didn't survive." She drew in a breath and went on. "When Mr. Briarcliff recovered, he visited my brother and me. He delivered a letter Christopher had dictated. Mr. Briarcliff brought it himself. Such a kind and thoughtful gentleman."

Mrs. Philpott and Mrs. Canning came in through the main doors. We were close enough that we should have exchanged greetings, but they both looked pointedly away. Hildy was preoccupied, and I was glad she didn't notice their snub. "Well, perhaps there are two men named Mr. Briarcliff. The man I met was very cold and arrogant."

"Really? How curious. It is a rather unusual name, but I suppose that's possible."

CHAPTER TWENTY-NINE

*H*ildy and I followed a nurse down a long corridor, the swish of our skirts and the click of our shoes ringing loudly on the tile. Closed double doors lined one side of the hallway. On the other side, sunlight came in through tall windows spaced at intervals. It was disorienting moving through the alternating patches of blazing light and cool shade. I swallowed down the spark of anxiety that being in a hospital brought on. I found the silence unnerving. The hospital where I'd worked during the war had been full of busy movement and noise, always bordering on but never actually tipping over into chaos.

The nurse paused at a pair of double doors. "Wait here, please."

She entered the ward, and before the door swung closed, I caught a glimpse of two rows of iron beds made up with white blankets. A nurse trundled past pushing a trolley. The aroma of bandages floated in her wake, causing a surge of memories that I promptly pushed down. It wouldn't do to dwell on those things today.

The door swung open, and the nurse came out. "I'm sorry,

SARA ROSETT

but Doctor is with the patient at the moment. You may wait there." She indicated a backless wooden bench at the end of the corridor. "The ward matron will let you know when you may enter."

The nurse left, and as we settled on the bench, Hildy said, "Joyless creature. At least she works the desk and not with the patients."

A few moments later the same nurse appeared at the end of the hall with a tall dark-headed man towering behind her. She nodded in our direction, then returned to her station. The man continued down the hall toward us, moving through the flickering sunlight and shadows.

Hildy looked up from fastening a loose button on her glove and glanced idly down the corridor, then she popped up. "Mr. Briarcliff! It *is* you. How wonderful."

A smile transformed his face, softening it a degree or two from its usual stony expression.

She patted him on his upper arms as he kissed her on the cheek. "Blix tells me that you've been in Cairo for quite a while. You should have sent me a note. You could have come around for tea."

"I would have enjoyed that, but I didn't want to stir up any sad memories of our prior meeting. You are on holiday after all."

"That's thoughtful of you, Mr. Briarcliff," Hildy said, "but your presence would only be a delight."

He glanced over her shoulder and caught my expression. "Apparently, Miss Windway finds your opinion rather unbelievable."

I did my best to wipe the incredulous look from my face. "No, it's not that at all—" Flustered, I stumbled to a halt as he leaned toward Hildy. "I must admit, Miss Windway and I got off on the wrong foot. She thinks I'm a disagreeable sort."

Hildy said, "But nothing could be further from the truth!"

"I can't say I blame her. It's my forthright nature. It tends to put people off."

I had the most awful feeling that he was laughing at me. Irritation jabbed at me like the pointy tips of the low-growing palm fronds that scratched my arms when I didn't sidestep them in the gardens. I'd been nothing but polite to him. In Sir Abner's office, *he'd* been the one to take offense, assuming I was an empty-headed socialite. "Forthright? No, I wouldn't describe you that way, Mr. Briarcliff. Rather, I'd say curt to the point of bordering on rudeness. And I suppose mentioning our little contretemps is an example of your *direct* manner?"

"I refuse to play polite society's games. I have no use for them. Much better to say exactly what one means."

I raised my eyebrows, incredulous. "Because being well-mannered and respectful is so very tedious?"

"Yes, it often is," he said, his tone matter-of-fact and without a trace of apology.

I'd forgotten that Hildy was standing there with us until she cleared her throat. She gave us both a long look, and I felt as if I were ten years old, standing in front of my governess Megs. I could see her now, sweeping her gaze over me as she said, "Blix, I'm disappointed in you."

Hildy said, "I'll see if there is word on the patient, shall I? Try not to come to blows."

She poked her head in the double doors, and Mr. Briarcliff turned to me. "Truce? For Hildy's sake?"

I blew out a breath through my nose. I didn't want to agree. Something about Mr. Briarcliff "put my back up," as Megs would have said, but I nodded. "For Hildy."

Hildy disappeared through the double doors, and Mr. Briarcliff said, "I received your note. The desk clerk heard you mention you were on your way to the hospital, so I came here, hoping I wouldn't miss you. Do you think this attack on Mr. Noviss," he tilted his head toward the ward, "has something to do with the diary?"

All traces of humor were gone and his face was back to its monolithic state, but he wasn't treating me like I was silly and seemed to be genuinely interested in my answer. I pushed away my annoyance with him, glad to shift the conversation to Timothy. "I'm not sure how everything fits together, but the diary was missing from Vita's things, and it turned up in Timothy's satchel, so it's certainly possible. As soon as we've seen Timothy, I can return to the hotel and retrieve the diary from the safe."

"Excellent. I'll hand it off to Sir Abner."

Hildy opened the door and beckoned to us. A young nurse said in an Irish brogue, "You can come through to see Mr. Noviss now."

"How is he today?" I asked as we followed her down the central aisle.

"He's resting comfortably. I expect he'll come around in a few days."

"He's unconscious, then? Not asleep?" Hildy asked, her gaze on the far end of one of the rows, where Timothy lay motionless.

"It's not uncommon after a head injury. Just a short visit today, please."

A white bandage swathed Timothy's head, and his hands rested on top of the blankets on either side. Ned sat hunched over in a chair beside the bed, his elbows on his knees and his face in his hands. At the cavalcade of our steps on the tile floor, he gave a little jerk and looked around as if he didn't remember where he was. When he saw us, he stood. Dark circles shadowed his eyes. His clothes were rumpled, and stubble covered his cheeks and chin. He moved slowly, like an automaton with stiff joints.

After we exchanged greetings, Ned offered Hildy his chair. She drew it up to the side of the bed and took one of Timothy's hands in hers. "Timothy, it's Hildy Honeyworth," she said as if she was conversing with someone across the dinner table. "Blix Windway and I have come to see you. Mr. Briarcliff is here as well. I must say, you gave us quite a fright yesterday, but Nurse tells me that you're on the mend. We wanted to stop by today and let you know we're thinking of you and looking forward to seeing you once you feel more the thing."

Hildy paused and searched Timothy's face, but it was still slack as if he was sleeping. "We don't want to tire you, so we won't stay long. I'll let Blix have a word with you now." She stood and motioned me over to her chair.

I gave a little head shake, indicating I'd pass.

She drew me a step away from the bed. "You should speak to Timothy before we go. It's good to talk to patients. Even if they don't seem to be responding, they can often hear what's said to them."

With anyone else, I would have insisted on declining, but there was something about Hildy's steady, encouraging gaze that propelled me to the side of the bed.

I sat down in the chair she'd vacated. I couldn't bring myself to hold Timothy's hand. Hildy had such an easy way about her with people. I would have liked to imitate her manner, but it was beyond me at the moment. I leaned forward, and said in a low voice, "I don't know if you can hear me, Timothy, but Hildy says you might be able to. If that's the case, then just know that Hildy and I came to visit you. We look forward to your speedy recovery."

And asking you lots of questions.

Timothy's face remained impassive. Not a flicker of change. I waited a few seconds longer, feeling awkward. "Well, good-bye, then."

The nurse stopped at the end of the bed and tucked the blanket more securely around the mattress, then joined me as I walked to the central aisle, where Hildy, Mr. Briarcliff, and Ned waited. "That's enough excitement for today."

Her gaze washed over Ned in a professional capacity. "You should get some rest. You won't be any help to your friend if you're worn out. Sleeping on the bench out in the corridor is no way to spend the night. And Matron will be cross if she returns and finds you still here."

Then she turned to Mr. Briarcliff. "I'm afraid you'll have to wait until tomorrow to sit with Mr. Noviss."

"That's fine. I'm not a close friend of his, only an acquaintance."

"I see. Well, visiting hours begin at ten tomorrow, if you'd like to return."

Mr. Briarcliff asked, "Has your patient said anything about the attack?"

"No, nothing like that."

One of Mr. Briarcliff's eyebrows rose. "He has spoken, then?"

"Nothing sensible. He was quite restless when he first arrived. He was in and out for a while—perhaps a quarter of an hour—before slipping into unconsciousness. He kept murmuring something that sounded like the word *blue* over and over again, along with some other words. One of them sounded very like *milady*." A line appeared, wrinkling her smooth brow. "His words were very garbled, though. I didn't understand anything else, but it's obviously something that's preying on his mind." Someone on the other side of the ward drew the nurse's attention, and she didn't see Ned's reaction.

He looked as if he'd been punched in the gut. Hildy sent a quick glance at me, her expression questioning. I lifted a shoulder to indicate I wasn't sure why Ned looked so devastated.

The nurse said, "I must attend to another patient. Only a few more minutes, please, and that includes you, Mr. Breen. We've already bent the rules for you, letting you stay so long this morning."

Ned looked dazed and didn't respond, so I said, "Certainly," to the nurse before she left.

Mr. Briarcliff took Ned's arm and turned him toward the door. "What's the trouble, Ned? Does the word *blue* have something to do with why your friend is laid out unconscious?"

As our group moved to the door, Ned scrubbed his hand over his face, making a raspy noise as his palm traced across the stubble of his chin. "No, I don't see how—" He shot a quick guilty glance over his shoulder at Hildy. "It's probably not that. It happened weeks ago."

Ned swayed a bit, and normally I would have put it down to drink, but I doubted that was the problem today.

Mr. Briarcliff stepped closer to Ned, looming over him. "Why don't you let us be the judge of whether or not it's important."

Ned gripped the iron frame at the foot of one of the beds to steady himself and shifted a step away from Mr. Briarcliff, who inched closer. "Well?"

Hildy stepped between the two men and gave Ned a searching look. "How long has it been since you've eaten?"

Ned stared at her, his swaying intensifying. "I don't know. Breakfast yesterday? I remember kippers."

Hildy made a tsking noise. "No wonder you look frazzled. Food first, and then you can tell us what's on your mind."

MR. BRIARCLIFF KNEW of a café less than a block from the hospital, and the four of us set out on foot for it. Hildy eyed Ned with concern. He looked quite droopy. "Mr. Breen," Hildy said, "might I lean on your arm? I find walking tiring."

Ned rallied and extended his arm. She looped her hand around his, and I suspected Hildy was doing more to support Ned than the opposite. Mr. Briarcliff and I fell into step behind them.

As we moved away from the hospital, Mr. Briarcliff drew in a deep breath, and his shoulders, which had been bunched up tight to his neck, inched down.

I said, "Glad to be out of there?"

"Yes," he said, his tone so curt that Ned and Hildy both glanced over their shoulders. Mr. Briarcliff grimaced. "Sorry. Ah, here we are. Best table is at the back, out of the sun." Mr. Briarcliff nodded to the deep shade at the back of the café. As we took our seats, he said, "You're a good chap, Ned, to sit up with your friend at the hospital for hours. I don't think I could do it."

Hildy patted Mr. Briarcliff's arm. "Hospitals hold some very unpleasant memories for you. It's quite understandable. I believe I'll have a tea and toast."

Hildy insisted Ned order a full breakfast. She and I decided to share a pot of tea. Mr. Briarcliff only wanted coffee.

We talked of the weather, the upcoming fancy dress ball at Shepheard's, and the benefits of an open-ended return ticket when visiting Egypt while Ned wolfed down a plate of food. Hildy nibbled at her toast, and I suspected she'd ordered it only so that Ned wouldn't be the only one eating.

Once Ned had finished eating, he looked more like himself, only it was a faded, lackluster version. He didn't look well rested, but he certainly didn't look as if he was about to keel over any moment.

When his plate was removed, Hildy said, "Now about what Timothy said . . ."

Ned cleared his throat. "Right." He stared into his coffee cup. "It was a scheme we had. Rather a foolish thing. I can see that now. At the time . . ." He rasped his hand over the lower portion of his face, then squared up his shoulders. "I'd better start at the beginning. Timothy wasn't saying *milady*. He was saying *lady—the lady in blue*. It was supposed to be you, Blix. You were the lady in blue."

"What? Me?" I put my teacup down. "A lady in blue? What are you talking about?"

"When you took the ferry. I'd heard at my club about the diary and that you'd be traveling to Egypt with it." The cadence of his speech increased, words tumbling out as if he wanted to get the story out as quickly as possible. "Timothy knew about Egyptology, so I convinced him to come with me. We came up with a scheme to get it."

CHAPTER THIRTY

"*I*t wasn't a good scheme," Ned added in his breathless, headlong monologue. "I see that now, but at the time—"

I scooted my chair forward. "Wait, Ned. Slow down. Are you saying you heard about the diary, that I'd be carrying it to Egypt before I left England?"

"Yes, that's right."

"From Percy?"

Ned drank the last of his coffee in a gulp. "The chap was blotto."

"You say that as if it explains everything," I said.

"Well, it does. I'm sure Percy has no memory of the conversation. Shocking that I remember it as well as I do. I'm not one to go easy on the bottle." He chuckled, but no one else joined in laughing. He tilted his empty cup and stared into it. "Right. Yes, well, you see, at the time Percy was pleased with himself, bursting to tell someone."

"And you obliged him," Mr. Briarcliff said.

Ned shifted in his chair. "I didn't realize what it would mean —that it would come to this." He lifted his chin in the direction of the hospital.

"As is so often the case." Mr. Briarcliff's voice was resigned, laced with regret and pessimism. "The lack of ability to see the consequences seems a trifling thing—until one is steamrolled under events that have been set in motion."

Ned looked at Mr. Briarcliff out of the corner of his eye. "Not sure I follow you there, chap."

"No, you wouldn't."

Hildy refilled Ned's cup. "What happened next?"

Ned took a sip and apparently scalded his tongue because he jerked the cup from his lips. He put it in the saucer and motioned to me. "I knew the day you were traveling. I waited outside your flat that morning until you came out. Once I saw you were wearing a blue coat, I sent a telegram off to the man I'd found, someone who would get the diary."

I was so shocked I couldn't speak for a moment, but I finally managed to say, "You spied on me?"

"I couldn't very well get into your flat, could I? Your doorman is a veritable Cerberus."

I leaned forward over my place setting. "And a good thing too, seeing what unsavory characters might be interested in getting in."

Hildy tugged at my arm and said mildly, "You're about to dip the cuff of your sleeve into your tea, my dear."

Ned scooted his chair away from me.

"Who did you hire?" Mr. Briarcliff asked.

"No idea of the chap's name. A friend said his mate would get the job done." Ned's mouth turned down in dismay. "But that didn't happen. Instead, he queered the pitch in a grand way."

Anger bubbled up, choking off my words. Mr. Briarcliff glanced at me, then said quickly, "What did you employ this rotter to do?"

"He wasn't a rotter—" Mr. Briarcliff leveled a look at him. Ned cleared his throat. "He was waiting in Calais for the ferry's arrival. I sent him the telegram with a description of Blix. Then I met Ned, and we caught the same ferry. It all should have been a breeze. I told the rotter to look for a woman in a blue coat, but the idiot couldn't even get that right."

I felt my eyes widen. "He thought it was Hildy," I said, remembering her cobalt-blue coat.

She'd been about to pour herself more tea, but she set the teapot down with a thunk. "The ferrety man!"

Ned sighed. "Yes. That was him."

"I take it the man failed?" Mr. Briarcliff asked.

"Miss Honeyworth—um—put up an admirable defense," Ned said. "I do apologize. I had no idea he'd go after you like that. He was supposed to swipe Blix's handbag, take the diary, and leave the handbag behind."

I gripped the edge of the table and leaned forward. "You sound as if the fact that he got the wrong woman was his major failing. Good heavens! He attacked Hildy."

"Young man, your morals are deplorable," Hildy said, her tone as frigid as the desert night.

"Yes, ma'am," Ned said, his voice small.

"Well, you'd better tell us the rest," Hildy said. "Was it you or the ferrety man who searched my room on the ship?"

Looking like a cowed schoolboy who'd been called to the headmaster's office, Ned said, "Me. I shouldn't have done it. I should have walked away, but a quick peek was all I needed."

"And I imagine you searched my cabin on the ship as well," I said. Ned's chin dipped lower. "I thought so." I sat back with arms crossed. "I can't believe you were so intent on it. I was bringing the diary to your aunt. Surely you'd have had the opportunity to see it once I gave it to her?"

Ned, head still drooping forward, looked up at me and shook his head. "You didn't know Aunt Vita. She was obsessed with that chap Duncan. Once she got her hands on that diary, she'd treat it like a—well, I'm sure you'll think this is blasphemy—but like the Bible. And not just a copy of the Bible, but an original text." He wiped his hands over his eyes, then down across his face as he straightened. "And I was right. She guarded that diary like it was more precious than gold. She wouldn't let anyone else examine it—too delicate, she said. She kept it in the hotel safe and only took it out when we went to the pyramids."

"But you didn't stop after you arrived in Alexandria." Mr. Briarcliff's voice was so quiet and silky that I glanced at him. The anger in his brown eyes made me glad I was on the other side of the table from him.

Ned shifted his chair away from the table, apparently deciding he didn't want to be too close to either Mr. Briarcliff or me.

"You also entered their hotel suite in Alexandria," Mr. Briarcliff continued, and Ned stared at him, clearly surprised.

"You shouldn't be shocked that we know about your activities. Keeping tourists happy is a great priority for all hotels. Any little hiccup draws attention."

My thoughts were whirling, spinning like a top. I'd thought that Ned was just a foolish young man and that Timothy was a milquetoast toady. And all the while they'd been plotting and planning to steal the diary from me. It was only a coincidence that the ferrety man had targeted Hildy and that I still had it in my possession when I arrived in Egypt. If I hadn't carried it in my handbag, they would have found it in my room on the ship. Storing it in the hotel safe in Alexandria had prevented them from getting it there. "You do realize you're talking about theft?" Ned's shoulders sloped as I went on. "Stealing another person's property. That's not something to launch into lightly. It's not a lark or a schoolboy prank."

Hildy frowned. "Indeed, it's a very serious thing, young man."

Ned looked even more miserable. "I apologize. I know that's inadequate—words alone, I mean. But I do see now how serious it is. I'm very sorry. Truly, I am."

I wasn't feeling very generous, but Hildy said, "I accept

your apology, but see to it that you mend your ways. You won't get far in life if you're set on cheating and theft."

"Yes, ma'am," Ned said.

Hildy gave a nod. She was more optimistic than I was. I doubted Ned's remorse would last more than a day or two. I took a sip of my tea and then returned it to the saucer with a sharp click. "What's done is done—no matter how despicable it was. You said the diary was valuable. Suppose you tell us why you thought that. The truth will go a little way toward making amends with me."

"It was a record of Cornelius Duncan's travels."

"Yes, I know that. Why would you steal the most tedious travelogue I've ever had the misfortune to read?"

Ned sat up straight. "You don't know about Duncan?"

"Yes, of course I do. He toured Egypt and was interested in pyramidology. He created a following in England, wrote books, et cetera." I rolled my hand as I sped through the list.

"But he wasn't a tourist," Ned said.

CHAPTER THIRTY-ONE

*N*ed scooted his chair closer to the table. "Cornelius Duncan came to Egypt with the group that prepared for Prince Albert's visit in—what was it?—1869, I think it was. Timothy looked it up." He tossed off the last sentence, then his face fell as if he'd momentarily forgotten that his friend was laid up in a hospital ward, bandaged and unconscious.

Mr. Briarcliff had been watching the conversation between Ned and me, his gaze darting back and forth, but now he leaned his elbow on the table as he swiveled to face Ned. "A royal delegation?"

"Yes. Duncan's job was to prepare things for the prince's tour. Prince Albert was a collector. Apparently, he'd visited Egypt before and acquired a mummy along with some other antiquities. On his second visit, he wanted to try his hand at excavation."

"And if a prince digs for antiquities, a prince must find antiquities." Mr. Briarcliff let out a snort. "Can't have a royal personage only find sand on an archeological dig. It would be too embarrassing for the host country."

Ned sipped his coffee. "Quite. One of the duties of the group was to acquire antiquities and bury them at a location outside of Cairo so the prince could *discover* them."

I sat back, stunned. "But in all Duncan's entries, he never mentioned anything about a prince or a royal tour or . . . seeding antiquities for someone to dig them up."

"It was a personal diary. At least that's what Timothy said after he did some looking into it. After Percy told me about Duncan's diary, I happened to mention it in passing to Timothy a few days later. Timothy went and looked up the fellow. Timothy's like that—bookish. The next day Timothy told me about Duncan. Timothy's the sort of chap who goes into long-winded explanations, even if you're not at all interested in the topic. I'll admit my mind wandered, and I didn't catch all of it, but when he said Duncan was part of a group whose job it was to hide antiquities for the prince to dig up, my ears pricked up."

"I bet they did," I said. A vague memory stirred of one of the diary entries. Sandwiched in between Duncan's multiple entries rhapsodizing about the pyramids, there had been one description of an afternoon watching men dig on the Giza Plateau. I'd assumed he was visiting an archeological dig, but perhaps he'd been observing the burial of the antiquities. I couldn't recall any other entries about digging or excavations. Duncan's accounts of the famous sites had only described the architecture.

Hildy said, "But didn't Prince Albert dig them up and take them to England?"

"No, he didn't." Ned couldn't keep a smile off his face. "That part of the prince's tour had to be scrapped. Some sort of problem with the transportation."

Mr. Briarcliff swirled his coffee around in his cup. "These antiquities, they were valuable?"

"Some very fine specimens from the Egyptian Museum, put into service for the purpose, according to what Timothy learned. The plan was to reroute the royal tour back to the dig later, but that proved impossible. Then there was talk of another visit from the prince in the next year—according to Timothy, the

Suez Canal had just opened and that was the draw—so they left everything as it was. But the prince didn't return the next year. Apparently, the retrieval of the antiquities wasn't a high priority. There was a shuffling of the British personnel about that time. Timothy did quite a bit of looking into it and found a note reprimanding some poor bloke for losing the coordinates of where they should dig to recover the items."

"You think they're still buried in the desert somewhere outside of Cairo?" I realized I'd spoken too loudly when the waiter turned toward us. I lowered my voice. "With all the looting that's gone on? That's absurd. Surely someone would have found them sometime during the—what would it be, fifty years?"

Ned didn't look the least perturbed by my disbelief. "Fifty-five. And no, I don't think they've been found. Timothy couldn't find a record of the antiquities ever being returned to the Egyptian Museum. They haven't turned up on display in any other museums or been listed for sale through dealers. Ergo, there's a good chance they haven't been dug up. Timothy found a reference to the burying of the antiquities in a letter from Duncan to a friend. Apparently, word got out that the British had lost the location of where they'd been buried. Duncan had said it was a good thing he'd put it down in his diary at the time. He'd be able to go back and pinpoint the place. Of course, he never returned to Egypt. Timothy said Duncan fell ill shortly after he wrote the letter. His family wasn't keen on his pyramidology jiggery-pokery and did their best to squash interest in Duncan's association with it."

Hildy said, "They didn't do well on that front, if Vita was any indication of the devotion the man inspired. She was an ardent follower—one of many, apparently."

At the mention of Vita, Ned hunched over his coffee cup. His leg jounced up and down, the ball of his foot barely touching the floor. The tiny movements vibrated through the table and caused ripples on the surface of my tea.

My thoughts went to Rose. Maybe her interest in the diary had nothing to do with her mother's health. Hieroglyphics fascinated her. Had Rose somehow learned of the diary and wanted it because it might lead her to lost artifacts, artifacts that might have hieroglyphics on them? "What were the artifacts that were buried?"

Ned lifted a shoulder. "No idea. Timothy couldn't find a list of them anywhere." Ned curled over his cup again, obviously mulling over what had happened to Timothy because he said, "Timothy took Vita's death hard. Very hard. He's been quite worked up about it. It's understandable. He and I were too young to be in the war, so hers was the first dead body he'd seen."

My thoughts still lingered on Rose, but Ned's words focused my attention on him. I sat up straight. "Timothy saw Vita's body? Are you sure about that?"

Ned's leg stopped bouncing as his gaze jerked up to mine. He put up his hand, palm facing me as if trying to tamp down my intensity. "It's not what you think. I swear. After dinner at the campsite, we had quite a lot to drink. We were completely blotto that night. Honestly, we were. We went back to the tent to sleep it off."

Ned fell silent for a moment, then he said, "Timothy must have woken up in the early hours of the morning and gone to—um—" He flicked a glance at Hildy, and his fidgety heel bounce returned.

"Relieve himself?" she guessed, her tone practical. "We understand. Go on."

Ned drew a deep breath. "He woke me when he returned. Stumbled in, actually. His hands were shaking, and he could hardly say anything. Something had terrified him. I made him sit down and gave him a stiff drink, and then he told me he'd woken and gone out of the tent to—" He stopped, cleared his throat. "Well. Anyway, he said he noticed the light in Vita's tent, but no sound and no movement. He thought that perhaps Vita was away from her tent as well and decided he'd nip along and have a look at the relevant passages in the diary. Timothy said the moment he poked his head into the tent he could see she was dead. He abandoned the idea of looking for the diary and got out of there as fast as he could."

Mr. Briarcliff said, "What time was this?"

"No idea. It was still dark."

Hildy asked, "Were the servants about? Could you smell smoke from the servants' fire as they prepared breakfast?"

Ned stared at the table for a moment. "No, I don't think so. I don't remember anything like that, but what Timothy had told me pushed everything else out of my mind. It wasn't long before Mr. Chambers came along and told us we were needed in the lounge tent. We knew what it was about, of course. We thought it best to just keep quiet about it."

"Timothy didn't want it to come out, that he'd been near Vita's tent," I said.

"No. He was terrified. Begged me to keep quiet about it, and I agreed." Ned's manner was more subdued than I'd ever seen him.

Mr. Briarcliff said, "I'm sure you understand that it all has to come out now. The police need to know all of it."

The surface of my tea stilled as Ned's leg stopped jiggling. He sighed and nodded. "Yes, I do know that."

Hildy had been silent, sitting with her fingers laced together, watching Ned as he told his story. "Ned," she said as she tilted her head to the side. "Why do you think Timothy was attacked?"

His lips turned down in an expression of bewilderment. "No idea. Maybe it was one of the rabble-rousers? There's been rioting and unrest here for the last couple of years. Or perhaps it was just a thief. Was anything taken?"

Mr. Briarcliff said, "It doesn't sound as if it was a robbery. His satchel was still there."

I didn't mention the fact that I'd discovered the diary in

Timothy's satchel. Hildy and Mr. Briarcliff also stayed silent on the subject, so they must have felt as I did, that it was better to keep the discovery of the diary quiet for now. Timothy must have taken it from Vita's tent, then lied about it to Ned, claiming he didn't take anything.

"I think we're done here." Mr. Briarcliff glanced at Hildy and me. We both nodded our agreement, and he turned to Ned. "Let's get you back to Shepheard's so you can change your clothes. Then you'll accompany me to the police station and repeat everything you told us." Mr. Briarcliff pushed back his chair. "Shall we?"

~

WE TOOK two horse cabs back to Shepheard's as it would have been rather a squeeze in one. Hildy and I arrived first. I went to the front desk to request the diary be removed from the safe. Mr. Briarcliff strode into the lobby a few moments later with Ned lagging behind. Mr. Briarcliff said something to Ned, who nodded and headed for the stairs, his steps slow and deliberate. He moved more like Mr. Chambers than a man in his twenties.

Hildy waved Mr. Briarcliff over as the manager arrived, diary in hand.

I thanked the manager and took it quickly before Mr. Briarcliff could reach for it. "I think we should have a look at it before you hand it off to the police." I drew a breath to lay out my argument, but Mr. Briarcliff cut in.

"I agree."

Surely I'd heard him wrong. His reply was so jarring that I felt as if I'd missed a step on the stairs and stumbled. "You do?"

"I know you have little trust in Sir Abner and his methods. I've seen firsthand the way he works. I must say your concerns are well placed."

Hildy swung toward him. "I'm surprised, Mr. Briarcliff. You don't trust him?"

Mr. Briarcliff looked up at the elaborate ceiling decoration for a moment. "Items can be lost or misplaced . . . or destroyed or ignored. I'm not saying that's what will happen to the diary, but," Mr. Briarcliff motioned to the Arab Hall, "I propose we find a quiet spot and make some notes on the 'relevant passages,' as Ned called them."

"I think that's a good idea," I said, "but I can do one better. I'll photograph every page. Then we'll have a permanent record. I should have enough film to do it."

Hildy said, "Oh, excellent idea, Blix."

Mr. Briarcliff hesitated a moment, then nodded. "Yes, it is."

I handed the diary to Hildy. "I'll get more film and join you in the Arab Hall."

I darted upstairs, snatched a couple of film canisters from my stash in my room. I was able to photograph each page before Ned returned. By the time he rejoined us, the diary was tucked away in Mr. Briarcliff's suit pocket and my camera was back in my handbag.

Mr. Briarcliff said, "Ladies, perhaps we should meet up after lunch?"

"Yes." I patted my handbag. "Hopefully something will have developed by then."

CHAPTER THIRTY-TWO

*A*n hour and a half later I burst into the hotel suite, waving a thick envelope. "I've got them!"

Hildy sat in an armchair, her writing desk on her lap.

"The photographs? How did you get them so quickly?"

I dropped my handbag and the envelope on a side table and took off my hat and gloves. "I took the film to that little shop across the street and paid an exorbitant fee to have them rushed."

I snatched up the envelope. As I moved around to sit on the sofa, I noticed Hildy had one foot propped up on a cushion and her ankles were puffy. "What happened?"

"I'm fine. With all the walking we've been doing, my feet are achy and a tad swollen." She set aside her writing desk. "How did they turn out?"

"They're grand." The prints were glossy and enlarged, which actually made it easier to read the entries. "Would you like to help me look for Duncan's description of the men digging in the desert?"

"Yes, of course." Hildy settled on the sofa beside me, and I handed her half the photos. The only sound in the room for a while was the soft clack of the photographs knocking against each other as we flipped from one to the other, scanning the handwriting. I paused each time I saw the mention of the pyramids or Giza Plateau, but none of the entries were the ones we were interested in. I'd reached the end of my stack when Hildy took a photo from her group and put it on the coffee table. "I believe this might be it."

She read aloud, "'Spent the morning on the plateau. Today's work was simply watching the diggers. Harris is in charge of this bit, so I spent my time studying the pyramids as best I could from a distance. I'd prefer to be among the pyramids proper, but the requirements of the day meant that our caravan of donkeys left from the southeast corner of the pyramid. We traveled due south out into the desert for a quarter of an hour. We traversed the rocky sands until we came to a rather large ridge that dropped down into a more sheltered area, a sort of valley with a broken-down dwelling. Harris tells me it was a temple, but from the sad state of it today it's difficult to believe that. He marked off an area near the structure and took down the exact coordinates so the place could be found again. Then he set the diggers to their task. I perched on a rock in the shade of the little tumbled building and worked on my mathematical equations regarding the various sizes of the Giza pyramids. Once the deposits were made in the sand and covered over, we departed. The whole exercise took a few hours.'"

"This has to be it, Hildy."

"It does sound promising, but I have a few more entries. Let me check the last ones and make sure that's the only reference to digging near the pyramids . . ." She was already scanning them as she spoke. She reached the last one and shook her head. "Nothing else here."

I tapped the edge of the photo on the coffee table. "This has to be it." I stood up and headed for my room. "Do you want to come with me?"

"With you? Where?"

"To the Giza Plateau to look for the location that Duncan described."

"Why would we do that?"

I paused at the door to my room. "To see if the tumbled-down building is visible."

Hildy gave a little shake of her head. "I'm afraid I still fail to see why one would want to traipse about the desert." She glanced at the window, where the stark midafternoon sun beat down on the palm fronds, highlighting each sharp green blade. "Especially now in the heat of the day."

"Well, the first—and most compelling—reason is buried treasure. Who wants to wait for the cool of the day when we might know where to find an undiscovered cache of Egyptian antiquities?"

Hildy tilted her head down and gave me a rather governessy look. "Blix, it sounds as if you've succumbed to Egyptomania."

I chuckled. "I promise I'm not about to become obsessed with mummies or scarabs. But you have to admit it is an intriguing situation." I went into my room but left the door ajar. I raised my voice as I pulled out my pyramid-climbing clothes —riding breeches, tall boots, and a light jacket over a long-sleeved shirt—and began to change. "The other, less exciting reason is to see if anyone has trekked out there and had a poke around."

"But the diary has been missing since Vita died. If anyone has been out there, the wind would have erased any trace."

"It wouldn't erase a trench in the ground. If Timothy has been digging in the desert on the sly, I doubt he'd take time to fill in any holes he's made." I shrugged into my jacket and retrieved the dark-tinted spectacles I'd purchased at the bazaar along with my silk scarf. I knotted the scarf around my throat and returned to the sitting room.

Hildy said, "But shouldn't we wait for Mr. Briarcliff?"

"He could be hours."

"But I think it would be a better idea to wait for him."

"Why? He has access to the diary itself. I'm sure he's already skimmed it and located the same passage. For all we know, he'll go there first and then return here to tell us."

Hildy glanced at the window and squinted against the harsh sunlight. "Honestly, I'd prefer that. I don't have your energy. Climbing sand dunes doesn't appeal." She wiggled her toes on the soft carpet. "And I'm not fond of the idea of putting my feet back in my shoes."

"Then you stay here." I slipped my camera, some money, and the tinted spectacles into my jacket pocket and put on my hat.

"But I can't let you go alone."

"I'll stop at the desk and arrange for a dragoman and a donkey. They arrange tours of this sort every day. And if I can't find the location, I'll still be able to take more photographs of the pyramids. One can never have too many photos of the pyramids."

"You intend to go off alone? Just you and a dragoman? Blix, I don't think that's safe."

"You don't have to worry about me. One of my governesses, Miss Weldon, had five older brothers. She was well trained in the art of self-defense and showed me everything her brothers taught her. 'A lady must know how to fend off unwanted advances—even the most aggressive sort,' she'd said. Believe me, that was a lesson I paid close attention to. I'll be careful. You rest up, and I'll be back before dinner."

It took much longer than I expected to arrange the transportation. The desk clerk had informed me that a donkey and dragoman could be brought to Shepheard's and I could ride it from the hotel to the pyramids, but I opted to take a faster route. I'd ride the tram to Mena House and collect my donkey there.

My dragoman, Ibrahim, was a spindly young man who was amiable to going beyond the typical tourist route around the pyramids. I'd marked the approximate location Duncan had described on the map I'd purchased at the Mena House Hotel, and Ibrahim said, "There is nothing there. No pyramid, no dig. Nothing but sand. Only sand."

I tapped the tiny X on the map. "But this is where I need to go."

Ibrahim shrugged and nodded, then set a straight course between the pyramids to the corner of the Great Pyramid. My donkey obediently trotted along in Ibrahim's wake as we cut through the throngs of tourists, the bulk of the pyramid towering over us. I checked my watch when we reached the corner. As we moved beyond it, the wind buffeted us, tearing at the sleeves of my jacket and riffling the donkey's short mane.

Once we were beyond the immediate area around the pyramids, we had the desert to ourselves. It stretched out a vast, undulating brownish-gold surface scattered with rocks. The sun scorched through the scarf I'd tied over my head and neck. Wind-driven grains of sand stung my cheeks and pricked at the back of my neck. I was glad for the spectacles that protected my eyes and cut down on the bright glare. The wind made it too difficult to speak, but occasionally Ibrahim would twist around in the saddle and give an inquiring glance. I'd smile and wave, indicating we should keep going.

A glance at my watch showed a quarter of an hour had passed. A sinking feeling hit the pit of my stomach as I surveyed the endless desert, only sand and rocks. The mounds of Sakkara shivered in the hazy distance. Hildy had been right —I'd gone on a wild goose chase, but I'd been snapping photographs as we went, so the excursion hadn't been a waste.

I spurred my donkey on to catch up with Ibrahim and tell him we could turn back. I came even with him as we crested a ridge. In the sheltered hollow below the outcropping, an ancient structure poked out of the sand.

"This is what you wanted to see, miss?"

"I believe it is." Sand surrounded the building, almost

reaching its lintel. Even more interesting than the structure was the network of holes dotted around the area. I felt Ibrahim's gaze on me, but I kept the camera in front of my face and took several pictures as I asked, "The holes are unusual?"

"Yes. Someone has been looking for relics, but it's useless. Nothing will be found here."

He flicked the reins and moved down the slope. Stones scattered away from my donkey's hooves as we descended. We dismounted, and Ibrahim held the donkeys while I picked my way around, checking the holes. They were all a few feet deep, a pile of displaced sand beside each one.

I went to the building, which the sand had almost buried. I was able to scramble up the incline and peer through the gap between the engulfing sand and the lintel. I removed my tinted spectacles and shaded my eyes. It was an empty shell inside. If there had been anything, decorations or hieroglyphics, they'd been stripped away.

A mechanical whine cut through the whistle of the wind. A small plane swooped overhead, made a loop, and came back again, dropping in altitude. It whipped up the sand as it roared overhead. The donkeys shied, but Ibrahim held tight to the reins and soothed them.

The plane made another curving turn and came back toward us, descending quickly. I caught my breath, thinking I was about to witness a crash, but it leveled off and touched down, creating a screen of dust that billowed out behind it as it rolled to a stop over the bumpy ground about thirty yards away. A man emerged from the cockpit and took off his goggles as he crossed the sand toward us. I knew exactly who it was. The tall figure with wide shoulders that tapered to a narrow waist and the easy, rolling gait were unmistakable—Mr. Briarcliff.

CHAPTER THIRTY-THREE

*A*nother man climbed out of the plane, and he jogged to catch up with Mr. Briarcliff as they crossed the desert toward us.

Ibrahim glanced at me, his brow lifting toward his turban in a questioning look, then his gaze shifted to the ridge above us as if he was calculating how to keep the distance between the two men and us.

"It's fine. I know one of the men." I couldn't bring myself to say that Mr. Briarcliff was a friend, but we didn't need to retreat from him.

The other man barely came up to Mr. Briarcliff's shoulder. With his stocky build, he reminded me of an English bulldog. He'd removed his goggles, and the wind was tossing his fair hair in every direction, but the substantial mustache that framed his mouth was completely gray. He paused to tie the lace on one of his knee-high boots, which was flapping in the wind, slapping against his rough trousers.

I went to meet Mr. Briarcliff, who was shading his eyes with one hand, his gaze running over the structure in the hollow of the ridge. Despite the shelter of the little valley, he had to raise his voice to be heard over the whistling of the wind as it buffeted us. "Hello, Miss Windway. I can't say I'm surprised to see you here."

"The feeling is mutual."

"I take it you were able to get the photographs developed," Mr. Briarcliff said.

"Yes, I take it that you read the diary before turning it in to Sir Abner. Did you intend to return to the hotel and share what you'd found with Hildy and me, or has our appointment completely gone out of your mind?"

"I'm on my way there. I just made a little detour." He motioned over his shoulder toward the plane.

"I suspected you'd come here first."

"So you decided to make the trip yourself and indulge in a bit of solo detective work? Well, you could have saved yourself the effort. I would have shared whatever I found with you and Hildy."

"I prefer to do my own research."

"As do I."

"Well, seeing as we're in agreement on that, I suppose neither of us can be upset with the other." The sun was tracking toward the horizon. Arguing with Mr. Briarcliff would only waste time that could be spent examining the area before we had to return to Cairo.

The older man joined us, and Mr. Briarcliff said, "This is Henry Listergraff. Henry, meet Miss Blix Windway."

"How do you do?" How odd it was to observe the social niceties in the middle of the desert. We might have been on the terrace at Shepheard's instead of standing in the sand with a tumbled-down ancient building peeking out of the ground.

He gave my outstretched hand a single firm downward tug. "Pleasure is all mine." A faint German accent filtered through his words.

"I brought Henry along to take some snaps of the area on our way in."

"Photographs? From the plane?"

Listergraff nodded. "Aerial photography is my specialty."

"How interesting. I haven't heard of that."

Mr. Briarcliff said, "The archaeologists find it rather a help in their work. I ferry the photographers like Henry around so they can get their images. You and Miss Windway have a lot in common, Listergraff. She's a photographer as well."

"I'm aware. I saw the advertisement for your lecture next week at Ladies' Auxiliary. I plan to be in attendance." He gestured toward Mr. Briarcliff. "Rafe says he'll attend as well."

"But you work for the hotel, Mr. Briarcliff, and the talk is during the day."

"I do work for the hotel, but not all the time. I'm a free agent. I do a little work here, a little there. A jack-of-all-trades, you might say."

"And master of none?"

Mr. Briarcliff sent me a tight smile, but before he could respond, Listergraff, who had been surveying the area, said, "Look at all these trenches. Has someone begun work here?"

"I doubt it," Mr. Briarcliff said. "More likely it's an amateur."

I took that comment to mean that Mr. Briarcliff hadn't shared any information about the diary with Listergraff, who was now circling around, studying the holes.

Mr. Briarcliff leaned in. "Don't mention the diary—"

"I didn't intend to. The fewer people who know about it, the better."

Mr. Briarcliff pulled back as one did if one didn't want to be scorched by a hot flame. "Fine."

Listergraff scrambled up the dirt incline to look inside the structure, then called back to us, "Nothing inside here, but interesting. Perhaps an old funerary temple." He got down on his knees and poked his head inside the dark gap between the lintel and sand.

Hands on hips, Mr. Briarcliff turned, taking in the whole area. "It appears that secrecy isn't especially needed, though.

Quite deserted out here. Looks as if Timothy was busy, but it doesn't appear he found anything."

I shaded my eyes and surveyed the area again. The sun was dipping lower. Shadows of the little mounds were lengthening. "It does seem that way; none of the holes are more than a few feet deep and only a shovel-width or two across. He went about it in a rather haphazard way."

"Well, there were no specific instructions about where to dig beyond the general location near the ruined temple."

"If Timothy had found something, I suppose he would have dug a trench—unless the antiquities were small items."

Mr. Briarcliff used his scarf to polish his goggles. "They had to be fit for a prince. I can't imagine they'd be insubstantial things. Did you notice the earlier entry that described the requisition of an additional three donkeys to carry the artifacts? I think we're safe to say that whatever was buried would have been bigger than any of these divots."

Galled that I'd missed that detail, I said, "So we can be fairly safe in assuming that Timothy didn't find anything."

"Or the antiquities were removed long before Timothy started digging."

"I don't think there's anything else to be done here," I said.

Mr. Briarcliff said, "I'd offer you a ride back, but I don't have another seat in the plane."

"Thank you, but I'll return the way I arrived." I said goodbye to Mr. Listergraff and climbed up the slope to where Ibrahim waited with the donkeys. He'd been eyeing the sun in the west, which was tracking toward the horizon.

CHAPTER THIRTY-FOUR

*T*he tennis ball sailed over the net. I stepped into my swing and whacked it back across the court. Ned lunged for it, but he wasn't quick enough. The ball hit inside the line, then bounced away.

To my right, Rose, who had been tense and poised for the volley, straightened. "Jolly good hit, Blix."

"Thank you." I bounced a new tennis ball to her as she set up to serve.

When I'd first met Rose, I'd thought she was an academic sort of girl, but this afternoon I'd discovered she was quite good at lawn tennis. Mrs. Jenkins hadn't been pleased with the idea of Rose playing tennis. When they'd joined us in the hotel lobby before we departed, I'd overheard Mrs. Jenkins say to Rose, "You become so wrapped up in the game. You're too intense on the court. It's not ladylike to perspire!"

"Oh, Mother. Don't be such an old-fashioned goose," Rose had said.

I hadn't been looking forward to the outing to the Gezira Sporting Club. My thoughts were still occupied with all the questions around the deaths of Vita and Tadros as well as Timothy's attack. Lawn tennis seemed a trivial thing compared to murder and assault, but I'd agreed to George's suggestion of a tour of the club, and it wasn't the done thing to cry off after committing. In fact, my social schedule was full. Tennis today and then a fancy dress ball at the hotel tonight. I'd also managed to convince Hildy we really should see the pyramids properly, and I'd asked the concierge to plan an excursion to Giza for us tomorrow. Once Hildy was on board with the idea, she'd invited several people, and we now had a small party scheduled for a morning excursion, including Mr. Chambers, Mrs. Jenkins, and Rose.

It felt strange to plan events and tours while a murder investigation went on around us. But neither Hildy nor I had heard anything from the police about an interview concerning the attack on Timothy or the diary, which Mr. Briarcliff had handed off yesterday afternoon, so we didn't have a reason to cry off from today's outing.

I'd been surprised to see Ned accompanying George to the sporting club today. When George had sent Ned off to arrange the horse cabs, he'd said, "I convinced Ned to come along. The boy's spending too much time at the hospital." Each day George was looking a little better. His shell-shocked manner had dropped away. Now the only outward sign that he'd been through something traumatic was the dark circles under his eyes.

Hildy had said, "George, I'm surprised at you. Ned's concern for his friend is an admirable thing."

"I agree the boy should visit his friend, but there's no need for Ned to sit at the hospital hour after hour, getting in the way of the nurses. The change of scene will do him good."

On our arrival, George had given us a tour of the club, then Hildy had convinced Mrs. Jenkins that a turn around the botanical gardens wasn't to be missed. Once they were out of earshot, Rose had bounced on her toes as she spun her tennis racket. "Who'd like to play?"

I hadn't intended to play lawn tennis, but Rose had looked

so eager for a game that I volunteered. George had agreed to play, and Ned wasn't one to turn down any competitive activity. Although Ned's manner was still subdued, he'd picked up a racket and joined us for a game of doubles.

Rose and I were currently tied with the men. Rose bounced the ball a few times as she squinted across the court. Many of the courts around us were in use. The shouts of the scores mingled with the ping of tennis balls and the swish of rackets.

Rose served, sending the ball into the net.

Ned, who was playing at the net, looked over his left shoulder at George and jerked his head toward the net. George moved a few steps forward. Rose watched them, but she didn't seem worried. She rotated her shoulders, lined up, and served again, sending the ball down the center of the court. It zipped by Ned before he could react. George lunged. Arm extended, he hit it back across the net in a high arc.

I darted forward and slammed the ball into the court, just out of Ned's reach. Ned and George groaned.

I turned to congratulate Rose on the point, but her gaze was fixed over my shoulder. "Look, it's Mr. Briarcliff."

He wasn't dressed for tennis. He was in his dark trousers, tall boots, and khaki jacket, which contrasted with everyone else on the courts, as we were all dressed in tennis whites. "Sorry to interrupt." He crossed the court to Ned and had a quiet word with him. Ned wiped his hand over his mouth as he nodded. Mr. Briarcliff patted him on the shoulder and reached for his racket. Ned called out, "Sorry! Must go!" Then he jogged toward the clubhouse.

Mr. Briarcliff and George came across the court to us. Rose and I met them at the net. Mr. Briarcliff said, "Timothy has regained consciousness. I thought Ned would want to know."

"Quite right," George agreed.

Mr. Briarcliff tested the tension of the racket strings. "I told Ned I'd finish the game in his place, if that's all right."

George turned and looked at the clubhouse. "That's sporting

of you, old chap, but Timothy has no relations here. I should go along with Ned to the hospital." He also handed his racket to Mr. Briarcliff. "Ladies, thank you for a lovely and challenging game. Apologies for abandoning you like this."

"It's absolutely fine," I said.

Rose agreed, and then, as George hurried after Ned, Mr. Briarcliff said, "May I fetch you ladies a lemonade?"

Rose said, "Oh, that sounds lovely," before I could respond.

CHAPTER THIRTY-FIVE

A few moments later I was seated at one of the tables in the shade. Mr. Briarcliff had gone to arrange for the refreshments. He emerged from the clubhouse and scanned the tables, then headed toward me with a waiter following him, carrying a tray with a pitcher of lemonade and three glasses.

As he pulled out a chair, I used my eyebrows to indicate a tennis game that was forming. "Some acquaintances of Rose's came along and drafted her to play doubles. Apparently, she doesn't get to play that often and didn't want to miss the opportunity." The four young women scattered to their positions, and Rose lined up to serve. Her racket swept through the air, and the opposing pair both lunged for the ball but missed it.

"I can see why she'd want to play. She's talented," Mr. Briarcliff said as the waiter set down two tall glasses and poured lemonade. The ice cubes cracked as the cool liquid hit them.

"Indeed. Hopefully, her mother doesn't return from touring the gardens until after the game." Rose used the back of her hand to wipe her damp forehead in an absent-minded manner as she talked with her partner.

Mr. Briarcliff picked up his glass. "Why is that?"

"Mrs. Jenkins doesn't approve of young women playing in such an intense way."

"That's absurd. There's only one way to play—to win."

I raised my glass an inch. "I quite agree. It's rather shocking to find ourselves in agreement."

A shadow of a smile might have traced across Mr. Briarcliff's face at my quip, but I couldn't be sure. He turned away from the courts and settled back in his chair, his glass clasped between his hands. "I didn't want to say anything in front of anyone else, but the news about Timothy isn't good."

"Has his condition worsened? I thought regaining consciousness would be an improvement."

"It is. Physically, he's improving, but I received word from Sir Abner that Timothy will be charged with murder. His physician says he'll allow it as long as he can check on his patient twice a day. Timothy will be taken into custody later today and moved to jail."

"How terrible for him—"

A voice from behind me said, "Trust you, Briarcliff, to see the dark cloud instead of the silver lining."

I swiveled. "Mr. Denby, good afternoon. Would you like to join us? You look like you could use a cool drink."

His cream-colored linen suit was rumpled, and he loosened the knot of his green tie a bit as he swabbed his neck with his handkerchief. "Goodness, yes. Thank you." He waggled his handkerchief toward the courts. "It boggles the mind that some people actually want to play tennis in this heat."

The waiter had left the pitcher of lemonade, and I filled the third glass.

Mr. Denby put away the handkerchief and clinched up his tie. "Lemonade wasn't exactly what I had in mind as a refresher, but bottoms up." He downed half the glass, then took out a notepad and pencil.

"Oh, that's right." I inched my chair forward. "I promised you an interview."

"It's not that. Of course, the readers of *The Nile* will absolutely devour the details about your tour of Cairo, but I'm here on another matter." He swiveled to Mr. Briarcliff. "Any remarks you'd like to make about Mr. Noviss?"

"No comment." Mr. Briarcliff watched Mr. Denby over the rim of his glass the way one would watch a spider discovered in the bath after switching on the light.

"Don't be shirty, Briarcliff. One must ask." Denby swiveled to me. "Miss Windway?"

"No, of course not. I'm happy to talk about Cairo, but not about Mr. Noviss." I sipped my lemonade and watched him for a moment. "But you know something else, don't you?"

"Moi?" His head reared back as he looked at me sideways. "What would *I* know? I only ask questions."

He looked as if he was holding a secret close. "You have a scoop, don't you?"

He drew a breath, but I cut in. "Don't bother to deny it. I saw that same look on your face when we discovered Tadros' body. You were as horrified as I was, but you were also secretly excited to be aware of the news before anyone else." I set my glass down. "Now what is it?"

He dropped his mock innocent look. "You frighten me a bit, Miss Windway, you do. You both must promise not to breathe a word."

"I promise," I said.

Denby looked at Mr. Briarcliff, who also put his glass down. "You can count on me as well."

Denby narrowed his eyes. "For what exactly?"

Mr. Briarcliff sighed. "To be as silent as the grave."

"Hmm. Not sure I believe you, but you don't have many friends. Just stay quiet until after the paper comes out tomorrow."

Mr. Briarcliff nodded. "You have my word."

"All right." Denby leaned over the table. "Young Timothy says that he didn't do it. Insists he's innocent."

"And how do you know this?" Mr. Briarcliff asked, suspicion lacing his tone.

"I happened to be visiting the patient when he came around."

"And I suppose you had a little chat with him before summoning a nurse?"

Denby drew himself up. "Of course not." Then his posture sagged a bit under Mr. Briarcliff's steady gaze. "Afterward. The nurse and doctor hovered around him and declared him fit enough to speak to a visitor. *Then* I talked to him."

"But before the police arrived," Mr. Briarcliff said.

"Yes, and good thing too. You know Sir Abner has an itchy trigger finger when it comes to shutting down anything that doesn't reflect well on the European community here. If I hadn't been there to hear the boy's story, it might have been squashed by *officialdom*, let's say."

Mr. Briarcliff gave a small nod. "You're probably right there."

"Indeed, I am. If I hadn't heard his side of it, Timothy Noviss would have been accused and convicted with the whole thing tidied away as quickly as possible. But that won't be the case now. His story will be in the newspaper tomorrow. I had a chat with Ned the other day, and Timothy's story lines up with it exactly. Timothy says he didn't kill Vita. He said he went to her tent to look for valuables—Timothy admits he was stony at the moment—but Vita was dead when he arrived at her tent. He's adamant that he didn't take the jewelry. He says he left empty-handed and kept quiet about knowing she was dead because he was afraid he'd be blamed."

Clearly, Mr. Denby believed the jewelry was a major motivation for the crime, but the lure of the diary with its possible location of lost antiquities would have been even more valuable.

I didn't voice my thoughts. The diary wasn't public knowledge, but my gaze caught on Mr. Briarcliff's, and I imagined he was thinking the same thing.

Mr. Denby looked from Mr. Briarcliff to me. He wagged his pencil back and forth between us. "Now you're the ones keeping something back. You two know something more about this."

Mr. Briarcliff refilled his glass and said in a mild tone, "How could I know more than you? You have it directly from young Timothy."

Mr. Denby surveyed us again, then said, "Mr. Briarcliff, I know you won't budge. You're a stubborn old chap. But Miss Windway, perhaps you might enlighten me?"

"Whatever do you mean, Mr. Denby? You're the one with the inside information."

"I see. It's that way, is it? Right. Fine." He closed his note-book. "I believe I see Mrs. Gelhorn. I'm sure she'll have a comment on the situation. She has a comment on *every* situation. Excuse me."

We sat in silence for a few minutes, then Mr. Briarcliff tipped up his glass and finished the last of the lemonade. "I think I should pay Mr. Noviss a visit."

"I'd like to hear what you learn."

Mr. Briarcliff gave a little preoccupied nod, his gaze fixed on his empty glass. "I'll have to convince Sir Abner to allow me to see Timothy, which will take some time. It might be late."

"That's fine. I'll be at the fancy dress ball tonight at Shepheard's."

His gaze cut back to me. "Of course. The frivolities must go on."

"It's not for me. I didn't come to Egypt for the social life. It's for Hildy. She's never been to a fancy dress ball. She's inordinately excited."

Mr. Briarcliff's face softened. "Ah. I hope she enjoys it. Until tonight."

"Until tonight. And, please, no detours this time."

"You'll abide by the same rule, of course? No detours of your own? Either of the detective variety or—what did you call it?"

"Research. I'm quite keen on doing my own research." But I didn't have much choice in the matter this time. I imagined that Sir Abner would make it impossible for me to visit Timothy. I'd have to depend on Mr. Briarcliff passing on what he learned, which rankled. But there was no help for it. "I assure you I'll be dancing, not detecting, tonight."

LATER THAT EVENING I came out of my room, the long skirt of my costume shushing as it brushed against the furniture of the sitting room. The little carriage clock on the table chimed the top of the hour. I checked my appearance in the large mirror that hung over a console table.

Hildy's door was cracked, and her voice floated out. "Oh goodness! Is it time to go down already? I'm sorry, Blix. I'm running late."

I'd told Hildy about Timothy's recovery, but none of the details about his arrest, which wasn't public knowledge—yet. After tomorrow's edition of *The Nile* came out, everyone would know. I would have liked to talk through the developments with her, but I was also glad not to be obligated to share the news tonight. Hildy had been looking forward to the fancy dress ball, and I didn't want to spoil her evening.

She emerged from her room in a dressing gown, her hair in paper curlers, giving her the look of the prickly cacti plants I'd seen in the American desert. "It's taking quite a bit longer to get ready than I anticipated—oh! Your fancy dress costume is perfect."

I turned from the mirror where I had been buttoning the cuffs of the leg-of-mutton-sleeved white shirt. "Do you think so? It feels too snug and, oddly, revealing, even though I'm swathed in fabric." I'd stitched a simple skirt from a length of dark material that I'd found at the bazaar. I tugged at the waistband, which cinched in the shirtwaist blouse, causing it to hug the curve of my breasts. The current styles were loose, and it felt odd to wear something so figure-hugging.

Hildy raised one eyebrow. "The Edwardians did know how to show off a bust and a trim waist."

She held out a large hatbox. "Of course, an Edwardian lady must have a hat. I'm only sorry it isn't bigger."

I took it out and turned it around, too fascinated to speak for a moment. "But this is absolutely enormous!"

"Enormous by the standards of a Bright Young Person who wears tight little cloches, but by the standards of an Edwardian lady, this would be piffling at best. The larger the hat, the better. At least that's the way it was before the war. I found the hat at one of the shops, but it was too plain. I embellished it a bit for you."

"A bit? I don't know if *embellished* is the word for it." I rotated the hat. "It's like one of those sideshow attractions. There's so much going on that you don't know what to look at first." The hat was wide brimmed with a low crown, and every inch of it was covered with an explosion of feathers in every color of the rainbow. Tucked among the bobbing feathers were several other ornamentations. "Wherever did you find the fruit?"

"They're papier-mâché. Leftover decorations from a fancy dress party a few weeks ago. I asked Fidel to check the hotel for small decorative things, and he found the fruit. They were destined for the rubbish, but he rescued them for me."

"How very resourceful." I settled the hat on my head and turned back to the mirror. I leaned closer to the mirror and tilted my chin down to get the full effect of it. "Is that . . . ?"

"A bird's nest? Yes, it is. It was part of last year's Easter decoration—another of Fidel's finds. I fashioned the robin from a bit of wire and some material from an old shawl that I didn't need anymore."

I tilted my head and admired the creation from all sides. "You've outdone yourself, Hildy. It's perfect. It's mad, absolutely mad. Thank you."

"I had such a wonderful time making it for you. It's actually tame compared to some of the hats I saw in my youth. A friend of mine once had a hat with a chicken—her family was quite fond of taxidermy—while another friend had a hat with seventeen oranges. She was so disappointed she couldn't get to twenty. I'm glad you like it. Perhaps you could do a small favor for me in return?"

"Of course."

Hildy retrieved a book from her room, a volume of Sherlock Holmes stories. "Would you mind returning this to Mrs. Jenkins? She lent it to me a few days ago, and I've been reading it in the evenings. I promised I'd return it today, but I don't believe I'll have time before the fancy dress ball."

"I'll take it right now."

"Excellent. Mrs. Jenkins and Rose are just three doors down the corridor. Same side as our rooms. I saw them returning from dinner one night. Tell her I'm sorry that I almost forgot to return it today. Oh, and I wrote a thank-you note. Let me get that." She dashed into her room, her dressing gown flapping around her legs.

I removed my hat and placed it carefully back in the hatbox. I didn't mind wearing my white shirt and ankle-length skirt through the hotel, but I didn't want to reveal the hat until we went down to the ballroom.

Hildy returned with an envelope. "Thank you. Now to get these paper curlers out and lace up my sandals."

On my way to Mrs. Jenkins' room, I passed a couple going down to the party. The man was dressed as a strong man in tights and carried a bar with balloons attached to each end. An angel with feather wings and a halo drifted along at his side.

I tapped on the appropriate door and put the envelope inside the front cover of the book so that it peeped up higher than the pages. I closed the book, then promptly flipped it open again to take a longer look at the handwritten name on the inside, *Louise Adeline Duncan Jennings*. The door opened, and I snapped the cover closed.

It took me a moment to recognize Rose. "My, you look lovely." She wore a long sheath dress in a silvery shimmering fabric. There wasn't a bow or ruffle anywhere in evidence. The cap sleeves showed off her slender, tanned arms. A headdress with a small red disk rested like a tiara in her short hair.

"Do you think so? I mean, thank you. Mother thought that I should go as Alice from *Through the Looking Glass*, but fortunately that costume had already been reserved."

"Very fortunate indeed."

Pink came into her cheeks. "Don't tell Mother, but I may have encouraged one of my friends to visit the costume shop the day before we did."

"Well, very good choice on your costume. It suits you. Isis, isn't it?"

"Yes. Do you know her story?"

"Hmm. It's a bit fuzzy. Traveled through Egypt collecting body parts, I think."

"That's right, but don't tell Mother the racy bits of the legend."

"Who is it?" Mrs. Jenkins called from another room of the suite.

"Wouldn't dream of it."

Rose raised her voice. "It's Blix."

"Returning a book you lent to Hildy."

Mrs. Jenkins came in, her gold lamé skirt clinging to her thighs as she walked. "Oh. I thought it was George. He's to escort us tonight." She wore a flat-topped conical hat with a gold cobra fixed above her forehead. Thick coal outlined her eyes. The strapless design of the gown's bodice combined with the fact that she wore an Egyptian-style beaded collar heightened her resemblance to the famous bust of Nefertiti.

"Mother, Blix was just saying how much she likes my costume."

Mrs. Jenkins sent me a tight smile. "How kind. It turned out surprisingly well. Although I think one famous Egyptian in the family would have been enough. We didn't need a goddess as well as a queen."

I couldn't think of a diplomatic reply, so instead I gave her the book, and I conveyed Hildy's apologies for leaving it so late to return it.

"It's of no matter." Mrs. Jenkins tossed it on the sofa as she picked up a beaded handbag. "I do hope the ballroom is better ventilated than the guest rooms. It's so horribly hot." She took her handkerchief from her handbag and patted her throat.

"I'm sure it will be fine, Mother."

"Rose, fetch me some water. And make sure it's cold. Thank you, Miss Windway. I'm sure we'll see you later this evening," she said before closing the door.

I walked back to our suite slowly, my thoughts preoccupied with Mrs. Jenkins and Rose. When I returned to our suite, Hildy was standing in front of the mirror. "Almost ready." She'd taken the paper twists out of her hair, and springy curls surrounded her face. Gold sandals peeped out below the hem of her long white dress. She was pinning a white veil-like headdress over her curls. The white material draped down and fluttered around her shoulders as she twisted her head from one side to the other. "What do you think?"

"Perfect. Regal and serene. Mrs. Jenkins said thank you for returning the book. By the way, you won't be the only goddess at the ball tonight."

"I'm not surprised. Funny how no one chooses to go as a scullery maid, isn't it?"

"Costume balls are the very definition of fantasy."

I took the Edwardian hat Hildy had made and positioned it on my head.

"Wait a moment." Hildy bustled away, saying over her shoulder, "I have some hatpins for you. Real hatpins. Not those flimsy ones you young things use today."

She returned, the long folds of her skirt undulating and veil swaying, and handed over two wicked-looking pins, each about five inches long. I balanced them on the palm of my hand. "I remember my grandmother using these. I always thought they were rather frightening."

Hildy nodded. "Excellent for self-defense."

I carefully inserted the pins, weaving them through my hair to hold the hat in place. "I hope Mrs. Jenkins feels well enough to make it through the evening. Rose will be so disappointed if they have to retire early."

"Why would Mrs. Jenkins retire early?"

"She has some sort of illness. Remember, she had Rose fetch her medicine when we were in the lounge tent after Vita died. I don't know what illness Mrs. Jenkins has, but she's often flushed as if she has a fever. Surely you've noticed. Her face was bright red just now."

Hildy had been looking in the mirror as she adjusted the curls around her forehead. "Blix, don't you realize that she's going through the change?"

"She's what?"

Hildy turned away from the mirror, her hands falling to her side. "You know . . ." She waved her hand up and down her body in the region of her hips. "Women . . . go through certain —um—transitions as they age."

"Oh." I stopped worrying about the angle of the hat brim and focused on Hildy. "Are you sure?"

"Well, it all fits. She's the right age for it. Feeling flushed and overheated is common when you're that age, and I did see the tonic bottle that Rose brought to the lounge tent. It can be purchased at any pharmacy, and it's supposed to help with the symptoms, although personally it didn't do a thing for me." Hildy suddenly laughed. "That's probably far more detail than you ever wanted to know on that subject."

"No, I find it extremely interesting. After Vita's body was discovered, I thought Mrs. Jenkins was ill and that was why Rose arrived in the lounge tent out of breath, but it sounds as if there was no need to rush."

"Perhaps Mrs. Jenkins is impatient. One is at that stage of life. It's most inconvenient and uncomfortable. We should go now. We want to be fashionably late, but not so late we miss any more of the ball."

CHAPTER THIRTY-SIX

$\mathcal{S}$everal hours later the dance floor was still crowded and there was no sign of Mr. Briarcliff. I'd kept an eye out all evening for his tall form. It was nearing midnight, and I'd just made a circuit of the room, confirming that he wasn't lurking behind any of the scenery—enormous pyramids and a papier-mâché Sphinx—but I hadn't found him. Mrs. Treeford was sitting alone on the edge of the dance floor, so I'd taken a seat between her and another chair that was heaped with discarded costume props the guests had abandoned while they danced. I settled my prop, a box camera, on the chair beside me and turned to Mrs. Treeford. "Enjoying the evening?"

Her hands were clasped together on the handle of the basket in her lap, her gaze fixed on the dancers. "I don't understand these dances. What is a shimmy?"

"The latest craze," I said and then quickly changed the subject so I didn't have to describe the dance to her. "I don't suppose Mr. Chambers is here this evening?"

"Oh no." She rearranged the folds of her red hooded cape. "I daresay he would have been if Vita were alive. She did require one to dance attendance." She giggled. "Oh my. That was a pun, wasn't it?"

246

It appeared Mrs. Treeford had consumed a generous helping of the punch this evening.

"But events such as this are not foremost on his list of interests," she added. "He likes a cup of tea and a book of medieval poetry. I prefer a nice sonnet myself, but to each his own."

The song ended, and the tempo of the music shifted to a more sedate waltz. Several of the younger couples left the dance floor, but Hildy, who had been chatting with George at one side of the room, took his extended arm and moved to the center of the room. They made quite an eye-catching pair with her in her bright white dress and veil and George in a pale blue kaftan worn over a white gallibaya. A white beard completed his outfit.

"Something wrong, my dear?" Mrs. Treeford asked.

"No, not at all."

"Then you shouldn't frown so. It drives away the gentlemen. My mother always said that a man doesn't want a lady with furrows in her brow."

I had several thoughts on her mother's advice, but I refrained from commenting. I was happy to see Hildy enjoying herself, but I hadn't missed the pointed glance that Mrs. Philpott and Mrs. Canning exchanged as George led Hildy onto the floor for their second dance of the evening.

Mrs. Jenkins and a military officer swung into view, blocking Hildy from my line of vision. I'd watched Mrs. Jenkins during the evening, and it seemed Hildy's assessment of Mrs. Jenkins' health had been correct. She'd danced all evening and didn't seem to be sickly or fatigued, but between sets she stood fanning herself near the open windows, where the cool desert breeze wafted in. I'd tried to talk to her or Rose, but each time I happened to spot them, they were either dancing or the crowds thwarted me. I had a little detail I wanted to clear up—something that had been on my mind all evening—but I had yet to run either of them to ground.

A figure materialized beside Mrs. Treeford, and she gave a

startled yelp. Hand pressed to her flat chest, she said, "Goodness, Mr. Briarcliff, you gave me quite a start."

"I apologize. However, that reaction is perfect for your character. Little Red Riding Hood, I presume?"

Mrs. Treeford giggled again as Mr. Briarcliff bowed over her hand.

I said, "You fall into the role of the big bad wolf quite nicely, Mr. Briarcliff."

Mrs. Treeford's gaze swept up and down Mr. Briarcliff's figure, then she shook her head. He wore his usual dark trousers, tall boots, and a khaki jacket. "That is a sad effort, Mr. Briarcliff, if that is supposed to be a wolf costume. No, you must be someone else." She tilted her head to the side and considered for a moment, then shook her head. "I'm afraid you've stumped me. Who are you?"

"Simple. Myself."

Mrs. Treeford gave him a mockingly severe look. "No, tell me. Who are you?"

"It's exactly as I say. I'm myself."

"Fiddlesticks. No one comes to a costume party as themselves. That spoils the fun."

"I'm not a tourist here. I don't deck myself up in fancy dress."

"That's not sporting at all, young man." Mrs. Treeford seemed to sink down into herself.

"Hildy will also be quite disappointed that you didn't make an effort," I said to him, then turned to Mrs. Treeford. "I'm sure he's just having you on. Mr. Briarcliff is . . . um . . . a free agent, wasn't it?"

Mrs. Treeford looked over his clothes again. "I'm not familiar with that term."

"I believe that means he does whatever he wants," I clarified.

Mrs. Treeford's spine straightened as she sat up. "That's not a costume. It's an attitude."

"Yes, you're right," I agreed.

Mr. Briarcliff was actually looking a bit uncomfortable, his gaze shooting out and scanning the room. I took pity on him—but only because I didn't want anything to spoil Hildy's evening. I snapped my fingers. "I know. Henry Morgan Stanley, the explorer. All you need is a pith helmet. Surely you can find one somewhere. Ask the front desk for them to check the Lost and Found. Someone probably left one behind."

Mrs. Treeford stood and swayed briefly as she settled her basket on her arm. She inclined her head to me. "It's been delightful chatting with you, Miss Windway, but I believe it's time for me to retire."

The music was fading. "Hildy will certainly come over to say hello to you, Mr. Briarcliff. If you hurry, you might be able to find a pith helmet before she gets through the crush."

Mrs. Treeford tucked her hand through Mr. Briarcliff's elbow. "Come along. Let's see that you're outfitted properly for this event. You may escort me to the lobby, and we'll stop at the front desk to find a pith helmet. I'm sure this young lady is right. There's probably one discarded somewhere that you can borrow."

Despite her small size, Mrs. Treeford bore Mr. Briarcliff away. He looked over his shoulder and motioned he'd return, then shortened his long gait to match the stride of Mrs. Treeford.

I danced the foxtrot with a plump military officer who was surprisingly light on his feet, then returned to the chairs at the side of the dance floor to find Mr. Briarcliff now sitting beside the pile of discarded costume accessories. A pith helmet that was a bit too small for him rested on his head at an angle, giving him the look of a bottle with the lid screwed on crooked.

I sat down beside him, and he leaned back to give my hat plenty of clearance. "Sorry." I shifted to the side. "I'm not used to wearing such monumental headgear."

He eyed the hat. "Now that we've settled my costume, who are you?"

I motioned to the pile of costume props. "That box camera goes with my costume. Who do you think?"

"Hmm . . ." He picked up the camera. "I'll hazard a guess of lady photographer."

"Well, of course, but *which* lady photographer?"

"I'm afraid I'm not well versed in lady photographers."

"Surely you've heard of Mrs. Beals—Jessie Tarbox Beals—the photojournalist?"

"Can't say that I have."

I realized I was probably frowning at him in a way that Mrs. Treeford would disapprove of. "She's an American photographic journalist. She's very talented and has photographed loads of famous people—presidents and authors and actors—but she really shines at outdoor photography. She's full of pluck, lugging around a camera much bigger than that one. She climbs up on tall ladders and even rides in hot air balloons to get the best images, rather like your friend Mr. Listergraff. She often gives talks. I heard her speak when I was in America."

"Interesting. Sounds like an admirable person."

I searched his face for signs of mockery, ready to jump in and defend my statement, but I didn't see anything like that. "So you do think some people are admirable?"

"It depends on what they do, doesn't it? Your Mrs. Beals sounds like a good egg."

"Oh. Well." Hildy was now dancing with the same portly soldier who'd partnered me earlier. Once she noticed Mr. Briarcliff, she'd make her way over, so I said, "Were you able to speak to Timothy?"

Mr. Briarcliff had picked up the box camera. He turned it over in his hands. "Timothy says he never found the diary. He says he went into the tent to look for it but was so shaken by what he saw that he left without even looking for the diary. He's adamant about it. He says it was never in his possession."

"He must be lying. When faced with jail in Egypt—even the British jail—I'd think one would proclaim innocence."

"No, I don't think he's lying. He was very clear in his statement." Mr. Briarcliff replaced the camera on the chair, carefully positioning it so that it was braced against the back of the chair and wouldn't tumble off. "I've seen people lie with a smile, careless bastards who tell untruths without a second thought." While his voice was quiet, his inflection had a fierce timbre to it, an undertone of anger. "Timothy wasn't like that. Ernest and frightened, yes. But not glib at all."

I put aside my questions about the liars Mr. Briarcliff had encountered and pulled my thoughts back to the topic at hand. "Then how did the diary come to be in Timothy's satchel?"

"I asked him about that. The police had already told him it was found in his belongings. Timothy insists it wasn't there when he went to the museum. He says someone placed it there."

I watched the dancers as they swirled by, a kaleidoscope of color and movement. "Then he's saying someone attacked him at the museum and put the diary in his satchel."

"To frame him, yes."

"What about the site in the desert with all the exploratory digging?" I asked.

"He claims he's never been there. Sir Abner wants to keep that quiet, by the way. He says they have enough trouble with treasure hunters as it is, so he doesn't want anyone to know about a possible undiscovered cache of antiquities."

"Yes, I can see why he'd want that kept hush-hush. I haven't told anyone." I stared at the mock-up of the pyramid and the Sphinx a moment, then said, "Something about the site in the desert has been bothering me. It was all very haphazard with holes dug in random places. The contents of Timothy's satchel as well as his notebooks were neat and orderly. Timothy has experience working on excavations. If he were searching the desert for buried antiquities, surely he'd go about it the right way, creating a grid and working from a pattern so that nothing was missed. That's how it's done, isn't it?" I'd seen photos of excavations, which were approached in an organized and methodical manner.

"Yes, that's what I've seen on local digs. I agree. Timothy doesn't seem to be the sort who would plunge in and go about it in that haphazard manner. The police are questioning the various guides to see if anyone contradicts his statement."

"But you don't think that's going to happen, do you?" I could tell from his tone that he was doubtful.

"No, I find it hard to believe Timothy murdered his hostess, stole from her, and then went about digging in the desert on the sly while touring Cairo with Vita's nephew. From the beginning, he struck me as a circumspect young man."

"That's my impression as well," I said, surprised that he and I agreed. "When did you meet him?"

"Ned frequents the Long Bar. He usually had Timothy in tow. It's my job to keep an eye on things there. We've played a few card games, and I've advised them on hunting areas." A young couple collapsed into the row of chairs a few feet away from us. Their chairs bumped against the row, and Hildy's costume prop, a flowered branch, slid to the floor. Mr. Briarcliff picked it up and absentmindedly twirled the slender limb. "I can't see Timothy committing murder—unless he could be absolutely sure he would get away with it, and even then . . ." He shrugged. "Well, I find it difficult to picture him having the wherewithal to do such a thing."

"Especially on his own," I said. Timothy seemed to constantly be in Ned's shadow. It was hard to picture him acting on his own.

"Exactly." The branch bobbed toward me as Mr. Briarcliff emphasized his word.

I floated an idea that struck me. "Perhaps they did it together? Timothy and Ned, that is." I'd been trying out possible suspects, fitting them into what I knew of the crime, but I'd only considered each person individually until that moment.

"A team rather than a solo effort?" Mr. Briarcliff looked away a moment, then shook his head. "No, I don't see it. In fact, I was thinking that perhaps it's Ned who should be under suspicion instead of Timothy."

"You mean because of his personality?" I asked.

"Yes, in part. Ned seems to be someone who'd be able to act alone. And also, if Ned ventured out of the tent before Timothy woke, he could have killed his aunt and taken the diary. He could have taken the jewelry to cover the theft of the diary. Then later Ned could have planted the diary so that Timothy would take the blame. He'd know Timothy's movements, that he'd be at the museum. A swift crack on the head to knock him out, then all Ned had to do was slip the diary into Timothy's satchel and get out of the area."

I nodded, but the wide brim of the hat knocked against the wall behind me, pushing it forward over my eyes. Did Mr. Briarcliff's lips twitch slightly? It was difficult to tell because he kept his features so immobile. It seemed his attention was on the branch, which he was idly moving back and forth in time to the music, but I could have sworn he'd very nearly grinned.

I adjusted the hat so that it wasn't sitting on my eyebrows. "Ned was at the café nearby."

"So I heard," he said. The branch swished to the right, and he added, "Ned is right-handed, and the way Vita's throat was slit indicates the murderer was as well." He sent me a quick, apologetic smile. "I'm sorry. That's too gruesome to discuss."

I inched my chair forward so that my hat wouldn't hit the wall. "Not at all. Sir Abner explained it to me."

Mr. Briarcliff stared at me. "You're quite a curious woman, Miss Windway. Most women would have the vapors at the mention of the technical details of a slit throat."

"Or at least pretend to have the vapors," I said. "But it's a fact of the case. Besides, I make it a policy not to have the vapors."

"Sound strategy for the modern woman. But to get back to Ned and the case, most people are right-handed, so that indicator isn't much use. However, the last point—and it's a major one—as an augment to Ned potentially being the culprit is that he benefits from the crime. He's inherited a bequest from his aunt."

"A substantial bequest?"

"Extremely."

"Ah. I see."

"Not as substantial as what George receives. The bulk of her estate goes to him, of course, but Ned's portion is a large amount for a young man to receive. However, that isn't proof. Not like the evidence pointing at Timothy."

I adjusted the brim of my hat again, which was weighing on my skull. How had women worn such things daily? "Another thing I've been thinking of is this—why slit Vita's throat?" Mr. Briarcliff looked startled at the abrupt change in topic. "I've shocked you, I see. It's just that it's something I've wondered about. The way Vita was killed—it's extremely . . . messy. If the murderer had waited until she was asleep and suffocated her with a pillow, there would be no risk of incriminating blood."

Mr. Briarcliff leaned slightly away. "Do your thoughts usually run along tracks such as this?"

"You're teasing me. I saw that tiny flicker of movement at one corner of your mouth a moment ago. In someone else, it might have been a half smile, but on your face it was more like one-sixteenth of a smile." He did grin at that, one of his brief lightning smiles that flashed across his face and was gone. "See, I knew it. You *are* teasing me." I turned serious. "Surely the same thought about Vita's manner of death has occurred to you too?"

"Yes, but slitting someone's throat is quick and fairly quiet, two things the murderer needed. The tents were close together. A struggle might have been heard."

"I suppose that's true."

The musicians launched into another rendition of the chorus. Careful of my hat, I settled back against the chair, amazed that I was having this discussion with Mr. Briarcliff of all people. He was a surpassingly good sounding board, and he knew all the details of the investigation. "Let's approach it from another direction. We know it had to be someone at the camp-site that night. I know it wasn't Hildy or me." A little spark of discomfort flared as I thought of the letter opener that had been found in Vita's tent, but I wasn't about to offer up that tidbit of information to Mr. Briarcliff. If the police hadn't figured out who that letter opener belonged to, I wasn't going to give it to anyone on a platter. "Other than Ned and Timothy, there was also Mrs. Jenkins, Rose, and Mr. Chambers."

"Each more unlikely than the last."

"Yes," I murmured, but my thoughts were on the book that I'd returned to Mrs. Jenkins. I searched the crowd for her and saw her dramatic headdress bobbing among the dancers. She towered over her elderly partner, a Renaissance courtier.

"You look contemplative."

"It's nothing," I replied with what I hoped was a dismissive tone as I scanned the room for Rose. I wanted to speak to her. "It does seem as if Timothy is the logical choice," I added because I didn't want Mr. Briarcliff to ask any questions about what I was thinking about.

"It does," Mr. Briarcliff said as the music ended, and Hildy and George made their way over to us. "But it doesn't feel quite right. Rather like a suit jacket that's too snug." Mr. Briarcliff stood and held out the branch to Hildy. "I believe this is yours?"

"Oh, did Blix tell you who I am?"

"There was no need. Hestia, goddess of home and hearth, is an excellent choice."

She tilted her head and thanked him for the compliment.

"Diana, the huntress, and Aphrodite were certainly inappropriate for me." Her gaze traveled up to his hat. "I'm glad to see you in costume."

"A minimalist effort, I must admit."

Hildy pressed a finger to her lips as she considered him. "Either an archaeologist or an adventurer." She snapped her fingers. "Mr. Stanley, I presume?"

"Well done! Got it in one."

I said to George, "Your stone tablets are in the chair." I was glad to see he looked more well rested. The shadows under his eyes were gone, and he'd danced as energetically as Hildy.

"I don't blame you for not holding them. I didn't realize they would be such a heavy prop." Hildy was moving her eyebrows, trying to convey something to Mr. Briarcliff. He looked confused for a moment, then said, "Oh. Yes, of course." He turned to me. "I've been remiss. Would you like to take a turn about the dance floor, Miss Windway?"

I tended not to dance, especially since my disaster of a season, but Hildy was looking at me with such a happy, expectant expression that I agreed. Then Hildy said, "But you'll never be able to dance to that tempo with your hat. Leave it with me."

The dance was a quickstep, and the floor was crowded. "I expect you're right." I removed the hatpins, stuck them in the crown of the hat, then handed it over to Hildy.

Mr. Briarcliff's steps were a bit stiff and rote in the beginning, but after a few bars he seemed to relax, and I found myself leaning into the turns with a confident abandon that I hadn't felt all night as he navigated us through the swirling couples. As the music came to an end, our steps stilled, but we remained in the close embrace of the dance pose.

"Goodness, Mr. Briarcliff, you're a first-rate dancer. That was lovely. I didn't think dancing would appeal to you."

He didn't speak for a moment, just studied my face. I was suddenly very aware of his hand, still warm under my shoulder blade, and how little space there was between our faces.

"I rarely have such an excellent partner." Someone jostled against us, and we broke apart. "Most women chatter so much that one can hardly hear the music."

"Well, no fear of that from me. I have to concentrate on the steps to keep my two left feet in check. It's been ages since I danced."

"But you're a natural."

"Only with you, it seems." We were promenading around the room, and I was glad that at that moment we were passing in front of one of the open windows, where the air was cool and refreshing. I surveyed the room. "Do you see Hildy?" My hat had joined the pile of discarded costume props, and Hildy was nowhere to be seen.

"There. Dancing with Major Kettering."

"Ah. I'll wait for her here." I paused as we came to the next open window, letting the crisp desert air sweep over my back and through the thin layer of my shirtwaist. We watched the dancers swirl by. A woman dressed as Cleopatra caught my attention, my gaze on her elaborate collar necklace of gold and turquoise. It made me think of the jewelry that was stolen from Vita's tent.

I turned to Mr. Briarcliff. "How does Tadros' death fit into the whole situation? Did he steal the jewelry? Was it a completely separate crime from Vita's murder? Or was Tadros someone's partner?" I asked, returning to one of my earlier theories. "Perhaps Tadros carried the jewelry away and the murderer later took it from him and buried it in the Ezbekiyeh Garden, intending to retrieve it after the inquiry into Vita's death was over."

"All very good questions."

"And then did the murderer kill Tadros to remove a witness?"

"That's Sir Abner's opinion, but he doesn't have evidence to support it. He's doing his best to link Timothy to the deaths of both Vita and Tadros, but Timothy claims he was at the museum the entire day that Tadros was killed. I intend to check on that tomorrow."

"I can see why Sir Abner is attempting to link the three things. Since Timothy was staying with Ned in Vita and George's hotel suite, he would have known Tadros."

Mr. Briarcliff stepped back to allow another couple to pass by. "But that argument can be flipped the other way as well. Ned could be just as likely to be the guilty party. Perhaps even more so when one takes into account the bequest from Vita's will."

There was a hiccup in the hum of the crowd, then the throng rippled, falling back as Mrs. Jenkins and Rose made their way across the room. Rose wasn't trailing along with rounded shoulders behind her mother. Tonight her back was straight, and she looked just as elegant as her mother. "Mrs. Jenkins and Rose are leaving. I must speak to them before they retire."

His expression became distant again. "Planning your outing tomorrow?"

I had taken a step away, but I halted. "How do you know about that?"

"I always have a look over the list of excursions the concierge sets up. All part of the job."

"Hildy plans to depart on a steamer soon. I want to make sure that she sees the pyramids before we leave, but that's not what I want to speak to them about."

"You have a few questions to run by them about Vita? What could they possibly know? Their tent was far from hers."

They'd stopped to talk to a knot of people, so I lingered a moment more. "As we discussed earlier, they were there on the Giza Plateau. Each of them is as likely a suspect as Timothy or Ned."

"Mrs. Jenkins, the fading society beauty, and her bookish daughter? Involved in a murder?" Incredulity bubbled in his voice, but it drained away as he studied me. "You do. You suspect them."

"They were there. Why couldn't one—or both of them—have done it? Perhaps they were the partners instead of Ned and Timothy."

"What on earth is their motive? Mrs. Jenkins wanted Vita's jewelry? She can buy as much jewelry as she wants at any shop from here to London. That's ridiculous."

"I didn't say their motive was to steal the jewelry. I think it's something else entirely."

I cut through the crowd, pausing only to snatch up my hat from the chair. Mrs. Jenkins and Rose were already climbing the stairs when I reached the lobby. I called their names, moving as quickly as my cumbersome skirts allowed.

Mrs. Jenkins said something to Rose, then continued to the upper floor. Rose came down to meet me at the foot of the stairs. "Mother's a bit fatigued, so she's gone on. Don't worry, though, we're looking forward to the outing to the pyramids tomorrow. Perhaps we should meet for breakfast?"

"That's not what I wanted to speak to you about. And I don't think you'll want to discuss this at breakfast."

"Whatever do you mean?" A note of worry threaded through her words.

"How exactly is your mother related to Cornelius Duncan?"

CHAPTER THIRTY-SEVEN

*R*ose's gaze darted around the lobby. "Whatever do you mean?"

"I can't imagine your mother is Cornelius Duncan's daughter," I said. "The gossips here wouldn't have let that connection go unnoticed, so it must be a more distant relationship. Cousin, perhaps?"

"How ridiculous." Rose laughed, but it sounded forced.

"Or is she his niece? The hotel library will be open tomorrow. I'm sure they have a *Debrett's*. I'll find out eventually."

"Why are you saying these things? I think you've had too much punch."

"I saw the name written on the inside cover of the book. Louise Adeline *Duncan* Jenkins. The first three names were more faded, but the word *Jenkins* was darker. All the words had been written in the same handwriting. Your mother had obviously owned the book for years. Instead of crossing out her surname, she simply added her married name. That's why *Jenkins* was in darker ink."

Rose's hand shot out and gripped my wrist. "You mustn't tell anyone. Please."

Instinctively, I pulled away, but her fingers dug in, her nails biting into the thin layer of skin around my wrist. She towed me around one of the two plinths on either side of the staircase that supported two ebony caryatids. Even though I'd argued with Mr. Briarcliff that Rose and Mrs. Jenkins could have had a part in Vita's death, until that moment they'd been on the lower end of my suspect list.

Deep down, I'd thought they were an outside possibility—something to be cleared off of my list rather than something to be frightened of, but Rose was a sturdy girl, and, caught off guard, she'd easily maneuvered me to the secluded spot behind a tall lotus-topped column.

I jerked my arm away as I reminded myself that we were in a busy lobby with guests moving about, and I only had to call out for help and a porter or desk clerk would hurry over.

Rose held up her hand, palm flat. "I'm sorry. It's just that if Mother knew you'd worked out she's related to Cornelius Duncan—she won't even say his name, she calls him *that man*," she infused her words with disgust as she imitated her mother, "she'd be frightfully embarrassed."

"What?"

Her words were unexpected, like a stumbling block that caused my thoughts to jumble up. I'd thought Mrs. Jenkins and Rose might be angry that I'd figured out their secret, but Rose looked miserable as she shot a quick glance up the stairs as if to assure herself that her mother was out of earshot. Her next words were barely above a whisper. "It's true. Cornelius Duncan was my mother's uncle." She said the word *uncle* as if the relationship was something shameful.

Clearly, there was more going on here than I'd realized, so instead of airing my theories, I said, "And you wanted his diary."

"I didn't! I don't give a hoot about it. I think it's rubbish—and Mother does too, actually—but she doesn't want the news about the diary to get out. She's afraid it will stir up interest in her uncle. She does not want anyone to work out the connection between her and Uncle Cornelius. I believe he would be my great-uncle, but we just call him *that man*—if we speak of him at all."

"But why wouldn't you want his diary? It could be worth quite a lot. You could sell it to some ardent follower of Duncan's, or you could publish it."

"Publish it?" She made a scoffing sound. "Mother would *never* publish it. If we can find it, she'll destroy it."

"What? Why?"

"Uncle Cornelius is an embarrassment to the family. His stupid jiggery-pokery! I think the whole thing is foolishness and we should ignore it, but Mother's determined to find the diary and destroy it. She's ashamed of Duncan. Mortified, actually. She thinks if we can find the diary and get rid of it, then we'll prevent a gossip-storm."

"Goodness. She's quite fixated on it."

Rose heaved a sigh. "I'll admit she's a tad unhinged over it. It's such an old-fashioned thing, to be worried about your reputation, but there it is. I know it sounds absurd, but Mother lost two marriage proposals because of her uncle. Her suitors didn't want to be associated with a family that had a relative spouting barmy theories, never mind that her uncle was estranged from the family. Now she's afraid the diary will stir up interest in all the pyramidology nonsense and bring Uncle Cornelius back into the spotlight. Mother is petrified that interest in her uncle will hurt my marriage chances—not that I want to marry right now. I don't even have any suitors at the moment, but once Mother sets her mind to something—well, it's easier just to go along. The diary is the whole reason we're here in Cairo."

"You traveled all the way to Egypt because of the diary? Good grief, it's been such a boost to travel to Cairo that Cook's should put it on their advertisements, it seems." Rose frowned, and I said, "Never mind about that. How did you even know about the diary? It was supposed to be a secret." Although the number of people who knew about it kept growing. Did it even qualify as a secret if half a dozen people knew of it?

"Not if Percy is supposed to be keeping the secret."

"Indiscreet, was he?" I already knew Percy hadn't kept details of the diary to himself, but I wanted to hear how she and Mrs. Jenkins found out about it.

"I'll say. One of mother's friends came to tea and mentioned there were rumors circulating that Cornelius Duncan's diary had been found, and wasn't that exciting? She hoped it would be published soon so she could see what all the fuss was about. Mother nearly upended the tea tray. The woman was Percy's aunt. He'd told her all about it and sworn her to secrecy, but she was giddy with the news. She couldn't wait to share the secret —in complete confidence, of course. She was sure Mother would want to know since she was a relative."

It was a good thing Percy was in England. I had a few things I wanted to say to him. I'd been so earnest and so vigilant about my commission to carry the diary to Egypt. What a fool I'd been. "So you knew I had the diary? Why didn't you just ask me about it?"

"Who was actually transporting it to Egypt *was* a secret. Percy did manage to keep that detail to himself. We only knew that it would be delivered to Vita, who wanted it to verify certain locations. Mother went to Percy and offered to buy the diary, but Percy is a follower of pyramidology. I think he must have sensed that Mother would destroy it, so he sent it to Egypt to preserve the knowledge in it." Rose rolled her eyes. "Mother decided we had to come here. She hoped to convince Vita that the diary should be in the family's hands."

"But Vita was so passionate about it. I can't imagine her selling it. Did your mother offer to buy it?"

"No. We never got the chance. Mother thought it would be best to wait until after Vita tried to replicate Uncle Cornelius' stunt at sunrise. When nothing otherworldly happened, Mother knew Vita would be disillusioned, and then she'd approach her."

"If Vita had refused, what would you have done?"

"This is a terrible thing to say, but mother was all for . . ." Rose mouthed the words, *Taking it*. She shook her head so hard that her Egyptian headdress wobbled. "Of course, we never had the opportunity. That's why I was so distraught when I spoke to you in the Arab Hall. I so wanted this whole thing to be over so I could go back to my hieroglyphics. But when Vita died, that changed everything." She broke eye contact, her gaze darting to the side.

"Yes, it did." I'd been rearranging my theories, dismantling my original ones because I believed Rose. She'd been open and forthright, but now she seemed to draw into herself.

"I should be getting back to Mother."

"Something happened after Vita died, didn't it? It was when you went to get your mother's medicine. Did you make a little detour?"

Rose's eyes flared, and she gripped her hands together. "What are you talking about? I got the medicine and came back."

"I think you went into Vita's tent. Were you worried about what your mother might have done? You said she's a bit unhinged when it comes to the diary."

"No. Of course not." The confident cadence of her words had disappeared. "I really must go."

She tried to brush past me, but I stepped into her path. "You were out of breath when you got back to the lounge tent. You'd been running. Why was that?"

Rose looked down at her interlaced fingers, then back up at me. "I lost my head and did something incredibly stupid. I was afraid Mother had been in Vita's tent and had taken the diary. Of course, now I know she hadn't, but all I could think of when I went to get the tonic for her was that if she'd been in there—if she'd left some trace of her presence and the police found out about the diary, well . . ."

"She'd have a motive."

Rose's fingers were now contorted into a claw-like grip. "A weak motive. I see that now. Who kills over a book? But at the time, I panicked. I knew I didn't have the time to search Vita's tent for any trace Mother might have left. And honestly, I don't think I'd have had the constitution. I've never seen a dead body, and I'd overheard Mr. Chambers say her throat had been slit. Going into her tent was out of the question, but I could do something to distract attention from Mother." She paused, looked around as if she'd like to duck under the stairs and hide.

In her hesitation, it dawned on me. "You took Hildy's letter opener and put it in Vita's tent."

"Yes," she said with a miserable sigh. "I darted into her tent and snatched up the first thing I saw, which was that letter opener. I used a fold of my skirt to pick it up, then I raced to the opening of Vita's tent and tossed it inside before I ran back to the lounge tent." Her eyes were glassy, and she looked away from me. "I've regretted it terribly, but I couldn't say anything because that would complicate the situation even more. I'd have to explain about the diary and my family's strange obsession with it. And Miss Honeyworth is so sweet, which only makes everything worse. I so wish I could turn back the clock and change what I did." She unclenched her hands and rubbed her fingers under her eyes as she drew a shaky breath. "I suppose I'll have to tell all of this to the police."

"It was a foolish thing to do." But I could sympathize. I'd been foolish too—letting Percy take me in with his hints. She'd been punishing herself with her mental anguish. "I'll tell you this: the police haven't asked one question about Hildy's letter opener. As long as they're not interested in it, I don't see why you need to come forward."

She sagged against the pillar. "Really? Oh, thank you. That's such a relief."

"Your mother doesn't know?"

Rose shook her head. "I couldn't bring myself to tell her that I might have set in motion the very thing she most wanted to avoid, notoriety around her relationship to Cornelius Duncan." She straightened and seemed to gather herself, then she looked up the staircase. "I'd better go. Mother will wonder what happened. I'm so sorry that I tried to implicate Miss Honeyworth. She's been nothing but kindness itself to us, and I feel dreadful about it."

"I won't say anything to her about it."

"Thank you." She took a few steps, then turned back. "I'll make some excuse tomorrow so we can bow out of the excursion. I'm sure you don't want me around."

"No, don't do that. What you did was rash and impulsive, but you were trying to protect your mother. Please do come. It will raise questions if you don't."

"Yes, that's true. All right, then. See you tomorrow morning."

CHAPTER THIRTY-EIGHT

*E*arly the next morning, dressed in my climbing clothes, I went down to the lobby, my camera strap swinging from my shoulder. I was still mulling over what Rose had told me about Mrs. Jenkins' desire to find the diary. What amazing power that book possessed. Just strings of words arranged on the page, but their existence had swayed people's opinions and also influenced behavior—both of Mrs. Jenkins' long-ago suitors as well as her own actions in coming to Cairo to track down the diary. I believed Rose's story that she and her mother were only interested in obtaining the diary and hadn't done anything more than wait for an opportune time to offer to buy it.

I seriously doubted that either of them was involved in Vita's death. As Rose had said, after the sunrise reenactment ceremony failed, Mrs. Jenkins could have offered to buy the diary from Vita—and probably been successful. She might have rejected the offer, but even if it failed, waiting was a much saner plan than murdering Vita. Why would you murder someone when there was an easier way to achieve your goal?

As much as I disliked admitting it, it seemed Mr. Briarcliff was right, and the two ladies weren't involved in Vita's death. I rounded the landing and scanned the lobby for Mr. Briarcliff. I was sure he'd ask about why I'd rushed off to speak to Mrs. Jenkins and Rose last night, and I'd rather put off a conversation with him. I'd have to admit I was wrong. I hated to be wrong. However, there was no sign of his imposing form.

I trotted down the last set of stairs, feeling light without the heavy hat and thick skirts I'd worn to the fancy dress ball. I had salvaged one of the hatpins from my costume to secure my cloche. I could have tied a scarf around my head, as I did last time I went to Giza, but I intended to take copious amounts of photos, and I didn't want to deal with the ends of a scarf flapping up from under my chin and into the frame of the viewfinder. I'd picked a hat with a brim that would shade the back of my neck and used one of the skewer-like pins to make sure I wouldn't lose it to the stiff winds on the plateau.

The concierge met me at the bottom of the stairs. "Good morning, Miss Windway. I've been in touch with the Mena House Hotel. Everything is ready for your group. Once the tram arrives at Mena House, you'll find donkeys waiting for you at the hotel along with the dragoman you requested, Ibrahim, for your tour of the pyramids. Lunch reservations have been made for your party at Mena House as well."

"Excellent. Thank you for coordinating everything."

He gestured to the main doors of the hotel, which were thrown open. "Some of your party is already outside." An oblong of sunlight streamed in, falling on the patterned rugs and highlighting dust motes that drifted in the air. A figure came through the doorway, and even though he was backlit by the sunlight, I could tell from the small stature, the light-colored linen suit, and the pith helmet who it was.

"Good morning, Mr. Denby."

He returned my greeting and tucked his pith helmet under his arm. He tilted his head toward the doorway. "I see you're reassembling the suspects. Planning to reenact the crime?"

A cool morning breeze wafted through the main doors.

Hildy and Mr. Chambers stood chatting on the terrace while the vendors, a thin crowd this early in the day, called out about their wares on the street below. George arrived and joined them, shaking hands all around. "I hadn't thought of it that way, Mr. Denby, but you're entirely correct. Although it's actually an outing to the pyramids, not the campsite. Hildy never did get to see the pyramids properly. She invited Mr. Chambers, Mrs. Jenkins, and Rose."

Mr. Denby's eyes narrowed against the sun as he watched George's small figure maneuver through the group so that he stood beside Hildy, shaking her hand and then holding it a few moments longer than was called for. "And George is never far from Mrs. Jenkins or Hildy these days, so of course he's going. And if he's one of the group, that means Ned will be there as well." He leaned to the side and peered down the street. "Yes, I see young Ned."

Ned shuffled along, hands in his pockets, eyes on the pavement. I felt a pang for Timothy, sitting in jail, even if it was a British jail. "It will be everyone except for Timothy."

Mr. Denby, his gaze still on Ned, said, "I interviewed him again—Timothy, that is—yesterday."

"How is he?"

"He continues to maintain that he's completely innocent. Looked remarkably healthy for someone in jail."

"I'm glad he's had no lasting effects from the attack."

Mr. Denby held out a newspaper. "I brought you one of the first copies of *The Nile*'s special edition. Hot off the press, as they say."

The headline read, *British Traveler Held for Murder Inquiry.* "A byline on the lead story. Congratulations."

"Thank you, but I can't help but feel it's macabre to celebrate a front-page news story, seeing as it's based on death and suffering. But there you have it, the workings of the press." He grimaced. "Of which I am one, for my sins."

"I thought you were a novelist?"

"Unfortunately, being a newspaperman pays the bills at the moment."

"You're still working on your novel though?"

"Of course. A writer is always working on a novel—that's the easy part. It's the finishing of the novel that's the trick."

His tone was dry, and I smiled at his joke as I skimmed the text. I lingered over pictures. The first and largest photograph showed Timothy, standing on a stone ledge, holding a large drawing pad as he sketched rows of hieroglyphics that lined the monument above and below him. Under his floppy white hat, his expression was one of concentration as he focused on his drawing. "Timothy looks so young."

"It's not surprising they picked that photo. The contrast between his image and the words *murder inquiry* makes it all the more scintillating. I'm sure the publisher is fairly salivating over the sales that will come from that combination."

"A rather sad commentary on our world."

Mrs. Philpott and Mrs. Canning walked by, their attention fixed on the front page of their copies of *The Nile*. Mr. Denby said good morning to them. They returned his greeting but ignored me. I barely noticed their slight. I'd moved on to the second photo. George sat at a desk, its highly polished surface covered with documents, pen in hand. The photographer had caught George in a candid moment as he took a break from his paperwork, reaching for his coffee cup.

Mr. Denby tapped the photo. "They couldn't find anything more recent of George. I should've told them to check with you. You probably have something from here in Cairo. That picture was in the archives. It's from when he was in his former post in Alexandria."

I had to admire the skill of the photographer. The papers, pen, and that glossy surface of the desk combined with the slightly blurred background of bookshelves gave the impression that this was a busy man in an important position. His extended left hand, caught mid-movement, gave the feeling of intimacy, as if we were sitting across the desk while chatting with him. The paper crinkled as my grip tightened as a thought struck me.

"But that can't be," I said.

Mr. Denby sidled closer. "Ah, you found an error. I must say, typos are the bane of my life."

"What? No, nothing like that. Look at this photo. George is holding the pen in his right hand."

Mr. Denby looked from the paper to my face, then took my arm. "Perhaps you'd better move out of the direct sun."

I shook off his arm. "George is left-handed."

"Are you sure? Perhaps you're mistaken."

"No, I'm not. When we met him in Alexandria, he wrote on a business card, giving us his address here in Cairo, and I distinctly remember him curving his left hand around to write, angling his wrist so that it wouldn't drag through the ink."

"Then the photo must have been posed. Perhaps the photographer directed him to take the pen in his right hand for the sake of the composition. Being a photographer, you'd be aware that photos are often staged."

"But this one isn't. I'd bet all the gold in Tut's tomb. Look, see that slight blur along the edge of his sleeve? The shutter clicked as he was moving."

Mr. Denby scrutinized the photo and shrugged. "I know little of photography beyond how to click the button on a Brownie camera. I'll bow to your knowledge."

"The photo isn't the only thing." My brain, firing away now that I was running down this track, had pulled up another memory as clearly as if I were watching it on a newsreel. "When Rose and I played doubles lawn tennis with George and Ned, they discussed which side of the court George should take since he was a *leftie*."

A prickle traveled along my spine as another memory from that day surfaced. I looked over Mr. Denby's shoulder. George, Hildy, and Mr. Chambers were still talking. Ned stood over to the side, smoking a cigarette. I took a step out of the slanting sunlight into the cool shadow of the lobby, beckoning Mr. Denby to move with me. "I've remembered something else— something very important, I think. It happened when we were playing tennis right before Mr. Briarcliff arrived with the news about Timothy."

Mr. Denby made a humming noise that indicated he was listening, but he was dividing his attention between me and idly scanning the lobby, looking for tidbits of news or gossip, I supposed. Clearly, he didn't see the importance of what I'd discovered.

I tapped his pith helmet to draw his attention. "It was Rose's serve. The ball hit on the centerline to the right of George." I folded the newspaper and used it to demonstrate. "George had to strain to reach the ball, but he managed it hit it back *with his right hand.*"

"I confess I'm baffled." He tilted his head down and leaned so that our foreheads nearly touched. "Why does any of this matter?"

He was teasing me, but I didn't care. What I'd figured out was too important to bring him down a peg. "Perhaps George is ambidextrous," I said in a low voice.

Mr. Denby shrugged and stepped back. "It could very well be. Left-handedness is not cricket, you know. Had a chap at school who preferred to use his left hand. The master slapped a ruler down on his hand whenever he caught him at it. They finally had to tie his left hand behind his back to force him to use his other hand."

"How cruel."

"The British education establishment isn't known for benevolence—or tolerance."

He still didn't understand. I drew him a few steps farther away from the terrace. "Don't you see? Vita's murderer was right-handed. George is left-handed—something that, as you say, is rather frowned on—but I've seen him using his right hand at least twice. And now there's photographic evidence of it as well." I shook the newspaper open and pointed to the photo.

Mr. Denby had gone back to surveying the lobby over my shoulder, but his gaze snapped back to my face as he went still. He stepped closer. "You're saying that George could have murdered Vita?"

"Except for the bequests, he inherits. It wouldn't be the first time a man killed his wife for her money."

"She did keep a tight grip on the purse strings," Mr. Denby said, then stepped back, shaking his head. "But he was here in the hotel when she was killed. He was in the bar with Mr. Briarcliff. And you and I know he didn't leave the hotel."

"Yes, that's true," I said, my gaze on the main doors, where tourists were ambling out to breakfast on the terrace. One of the waiters glided by. I watched the section of the terrace for a moment, then turned in a slow half circle, scanning the lobby. "Not by the front door—" I gripped Mr. Denby's arm.

"Miss Windway, please. Linen wrinkles so."

I murmured, "'Attendants must not be seen unless absolutely necessary.'"

"What?"

"It's something Fidel, our floor attendant, said to me." I swept my hand around the lobby. "Look around. Do you see any attendants? No. Only the desk clerks. And you don't see anyone upstairs in the corridors except for a brief glimpse. These grand hotels function in many ways like an English manor, where servants are to do their work without intruding on the family, taking back staircases . . ."

Mr. Denby's face transformed as understanding dawned. "So they can move through the house without being seen."

"Exactly. I know Shepheard's has back staircases because Fidel mentioned them. I can't believe I didn't think of this earlier!"

"When you're part of something, it's hard to see it from the outside. But before you get swept away, how would paunchy George get back to Giza and find the campsite in the dark?"

"He'd get there the same way our party will today, on a donkey—or even a horse. They can be hired and brought right to the hotel. And as for getting back to the campsite, he knew its location. He's a hunter. Navigating through the desert must be something he's done. Surely he could get to the pyramids and cover the short distance from there to the campsite, even in the dark."

"I suppose you're right."

I checked my watch. We still had a quarter-hour before we were to leave for the tram. I set off across the lobby. "Come with me."

CHAPTER THIRTY-NINE

*M*r. Denby caught up with me just as I reached the front desk. "Good morning!" I said to the desk clerk. "Just a quick question. Mr. Denby is a reporter working on a story about the grand hotels of Egypt." I felt Mr. Denby's gaze on me. I was sure it was disapproving, but I plowed on without glancing his way. If I was on the right track, he'd want the story. "I was telling him how much I've enjoyed my stay here at Shepheard's."

The clerk removed his pince-nez. "We are happy to hear it, Miss Windway."

"In fact, Mr. Denby was saying that if he could learn more about the hotel—its inner workings—it would make his piece distinctive. Really set it apart."

"I see," the young man said, but he looked puzzled. "How may I be of assistance?"

"Mr. Denby was reluctant to ask, but I told him Shepheard's is marvelous and that I was sure you'd be willing to help."

"Of course, mademoiselle."

"Mr. Denby is interested in seeing behind the scenes of the hotel. It runs so flawlessly, yet we hardly ever see the attendants, the staff that makes it possible. How is that accomplished? How do the attendants move about the hotel? There are back staircases and corridors, correct?"

"Oh yes. In fact, let me summon Mr. Thayer."

As soon as the clerk stepped away, Mr. Denby said, "Working on a piece, am I?"

"Shush. You want the story, don't you? If I'm right, it will be a scoop."

The clerk returned. "Follow me, please." He led us down a corridor, knocked at a door, then motioned for us to enter. A slender man of about fifty with gray sideburns that would have been the style before the war came around the desk and shook our hands. "Mr. Thayer, at your service."

We introduced ourselves, and I gave the spiel about the news story, but this time Mr. Denby jumped in, adding, "The inner workings—the secrets—of the grand hotels, that's what I'm after. What unseen elements keep this hotel ticking along like a fine Swiss timepiece?"

"We're flattered to be included in your article. I'd be happy to arrange an interview with Mr. Martin, the owner of this hotel, as well as many other fine establishments in Egypt from Alexandria to Khartoum. He'd be delighted to speak to you."

Mr. Denby ran his finger around his collar. "What a generous offer. Perhaps later."

He looked a bit worried, so I said, "I imagine that Mr. Denby will be keen to speak to Mr. Martin after the article takes shape."

"Quite. Yes, wouldn't want to waste the gentleman's time at this point as I'm only gathering general information. Now I assume you have some sort of system of back stairs and corridors for your staff?"

"That is correct. Here, let me show you." He gestured to the wall behind us. I turned and studied several large framed architectural drawings, each showing a different floor of the hotel. He pointed to several stacked lines at the corners of the square block that made up the hotel. "Here are the staff staircases." They were much smaller than the main staircase in the lobby.

"And what is this diagonal corridor?" It ran from corner to corner across the central portion of the hotel under the Arab Hall.

"Ah, that is our underground corridor. One of our earliest efficiencies. Before the Arab Hall was built, the center of the hotel was a courtyard. The underground passage allows staff to move between the kitchens and the laundry, which are located on either end. It saves quite a few steps, I assure you."

The interior corner where the laundry was located wasn't far from the staircase that would access George and Ned's suite of rooms. I glanced out of the corner of my eye at Mr. Denby. He must have noticed the same thing because I saw a spark of excitement trace across his expression before he masked it.

"And this underground passage is still in use today?" Mr. Denby asked.

Mr. Thayer smiled. "Constantly."

"May we see it?" Mr. Denby asked.

"I'm sorry, but guests aren't allowed. Staff only."

I said, "Perhaps you'd make an exception this once? The publicity from Mr. Denby's article could be rather significant. Today, in fact, he has a story on the front page of *The Nile*."

"Well . . ."

Mr. Thayer was wavering, so I gave him my most blinding smile. "Just a quick peek. That's all Mr. Denby needs. Isn't that right?"

"Yes. Just a glimpse."

"All right, yes. Come with me."

Once we were in the hallway, Mr. Thayer closed his door and motioned for me to precede him down the corridor. "This way. Just before the exit to the gardens, you'll see an unmarked door on your right."

Once we reached it, I stepped back and let Mr. Thayer open it. We followed him down a flight of stairs, then he opened

SARA ROSETT

another door. Compared to the opulent decoration and finishings in the lobby, the passage was utilitarian with a stone floor and bare white walls. It was well lit with a row of overhead electric lights. Our heels rang out on the flagstones as we walked along. "As you can see, there's quite a parade through here."

The corridor was indeed busy as attendants moved back and forth, hauling stacks of towels or balancing trays of food. They paused when they saw us, clearly surprised to see Mr. Thayer and two guests. He waved them along. "Don't mind us. Go on about your business."

As we approached an open door, the air became palpably warmer. The click of crockery along with the buzz of voices emanated from the room. We passed the kitchen, and the aroma of roast beef and fresh bread drifted through the air.

"Is it always this busy?" I asked. "Even at night?"

"We use it around the clock. A hotel never truly sleeps. Bit of a paradox there. Perhaps you can use that in your article, Mr.—ah—Denby, wasn't it?"

"That's right. Yes, perhaps so."

With a sinking feeling, I scanned the flowing tunics and billowing pants of the staff. Some wore turbans, while others had tarbooshes, but not one of them was in Western dress. George wouldn't have been able to pass along the corridor without someone noticing him. Mr. Denby must have worked out the same thing because a frown etched across his forehead.

Once we reached the other end of the corridor, the scent of bleach filled the air. "Laundry here," Mr. Thayer said, then climbed another set of stairs, opened a door, and we emerged into the cool hallway of the guest chambers with its brightly colored rugs, potted plants, and scattered rattan chairs. The quiet, nearly deserted passage contrasted with the bustling, humid underground passage. One of the smaller staff staircases that led to the upper floors was located only a few steps away.

Mr. Denby, smiling now, pumped Mr. Thayer's hand. "This

has been most helpful. Thank you for taking the time. I'll be in touch soon."

I was barely able to get in my own thanks before Mr. Denby bustled me away.

"Don't be angry," I said. "I'm sorry I dragged you into this, but you have to admit that when he said there was an underground passage, it truly did sound like it would be the key that unlocked the mystery. Admit it. You thought the same thing."

Mr. Denby sighed and tilted his head from side to side, moving it just a fraction. "Yes, I suppose so. But George would have stood out like a searchlight on a foggy night. Someone would have noticed him if he left that way."

As we returned to the lobby, Hildy came through the door from the terrace. The burst of feathers on her hat created a spiky shadow that stretched across the carpets. "There you are, Blix. And Mr. Denby. Good morning. Are you coming along with us today?"

"Unfortunately, no. I have an appointment this morning, and then," he cut his gaze to me, "I have to speak to my editor about an article on the grand hotels of Egypt."

"What a shame," Hildy said. "Well, on the off chance that your plans change, we'll be at the Mena House for lunch and would be happy to have you join us."

"You're too kind."

"I'll tell the others we're ready," Hildy said and went back out the door.

Before I followed her, I said, "I believe I owe you an interview."

"I'll say."

"I'll answer questions for as long as you like. After dinner?"

He nodded. "Meet me in the bar? We can find a quiet corner somewhere in the hotel." I agreed, and he said, "Enjoy the pyramids."

∼

WHILE SEEING the pyramids from the ground was amazing, the experience was altogether different when one was at the top. I'd put aside my mental suspect list and all my questions around the deaths of Vita and Tadros. I intended to soak in the experience of the pyramids with single-minded attention. We'd found Ibrahim waiting with our donkeys as promised at Mena House and set out on a tour that wove around the base of the pyramids, viewing them from all sides. Then George had turned in the saddle and called out, "Who's for going up?" He'd flung his arm out at the Great Pyramid, where a few people in ant-like lines were inching up the great blocks of stone.

I certainly wasn't about to pass up the experience, and now I stood, buffeted by the wind, taking photographs in all directions. The view was spectacular with the other pyramids and the Sphinx spread below, then the yellow and brown tones of the desert sands and rugged escarpments, and finally, in the distance to the east, the strip of green and the blue sparkle of the Nile.

I shifted to the opposite side, taking care as I crossed the slightly uneven surface of wide stone blocks. The pinnacle was about twelve yards square, and there was plenty of room for our party along with another group, who'd brought a set of golf clubs and were taking turns hitting golf balls that arced through the air and hit with a faint thump on the lower stones.

I took several photos of the dig to the west. From above, the trenches and tombs were clearly delineated. I began to see why aerial photography could be useful to archeologists.

Rose came up to my elbow. "I wish I'd known we'd climb to the top. I would have brought binoculars. Do you think that's Miss Honeyworth and Mr. Chambers?" She pointed to a pair of minuscule figures, small dark dots in the sea of sand below us.

"I suppose it might be them."

Hildy had said she would stay on the ground rather than climb. "I can admire the pyramids just fine from here," she'd said. Mr. Chambers had agreed. When we left to begin our ascent, Hildy and Mr. Chambers had already turned their donkeys and were heading back across the plateau toward Mena House.

Mrs. Jenkins sat in a camp chair at the center of the flat area. "Rose, come away from the edge. You're frightening me."

Rose's gaze went skyward, but she inched back a few steps.

I'd been surprised Mrs. Jenkins said she'd make the trek up the side of the pyramid, but her reason became clear when she'd extended her hand to George and said, "You'll help me, won't you? Mrs. Philpott said that every year a few tourists fall to their death while pyramid-climbing, but I'd so hate to miss the experience."

George had waved away her concern. "Foolish chaps taking it too fast on the way down, usually. There's nothing for you to worry about. I'll stay by your side the whole time." And he had. He'd assisted the chain of Bedouins who helped us scramble up the tiers made of three- and four-foot-high stones, passing us from hand to hand, pushing and shoving as required to get us to the top. I'd felt rather like I was in a fairy tale, clambering up a giant's staircase.

By the time we reached the top, Mrs. Jenkins' color was high, and she'd spent the entire time at the top fanning herself with her handkerchief. Rose moved back to her side. "This is all amazing, but I don't see why I can't go inside the pyramid."

"Rose, we've been over this again and again." Mrs. Jenkins' voice was weary. "I won't have it. It can't be safe in those passageways. One hears they're quite unsanitary. Now George had the foresight to bring flasks of tea and water along with a tin of biscuits. I'd like some water, please, Rose."

George had brought the food but had handed it off to Ibrahim to tote up the pyramid. Ibrahim had spread out a blanket and arranged teacups and saucers as well as trays with biscuits. He now stood a few steps away from us, waiting. When we were ready to go back down, he'd negotiate the cost of our "passage" down the pyramid with the Bedouins.

Rose removed a tumbler from the basket and poured water for her mother. I settled down on the blanket, took a biscuit, and poured myself a cup of tea. George, who'd been admiring the view, settled into another camp chair beside Mrs. Jenkins.

Ned had been talking with the men hitting golf balls. They offered him a club. He took a few swings, then shook hands all around and returned to our group. He dropped down on the blanket beside me, hunched over, and sheltered a cigarette from the wind as he lit it. He straightened and pointed the cigarette at me. "Have you heard anything about Timothy?"

"Me?" I asked, surprised that he'd addressed me.

He nodded, and the tip of his cigarette glowed red as he drew on it. "You're in touch with that Mr. Briarcliff chap. He's in the police's pocket, isn't he? What does he say?"

"I'm barely acquainted with him."

"You two looked very chummy last night."

"We were simply passing the time while Hildy and your uncle danced."

Ned's gaze cut to George. "Yes, all the ladies chase after him. Hard to understand."

"Perhaps it's his good manners and pleasant disposition that attract them." It was hard to reconcile my suspicions of him with the solicitous picture he presented. He leaned toward Mrs. Jenkins, refilling the tumbler for her, his gold watch chain and waistcoat straining against his slight paunch.

Ned scowled. George said something to Mrs. Jenkins, and she let out a peal of laughter.

"I rest my case." I reached for another biscuit. Climbing four hundred feet was hard work, even if you were being helped along.

I expected Ned's scowl to deepen, but he let out a huff and a small laugh. "Perhaps you have a point." He stubbed out his cigarette on the sole of his shoe and reached for a biscuit. "I would like to know about Timothy, though. Have you heard anything? They're not letting anyone see him right now."

"I'm afraid I can't help you there. Your uncle is in a position to know more."

"He won't tell me anything, except that the whole thing is wrapped up. Done and dusted. Timothy's guilty, and that's all there is to it. Uncle George says it's best to forget the whole thing." His head dipped forward as he turned the biscuit over in his hands, but he didn't eat it.

"But you don't agree?"

"No." He straightened. "Sure, Timothy isn't family, but that doesn't mean you just leave him to rot in jail."

"You don't think he did it?"

He scoffed. "Timothy? He's so blinking soft that he can't even hunt properly."

"What do you mean? I thought you both hunted."

"Oh, we did, but he never hit anything. Missed by a mile every time. And it wasn't that he was a bad shot. He didn't want to kill anything. Doesn't like it, apparently," he said with a shrug. "So there's no chance he—um—I mean, there's no chance at all that he killed Aunt Vita. He's what the ladies call a *sensitive soul*." Ned's scathing tone indicated he thought the words were far from flattering. "But he's my friend," he added on a sigh. "He stood by me at school, and I'll not desert him."

Was that a grudging feeling of respect stirring in me for Ned? Maybe a tiny ember of it. I supposed the boy did have at least one redeeming quality. Unless he was an excellent actor, Ned seemed to be genuinely upset and worried for Timothy. It seemed he wasn't likely to take George's advice and forget about Timothy. "Well, I'm afraid I really can't help you. You might approach Mr. Briarcliff directly. Tell him your concerns."

Ned had shoved his whole biscuit into his mouth, and he nodded.

Mrs. Jenkins addressed Ned as she dipped her handkerchief into the water in her tumbler. "I heard you mention Timothy. Shocking. I must say I never would have believed it of him."

George moved the tray to anchor the blanket from a gust of

wind. "It just goes to show how difficult it is to judge character."

Ned ran his hand over his forehead. "Uncle George, I've told you. Timothy couldn't—"

Mrs. Jenkins, in the process of sweeping her damp handkerchief across her wrists, must not have heard Ned because she spoke over him as she said to George, "I don't understand. Was Timothy in league with this person who stole Vita's jewelry?"

"It appears so." George took out his cigarette case and offered one to Mrs. Jenkins, who shook her head. He selected one for himself and tapped the cigarette against the lid. "And apparently Timothy wasn't satisfied with the jewelry. The foolish chap was digging in the desert, looking for more treasure."

Mrs. Jenkins' handkerchief stilled as she stared at George. "What's this about digging in the desert for treasure?"

George's quick tattoo on the cigarette stopped for a moment, then resumed. "That's what I heard. Probably another rumor. You know how these things become exaggerated."

"I'm sure you're right," Mrs. Jenkins looked at Rose, who'd wandered back to the edge. "But please don't mention it to Rose." The wind whipped a curl across Mrs. Jenkins' cheek. She tossed her head, shaking it out of her face. "But enough about that sordid subject. There's another fancy dress ball next week at the Savoy. Will you attend, George?"

George replied, but it was as if his voice was filtered, a muted murmur as my thoughts whirled around like little spirals of sand kicked up by the wind. No one knew that Timothy was suspected of digging in the desert except Mr. Briarcliff and me—and Sir Abner, of course, but he wasn't publicizing that detail.

284

CHAPTER FORTY

*M*rs. Jenkins spoke my name, drawing my attention back to the conversation. "Will you attend?"

I scrambled to remember the topic of conversation. "The next fancy dress ball? I'm not sure." I didn't like the way George was staring at me, so I turned to Ned and cast about for something innocuous to say. "Your costume last night was rather impressive." He'd come as a gangster in a suit with a loud pinstripe, flashy tie, Homburg hat, spats, and a cane.

"Thank you. The costume shop in the hotel had everything except the cane. I had to borrow one of those from Uncle George."

"I've already decided on my costume for the next fancy dress ball. I'll give you a hint." Mrs. Jenkins leaned over to whisper in George's ear.

I knew the place Ned had mentioned, a row of shops that adjoined the hotel. "The shop must be well stocked. Is that where George got his Moses costume?"

"Only the stone tablets. The rest he had. Aunt Vita arranged the Christmas pageant and said he had to be in it." His smile was brief. "Aunt Vita was a big arranger, you know. Liked to tell people what to do."

"She was quite good at organizing," I said, thinking of the campsite. "What part did your uncle have in the nativity pageant?" I expected him to say one of the wise men.

"He's always one of the shepherds."

Despite the hot sun drilling down, a prickling sensation radiated out from my spine and traveled through my body. "So George already had a long tunic?"

"Yes, and the cloak thing that goes over it. What do they call it?"

"Gallibaya."

"Yes, that's it. And the turban too. He went completely native with the costume for the Christmas pageant. Learned how to wind the turban properly and everything."

My gaze shot over to George. If he owned a costume like that, he could blend in with the servants at the hotel.

His head was still tilted close to Mrs. Jenkins as she spoke in a low voice, but his gaze was fixed on me. He couldn't have overheard what Ned had said, could he? Surely Mrs. Jenkins' words would have drowned out Ned's quiet tones. But my heartbeat sped up because George's focus on me didn't falter as he nodded at something Mrs. Jenkins said.

I shot to my feet. "Ned, would you introduce me to the group with the golf clubs? I'd like to get some photos of them, if they're agreeable."

Ned said he didn't think they'd mind, and I followed him over to the group, the weight of George's gaze heavy on my back.

The other group had tired of hitting golf balls and were having lunch from a picnic basket. They handed off the golf clubs to Ned and suggested he pose for me. I took several photos of him at the edge of the stone blocks with Cairo in the distance, then I snapped a few more as he swung the club, sending golf balls sailing off the side of the pyramid.

I moved through the familiar motions, framing the shots and adjusting for the glare of the sun, while my thoughts buzzed. I mentally edited my list of the various people who'd been on the Giza Plateau the night Vita died. George had to be on that list now. He could have used the clothes he wore to the fancy dress ball to move through the hotel's underground corridor unnoticed to the door that accessed the gardens.

And once George was on the list, I had to rearrange the lines I'd penciled in between people on the list. Were George and Timothy accomplices? But if that were the case, why hadn't Timothy accused George? Faced with the prospect of prison in a foreign country, I couldn't believe that if Timothy and George were in league that Timothy would keep quiet about it.

What if George's accomplice wasn't Timothy, but Tadros? The details that hadn't made sense earlier suddenly fit together seamlessly like a key sliding into a lock with a smooth click.

With his alibi at the hotel established, George had slipped out through the underground tunnel and returned to the campsite. He could enter Vita's tent, kill her, and return to Cairo. Tadros had either been George's partner or George had duped him into helping him. With both Tadros and the jewelry missing, the police had assumed Tadros was a thief and murderer.

My heartbeat kicked, and I felt as breathless as I had after the climb up the pyramid, but I forced myself to go through the motions of taking a few more photos. The viewfinder trembled as I tried to frame the shots, my hands jittery. George and Mrs. Jenkins weren't that far away, and as I stepped back to get a wider photograph, I caught a snatch of their conversation.

Mrs. Jenkins' voice carried above the wind, "How are the repairs coming along at Silverthorne?"

"In fits and starts. The workmen cry off for one reason or another . . ."

I clicked the shutter a few times, then moved closer to Ned. As he lined up to swing the club again, I asked, "How did your aunt feel about the renovations at Silverthorne?"

"Originally, she was all for it, but that changed recently."

"How so?"

Ned dropped out of the stance. He looked over at George, then stepped nearer me. "Silverthorne requires pots and pots of money to run day to day. And that's not considering all the repairs that are needed. George would get something squared away, but then another part of it would tumble into disrepair. Aunt Vita was all for selling the place and moving to a modern flat in London. She said keeping Silverthorne was throwing good money after bad."

"Your uncle didn't agree?"

"No. Uncle George has a fondness for the old pile." Ned swung the club idly. "Don't understand it myself. Bad drains and drafty rooms and moldy tapestries. Can't see how that compares with hot water, electric fires, and the theater, not to mention the finest restaurants a few blocks away."

Was that it? Did it all come down to money? George had inherited Vita's fortune and could spend it on whatever he wanted—repairs and renovations to Silverthorne. And then there was also his recently acquired motor, another expensive purchase.

I thanked Ned for posing for the photos, then said, "The sun is too intense for me. I believe it's time for me to make the descent."

I kept my face turned away from George and Mrs. Jenkins as I crossed to Ibrahim. If I looked at George, surely the thoughts running through my mind would be visible on my face. How could I pretend my attitude toward him hadn't gone through a sudden metamorphosis?

Ibrahim stood as I approached. "I'm ready to go down. Can you arrange it, please?"

He looked over my shoulder at the spread of the blanket and food. "Now, miss?"

"Yes. I know the rest of the party would like to stay a little longer." In fact, it was my greatest desire that they stay exactly where they were while I made my way down. "It's the heat. I'll go down alone if you can coordinate with the Bedouins for me." They were waiting, seated a few feet down from us, ranged around on the tiered blocks of stone that made up the northeast corner of the pyramid.

"Of course, mademoiselle."

I tucked my camera into its case. As I settled the strap on my shoulder, George's voice sounded behind my ear as his hand closed over my arm above my elbow. "Surely you're not leaving so soon, Miss Windway?"

"I'm not feeling all the thing." I stepped back in a jerky movement, rotating my arm, an indication that I wanted him to release me, but his hold tightened.

"Careful there. Sudden movements like that can be dangerous up here. You must stay. It'll ruin the afternoon if you leave."

Ibrahim looked back at me, an uncertain expression on his face.

"I'd rather not." I pulled away harder, stepping back and putting all my weight into wresting myself away from his grip, but George yanked my arm, pulling me close to him, then he propelled me toward the blocks at the outer edge, away from the corner where the Bedouins were seated.

"What are you doing? Let go!" My foot caught on one of the blocks, and I stumbled. George wrenched me back to his chest as his raised voice carried across to everyone. "Calm down, Miss Windway. No need to panic. Let me help you."

I struggled, breaking his grip for a moment, knocking my hat askew, but his hand clamped down on my wrist. Hildy's sturdy hatpin kept my hat fixed to my head, albeit at an odd angle that almost covered my eyes.

I reached up with my free hand to push the hat back into place as he forced me back another step. My stomach lurched, anticipating the drop off the side of the pyramid.

He raised his voice so that it carried over the wind. "I know you're prone to bouts of melancholy, Miss Windway, but there's no need—"

He let out a high-pitched screech as I plunged the hatpin into the back of his hand.

He released me, and I scrambled over the blocks, away from the edge, as the wind whisked my hat away. "He tried to push me off the edge." Despite the sun boring down, I shivered. Holding the hatpin up like a tiny sword, I shifted around behind the empty camp chair.

"Miss Windway! What has come over you?" Mrs. Jenkins leaned away from me.

George had clasped one hand over the back of the other and held both of his hands pressed to his paunch. A thin red dribble appeared between his fingers. "Now, Miss Windway, you're overwrought. You've had a mental breakdown before. I'm sad to say it's happened again. You've lost your grip on reality—"

"No, that would be *you*. You killed your wife."

He looked at me with a sorrowful expression. "Miss Windway, please. If you'll let me get you down the pyramid, I'll see you get the help you need. Just as your family did last time when they sent you to Switzerland."

I closed my eyes. Of course he'd rake it all up again.

Mrs. Jenkins said, "Oh, Miss Windway, do be sensible. Let George help you."

The familiar creep of mortification enveloped me. The wind tossed my hair over my eyes. I wouldn't let it happen again, the whispers, the rumors, the pitying looks. I shook my hair away and squared my shoulders. "You killed Vita, then you killed Tadros to confuse everything around her death."

Mrs. Jenkins looked as if she was watching a theater performance in extraordinarily bad taste. "Miss Windway, really!"

George's brow wrinkled into a sad but kindly expression as he looked from one person to another. "See, she's delusional."

"No, I understand everything now. It's all quite clear. Vita wasn't falling in with your plans. You saw an opportunity to remove her, and you took it. You made an appearance at the campsite, then returned to the hotel and established your alibi."

George chuckled and shook his head as if to say, *See, she's really in a bad way*, but I kept speaking. I had a moment or two to make my case, and instead of slinking away in shame as I had before, I had to squash George's lies.

"You dressed in the gallibaya that you own. You wore it to the fancy dress ball last night too. That night that you left the campsite early, the gallibaya allowed you to leave the hotel without attracting any attention." Would anyone believe what I was saying? George looked every inch the respectable British gentleman in his dark suit with the flash of his gold watch chain across his pouchy stomach. I went on quickly, "No one notices servants, do they? Once you were out of the hotel and into the gardens, all you had to do was make your way around to the side street, hire a donkey or horse, and return to the campsite."

Pink suffused George's cheeks. "Absolute rubbish!" His coddling manner had evaporated like water in the heat of the day.

Ned, golf club dangling from his hand, stared at his uncle as if he were a fascinating but strange creature. "But why? Why would he do that?"

"For Vita's money." I transferred my attention to Mrs. Jenkins for a second. "The renovations at Silverthorne. You know how expensive those are. And the new motor? I bet Vita didn't approve of that purchase either."

George sputtered. "Nonsense. Vita wanted Silverthorne to be a showplace."

Ned said, "No, she didn't. She wanted a flat in London with all the modern conveniences."

"So you slit her throat." My palms were sweaty, and the metal shaft of the hatpin was slippery. I gripped it harder. "And you were careful to do it with your right hand. You'd been using your left hand, like you had that day I met you in Alexandria. How long had you been waiting for an opportunity? How long had you been using your left hand? Weeks? Months? I bet only a few people know you are ambidextrous, don't they? But Tadros would have known. Was that why he was part of the plan? You couldn't have him around to tell the police that you could use both of your hands equally well. Did you pay Tadros to steal the jewels, then hand them over to you and disappear? I bet he didn't understand that his death was part of the plan, that he was a scapegoat who'd take the blame through his *suicide*. But when that didn't work, you had to come up with another person to take the blame—Timothy."

Ned rotated the golf club. "Is that true?"

George shook his head, but I spoke over him. "Timothy is adamant that he didn't take Cornelius Duncan's diary."

Mrs. Jenkins, who'd been tutting and motioning for Rose to round up one of the Bedouins to escort them down, froze.

"You must have taken it when you killed Vita and later planted it in Timothy's satchel after you attacked him. Did you dig the holes in the desert as well to implicate him, or did you have a lackey do it?"

Ned advanced another step, golf club swishing through the air. George held up a hand. His palm was bright red with blood from where I'd stuck him with the pin.

"Right. Yes. Fine. Stop right there, Ned." George gave a little irritated shake of his head. "I had to do it. Don't you see? It all comes back to that idiotic diary. Vita said repairing Silverthorne was a foolish investment, but she was going to fritter her money away on *pyramidology*. It wasn't enough to own the ancient jewelry and the diary. No, she planned to open an *institute*. She would have sunk every last penny into her daft hobby. There wouldn't have been anything left. I had to do it. It was the only way. She wouldn't listen to reason."

I felt light-headed with relief. No one could say I was barmy now. George had admitted it. His pudgy figure in his dark suit with his gold watch chain suddenly looked insignificant compared to the vast desert that spread out to the western horizon behind him.

I lowered my hand with the hatpin. "I think we'd better go down now and speak to the police, George. I'm sure you won't mind if I go first. I'd appreciate it if you stayed well away from me on the way down."

"You've no need to worry on that count," George said. "I won't be returning with you." He took a single step backward, which sent him tumbling down the side of the pyramid.

CHAPTER FORTY-ONE

*T*he terrace at Shepheard's was never deserted, but at the moment there was a lull between luncheon and tea. It was the heat of the day, and most of the guests had retreated inside. I'd chosen one of the tables in the shade and spread out all the photographs I'd taken over the last few weeks. I was sorting them, selecting the ones I'd have made into slides for my lecture about Cairo.

The motion of a street vendor waving drew my attention beyond the iron railing.

"Postcards, miss? Very nice postcards."

"No, thank you." I had made one purchase before I settled down to work, and it rested on the table in a slender blue box. I waved off an array of jewelry, scarves, and the ubiquitous stuffed crocodile, which was available in two variants—on a stick or as a hat.

"Oh, Miss Windway." I anchored the stacks of photos with my camera and my handbag. Miss Philpott was weaving through the tables. She nearly plowed down one of the waiters, but he performed a deft sidestep. She halted at my side, and I mentally braced myself for a dressing down. "I'm so happy to see you out and about. Are you recovered from your ordeal?"

I'd spent the last few days alternating between answering questions from the police and assuring Hildy I was fine. Now that she was closer, I could see Mrs. Philpott wasn't scowling at me, but I was still guarded in my response. "As much as I can be. I'm trying to focus on other things." I tilted my head toward the photos.

"Yes, I suppose you must. It's not every day one witnesses a bounder fling themselves off a pyramid and tumble to their death. I always knew there was something a bit off with Mr. Rhodes."

Hindsight was a beautiful thing, especially when applied to other people's actions. "Did you? I must admit I found the whole thing shocking and surprising."

"Oh, I didn't say it wasn't shocking. To think, I danced with him several times! But enough about that." She motioned to the photos. "I understand you give lectures. I'd like to invite you to the Ladies' Literary Club. Our next meeting is on Thursday. We'd be delighted if you'd join us as our guest speaker. We pay a speaker fee and provide light refreshments."

It took me a moment to reply. An invitation to speak to her club was the last thing I'd expected. "I'd enjoy that, but only if Miss Honeyworth is included in the invitation."

"Of course Miss Honeyworth is invited. Why wouldn't she be?"

It seemed notoriety covered a multitude of sins—at least in the eyes of Miss Philpott. "Then I accept. What topic would you like me to speak on? I have lectures with slides about the American West, the Scottish Highlands, Italy, the Swiss—"

"I'm sure they're all lovely, but we want to hear your first-hand account of what happened on the pyramid. Ten o'clock in the Ladies' Salon."

"But—" I raised my hand. "Wait! I don't . . ." She bustled away before I could finish my sentence. I let my hand fall to the table. ". . . have a lecture on that!"

"Then perhaps you'd better compose one." Hildy joined me

at the table. "That's the third invitation to speak you've received, isn't it?" She scooted her rattan chair into the shade, the lilac-colored feathers on her hat quivering with the movement.

"Fourth. Unfortunately, the only topic anyone is interested in is Vita's murder."

"Well, you can't blame them. There is great interest in true crime. It's ghoulish but so compelling. I keep going over and over my interactions with George. I still find it hard to believe that he had me completely taken in. I'm usually a better judge of character."

"Don't be too hard on yourself. He took everyone in, even the police."

I'd been concerned for Hildy, wondering if perhaps she harbored any romantic feelings for George. Apparently not. She'd been appalled at what he'd done, and she wasn't mourning him. The veil of sadness that seemed to drop over her when the subject of Vita came up was missing when the topic of George's death was mentioned. "Yes, well, the police didn't seem to be trying especially hard." She brushed dust from the table and took a thick packet from her handbag. "I think it's time for a change of scene. I booked passage for us on the Nile."

"And which steamer did you choose?"

"The S.S. *Cleopatra*."

"Good choice. That one sounded lovely."

She handed over a brochure. "Yes, and we're to have a nice group of people on the steamer. In fact, I met an older gentleman who was booking passage on the same steamer, a Mr. Listergraff. He does aerial photography, whatever that is."

"I've met him as well," I said, thinking of our unconventional introduction in the desert. "He seemed the amiable sort."

"Oh good. It's so important to travel with likable people since we'll be in close quarters with them for an extended amount of time."

I opened the brightly colored pamphlet that had a picture of a white multi-deck steamer and a temple in the background. "When do we depart?"

"Next Wednesday, which will give you time to do your lectures."

I handed the brochure back to Hildy. "Which will allow me to pay for my passage."

"Which I've told you that I'm happy to cover," Hildy countered.

"But I'm delighted to have the ability."

Hildy refolded the pamphlet. "I do understand. Having money of one's own is nearly as important as having a room of one's own." She removed a folded newspaper from her handbag and spread it on the table. "Oh, and I thought you'd be interested in this."

Mr. Denby again had the byline on the top story in *The Nile* with the headline, *Tragedy at Great Pyramid*. The smaller subheads read, *British Citizen Dies After Fall* and, even smaller, *Suspect in Murder Inquiry Released*.

I pulled the paper closer and scanned the article as Hildy said, "I believe that is what's called 'burying the lead.' The fact that George admitted to murdering Vita isn't mentioned until the fifth paragraph."

"Well, Sir Abner did say that George knew the editor. It must be difficult for him to run a story about his friend the murderer."

"Yes, but in my experience the press is usually quite willing to sacrifice personal relationships for dramatic and salacious headlines."

I looked up. "Your experience with the press?"

She began tidying up the travel brochures and pamphlets. "One hears things. Oh look, there's Mr. Briarcliff." She waved. "Do join us."

He glanced at the article as he pulled out his chair. "A very thorough whitewashing of the event."

I put the newspaper down. "Yes, must keep the tourist machine running without a hitch."

"Just so," he said.

I tilted my head. "I do find it interesting that you have a rather cynical viewpoint. You work for that machine." I looked pointedly at the facade of Shepheard's.

"Unfortunately, I'm not wealthy. I must earn my crust, and my work for *the machine*, as you call it, keeps me solvent. I have lines drawn that I will not cross, I assure you. One of those lines is working for any sort of rag."

Hildy said, "With all that's happened, I suppose it's Ned who is the wealthy one among our little group."

"What will he do?" I asked. "Have either of you heard? I haven't seen him during the last few days."

Mr. Briarcliff caught a waiter's eye and ordered coffee for himself, and Hildy requested a pot of tea. "Ned has been busy. He's planning to return to England to finalize the sale of Silverthorne."

"How sad." Hildy sighed. "It was a grand old house. But I suppose it's for the best, seeing that it was the root cause of the trouble between Vita and George."

Mr. Briarcliff swung one ankle up and rested it on his other knee. "Ned already has a buyer. A wealthy American purchased the house and the folly. He intends to disassemble it, ship it across the pond, and reassemble it in some Midwestern city. I forget where. Apparently, the folly will go in their back garden."

"How absurd," Hildy said, but then she smiled. "Although I can't help but think that Vita would be rather pleased. She was from the Midwest, you know."

Mr. Briarcliff went on, "Ned also inherited the diary, but he doesn't want anything to do with it. Mrs. Jenkins offered to purchase it from him, but he gave it to her since it was written by her relative."

"Very fitting." I'd filled Hildy in on all the information about the diary, including my unsuccessful attempt to retrace

Cornelius Duncan's steps and find the treasure. I took out the envelopes for my photos. "I'm sure the diary will conveniently disappear into their family library, never to be brought out again."

Mr. Briarcliff reached for the newspaper. "Speaking of the diary, have you seen the story on page three? No?" He folded it back and handed it to me. "I think you'll find it interesting."

Hildy strained her neck. "Is that a photograph of Rose?"

"It is." I angled the newspaper so she could see it. "The headline says *Rose* found the treasures that were buried for the prince?" The paper went slack in my hands as I stared at Mr. Briarcliff. "How is that possible? There was nothing in the desert."

"She read the diary, the whole thing. You and I both missed a small detail. The diary described Duncan's group starting from the southeast corner of the pyramid. We both assumed it was from the corner of the Great Pyramid, but she noticed a reference in a later entry. When they returned from burying the antiquities, Duncan mentioned that they didn't go back to the point they'd started from, the second pyramid, but cut across the desert toward the Sphinx."

"So they started from the middle pyramid, not the Great Pyramid." I turned the page, disappointed that no photos had been included. A note in large bold letters said pictures of the recovered artifacts would be in the next issue.

"Exactly," Mr. Briarcliff said. "Rose set out from the other pyramid. She hired a dragoman to go with her—your guide from the other day, in fact, Ibrahim. She laid out a grid, and they dug several test holes."

"Oh my," Hildy said. "I'm surprised Mrs. Jenkins gave her approval to do that."

"I don't believe she did. Mrs. Jenkins thought Rose was spending the day shopping with a friend."

"What did she find?" Hildy asked.

I read from the article, "'A very fine gold mask, a set of

Coptic funerary jars, and a statue of Isis.'" I skimmed ahead and summarized the rest. "It says here she's not keeping them. They're to go back to the museum." I handed the paper to Hildy, who'd taken out her reading glasses. "Now perhaps the Jenkins family won't be so embarrassed about Duncan. His diary was instrumental in finding lost artifacts."

Mr. Briarcliff looked doubtful. "Perhaps. I think you were right earlier. It will disappear, never to be seen again."

I began stacking my photos, tapping them into alignment on the rattan table. "You never know. They might donate it to the museum. It would make a nice display along with the recovered artifacts."

The waiter arrived with the drinks. Mr. Briarcliff indicated the travel packet as Hildy moved it off the table. "Heading up the Nile so soon? You've only scratched the surface here."

Hildy picked up the teapot. "I'm ready to move on."

"What about you, Miss Windway? What are your plans?"

I slotted the photos into the envelopes. "I'm going on with Hildy."

Mr. Briarcliff sipped his coffee. It must have been too hot because he returned his cup to the saucer. "You've certainly seen more than the average tourist." He pointed to one of the photos I'd taken the day we visited the orphanage. The children raced across the grass, their arms and legs a blur of movement. "You have a way of catching unusual moments. You make an effort to see more than the ordinary."

I picked up the last envelope. "Careful there, Mr. Briarcliff, that sounded suspiciously like a compliment."

"It was."

"But I've been around you enough to know that you never give compliments."

"I wouldn't say never. It's just that so few people deserve them."

Hildy picked up another picture of Mr. Chambers with a child on either side of him. "Mr. Chambers is another person planning his return to England. I spoke to him today when I was arranging our steamer tickets. He was booking passage from Alexandria, leaving next week for a well-deserved retirement. The orphanage will be in good hands with Mr. McKinney. Mr. Chambers said he'll return next winter for a visit. We're to dine with him tomorrow night, Blix. I hope that's all right with you."

"Yes, of course. You can give him those photos. I had extra made for him."

"How thoughtful of you." Hildy swept them up and uncovered the narrow box. "What's this? Last-minute shopping?"

"Yes. For you." I handed it to her.

"Oh, how exciting! It's not my birthday."

"It's to replace something that was lost."

Like a child on Christmas morning, she worked the lid off. Her face broke into a smile as she held up a letter opener with turquoise scarabs on the handle. "It's exactly what I need. I never did find my other one."

"I'm glad you like it. The vendor assured me there's not another like it in all of Egypt."

"Ah, there isn't?"

"One hundred percent unique. Guaranteed."

Hildy handed it over to Mr. Briarcliff so he could examine it. "It's probably from Tut's tomb itself." He handed it back to her, and she smoothed her hand along the scarabs before putting it away.

I picked up my photos and pushed back my chair. "I have to run. I must find Mr. Denby. I still owe him that interview."

Mr. Briarcliff scooted his chair back. "I must go as well. I have an appointment about a little issue on one of the steamers."

"Not on the S.S. *Cleopatra*, I hope," Hildy said.

"No, I never hear anything bad about the *Cleopatra*. I'm sure your journey will be completely uneventful."

. . .

The End

∽

THANK you for reading Blix's adventure in Egypt. To find out when the next book in the series is available, sign up for my updates at SaraRosett.com/signup, which will also include my favorite books and bookish things.

THE STORY BEHIND THE STORY

Thank you for joining me on Blix's first Egyptian adventure! I've wanted to write a novel set in Egypt for a long time. The country and its history have always fascinated me. Egypt was often my choice for school papers and book reports. Then I read Elizabeth Peters' Amelia Peabody series. I thoroughly enjoyed the fantastic characters and the marvelous sense of place that Peters brought to each story. Later I read *Death on the Nile*, a whodunit within the confines of a Nile steamer in the 1930s. Those books inspired me to dream that one day I'd write a mystery set in Egypt.

I tried out various ideas for a novel set in Egypt, but it was only after I wrote about Blix, the lady traveler, in the sixth book in the High Society Lady Detective series, *Murder on a Midnight Clear*, that I realized I'd found the perfect character for the Egypt books. I thought, *She's the one. Blix would definitely travel to Egypt.* Once I knew who Blix was, I needed a traveling companion for her. Warm and generous and slightly naïve in the ways of society, Hildy Honeyworth was the perfect counterbalance for Blix.

I began the long process of sussing out Blix's background and creating a cast of characters around her. Blix was a bit of a mystery to me, but as I wrote the first draft, her personality and her history became clearer. Her rather sad childhood and the constant parade of governesses (some eccentric and fun, others downright mean) as well as her wariness toward society gossip and her thirst for adventure gradually came into focus.

An array of female travelers inspired some details of *Murder Among the Pyramids*, including Eva Dickson, who funded some of her travel through bets on road races, as well as Osa Johnson, a photographer and videographer. Other women travelers and explorers who fired my imagination were Freya Stark, Rosita Forbes, Isabella Bird, and Aloha Wanderwell. My copy of *The Encyclopedia of Women's Travel and Exploration* by Patricia D. Netzley has many pages marked with inspiring women travelers!

To get the feel of Egypt in general and Cairo in particular, I read many travelogues from the time period. Egypt had long been a popular destination. There is a wealth of information about travel to Egypt. *Women Travelers on the Nile*, edited by Deborah Manley, and *Miss Brocklehurst on the Nile: Diary of a Victorian Traveler in Egypt* provided insights about the shipboard journey as well as the tours of Alexandria and Cairo. Guidebooks from the time provided details about the Egyptian museum and tours of the pyramids.

Another invaluable resource was *Shepheard's of Cairo: The Birth of the Oriental Grand Hotel* by Tarek Ibrahim. Shepheard's was *the* place to see and be seen, so I was delighted to find a copy of Ibrahim's book, which provided maps and detailed floor plans of the famous hotel, including a certain underground passageway that provides a major plot point. For an overview of the celebrated hotels throughout Egypt, I consulted Andrew Humphreys' *Grand Hotels of Egypt in the Golden Age of Travel*.

The germ of the idea for burying antiquities in the desert came from *A World Beneath the Sounds: The Golden Age of Egyptology* by Toby Wilkinson. In 1857, according to Wilkinson, Auguste Mariette, archeologist and future founder of the

Egyptian Department of Antiquities, was sent to Egypt to prepare for the visit of Prince Napoleon, a cousin of the emperor who wanted to take on the role of archeologist in Egypt. Wilkinson states that Mariette was to "unearth, and then rebury, a series of objects for the prince to 'discover.'" The royal visit was postponed, but the idea of seeding antiquities in the desert for a visiting royal to dig up was just too good to pass up. I knew I had to include something similar in *Murder Among the Pyramids*. I put my own spin on the situation and changed the royal dignitary, the dates, and the outcome, but the initial spark for the idea came from reality—an example that the truth is often stranger than fiction.

I enjoyed traveling to Egypt with Blix and Hildy. I can't wait to see what happens to them on their Nile tour! Sign up for my updates at SaraRosett.com/signup, and I'll let you know when the next book in the Lady Traveler series will be out as well as what books I'm reading.